THE RADOVAKS' WAR

An epic story of survival during WW2

by

Robert Wickson

ISBN 978-0-9548822-2-8

In association with
Quest Publications
14 HD BH22 9SW

Author's note

In case there is any doubt, the Radovak family – and all the characters surrounding them - are entirely fictitious, and the incidents and adventures they go through during WW2 are merely a figment of my imagination. But the historical background of WW2 is factual, and I have used whatever I thought was needed to enhance the story.

It is not known whether any Polish officers escaped the massacre at Katyn, but I hope some – like Igor Radovak – managed it. The Russians finally admitted in 1989 – to their eternal shame - that they were responsible. But Katyn was not the only mass grave. With other sites found, the total of Polish prisoners murdered on the orders of Stalin have been estimated to be 20,000 to 30,000.

The Todt Organisation was mainly responsible for the construction of Hitler's 'Atlantic Wall', and the *Batterie* at Azeville in Normandy is still there (as are all the other fortifications along the coast)'

'Popski's Private Army' under the command of Major (later Lieutenant-Colonel) Vladimir Peniakoff, was a small, secret, but formidable 'cloak and dagger' unit that operated behind enemy lines in North Africa and Italy.

Popski's book about PPA was first published in 1950 – copies can still be found. Sadly, Popski died of a brain tumour in 1956.

Acknowledgements

My grateful thanks to all the writers and aspiring writers that meet each month at Brockenhurst, who have given me so much help and encouragement with this, my first – and probably only – novel. They know who they are. But in particular to Judy Hall, who has spent many hours trying to get me to knock the book into a respectable shape. And, frankly, she would like me to do more.
Any imperfections then, are all mine. Even so, I hope you enjoy reading it.

CHAPTER 1

September 1st 1939

Anastasia Radovak was in the kitchen preparing the mid-day meal when the piano recital she was listening to on the wireless went silent. She glanced at it with a frown of annoyance.

'This programme is interrupted for a special news bulletin,' a male voice stated solemnly. There was a pause before the voice continued. 'Government sources have announced that German armed forces have this morning crossed the border into Poland, and German aircraft have bombed Polish airfields and other military installations.'

Her face paled. She stood motionless. The voice continued.

'As a consequence of this armed aggression, Poland is at war with Germany. The Polish Army and Air Force are fighting back ferociously. Everyone is urged to remain calm and not panic or cause havoc on the roads by fleeing. Further news bulletins will be made every 30 minutes.' The playing of martial music brought her back to life.

Her brain in turmoil, her hands shook as she continued to peel the potato she had in her hand, cut it in half and put it into the saucepan in front of her. Wiping her hands on her apron she walked across the farmyard and around the back of the barn, where her daughter-in-law Trishka and Josef the farmhand were busy stacking hay. They looked up as she approached.

'It's happened,' she said tonelessly. 'It's just been announced on the wireless, the Germans have invaded.'

Trishka turned; her eyes wide open in alarm.

'Invaded?' she questioned. 'Invaded Poland?' And when Anna gave a small nod she turned her face to the sky with eyes squeezed tight together. 'Oh *hell*,' she said quietly to herself. For a few seconds they stared at each other in silence with their separate thoughts.

Josef stabbed his pitchfork hard into the hay. 'The bloody bastards!' he said bitterly.

Trishka brushed back a few strands of loose fair hair. Her healthy outdoor complexion was now ashen. She slid down from the haystack.

'What now, Anna?' she asked, blinking back her tears.

The older woman shook her head slowly. She put her arm around the shoulders of her daughter-in-law and gave a comforting squeeze.

'I don't know,' she said, striving to keep her voice calm, and then turned back towards the farmhouse. 'Lunch will be in half an hour, we'll talk about it then.'

Back inside the house Anna blotted tears from her cheeks with her apron as she continued preparing the meal. Her insides felt knotted with fear. Igor would be in the thick of the fighting by now. And what about Max? He'd been called back to the Military Academy in Warsaw two months ago. In spite of what the news broadcast had advised, her first reaction was to flee to Warsaw to join him, and then for them all to try to get, somehow, to England, where Stefan, their youngest son, was at university.

She didn't think that the Polish armed forces, however bravely they fought, would be able to hold off the German onslaught indefinitely. The only question was, how long had they got? How long before the Germans took Warsaw and the rest of Poland?

She considered the alternatives. If they stayed where they were it would be with the hope that the Germans would allow them to get on with their farming. But whom would they be farming for, the Polish people, or the Germans? The German army more like. As much as she hated the thought of leaving the farm, she sensed that it would be more dangerous to stay, to be at the mercy of the invaders. They would be like prisoners on their own farm.

The second alternative was to head east, over the border into Russia, to her parents' farm ninety or so kilometres away. She'd been allowed to visit them whenever she wished, and so a longer, indefinite stay, might also be permitted. This alternative was tempting, it was certainly the easiest option, but she dismissed it. Although she was a Russian by birth, she did not trust Stalin and his communist regime. If she was on her own she might have chanced it, but she could not risk having Trishka and Josef arrested. No, somehow they must find a way to stay free, and that would mean staying clear of Germans and Russians alike. It also meant that they would have to leave the farm.

When the two came into the kitchen the next news bulletin was just starting. They listened to it in silence. It was not much different to the previous broadcast, except to add that, as a result of the German invasion of Poland, Great Britain and France had given an ultimatum to Germany. As the martial music started again, Anna served the meal.

'Well,' she said. 'It's nice to know that we're not now on our own, but I doubt that the English and French will be able to help us throw back the Germans. They're less prepared for war than we were.'

Chewing on their food the other two nodded in agreement. As they ate Anna told them what she had been thinking, the choices they had and the decisions they needed to make. They listened intently, until she finished with 'So, I don't think we should stay here, but if we go, which direction should we take?'

They finished the remains of the food, thinking over what she had said.

Anna looked at Josef as he put his knife and fork down. 'What do you think Josef? Do you agree that we should go?'

Josef hesitated with his answer. 'Well Anna, I can see how it makes sense to try to escape the Nazis, and if there was even a slim chance of getting over to England I'd willingly join you. But I don't think we'd do it. There'll be thousands of people who live much nearer the ports than we do, all trying for the same thing. It would be a long way to travel, risky all the way, and we would have to sleep in the open most of the time. It would be a dash with only one aim in mind – to get on a boat to England. If that fails, we would be stranded, and in a much worse state than if we'd stayed put.'

Pausing in thought, he glanced at them in turn.

'There might be another choice, if you're interested,' he said.

'Another choice?' questioned Anna. 'What do you mean?'

'Yes, well, this war's been brewing up for months now, and many of the farmhands around here - those without family ties - and some of the farmers as well, have talked about what they'd do if the Nazis came. The truth is that a few groups have been formed, and they've been quietly making camps in the forests, and laying in stores.'

Anna and Trishka looked at each other. It was certainly another choice.

'We're all used to living off the land,' continued Josef, 'and with traps and suchlike reckon we can survive as long as we like, so long as we keep out of sight.'

Anna nodded in agreement. There were vast stretches of forest along the borders of Poland and Russia that would hide them. There was plenty of wildlife and streams full of fish. The only drawback would be the winter months. It was the winters that would be the worst.

'But how would they feel about women joining them?' she asked.

'Up to now, we haven't even talked about women joining us, but nobody's said they can't either. So if you want me to ask if you can join us, I'll willingly do it'.

Trishka put down her knife and fork.

'I think I might have a problem with that one Josef,' she said, and paused. 'What I mean is, I might not be in any fit state for that kind of life for a few months.'

'Fit state?' said Anna, in surprise. 'Trishka, you're as fit as a fiddle.'

'I'm fit, yes, but what I'm saying is that over the next few months I may not be....' Her voice trailed off

'May not be?' Anna repeated again, looking bewildered.

A look of understanding came to Josef's face.

'I think I know what you're getting at Trishka,' he said gently, and paused, as though undecided whether to continue. 'Are you in the family way?'

Anna's mouth dropped open and her eyebrow's went up.

'Trishka! – *Are* you?' she gasped out.

Trishka, smiling slightly at Josef's insight, looked briefly from one to the other.

'Well, I could be wrong, it's still too early to be certain, but I think I might be.' Trishka coloured up. 'Anyway – I'll go along with whatever you think best.'

Anna went and put her arms around her. 'My dear girl' she said. 'My dear, dear girl.' The momentary joy that she was to have a grandchild was crushed by the stark reality that it was not the best time for any woman to find she was pregnant. Josef decided that

4

whatever they chose to do, he would stay with them. He had, after all, promised Max Radovak that he would 'keep his eye on things' during his absence, which included his family as well as the farm. He stroked his stubbly chin.

'It might complicate things if you let on you could be pregnant,' he said. 'Look, the group will be meeting tomorrow at the livestock market, why not come along and meet our leader, Jak Zenski, and the others, and if they'll let you join us, it's up to you to decide – but if you want to come, you'd best not mention your suspicions of a baby,' he paused. 'What d'you say?'

Anna looked at him for a second or two and then gave a nod.

'Yes Josef,' she said, 'we'd better come with you tomorrow. If we do decide to leave the farm we've got to see if our neighbours will take on our livestock, and the best place to meet most of them will be at the market.'

At first the livestock market the next day seemed to be much the same as it always had been. There was the usual bustle and noise, the usual faces, the usual stalls, the same auctioneer anxious to get on with the sale. But faces were more serious and preoccupied, and there was no banter and laughter in the small groups that gathered together.

By now even those who did not have a wireless had heard the news about the German invasion. Being spread out on remote farms, they had mainly come to market that day for the sole purpose of discussing with their neighbours what they should do. It seemed that most of them would stay and carry on. After all, they had livestock to attend to, crops to get in, and needed to finish preparing for the winter. It was not so easy to walk out on a working farm. As if to help them with their decision, the auctioneer announced that he would continue with the regular livestock sales until further notice.

Josef led Anna and Trishka to a wooden hut at the far end of the market square, normally used as an office by the auctioneer. Inside, about ten men had already gathered, a mixture of farmers and farmhands. The expressions on the faces of the men were serious as they talked together. They turned to greet Josef as he entered, but fell silent as they saw the two women that followed him. Anna and Trishka smiled nervously at the men as Josef went over to the tallest of them and spoke to him, pointing over at the women as he did so.

5

The tall bearded man was Jak Zenski, the group's acknowledged leader. When Josef had finished talking, he asked him one or two questions, and then turned to speak to one of the men standing behind him. After a minute Jak Zenski came over to the women, and Josef introduced them. The rest of the men made an attempt to carry on with their conversations, but cast curious eyes in the direction of Josef and the two women.

Explaining to Anna and Trishka what he was going to do, Jak Zenski turned around to face the men. 'Could I have your attention please?' He waited for them to face him.

'So far we've been preparing our camps and hoping that we wouldn't need them. Well, yesterday's news that Germany has invaded has brought our preparations to a head. It's time to act on our resolve to remain free. We've accepted that we'll not be strong enough to fight the invaders, so our intention remains the same – to keep out of sight and stay alive – and help others where we can.' Some of the men nodded as he paused.

Jak Zenski continued. 'However, I can now tell you, since hostilities have started, that we are not going to be so isolated and alone as we first thought. Three months ago a man from Polish Military Intelligence came to see me. Somehow they had heard about our camps, and they wanted us to join up with a number of other groups that were secretly being organised throughout Poland. In return they would help us with our supplies, provide someone to train us, and, if hostilities started, give us a radio transmitter so that we could keep in touch and report back any civil or military intelligence to a central unit.'

The men looked at one another, muttering to their neighbours. Finally, one of them spoke up.

'Well, they're a bit late with a trainer aren't they? Leon has been doing a good job up to now, do we need another one?'

Some of the men turned to the tall, lean, fair-haired man that Jak Zenski had spoken to earlier. Those nearest to him patted him on the back in support of what had just been said. Jak Zenski smiled.

'Men, you'll remember that I introduced Leon to our group about three months ago, as my new farmhand. And I can tell you that he's been very useful as a farmhand. But the truth is that Leon is our group trainer provided by Military Intelligence, and has been

6

working with us under cover. But I can now formally introduce you to Lieutenant Leon Denkov, who'll be remaining with us to help and guide us.'

There was a burst of excited chatter.

Leon Denkov held up his hand for silence.

'Thanks, Jak, for the formal introduction, and my apologies to the rest of you for having to remain under cover until now, but this was, as you will appreciate, my orders. Even so, please would you keep this information to yourselves? So far as anyone else is concerned outside of this room, I'm just Jak Zenski's farmhand.' He let these words sink in, and glanced over at the two women before continuing.

'Now, as Jak has said, we're now at war with Germany, so it's time for us to move to our camp. We're not certain how long our army will be able hold back the German offensive, but from information I've received this morning, it's not likely to be very long. We've been advised to be at our camp within the next five days, at most. Is there anyone who'll have a problem with this deadline?' He looked around, but there was no response.

'Good - thanks men. I suggest we leave over the next four days, which I hope will be enough time to get your affairs in order. You all know the route to take. I'll leave it to you to arrange between yourselves the days and times you leave to ensure that we don't draw attention to ourselves by travelling in convoy.' He stopped and looked over to Jak Zenski, who nodded to him to continue.

'Jak has asked me to make one final announcement, because it was a late request that came through my channels, and it was causing us some anxiety until this morning. It'll be one of the main functions of the groups to assist and escort any of our military that are trying to evade capture by the Germans. Through our chain of camps we've established an escape route out of the country. The late request we received was to provide two extra key people. One who was trained in first-aid, and one who could speak English and German as well as Polish, to use the radio transmitter. Well, as I have said, this was a problem that we arrived with this morning, but I'm pleased to announce that it has, hopefully, now been solved. As you are aware, Josef has brought these two ladies with him, who are interested in joining us. I think some of you already know them. One is Mrs Anastasia Radovak, whose husband is in Warsaw as an army instructor, and the other is her daughter-in-law Mrs Trishka Radovak, whose husband is at this moment fighting on the front line.' He turned towards the two women as he spoke.

'Josef has told us that Anastasia was a nurse in the last war, and, so far as I'm concerned, she'd be most welcome to join us in this capacity. And Trishka, Josef tells us, studied languages at Warsaw University, and was a languages teacher before she married. She's fluent in English, Russian and German, so she'd be the ideal person to train as our radio operator'.

Trishka felt herself blushing as the eyes of the men fell upon her. Anna seemed to be striving to look calm, but was clearly nervous.

Jak Zenski came to the rescue. 'Now men, don't embarrass the ladies by staring. They came to look us over and see if we would take them before deciding. Now, as Leon has said, we need their skills urgently, so I hope you will all agree with us that they can join the group if they so wish, and we will protect them and respect them to the best of our ability if they do.'

Josef watched with a satisfied smile on his face as the men in the room nodded in approval. The two women had a short whispered conversation before Anna looked up and faced them all.

'Thank you Mr Zenski, - Jak - and thank you all. Like you we don't wish to remain and wait for the Germans to arrive. It was our first intention to try to get to England, but we now realise that's not possible. Josef took a chance and told us about your group only yesterday, and we're both grateful to him for bringing us along. Yes gentlemen, we shall be pleased to join you - and thank you again for accepting us so readily'.

Josef was also relieved that they had been accepted. The alternatives would have been far more dangerous. And he was grateful to Jak Zenski. When he had asked what the two women had done before they were married, Josef had no idea why he needed this information. The way that he had conveyed the information about their past careers to Leon Denkov, had obviously helped in getting the rest of the group's approval. He could see how Anna's skills as a nurse fitted in, but he'd heard that Leon himself could speak English, as well as German and Russian, so he suspected that Trishka's abilities with languages were not so essential as he had made out.

Before they left, Josef introduced them to all the men and, as they travelled back to the farm, he gave them further details. Jak Zenski was a widower. His wife had died in childbirth about two years ago. His two brothers had decided to stay on the farm. Out of the others, only one was married, but his wife had left, taking the children with her. The rest of the men were younger and single.

When they arrived back at the farm, Anna sat down to make a list of what needed to be done. Her thoughts turned to Max. All she could do was write to tell him that they were leaving the farm and were in safe hands, and hope that he would receive it. There was no way that they could communicate with Igor.

Within the next three days they managed to sell some livestock and give the rest to neighbours who were staying behind. They had cleared out the house and buried some family possessions in a secret spot, and collected all papers and old correspondence and burned it. They did not leave anything that indicated who had lived there. They knew that it would not take the invaders long to find out the names of the owners, but they would not make it any easier for them.

At dawn on the fourth day they saddled up their horses and loaded the farm's big carthorse with provisions, extra clothing and blankets. Eating a final breakfast in the farmhouse, they locked the door and started off. They had a long way to go, much of it across open country.

Josef, with the carthorse in tow, led the way out of the farmyard. Having made their decision, they were glad to be on their way.

CHAPTER 2

When he regained consciousness, Igor's first thought was that he was blind. It was equally black whether he had his eyes open or closed. Also, something was holding him down, and he could not feel his right arm. With difficulty he reached over with his left hand. He could feel the top of his arm; the rest of it was under the neck of his horse. There was no sign of life. Anguish swept through him - his beautiful chestnut stallion was dead. He pushed against the horse's neck and slowly slid out his arm. The blood of his horse acted as a lubricant, and he screwed up his face at the pain as the circulation returned to his arm.

As his head cleared he understood why it was so completely black. It had been daylight when he was struck down, but now it was night. And he could hardly move because the branches of the tree that had killed his horse were pinning him down. He checked his legs. He could move both a few inches. His right leg hurt. Not broken, he felt sure, but probably gashed, and if he was losing blood he could do nothing about it. He wondered how the branches of the tree had killed his horse but had left him virtually unscathed, or so he thought.

He could hear the rumblings of gunfire. The battle had moved on. A black weariness engulfed him. Was he going to die here, with his horse? There was little chance of being found, either dead or alive, hidden from view under the tree. He had a raging thirst and a terrible headache. It occurred to him that he might be more injured than he realised. If he was not injured he ought to be struggling to get free.

These thoughts drifted through his mind as he tried to stay awake against an overwhelming tiredness. Visions of his wife floated before him. And then he heard her voice. She was leaning over him, a look of anxiety and pleading in her eyes.

'Come back to me Igor,' she whispered. 'Come back to me.' They were the same words she had spoken when they parted.

He tried to answer and reach out. He felt Trishka's hand smooth over his forehead and down his cheek. Her hand was cool and he smiled to reassure her.

'Don't worry, my Trishka,' he wanted to say, 'I will be back.' But no sound came. He only mouthed the words. He spoke louder, and then shouted, trying desperately to lift his arms to take hold of her.

The effort jolted him awake. The words he had been trying to get out left his throat as a strangled cry that echoed through the trees. A slight breeze ruffled leaves against his cheek.

All he could see was a cluster of white spots. It took him several long seconds to realise that the spots were sunlight filtering through the leaves of the tree. The dense blackness that had surrounded him in the night was now a deep green. He could see the shape of his horse. His eyes focused longingly upon the canteen of water hanging on the saddle. But it was at least half a metre out of his reach.

With an effort he began breaking off the smaller branches and twigs from around his head. His hands stopped suddenly, as a thought struck him. He slid his right hand down to his waist and after a brief fumble raised it up to his face. The blade of a hunting knife gleamed dully in the shaded light. His father had given it to him on his twenty-first birthday. It was strong and sharp and he now knew that he had the means to escape. With the first branch he cut he reached out and managed to unhook his water canteen and dragged it to him. Greedily, he drank half the contents. With renewed energy he started to clear the branches from his torso. Then, reaching down as far as he could, he cut a channel through which he could drag his legs. It was slow laborious work, with frequent stops to rest his arms.

He judged that the quickest way out was to pull his body up into a standing position. It was well past mid-day when, on his fifth attempt, with his uniform drenched with sweat, he at last stood upright, with his head emerging through the foliage. He scrambled over his dead horse and stepped down. As he did so the sharp pain in his leg prompted him to take off his boots, undo his belt and lower his trousers. The whole leg was a black bruise from the thigh down to the foot, but he was relieved to see that the skin was not broken, except for a bad scratch on his ankle.

Drinking the rest of the water from his bottle, he delved down into the foliage to find his saddle. There had been the remains of some food in his saddlebag, but this was under the horse. Instead, he filled his pocket with spare ammunition for his revolver.

Looking around he could see the bodies of horses and soldiers scattered amongst the trees. Less than twenty-four hours ago these same bodies had been his eager and courageous comrades, determined to 'throw the enemy back into Germany'. He found it hard to grasp that they were now gone. He inspected each in turn, not knowing what he would do if he found anyone alive.

They were all dead. As he looked closer from one to another his face darkened with anger. It was obvious that many had been wounded, some worse than others, but they all carried one wound that had been fatal. Each of them had been shot in the head. Rather than treat them as prisoners and tend to their wounds his comrades had been murdered. His anger boiled into a rage.

He raised a clenched fist towards the sounds of the distant gunfire.

'You murdering swine,' he shouted at the top of his voice, and cursed Hitler and the whole German race and swore to avenge his dead comrades until, breathless and choking, he slumped down sobbing against a tree. As his temper cooled he realised - too late - that the enemy might still be within earshot. He crouched on his knees, ears alert, and peered cautiously into the woods surrounding him - but all was quiet.

Anger still smouldering, he looked again at the bodies. Some advice from the past came back to him. Who was it that had told him? His father? Josef? His instructors? It didn't matter. At the time he had thought - 'I couldn't do that' - and dismissed it. But he recalled it now as his eyes swept over the carnage around him.

'As a soldier, take whatever you need from the dead to stay alive and keep fighting– it's common sense, not disrespect.'

He checked the saddles of each horse. He found more water bottles, and in the pouches a few bits of food and some army issue chocolate bars and a few boiled sweets. There was also a shaving kit complete with soap. He collected the identity discs of his dead comrades and placed everything into the pouches of a saddlebag. Taking a groundsheet from one of the saddles he slung them over his shoulder and started walking deeper into the wood, in the opposite direction to the scene of the battle. High above him filtering through the tops of the trees he could see glimpses of the sun to guide him. He wanted to get away from the death surrounding him.

Minutes later he came across another body. It was lying face down, but he recognized the uniform. It was his Captain – Ivan Gravik. The uniform still looked clean and well pressed. There was no sign of blood or injury, but as he turned the body over he realised why. The way the neck fell to one side could only mean one thing. His Captain had been thrown from his horse and broken his neck as he hit the ground. He looked around but there was no sign of the horse.

Taking the Captain's identity disk he slipped it around his own neck. Searching the pockets he found his wallet. Inside was a photograph of the Captain standing beside an attractive woman and two children, smiling happily. There were two or three letters from his wife and Igor placed the picture with them. These he did not take, but he removed other possessions that he needed, in particular, from around his neck, a pair of binoculars. And then, comparing his own dirty and bloodstained uniform with the clean one of his Captain, Igor murmured apologies to his dead comrade as he removed his uniform.

They were both about six foot tall, and a similar weight. There was little difference between the uniform of a Lieutenant and a Captain of cavalry, apart from the insignia of rank. He removed what he could of the Captain's insignia and replaced it with his own. Digging a shallow grave, he covered the body over, saluted briefly, and walked on.

It took half hour to reach the other side of the wood. The sudden light caused him to squint as he scanned the landscape of farmland and fields before him for a sight of the enemy. There was no sign of life at all. Through the binoculars he could see a small wisp of smoke in the distance that could be from a campfire or a chimney. There was no way of telling. It all looked peaceful. If the enemy had passed through on this side they had obviously met with no resistance.

He sensed, rather than heard, a movement to his left, along the edge of the wood. Instinctively he ducked back to the protection of the trees. Nothing was coming towards him, he felt sure, but if someone was out there he needed to know. Easing his revolver into his hand he cautiously looked out from behind a tree. Not realising that he had stopped breathing, he gasped with relief. There, fifty or so metres away, was a horse, quietly nibbling at the grass in the shade of the trees. Walking towards it he could see that it was his Captain's stallion.

As he got nearer he saw that the horse had suffered some injuries. There was a gash on its neck and blood had trickled down its front leg, and another flesh injury to the right flank. The horse lifted its head and watched the approach of the man in the uniform of his master. Igor murmured quietly to the horse, stroked his long nose and gave him one of the boiled sweets he had found in a saddlebag. The horse gazed at him softly as it crunched the sweet around its mouth.

As though accepting his new master, the horse bent down to continue his nibbling. Inspecting the wounds, Igor could see that the bleeding had stopped and he decided that he had nothing that would help. More importantly, he was relieved to see that the horse was not too injured to ride.

One pouch of the Captain's saddlebag revealed two slices of bread, a chunk of cheese and an apple. The water bottle was full and Igor poured half the contents into his hat and put it on the ground for the horse. Undoing the strap on the remaining pouch, he found that it contained real prizes. Inside were two maps, one of the local area, with pencilled notes, arrows and crosses denoting enemy and friendly positions of the previous day's battle. The other map was a larger one of Poland up to the Russian border. There was also a compass. Finding the horse, maps and compass had dramatically improved his chances of survival.

As they had been preparing to go into battle on the previous day, the news had come through that Great Britain and France had declared war on Germany. They had given a cheer and had gone into battle with fresh energy. But they knew that neither the British nor the French could do anything to stop the German invasion. They were too far away. It was too late for anyone to help Poland now. Having witnessed the combined ground and air power of the German forces, he knew that the Polish army would not be capable of stopping them for long. His plan, his only hope of continuing the fight for his country, was to get to England. This was what he and his comrades had talked about and decided to do if the Germans occupied Poland.

Sounds of distant gunfire still rumbled in the air. The horse was starting to walk out of the shade of the trees and Igor went over to it, gave it another boiled sweet, and led it back to the shade and tethered it to a branch. Opening one of the maps he sat down with his back to a tree drew his knees up and placed his elbows on his knees to steady the binoculars as he carefully scrutinized the landscape once again.

Occasionally he glanced down at the map. As the light began to fade he decided to stay where he was for the night, satisfied that he had a good idea what direction to take at daybreak. Not knowing the whereabouts of the enemy, he reasoned that it was pointless to rush and take unnecessary risks.

Returning to where the horse was tethered, he cut a few branches and pushed them into the soft earth to act as posts and formed them into a rough square. Hanging a groundsheet on the posts, he made a small fire. Walking around the outside, he checked to make sure no light from the fire could be seen. He was not concerned about the smoke; once it had filtered through the trees it would be invisible in the dark. He half filled a billycan with water and placed it on the glowing embers. He dropped pieces of the dry bread into the water, followed by slices of the onion and finally pieces of cheese.

With the hot food inside him, the exertions of the day caught up with him with an overpowering desire for sleep. Before wrapping himself in the groundsheet he checked the horse and the tether, gave the horse another drink of water and threw a groundsheet over its back.

CHAPTER 3

Igor woke to the sound of an impatient snort from the horse. It was still dark but the first glimmer of dawn was beginning to appear. He hobbled the horse and set it to graze as he busied himself packing. Breakfast was a small piece of bread and cheese and a few gulps of water. From habit he had a quick cold shave.

Saddling the horse, he strapped down everything securely, mounted, and then made his way down the long sloping field towards the thin line of trees at the bottom. From his scrutiny of the previous day he had judged that this was the line of a narrow country road. In spite of its injuries, the horse felt strong and solid beneath him.

Upon reaching the road Igor checked his compass. He was heading northeast, on a long journey towards his family farm near the Russian border to collect his wife and mother before attempting to get to England. That this might be construed, in military terms, as desertion, never entered his head. To him his plan was a very practical one of staying alive and free in order to continue to fight the invaders of his country. To stay would result in becoming a prisoner-of-war, a slave labourer, or being shot.

The road was leading him, he realised, in the direction of the wisp of smoke he had seen the previous day. As the sun rose he let the horse walk at its own pace. After a while the road went through a pine forest, and the trees gave him a strange comfort.

When he found a small stream running alongside the road, Igor dismounted and let the horse drink. Bending down, he refilled the water bottles. As he did so a sound caught his attention. It was a long way off and no more than a buzz. Slinging the water bottles over the saddle Igor led the horse into the forest.

He went in far enough to become merged with the gloom of the trees but where he could clearly see anything that passed along the road. It took a minute or two for the sound to materialize into the distinctive noise of a motor engine. The noise increased, it was travelling fast, and in a flash it passed his line of vision through the trees. It was a motorcycle and sidecar, and the cross on the side of it confirmed that it was German.

Because there had been no sign of the enemy since he had come out of the forest, Igor had believed that the Germans were not yet in control of this part of the country. Obviously he had been wrong. If a solitary motorcycle and sidecar carrying two Germans could feel safe travelling at speed along this small country road, then it followed that they were in control of it.

There could be no more leisurely progress, from now on he would have to keep out of sight and be on constant alert. For the time being the forest provided the cover he needed. Fifteen minutes later Igor heard the sound of two gunshots. He paused, another shot rang out, then another. The echoes reverberated through the forest.

After a while he moved on, trying to assess how far away he was from the shots. Of one thing he felt certain, they had come from the direction in which he was heading, and he would have to pass close to where they had originated.

Eventually the trees began to thin out. Igor tethered the horse and walked cautiously to a point where he could use his binoculars to scan the way ahead. There were several large fields stretching out before him, with a dozen or so cattle grazing. In the distance were more trees. It did not take him long to spot what he was looking for.

A little more than half a kilometre away, behind the trees on the other side of the road, he could see the top of a chimney with smoke rising from it. He walked fifty metres to his left and focussed again. There was, he thought, at least one other building there. At this distance they were only extra smudges of darkness amongst the trees. He was looking, he guessed, at a farmhouse with a few outbuildings, and it was from here that the shots had been fired.

Igor's first thought was to make a safe detour of the farm, but he needed to know if the two Germans were there, and whether there were more. If there were more, he would get an idea how many and then move on. If he met up with any Polish units, the information might be of some use

As the ground behind the farm sloped upwards Igor decided to approach it downhill from the rear. Mounting the stallion he made towards the road. He had to take the risk that it was not being observed, but he had to cross it. Urging the horse into a gallop they broke cover and in two quick strides were over the road and into the trees on the other side. As the ground rose up the trees thinned out.

He cantered the horse as quickly as he dared, the drumming of the hooves muffled by the soft ground. At the top of the rise he looked down onto sloping pastures.

He walked the horse down the other side of the slope for a few metres and then trotted it in the direction of the farm. After what he considered to be about the right distance, he dismounted and let the horse graze while he went to have a look. He had calculated correctly. The farm buildings were directly below him, about three hundred metres away.

Igor hobbled the back legs of the horse so that it could continue grazing but not walk far. He took extra cartridges for his revolver and set off. Moving from tree to tree he descended down the slope towards one of the outbuildings, a barn which seemed to be furthest from the farmhouse. Everything was quiet. Too late, he had the sudden thought that a farm dog would sense his presence. But no dog barked. He edged his way to a half open door at the back of the barn, and paused to listen before he sidled inside.

The only light was coming from the front of the barn where one of the double doors was wide open. He could see part of the farmhouse and he moved out of its line into the shadows. The barn had partitions down one side, originally, perhaps, to tether farm animals, but now used for storage.

In the first partition was piled sacks of potatoes. The second was filled with loose turnips, the next bales of hay. Igor froze as he came to the next partition. Loose hay was spilling from it, but jutting out of the hay was a pair of boots, toe downward. Inching forward his face was grim as the legs and then the rest of the body came into sight. In all, three bodies were lying there. He guessed it was the farmer, with his wife beside him, lying face down. They had been shot through the back of the head. Beside them lay the remains of the farm dog. Igor leaned down and touched the hand of the farmer. It was still warm. The point of death must have been when he first heard the shots less than an hour ago.

What kind of people were these Germans, he thought, who not only invaded peaceful countries but killed innocent civilians with such impunity? Why were these people shot? Did they resist or put up a fight? Obviously not, if they had put up any resistance they would have been shot from the front. No, they had been taken into the barn and murdered from behind. His knuckles turned white as he clenched his fists in silent rage. He walked to the front of the barn and stood behind the closed half of the double doors. Several chinks of light shining through the door revealed knotholes big enough to look through. He was now sure that there were no other Germans about except the two who had arrived on the motorcycle.

Igor concluded that they had been sent out as scouts, probably specifically ordered to check out the farm and secure it. They were still there, because he could see the motorcycle and sidecar parked on the other side of the farmhouse. From beyond the motorcycle, in the gloom of the overhanging trees, he could hear the faint sound of voices. Putting the lens of one half of the binoculars against a knothole, he focussed on the gloom. The two Germans suddenly leapt into his sight. They were working at something in the farm's wood-store, a simple structure of a roof supported by posts. Beyond the wood-store he could see a cowshed and a small pigsty. A dozen or so chickens were roaming about.

The Germans were constructing a parapet with the logs and he could see their heads and shoulders behind it. They came to the front to inspect it. One of them walked over to the motorcycle, lifted something from it and walked back. He was carrying a machine gun, a Spandau. They were, Igor realised, constructing a machine gun position. The barrel of the machine gun appeared through an aperture in the log parapet. It disappeared, and some rearrangement of the logs was taking place. A vague plan of how to surprise and deal with these two murderers formed in Igor's mind.

He would have to act quickly, before they finished. Creeping through the barn to the back door, he lifted down an iron crowbar and took it with him. Climbing up the slope he carefully worked his way around the farmhouse towards the back of the wood-store. The Germans were still working, their backs towards him. It would have been easy to shoot them both in the back with his revolver, which he thought was no more than they deserved. But remembering how far the sound of gunshots could be heard and not knowing who might be within earshot, he did not wish to make any unnecessary noise.

They had shifted the logs around to create a space big enough for two or three men to crouch in. Igor was about four or five metres away, observing them from behind a tree. They were talking and joking as they bent to their task, their tunics and helmets in front of them on top of the parapet.

Then they straightened up and looked briefly around. Satisfied with their work, they reached for their tunics. Igor braced himself. It was when they reached for their helmets that he sprang forward. As the ground was sloped down towards the wood-store he did not have to leap over the rear parapet, he could step onto the top of it. In his left hand he had the crowbar and in his right hand his hunting knife.

Before the Germans had time to turn around, Igor smashed the crowbar onto the head of one, jumped into the pit behind the other and sank the knife into his neck. It had taken no more than five or six seconds. The eyes of the soldier with the knife in his neck looked up at Igor in disbelief, and Igor noticed the skull and crossbones badge and the double lightning flash on his collar. These were soldiers belonging to Hitler's specialist Totenkopf, or Death's Head unit, the Waffen-SS.

Igor could speak German but only two words came to him that seemed appropriate. 'Heil Hitler,' he spat at the dying German. Recalling his murdered comrades and the bodies he had found in the barn, he felt no remorse. Checking to see that they were both dead, Igor pushed the bodies over the front parapet, and dragged them one at a time to the barn.

He carefully laid aside the bodies of the farmer, his wife and dog. Taking a pitchfork, he moved all the hay to the other side of the barn and pushed the motorcycle into the space he had cleared. Placing the bodies of the Germans on top of motorcycle and sidecar, he went back for the Spandau and pushed it beneath the wheels. Taking a pitchfork he covered everything with plenty of hay. Finally, satisfied that nothing of what lay underneath could be seen, he laid the bodies of the farmer and his wife and dog back onto the hay. With a bit of luck, he thought, no one looking for the soldiers would bother to check what was under the bodies of the dead couple.

Going back to the woodpile, Igor pushed the logs over until there was no sign of the blood that had been spilled. He walked slowly back towards the barn wiping up any signs of blood and covering any tracks between the wood-store and the barn. His idea was to create a small mystery for the enemy as to what had happened to the two soldiers. If they were found dead, the Germans would certainly kill

Igor if they caught him, and - if the event at this farm was an example of what they were capable of - they would no doubt kill more civilians in retaliation. By concealing the bodies, the enemy might be fooled into thinking they had been taken prisoner.

Glancing at his watch, Igor saw that it was over an hour since he had first discovered the bodies in the barn. He was anxious to leave, but he was hungry, and needed to see what food was in the farmhouse. Entering through the open door he looked around. The room reminded him of his own home

A solid old wooden table with six chairs dominated the middle space; a pair of comfortable looking old fireside chairs on either side of an iron grate with fitments for cooking, baking, boiling, smoking and drying. There was the familiar smell that all farmhouses shared; wood-smoke, smoked ham, cheese, apples and old leather dominated lesser aromas.

The farmer and his wife had obviously been disturbed at breakfast. Bread and other food were on the table and an unfinished plate of eggs and bacon. Igor cut two thick slices from the loaf, put the remains of the eggs and bacon between them and ate hungrily.

There was also a jug on the table containing a red liquid. Igor gave it a sniff, and then took a sip. It tasted like home brewed wine. Taking two or three gulps he carried the jug with him as he went into the kitchen. There he found a sack of potatoes, apples, freshly baked bread, and joints of ham hanging from the ceiling. Satisfied, he put down the jug and, still munching on the sandwich, set off to fetch the stallion.

As he walked across the farmyard a sound from the stable made him realise that it was occupied. Inside was the farm carthorse, a large dapple-grey, past its prime, but still a solid looking animal. His first thought was to turn it loose into the fields, but decided he could make use of it as a packhorse to carry provisions.

Finding the stallion still grazing contentedly, he un-hobbled it and rode it back to the farm, tethered it outside the stable and gave it a bucket of water. From the barn he sorted out a number of clean sacks and returned to the farmhouse. He knew that the enemy would take whatever he left behind, so he would take as much as the horse could carry.

Igor filled eight sacks, enough to last him several weeks. He led the carthorse from the stable and placed a horse blanket over his back. Tying two of the sacks together in turn, he slung them over the horse until there were four on each side

Over the lot he fitted a groundsheet and tied it securely under the belly of the horse. Finding a coil of rope, he cut a length off and made a loop in one end and fastened the other end to the nose harness of the carthorse. Taking a final look around, he took the farmers warm looking coat and fur hat, closed the farmhouse door and mounted. He led the carthorse across the road, over a small field and into the trees on the far side. It took only a few minutes for them to be swallowed up in the security of the forest. With a check on the compass Igor set his direction to the northeast.

Ten minutes after he left, a column of German army trucks filled with infantry came along the road he had so leisurely taken that morning and stopped at the farmhouse.

CHAPTER 4

The wide fields were grey in the early dawn light. By this time in late October the Polish countryside was usually covered with the first flurries of winter snow. Instead, this year, there had been cold hard frosts.

The surface of the frozen road seemed to echo to the hooves of the solitary horse. Igor was oblivious to the sound. With head dropped forward, eyes closed, shoulders hunched, he looked asleep. But the gloved hands holding the reigns were steady, even though resting on the saddle. Muffled with extra clothing against the cold, the earflaps of a fur hat tied under the chin, only the boots in the stirrups gave a clue to the rider's identity. The boots of a cavalryman

Small clouds of steam from the nostrils of the horse punctured the frozen air as it trudged along. Igor opened his eyes and raised his head. It had taken several weeks to travel across country towards his destination. There had been times when the only safe course was to remain hidden during the day and travel at dusk, or at the first glimmer of dawn.

During the first week he had seen a few Germans at a distance, but this part of Poland seemed to have avoided the worst of the German aggression. He pondered over the reason for this, and his conclusion was that the enemy had decided that the open spaces could be taken at will, once the capital and main cities had fallen.

As the food was consumed, or became unfit to eat, his need for the carthorse had grown less. The frosts had arrived early and there had been less and less grazing available for the horses, and the watering places, the ponds and streams, had become hard frozen.

A week ago he'd taken the last of the food off the carthorse and left it trying to nibble at the frozen grass within clear sight of a farm. He hoped that it would be taken care of and be of some use to a fellow countryman. The road he was now travelling was familiar to him. This was where he had grown up. Only two more kilometres and he would be home.

One of the consequences of avoiding contact with anyone was that he had no idea of how the war had been going against the invaders.

Two or three weeks had passed since he had last seen formations of aircraft heading towards Warsaw and heard the crump of bombs. On many nights he'd sat watching the horizon glowing red. In the daylight pillars of dark smoke had filled the distant sky.

The farm came into view. Only six months had passed since he'd ridden away, but so much had happened since then that he expected it to look different in some way. But everything looked normal and familiar in the early morning light. There was smoke curling from the chimney, and he anticipated a big welcome from his wife and mother.

He was looking forward to hot coffee and a huge cooked breakfast. He half expected to see Uncle Josef around the farm buildings, but all seemed quiet. He knew that his father would not be there. He also had been called up by the army, not to fight, but as an instructor at an army base near Warsaw. His father had fought in the last war, and had correctly forecast that Hitler would start another war and that Poland would be forced into it.

At last Igor entered the farmyard. He rode towards the stable block, dismounted, and tethered the horse. Giving it a pat, he started towards the farmhouse. Glancing around as he walked he was puzzled to see motor vehicles parked in the barn. The realization that they were military vehicles hit him at the same time as the door of the farmhouse opened and through it walked, not his mother or his wife, but a bullnecked and granite faced Red Army sergeant. From the shadows of the farm buildings on either side of him more Russian soldiers appeared, with rifles pointing at him. They had obviously been watching him approach and had lain in wait.

They all looked sullen and suspicious, but alert for any sudden action from him that would give them the excuse to shoot. But the main thing that he was to remember about them was that their uniforms all seemed to be one size too large.

His mind was in a whirl. Why were Russian soldiers here in Poland? Had they come to help them fight the Germans'? No, it was not likely.

A fearful thought gripped him. Where were his wife and his mother? He tried to keep his composure as he walked steadily on. From behind the sergeant a Russian officer appeared, pistol in hand, and calmly watched him as he approached the farmhouse. He was, perhaps, a year or two older than Igor, but an inch or two shorter. His face was pale and lean, rather than thin. He wore a long military officer's greatcoat, undone, which revealed a uniform of equal rank to Igor's.

Striving to appear relaxed Igor gave a brief smile at the officer and said 'Good morning' in Russian. The reaction from the Russian was a small upward jerk of the pistol as he continued to watch him approach. When there was no response from Igor, the pistol was jerked up again and remained levelled at him. It suddenly dawned upon Igor what this action meant. It meant that the officer wanted him to raise his arms up above his head. As he did so the officer went back into the farmhouse to await his arrival.

The sergeant stepped aside to let him pass and followed him in. Igor hardly recognised the once familiar room. The house had been ransacked. The table was littered with dirty plates, empty cups and bottles and discarded food. Piles of army equipment were strewn around and against the walls.

The officer indicated to the sergeant to search Igor. As he moved to do so Igor finally found his voice. 'Where are the people who live here' he said in Russian. The officer merely said 'Gone.' The thought flashed through Igor's mind that 'gone' did not necessarily mean 'dead.' But had the Russians taken them?

'Gone where?' asked Igor.

The Russian ignored the question as he watched the sergeant stand back after unbuttoning the overcoat that had belonged to the dead farmer.

Now the Russian officer could see the uniform beneath. Clearly he was not expecting to find that he had captured a Polish Army officer.

'Identify yourself,' snapped the Russian.

'I am Lieutenant Igor Radovak, of the Pomorska Brigade of Cavalry.'

'What are you doing here?'

'This farm belongs to my family, I was expecting to see my wife and mother here and try to get them away before the Germans came.'

The Russian scowled. 'Germans! There are no Germans around here.'

'No, but I thought they were coming this way, I was fighting against them several weeks ago in the west, I didn't expect to find Russians here.'

The Russian gave a thin smile 'Obviously not,' he said.

By this time the identity disks of his dead comrades had been found, together with his own pay-book and that of his Captain. For no reason at all, except to keep it safe, he had put his Captain's identity disk around his neck with his own.

They were taken from him and placed with the others on the table. The Russian looked over these finds and then at Igor.

'Why are you in possession of these?' he said, pointing to the pile of disks and pay-books.

'They belonged to my dead comrades; I took them so that their families could be told what had happened to them.'

The Russian leaned forward 'So, what did happen?'

Igor hesitated; but quickly decided to tell most of his story. He explained to the Russian how they had charged the guns and tanks of the invading Germans. He told how they had tried to take cover in a wood and how a falling tree that killed his horse had struck him down. How he had escaped from under the tree and found all his comrades dead, and later found his Captain's horse and decided to make the journey back to the farm.

He only omitted that he had killed the two Germans at the farmhouse. To cover this point Igor put the clock forward. He told the Russian that he had come across the farmhouse and the farmer and his wife had given him food and provisions to help him on his way.

The Russian officer listened in silence. When Igor had finished he looked at him for another half minute. Igor returned his gaze with steady eyes, waiting. Pushing his chair back, the Russian left the room, leaving him being guarded by the Sergeant. He returned with a map and spread it over the littered table.

'Show me where you were in battle with the Germans' he said.

Igor pointed to the spot where the battle had taken place. From there the Russian traced his finger along the route that Igor had indicated he had travelled over the past few weeks. Slowly folding the map the officer walked thoughtfully around the table and sat down facing Igor once again. He ran his eyes over his uniform. He leaned forward, elbows on table.

'Why do you not tell me the truth, Captain Gravik?' he said. 'You might as well, because the war is now over for you.'

'Captain Gravik? – I'm not Gravik – I've explained to you that I am Lieutenant Igor Radovak. This is the uniform of Captain Gravik, but I have explained that I changed my uniform for his because mine was covered in blood and he had no further use for it'

'So you say, so you say. You say you are Lieutenant Radovak, but you wear the uniform of Captain Gravik, that has been tampered with to make it look like the uniform of a Lieutenant, and the horse you have been riding seems to belong to Captain Gravik, because his name on the saddle. Not forgetting, of course, that the identity disk of Captain Gravik was around your neck, as well as that of Lieutenant Radovak.'

Igor was bewildered by the accusation of trying to change his identity. Why would I wish to do that, he thought. He could not think of any reason why the Russian should not believe his story.

'I have told you the truth, this is where I lived and I have told you why I came back'

'So you simply rode away from the battle scene and did not try to rejoin your regiment.' He slapped the top of the table hard. 'In the Red Army that would be classed as desertion and you would be shot.'

Igor, his temper rising, replied coldly. 'I would have rejoined my comrades if I could have found them, but by the time I got out from under the tree the fighting had moved on'

The Russian did not look convinced. 'Why were you hiding your uniform under a civilian coat and hat?'

'I wasn't hiding my uniform – I wore the coat against the cold. The farmer gave it to me. Look, if you don't believe me why don't ask the people from other farms around here, they will confirm my name and that I was brought up here'

'Unfortunately, I cannot do that. All the people who lived around here either fled before we arrived, or have been taken away.'

'But there must be something here, in the house, in the drawers of the cabinet, papers, letters, or something that will have the name of Radovak on it'

'There was nothing left when we came - but what would that prove? The Radovaks may have lived here, but you cannot prove to me that you are Lieutenant Igor Radovak, any more than prove to me that you are not Captain Ivan Gravik.'

Igor looked at the Russian. He simply could not understand why he should be accused of trying to take on the rank and identity of his dead Captain. The evidence the Russian wanted was lying far away in the wood where Igor had buried his Captain. In retrospect, it had been a mistake to leave the photographs with the bodies. He remembered that there had been two or three photographs in the Captain's wallet of himself with his wife and children. But even if he had brought the photograph, would this Russian have been convinced?

The photograph had no proof of identity on it; it could have been anyone wearing the same uniform. The only proof was the body and the photograph together. He could do no more than repeat his story.

'I am Lieutenant Igor Radovak and the details of my journey here are just as I have told you'

The Russian continued to look at him. 'Tell me then – Lieutenant - where did you learn to speak such excellent Russian?'

'Living so near the border, everyone around here could speak some Russian, but as my mother was Russian I learnt from her.'

'Ah! Your mother was Russian,' he exclaimed. 'And what was her name before she became a Pole'

'Anastasia Groski' said Igor. The Russian produced a notebook and fountain pen from his inside pocket and proceeded to write. After a few minutes he stopped writing, read through what he had written, and added a few more words. Satisfied, he tore the page from the notebook, rose to his feet, went over to the door and returned with two soldiers.

'Your story will, of course, be checked, but it is not up to me to loosen your tongue to get to the truth of why you are here.' Turning to the sergeant, he said, 'Take him away.'

As Igor was led out of the farmhouse the Russian officer handed the paper to the sergeant. Outside, with his hands tied together, Igor watched as one of the vehicles was backed out of the barn. It was a captured Polish Army staff car, with a small Russian flag now tied to

the bonnet. He noted grimly that it was a German made Mercedes –
Benz.

He was bundled inside and the two soldiers got in, one on either
side of him, both with pistols drawn. The sergeant climbed into the
passenger seat, he had with him the greatcoat and maps that had been
taken from Igor. There was a glass partition between the front seats
and the seats at the rear. The driver reached his arm back and made
sure the partition was closed before he started the engine.

As they moved towards the road the stallion, still tethered where
Igor had dismounted from it, turned its head and gazed at the car as it
passed

CHAPTER 5

Through powerful German binoculars given to him by a retreating Polish soldier, Jak Zenski scanned the distant valley that stretched out below him. Although invisible to the naked eye, he could just make out a column of mounted soldiers moving steadily along a track that he knew well. It had been the route taken by hundreds of escaping Poles over the past months. The track where, a few weeks ago, they had led the few remaining horses and released them. It had probably been a mistake, he thought, because instead of being picked up by fellow countrymen, they were more likely to have been picked up by the enemy.

At this distance he couldn't tell whether it was a Russian or a German patrol. It hardly mattered. What was more important was why they were there. Were they scouring the area looking for the last remnants of the defeated Polish army, or were they looking for partisans?

Ever since the secret camps had started operating no one from any of the groups had been back to the villages. The escaping soldiers had only been told the general direction they must take, and the partisans had watched them wind their way upwards and made sure that they were not being followed before guiding them to the camps. No one had ever gone back down the line. In this way the partisans had maintained their obscurity.

It was now October 1940, and there had been no further escapees for several weeks. Any stragglers were either being picked up before they could get through the last of the villages, or there were none left to help.

The light was beginning to fade as Jak put away the binoculars and walked back through the trees. Ten minutes later the tree line ended and in front of him was a steep incline of grass and rocks where, at some time, there had been a small landslip, exposing a rock face about fifteen or twenty metres high. Walking towards a clump of young bushy trees at the base of the incline he disappeared from view.

Behind the trees, Jak put his hand into what looked like a rabbit hole and lifted open the grass covered hatchway to the hideout. Turning around, he lowered himself down the few steps as he closed the hatch behind him. The hideout was half dugout and half log cabin. The inclined rock face against which it had been built was originally a horseshoe shaped hollow. Tree trunks had been placed vertically around the sides of the rock face and full-length tree trunks leant at an angle against them. On the outside, turfs had been laid on the trees, together with a few rocks, so that the overall effect looked like solid earth. The few odd rabbit holes that could be seen from the outside were, in fact, ventilation shafts and spy holes.

Arranged along the back of the hideout, in tiers of three, were bunk beds. In the centre was a black wrought iron stove with a pile of logs beside it, and between the stove and the bunk beds was a rough pine table with six stools around it. On the table an oil lamp provided the main lighting for the dim interior. The chimney from the stove stretched up to the roof where it was joined to three funnels that carried the smoke to filter through the outside trees. Several upturned wooden boxes were scattered around for sitting on, and upon one of these was perched an old wind-up gramophone.

Two partitioned rooms took up the far side - the smaller one for stores, the other bunk beds for the two women. Next to the two rooms a split pine log work surface jutted out from the wall, on which was a radio transmitter, in front of which Trishka was listening through headphones and jotting down a coded message in the light of two candles.

Hearing Jak arrive, Trishka put down the headphones and switched off the transmitter.

She sighed. 'No news of the evacuation yet – we're still being told to standby and be ready to leave at short notice'

Leon walked over from the stove and handed them both a mug of weak coffee.

'It's the weather' he said. 'Those 'planes need the right conditions. If there's a strong wind against them they don't have sufficient fuel to reach us, even with the extra fuel tanks they have. But if they can just get here we've enough fuel stockpiled for the return journey.'

With each journey from England, a 'plane had not only carried enough cans of fuel for the return journey, but an extra can or two for the partisans to keep for emergencies

They were the last three left in the camp. Over several weeks many of the camps had been closed down. The Polish partisans had themselves joined the escape route to England. Anastasia and Josef had gone out two weeks ago with Trishka's baby boy. Others in the group had joined up with one of the few remaining camps.

The 'planes that came over in the night could land and take off quickly on short improvised landing strips. So far they had been lucky. Flying low and arriving at dusk the 'planes had avoided being identified. Staying overnight, they had flown off at dawn, reaching the open sea at daylight. But German aircraft had started patrolling the forest areas, and it was only a matter of time before it became too dangerous to continue the flights.

The evacuation of the camps had also been decided for very practical reasons. At the time they had started operating, the camps were well provisioned. But the sheer numbers of escaping soldiers had reduced the provisions quicker than expected. So the rule they had imposed not to return to any occupied villages to obtain further provisions meant that they had run out of food and other essentials after a few months. So far, the flights from England had brought in enough to keep them going, but it was not likely that the flights would continue if there were no more soldiers to fly out.

The supply of meat from the traps had dwindled during the year. And as the food dwindled they had lost weight. They still had some oats, and a few withered apples, but they were out of flour for bread. Also, there was hardly any oil left for the lamp, and the battery for the radio transmitter was getting dangerously low. They would need so many essential supplies to stand any chance of surviving the coming winter. The alternative was to return to the occupied villages - and risk capture.

Jak finished his coffee and put the mug down.

'Did you manage to get the news from the BBC?' he asked.

Trishka shook her head. Her face looked pale and drawn in the light of the candles. She had worked hard at her job during the year, even though she had been pregnant. With her fair hair now cut short, the altered army uniform she was wearing made her look like a boy soldier. She was desperately worried that her baby son had made it safely to England with Anna, and whether they had recovered from the chest infection they had both been suffering from.

'I only heard the headlines Jak, I thought it best to save the battery. London is still being bombed - they are going through it over there.'

They looked solemnly at the radio transmitter, each trying to visualise what was happening in England. They could not help wondering what they would be escaping to if they got out. Would they again get embroiled in a German onslaught? Over the last few months, as they had listened to the news from England, they had marvelled that the British were still holding out. But the British were still in a high state of alert, thinking that Hitler might invade at any time. Earlier in the year Trishka had translated Winston Churchill's radiobroadcasts for them. They had been impressed with his declarations that Great Britain would never give in to Hitler - and with the way that the RAF had inflicted such losses on the Luftwaffe. But they still wondered how long the British could hold out.

Leon moved over to the stove and stirred the contents of a saucepan. Throwing in a handful of porridge oats, he gave it another stir and put the lid back on. On an enamel plate on the table was half a turnip. Carefully cutting three slices from it, he put one on each of the three plates set out. Lighting two more candles, he went back to the stove and looked into the saucepan.

'Okay, food up' he said. 'Rabbit and porridge stew on turnip'

'Thanks Leon,' they replied.

Before he sat down, Jak went over to the old gramophone, wound it up, and put on a record. As they ate, a scratchy rendition of Chopin's piano music echoed around them.

At first light the next day, Jak and Leon had a quick breakfast and went out into a frosty morning. They walked through the woods towards the vantage point from which Jak had seen the mounted patrol. Handing the binoculars to Leon, Jak pointed out the part of the track that needed watching and went off to check the traps.

Although well clothed against the cold, it was not long before Leon was stamping his feet to keep up the blood flow. At first there was little to see. An early morning mist was still hanging in the air of the valley. After an hour Jak re-appeared, carrying a small rabbit. 'Any movement?' he said.

Leon handed him the binoculars. 'Take a look', he replied, his face serious.

The mist had cleared, and as Jak focussed on to the track and followed it down he picked up the patrol immediately. Although still a long way off, it was much higher now. He handed back the binoculars. 'What do you think, Leon, are they looking for us?'

Leon lifted the binoculars to his eyes again.

'Yes, Jak, I think they might be. But it looks like a reconnaissance unit. They might have heard a rumour about us, or they might be just suspicious and wanting to know where all the retreating military have disappeared to. But they don't seem to be expecting any trouble. If they knew anything definite I think they'd be more than a patrol - and moving faster.' As he finished speaking, he stiffened and let out a curse.

'What is it Leon?'

Leon did not answer immediately. He adjusted the focus.

'They're not Germans, Jak,' he said quietly. 'They're Cossacks'

'Cossacks? My God! How long before they reach us would you say?'

'They're not hurrying – probably tomorrow at that pace. I'd better go down the track and set the detour, but I'll need a cup of coffee before I start out.'

They walked back towards the hideout, where Trishka was waiting for them in some excitement.

'I've just received the signal; a 'plane will fly in on Wednesday evening, but it will only stay long enough to re-fuel and get us on board. The forecast is a clear sky, and there'll be a full moon.'

Wednesday evening! It was now Monday, so they had another two days to wait. Leon was busy making the coffee as Jak explained to Trishka about the Cossack patrol coming towards them. Trishka looked from one to the other. She knew what they were thinking. She had heard what Cossacks did to any women they captured.

'Don't worry, no Cossacks will take me alive, but if it comes to it I'll make sure that I take one or two with me. How many are there?'

'Leon reckons there were ten; when they get a bit closer we'll know for sure' said Jak. 'I doubt if they'd find the hideout, the main danger is that they'll get close enough to mess up the flight out.'

'You're right Jak' said Leon, 'we can't allow them to get anywhere near the 'plane. If they get too close, we'll have to let off the red flare to warn the pilot and then take them on'

Jak nodded. So far they had not fired a single shot, but they had rifles and a revolver each, and a machine gun with two hundred rounds of ammunition - plus a box of grenades.

Leon finished his coffee and put the mug down. 'Well,' he said, 'first things first - I'll go and set the detour for them to follow.' Lifting the trapdoor, he said 'See you in about three hours,' and was gone. Jak lit a candle and went to the small storeroom, returning with a heavy rectangular box that contained the machine gun.

Twenty minutes later Leon was following the track down. It was hardly recognisable as a track; it was simply where the feet found it easiest to tread through the scattering of rocks. He kept to the cover of trees wherever he could, and after about an hour came to a larger outcrop of rocks.

This was the point that they had decided was the best place to block off should the need arise. It was calculated to make it seem that the best way up was to turn right at the rocks and take an easterly direction for a while. The rocks were about two metres high on either side of the track, and on the top were several loose rocks, which a careful scrutiny would have revealed were only held in place by a short piece of log.

Leon picked up a fallen branch and, standing as far back as he could, stabbed at the log. The branch was not strong enough and broke. He spent another few minutes finding one more suitable. With the stronger branch the log shifted at the third stab, and the rocks tumbled down. Turning to the other side of the track, he did the same. Looking at his work he was satisfied that it seemed natural, rather than contrived. To help the deception a little more, he stamped along the detour route for a little way to make it look used.

He glanced at his watch. Time to leave. It had taken him an hour to get there, he had been there for twenty minutes, and it would take him an hour and a half walking up hill to get back. He set off at a steady pace. Higher up, through the binoculars, Jak was keeping an eye on Leon and the Cossack patrol, and was pleased to see that Leon was on his way back without any sign that he had been spotted.

That night after they had eaten Leon set up the machine gun and gave a demonstration of how to load and fire it. He had given the same demonstration months ago, but he wanted to make sure they had not forgotten. He moved on to the handling of grenades, and finally they each took a rifle to clean. Nothing was said out loud - they knew that the consequence of using them and not getting away would be disastrous. The next day Trishka took the binoculars and watched the Cossacks while the two men checked the landing strip. They went along either side of the runway and uncovered the holes that would contain a rag soaked in petrol, which would be lit as soon as they heard the aircraft approaching. The holes ensured that the flames would hardly be noticeable at ground level, but would be clearly visible from the air.

Only the two small fires at the take off end would be above ground, but these would not be lit until the 'plane had refuelled and was ready to take off. They hid several hand grenades at the base of the trees lining the landing strip, together with spare rifles. They had decided that the only weapons they would take with them were a revolver each, and one grenade. The machine gun would be placed in a strategic position to protect the aircraft whilst it was on the ground, but if it was not needed they would leave it hidden under a piece of tarpaulin. Later, as darkness fell, they could see the patrol's campfire from the vantage point.

At nine o'clock, Trishka switched on the transmitter. There was a repeat of the coded message about the flight the next day. Tuning in to the BBC news, she listened for a minute before switching off.

'The message is still the same for tomorrow' she said, 'I couldn't catch much of the BBC, the battery is too low'. Going over to the stove she poured three mugs of coffee. No one spoke, but Trishka's words about the battery being low were in the thoughts of all of them. If they did not get out tomorrow they would be stranded. Even if London were prepared to organise another flight, they would not be able to contact them without the transmitter. The last bit of power left in the battery would be needed to signal England that they were abandoning the camp and making for the only other camp still operational - which meant a walk of over thirty kilometres.

They began to sort out what to take and what to leave behind. Trishka read the printed instructions that they had been given at the start of the flights. There would be no room for any luggage except a small haversack. The journey would be cold, so warmest clothing available was advised.

By ten o'clock they were sitting at the table with a hot drink listening to Chopin again. Leon produced a hip flask and measured a spoonful of brandy into each cup. Touching the mugs together, they wished each other 'good luck' for the next day, drank it down, and went to bed. But none of them got much sleep.

By six o'clock next morning they were sitting at the table again drinking coffee. Leon talked about his girl friend, Olga. She had been studying medicine in Germany when the war started. Although she had a German surname, her mother was half Jewish, and the last time he spoke to her she was trying to get out of Germany. Trishka spoke about her last telephone call from Igor, the day before the Germans invaded Poland.

Leon, a few months ago, had sent a message to England to see if they could get any information about Olga and Igor through the International Red Cross. They had received an acknowledgement of the message and that was all. With all that was going on they did not expect to hear anything for a long time, if at all.

Over the months, the close proximity of the camp had drawn them together. A fondness had grown between Trishka and Leon, and between Anna and Jak, which none of them dared to let develop into anything more than a platonic 'comradeship'. True feelings had to be suppressed.

On the table they gathered all the remaining food. It would last another three or four days at the most. Trishka made a good helping of porridge for breakfast, leaving enough to mix with the remains of a tin of corned beef for lunch - which would be their last meal before departure.

As soon as it was light enough Jak and Leon left the hideout. There had been a sharp frost during the night and a thick mist hung in the still air. Leon was anxious to get to the vantage point but they knew it would be pointless to try to see anything through the mist. Instead, they walked off in different directions to dismantle the traps.

When Leon got back to the vantage point an hour later he found Jak already there. The mist was thinning slowly but visibility down the track was still poor. Jak turned as he heard Leon approaching.

'It's still too thick to see anything, I doubt if it'll clear before mid-day'

They stared into the haze. Visibility was about three hundred metres. Above the mist the sun was trying to break through. They could only wait.

Their bearded faces were tight with tension. With only a few hours to go before the 'plane flew in they needed to know where the Cossacks were. The patrol should be near to the detour point, clearly in view, but in this mist they could only guess.

They spent the next hour going back and forth to the hideout; to get a hot drink and reassure Trishka. Leon went first, and then Jak, who returned with an equally anxious Trishka. It was just after noon when the sun had finally broken through to reveal a cloudless sky. Through the binoculars Leon carefully followed the track down towards the valley. He passed them to Jak.

'I can't see them Jak, you take a look'.

Jak took the binoculars and scanned the track up and down. Without lowering them, he cursed.

'Not a sign of them', he said. 'They must have reached the detour point and are out of view'

'Yes, but what we don't know is how long ago that was. They'll eventually turn north again, and if they keep going they could be getting dangerously close to the landing strip before nightfall'

'Well', said Trishka, 'we know that they're not heading directly for us, so is there any point in staying here any longer?'

'You're right, Trishka, but I think we'd better keep an eye on the track a little longer. You and Jak go and get something to eat - I'll give it another half hour and then follow you'.

It was two thirty when Leon returned to the hideout. After he had eaten, they decided to split up and walk carefully through the forest in the direction they thought the Cossacks might be heading. They would walk for thirty minutes, then turn around and retrace their steps. With two hand grenades in their pockets and a rifle each, they set off.

Trishka and Jak got back to the hideout at four o'clock. Fifteen minutes later Leon arrived. None of them had seen any sign of the Cossack patrol. Worried and tense, and needing something to do, they checked their haversacks. As the daylight began to fade they left the hideout for the last time and made their way to the landing strip.

Jak and Leon took a can of petrol each and walked down the runway sloshing a measure onto the rags in each hole, saving enough to light the torches. They stood just inside the cover of the trees near to where they had hidden the machine gun. Each with their own thoughts, they remained silent as the light faded. And then they all jumped as the quietness was shattered by a gunshot. The sound echoed through the trees and into the distance. They looked at each other.

'Rifle' said Leon, 'about one kilometre away, I'd say, perhaps less. The Cossacks have probably found something for their supper'

'I hope you're right, Leon,' Jak said, looking worried.

'Listen,' said Trishka, and held up a finger. Straining their ears they could hear the unmistakeable sound of an aeroplane engine. Leon started counting. The rule was that the runway was to be lit up thirty seconds after they first heard the sound of the engine. There was no point in remaining hidden any longer.

They each held a stick with a rag tied on the end and as Leon counted they dipped the sticks into the petrol can and lit them with a match. Running out to the holes they dabbed the torch into each one. Half a minute later the aircraft came into view, fast approaching over the trees. It touched down and bumped along the landing strip. Just before it stopped it swung around to face the way it had come.

As the aircraft flew over them they ran down the runway after it, and by the time it had turned around and stopped they were each carrying two jerry cans of petrol from the hidden store ready for the refuelling. The pilot and navigator jumped from the aircraft. In a broad Yorkshire accent, pointing east, the pilot spoke. 'Who lit bloody big bonfire o'er yonder? 'Til I saw runway light up I thought t'was landing strip'

Jak and Leon looked at each other, wondering what he was pointing at. They could not understand his odd English. Trishka, although not familiar with English spoken with a Yorkshire accent, managed to grasp what the pilot was saying.

'It's probably the camp of a Cossack patrol' she panted, 'we need to get out of here fast.'

The pilot raised his eyebrows. 'Bloody 'ell,' he said. He turned to the navigator.

'Get move on Freddy – they've got bloody Cossacks after them.'

Freddy was getting on with it. The only sound was petrol gurgling into the fuel tanks. It was a bright moonlit night and the runway was clearly visible. The pilot turned to Trishka.

'Don't bother t'light fires at end of runway' he said. 'Reckon there's nuff light to get off OK – it'll save a bit o'time'

The pilot squinted at his luminous watch, making rapid calculations. So far as he could judge, the campfire he'd seen from the air was about a kilometre to the east. If that was the campfire of the Cossacks, and they decided to investigate the sound of a 'plane landing near to them, they would, at best, only be able to canter through the trees, rather than come at full gallop. He still dare not risk being on the ground for more than fifteen minutes. At twelve minutes he looked up.

'Leave last two cans' he said. 'Let's get off' He clambered into the aircraft, and the navigator helped the others to get aboard before pulling himself up and shutting the door. The engines of the aircraft roared into life and the wheels started moving forward.

In the darkness of the fuselage, they could not see the grim face of the pilot as he hurtled the aircraft down the short runway. And behind them they did not see the mounted horses emerge from the forest and stop to watch what looked like the certain destruction of the 'plane as it hit the trees at the far end of the landing strip.

Instead, the passengers in the aircraft flinched as the one of the wheels touched the top of a tree as it soared over them, and the horsemen below watched curiously as the aeroplane faded into the night sky.

CHAPTER 6

The long drive had ended at Minsk, where Igor was handed over to the Soviet Secret Police, the NKVD. Stripped of his uniform, he was hosed down with icy cold water, and then thrown a set of prison clothes and a pair of canvas shoes. The prison trousers were too big, but no belt or other means of support was provided, which made it necessary to use one hand to hold them up. The top was a loose shirt-blouse, a Russian *rubashka*. There were no laces for the canvas shoes, so it was necessary to shuffle along to keep them from falling off.

The cell he was pushed into measured two metres by three, with a bench along one wall and on it a thin, dirty, canvas mattress filled with straw. One coarse blanket was folded up on the mattress, and there was a bucket with a wooden lid in the corner. In the far wall, half a metre above his head was a small square window with two iron bars.

The walls of the prison, corridors and cells alike, had all been painted a drab grey, the paint flaking off. In the corridors the smell of carbolic soap failed to stifle the stink of body odour, urine and excrement that came from the cells. The only heating was from pipes running along the corridor walls just above the cell doors. They did not extend into the cells. Prisoners soon found that the warmest place was against the wall next to the cell door.

The food each day was a bowl of watery cabbage soup and a hunk of dry rye bread, with a mug of tepid ersatz coffee. Occasionally, a piece of raw turnip or a small onion might be with the bread. After a while this meagre diet became the highlight of the day.

His interrogation at Minsk began in a deceptively straightforward way. Name, rank; serial number; date of birth; parent's names; education and training before military service. And there were endless trivial questions about his early days at school; the name of his schoolmaster, his school friends, his activities after school.

Being so near the Russian border, and able to speak Russian, surely he visited Russian villages? He was asked about the villages he knew and the names of the people he had met. His ability to speak Russian was clearly regarded with suspicion, and so his answers to the questions were guarded.

He didn't admit to the many hunting trips on the Russian side of the border he had made with his father. Nor to the summer weekend camping expeditions with his friends, where any thoughts of which side of the border they were on did not enter their heads. Instinctively, Igor blotted out any knowledge of anything or anyone that was Russian.

After two weeks his suspicion that the questioning he was being subjected to was not normal procedure for a prisoner of war proved right. He was not, to the Russians, a mere soldier. The realisation came to him when he was asked to sign a document that he was told '…just confirms the answers you have given to the questions.' But Igor noticed that the document was typed out, whereas the answers he had given had been written down in pencil. His replies had not been taken away and typed out; the typed sheets had been prepared before his interrogation.

When he requested to read the document before he signed it, his interrogator changed from being polite and almost affable, to an enraged and snarling tyrant. It was then that the reason why he was being treated differently was revealed. In exasperation, the interrogator shouted, '…sign it, you spying Polish swine - sign it!,' followed with a succession of slaps and punches to the head.

As he reeled from the onslaught, the word 'spying' echoed in his ears. So that was it. A Polish army officer with a number of different identity disks and pay-books, two identity disks around his neck, able to speak fluent Russian, and found wearing a civilian coat and hat near the Russian border, added up, to a suspicious communist mind, to only one explanation - he was a spy.

The merit that the Russian at the farm expected from capturing a spy had passed, in turn, to the NKVD, who had decided to share in the merit by getting him to 'confess'. Having accused someone of being a spy, the system, the Soviet system, demanded the culprits file to show the 'evidence' in the form of a signed 'confession'.

One of the things that he had grown up with; that his mother had constantly reminded him of, was that common sense and reason had been taken over and turned into an entirely different meaning in communist USSR. In 1917, at the start of the revolution, the Russian workers and peasants, the *proletariat*, had been urged by Lenin to fight against the forces loyal to the Tsar in return for 'land' and 'freedom'. And the *proletariat* had fought - but after the revolution the promises were forgotten.

In his teens, in the 1930's, Igor had heard dark rumours and stories coming across the Russian border about the regime Stalin had created after Lenin died. Rumours about the forced migration of the Kulaks to Siberia and other places far inside the Russian wastelands. There had been rumours of the imprisonment and starvation of untold numbers of people; of show trials and executions of those who, for some reason or other, did not agree with the system, or complained, or had fallen out of favour with someone in authority. So far as the people were concerned, the oppressive regime of the Tsar, taken over by Lenin in the name of the 'working classes', and inherited by Stalin was, in effect, just another ruling elite far more oppressive and cruel than the Tsar had ever been.

Igor was well aware that when countries went to war spies were invariably executed. So by signing a 'confession,' or even giving them anything that they could use as evidence against his story, would be like signing his own death warrant.

His frustration that he was accused of being a spy turned to a deep-rooted anger. He resolved that, whatever they did to him, he would not 'confess.' He realised that the whole process was aimed at reducing the victim to the lowest level of human degradation and despair, to turn each prisoner into the likes of a cowed and frightened animal.

His decision not to give in somehow elevated him above the final despair, as though his body and his brain were detached from each other. He could not analyse his feelings and spent no time trying to. His instincts were simply to maintain enough strength, mental and physical, to survive each ordeal. To this end he retained one single thought. If he were to die, he would die with his self-respect intact.

The interrogations were not continuous; sometimes there were gaps of several weeks. As the months dragged by Igor's tall, fit and muscular frame was gradually reduced to the posture and shuffle of a much older man. His hair became long and matted and the bottom half of his face was covered by a bushy beard. Even so, part of the posture that he had adopted was a deception.

He had learnt that to stand upright and try to walk with some measure of dignity attracted extra abuse and physical punishment from the guards. So, with his loss of weight he had adapted to appearing to be more dejected, depressed and mentally and physically worse than he actually was. The acting came out of his resolve, it gave him something to cling on to, something that kept his mind working and was all part of not giving in. He devised other small victories against his captors and tormentors.

One such victory was to do with his ability to speak Russian. When he was transferred to another prison at Kharkov, and was asked if he could speak Russian, he had readily agreed that he could. But when, during further interrogations, he was asked questions in Russian, he frequently pretended not to understand key words and phrases put to him. Only when the questioner was becoming dangerously frustrated with him not understanding did he suddenly pretend to comprehend the word or words that were needed.

In this way he found that he could reduce the number of questions put to him. His pretence was amply rewarded when, one day, his interrogator muttered in exasperation to one of the guards 'What fool said that this stupid Pole could speak Russian?'

Another victory he had over his captors was in the painstaking manufacture of 'string' to hold up his trousers and use as laces for his shoes. This was not ordinary string; it was made from his hair. He invented this string making ability by chance. With nothing else to do during his long hours of isolation, he started to plait small strands of his hair and beard. It took him a long time to plait one strand into the thickness of a thin twine. Several times he did this and then he would undo the strand and start again.

The idea of utilising the strands did not occur to him at first. He had no way of cutting them and to pull them out would have been too painful. But the breakthrough came one day when he was slowly puffing away on half a cigarette thrown into his cell by a friendly but unseen guard. He had plaited a few strands of his beard that day and as he stroked his beard he decided to singe them off with the aid of the cigarette.

Looking at the five or so strands he had in his hand, it dawned on him that he could use them as laces for his floppy canvas shoes.

From this, the next step was to make enough strands to go around his waist to hold up his trousers.

It took him weeks of painstaking work, and it rested on him being given another lighted cigarette. But the day eventually came when he carefully tied his hair string around his waist and, for the first time since he was imprisoned, he could stand and let go of his trousers without them falling around his ankles. When he went to be interrogated he had to pretend to hold his trousers and shuffle in the same way, but the psychological strength he had achieved from this additional 'victory' contributed to his continual survival. To survive, to live through it, was his constant thought.

And then came a day when two guards entered his cell and handed him an army issue towel and a small square of green soap.

'Time for you to wash, Polack', said one, and he was escorted to a crude concrete shower room. Igor was wary but fascinated by what was happening, but found that each cubicle was occupied by a fellow prisoner busy going through the motions of washing away the ingrained filth and grime of months of captivity. No talking was allowed between the prisoners, but a few grunts of pleasure amidst the running water could be heard.

Igor took off his dirty prison clothes and put them on the floor of the shower. He stood on them as the water cascaded over him. He lathered and rubbed his body until it glowed. He lathered the soap into his hair and beard and, finally, used the remains of the soap on his prison clothes and watched the brown dirt rinse away. After the shower they had their beards and heads shaved.

On the following day Igor was surprised to be given back his old uniform and told to change. Shortly after he was led out into the prison yard, a bleak square surrounded on three sides by cellblocks with tiny barred windows. Snow was beginning to fall as the yard began to fill up with other prisoners.

No one spoke, but they stared at each other in the hope of finding a face they recognised. It was a fruitless hope, since it was doubtful that even their own mothers would have been able to recognise their gaunt looking sons amidst so many shaven heads.

Eventually about three hundred prisoners were gathered together. They were told to sit in rows, and the snow fell steadily down and settled on them. When the rows were complete and they had been

45

counted, brown paper bags were distributed to each prisoner. Inside each bag was a small loaf of bread and a piece of dried fish.

A Sergeant blew a whistle and the prisoners focused their attention on him. He held up one of the brown paper bags.

'You have each been given one of these bags. It is food for the first part of your journey to your allotted camp. There will be no more rations for three or four days, so you are advised not to eat it all on the first day.' The massive doors of the prison swung open to reveal a convoy of army trucks waiting outside. He pointed to them.

'As your name is called you will get into the trucks in an orderly fashion'.

He nodded to a corporal holding a clipboard. As the names were read out the prisoners got up and brushed the snow from their clothes before getting into a truck. They did this in silence, but they all seemed eager to get on with what lay ahead. Just as daylight was disappearing everyone was finally aboard and two soldiers clambered into the back of each truck before they started off. At the rear of the convoy was an open truck with four soldiers manning a mounted machine gun.

The trucks sped along ill lit roads, most of which were lined with drab looking blocks of flats which stood out starkly from the fresh white snow that was still falling.

The roads were badly maintained and there was cursing and swearing among the prisoners as they were bounced about. The men did not talk, but Igor sensed that, like him, they were enjoying the experience of being in the company of other men once again. For those who wanted to, there would be plenty of time for talking later on.

They stopped at a small branch line railway station and were ordered out of the trucks. Not far away from the station the lighted windows of houses could be seen, but the station and its surroundings were deserted. A steam engine was drawn up at the single gas-lit platform. It was coupled at the rear to a long line of cattle wagons. Out of sight, at the other end of the wagons, the sounds of another engine could be heard at the front of the train. The guards strung out along the platform and the prisoners were ordered to sit in rows as another role call was made.

Two guards hoisted up each prisoner in turn and a further two guards inside the wagon allocated each prisoner his space. Working first around the walls, the guards gradually worked towards the centre until sixty men were wedged together, with just enough floor space to sit with their knees up to their chin, kneel, or stand.

No prisoner had the space to change a position without help. Each position depended upon the cooperation of those around him. Igor had been allocated a space near the wall, with his back to the engine, which was regarded at first as one of the prime positions, since those prisoners had something to lean on. His opinion changed when the train was on the move, since through the gaps in the walls came an icy draught that sent his back numb with cold.

After an hour the train stopped again, and through the few small gaps in the panels of the wagon, those who were able to see out reported that another batch of prisoners were getting onto the train. There were two further stops that night at small stations to take on more prisoners.

During the night Igor ate half of his food and placed his bag behind his shoulders. It not only provided some insulation from the cold, but would be more difficult to steal if he fell asleep.

Someone raised the question of where they were heading. All agreed that the destination was Siberia, but the discussion revealed hidden anxieties. Were they going to be forced to work in salt mines, or coalmines, or even gold mines?

Igor did not join in the speculation. He was so cold that his own thoughts were on how many were likely to survive the journey. The first night of the journey was bad enough, the train just crawled along, but it became a nightmare when they were kept locked up throughout the following day. It was thirty hours before they stopped again.

As Igor looked around he could see that many of the prisoners had injuries. At one stop he watched as a prisoner near him lifted his trouser leg to reveal a gruesome looking injury around his kneecap. It was crawling with maggots. Having inspected it, and in spite of the cold, he dropped his trousers and urinated on his wound. Looking around he invited others to also urinate on his wound. At first many of them grinned and thought he was joking, but he persuaded them that he was serious.

Although one or two came forward to help him out, very few had any liquid left in them. The man explained that the maggots had protected the wound from gangrene. Now he needed to keep it clean. Apart from the cold snow, all he could think of was urine, which contained salt.

Only occasionally did the train rumble through larger towns. The train usually remained stationery on branch lines during the day and started moving at dusk. But there was one day when the train stopped at a small station just before dawn. On this day some four thousand prisoners spontaneously erupted with such a noise of raging and roaring that would have woken the population of a town.

It happened because those with an eye against one of the spy-hole cracks in the sides of the wagon would report anything of interest to those sitting behind them. Sometimes hours would go by before anything of the remotest interest caught their eye. On the day that they stopped, another train of a similar type drew up alongside on a parallel track. Suddenly the lookout, reporting the arrival of the other train, let out a yell. 'There are women and children on it!'

There was a scramble inside as those who were nearest pushed and shoved each other to get a look at the other train. 'They're Polish women,' came the shout.

The train had small barred windows through which faces could be seen. The wretched pale faces looked confused at the noise coming from a cattle train with closed doors and no windows of any kind. The men who had a wife and children were in the worst state. They raged and roared out their despair and frustration. They hammered at the insides of the wagon with their bare hands.

Soldiers ran up and down the train banging on the sides with their rifles for the prisoners to be silent, and there was urgent shouting to the other train to get moving again.

When the trains moved on the men remained quiet for the rest of the day. The thought that their wives and children might be suffering the same kind of misery as themselves was the cause of many silent tears in the darkness. It brought into focus the sheer horror, degradation and hopelessness of being prisoners of the Russians.

At the next stop, before they were served with any food or water, officers went down the line of wagons and shouted about the need to remain silent during the journey. There was the threat of not being given any food or water if such an incident was repeated. The threat of starvation was enough to maintain discipline.

The train crawled along the next day, until, in mid-afternoon, it grinded to a stop. Those at the spy-holes reported that it looked like they were stopping early. Then the doors of the wagon were flung open with the shout 'All out, all out, end of the line'

There was some eagerness to get out of the train and they jumped down with fresh energy. But as they stood there with their heads bent low against an icy wind, they soon wished they were back in the comparative comfort of the stinking wagons. Where they had stopped was not a station but a siding with piles of logs and timber stacked on either side, fifty metres back from the track. As the train emptied they huddled behind wood-stacks out of the wind, and watched as several dead bodies were gathered from the trucks and carried away for burial in the snow.

The question on every prisoner's lips was the same. 'This is not Siberia – where are we?'

One or two prisoners knew, and word was quickly passed from mouth to mouth. They were near Smolensk, on the edge of the Katyn forest.

CHAPTER 7

With the rest of the staff at the military academy, Max was flown out of Warsaw a few days before it surrendered to the Germans. Tall and broad shouldered, with a full head of dark hair streaked with grey, he looked distinguished in the uniform of a Polish Colonel. But he still had the weather beaten complexion of a farmer. In England the Poles were allocated a country house about twelve miles north of London as a Divisional HQ, to which the soldiers who escaped from Poland were sent to be vetted and transferred to new units within the British Army.

As soon as he arrived Max wrote to Stefan to let him know he was in England. He was hoping his son would have some news about his mother and the others. But there was no reply to his letter.

A few weeks later when he got leave he travelled from London to Birmingham to look for him. He caught a bus to the suburbs and found the address of the house where Stefan had been lodging.

Five soldiers, Royal Engineers, who were in the area constructing anti-aircraft batteries, occupied the house. They had no idea who the previous occupants had been, but they gave him an unopened letter addressed to his son. It was his own letter written when he had arrived in England.

On the corner across the road was a newsagent and tobacconist shop, and he went inside to ask if they knew where the people from the house opposite had gone.

The woman in the shop told him that there had been three students from the university lodging there. She had heard that the students had all enlisted, and shortly after that the owners had gone to live with relations in Coventry.

Max returned to London. All he could do was to make enquiries through the appropriate channels to see if his son had enlisted.

*

Stefan recognised the German bomber as it flew through the thin clouds above him. A Junkers 88. He had spotted it break away from the main formation and head for the English Channel. About three hundred metres separated them, and he was certain that the German was unaware that he was on his tail. As the shadow of the aircraft darted from cloud to cloud he eased his Hurricane up towards its exposed underbelly and moved his finger to the firing button.

Taking a quick glance at his turn and bank indicator, he set his sights on the next break in the clouds. He started to fire before he could actually see it. The machine guns burst to life and, in the few quick seconds it flashed into view, he could see the bullets hitting home. A thin stream of black smoke appeared as his bullets followed it into the next cloud.

He stopped firing, determined to follow the trail of smoke. Two seconds later the cloud in front of him erupted into an inferno of orange and black and the Hurricane was thrown sideways by the blast. Instinctively, he pulled the stick towards him and the aeroplane soared upwards, bursting through the clouds and levelling out in a clear blue sky. He took an anxious look at each of his wings, but apart from several holes, they were all there, the machine was still flying.

In the distance he could see other enemy aircraft, not in any kind of formation, but flying singly or in pairs, heading back towards France. Glancing at his fuel gauge, he realised he had been in the air too long already; there was no chance of chasing them.

Once again a single squadron of British fighters had routed a much larger formation of enemy aircraft. Pleased with his kill, he was certain he had severely damaged two others. A few other Hurricanes broke through the clouds around him.

'OK, let's go home,' the voice of his squadron leader crackled over the intercom.

With a last wistful look at the departing enemy, Flight Sergeant Stefan Radovak turned his aircraft back towards his base at Hornchurch. He was the youngest of the four Polish pilots in the squadron. The others were Polish Air Force pilots, who had flown their aircraft to England when it became obvious that Poland had fallen.

Somewhere there was a whole squadron of Poles, and also Czechs; French; Dutch, Canadians, Australians, New Zealanders and motley others from the British colonies, all keen to score a 'kill' against Hitler and his Nazis. But it was the Poles who had the reputation for being the most bloodthirsty. For what the Germans had done to their country, for all the atrocities they had committed, the Poles were obsessed with killing Germans. Unlike his fellow pilots, Stefan had not witnessed the bombing and misery caused by the German blitzkrieg; but he was left in no doubt about what had happened in Poland by those who had escaped, and he continually grieved at not knowing what had happened to his family.

As a student in England Stefan had listened to the wireless and read the newspapers with growing alarm as Hitler had bullied his way into Czechoslovakia before turning his attention to Poland. The week before the Germans invaded all his efforts to contact his family had failed. He had written to his mother at the farm; sent a telegram to his father at the military base near Warsaw, but had received no replies. He had no idea where Igor was, except that he would probably be fighting somewhere in the front line. Until the invasion, Stefan had kept in regular touch by a weekly letter, but as news of the German onslaught came through he had lost all hope of further correspondence.

When it was announced that Britain had declared war on Germany, Stefan had travelled from his student lodgings to the centre of Birmingham to join the queues of men enlisting for the army. It was only when he met some fellow students waiting to join the RAF that he signed up with them.

Within two weeks a letter arrived enclosing a travel voucher and instructions to report for training to RAF Station Uxbridge, in Middlesex. On a crowded train from New Street station, standing most of the way, he travelled to London, then on to Uxbridge.

The view from the train gave him an insight of Britain preparing for war. Trenches were being dug, sandbags piled up to protect windows and doors against bomb attacks. Soldiers were marching along roads; others drilling on parade grounds. People were fitting blackout curtains to windows; signposts were being taken down, and air raid shelters were being built.

Stefan had noticed how the British made jokes about Hitler; ridiculed him, and treated him with contempt; but underneath they were deadly serious, and he did not think that they would be easily beaten. He was glad that he was joining them in their fight. Now Poland had fallen to the Germans, he could take revenge by helping the British defend their island.

The airfield came into view. As he approached the landing strip Stefan could see that several of the squadron had already landed. It was too early yet to see if any were missing. He noticed that the aeroplane fitted with the extra fuel tanks was tucked away in a corner of the airfield. They all knew that this aircraft was used to fly to Poland and back, bringing out soldiers and civilians keen to continue fighting the Germans. It had not been there when they flew out earlier, so it must have arrived back recently. He wondered if the passengers would still be on the airfield. In the past he had met several, mainly soldiers and partisans, in the mess or in the canteen, after they had been given a bath and clean clothes. He had managed to have a quick conversation with some of them at the bar about the conditions back in Poland before the army took them off.

At the debriefing he claimed his kill, and learnt that the squadron had lost two aircraft, against six confirmed enemy losses, and several damaged. One pilot had been killed, but the other, Mike Townly, a Canadian, had parachuted safely into the middle of a hockey match at a girl's school.

After a quick shower and a shave Stefan made his way to the mess, in the hope of meeting with the fellow Poles who had arrived during the morning.

As usual, most of the pilots who had flown that day were already there. The talk was usually about the most recent dogfight, or going to meet girls at the village pub. Both involved drinking lots of beer.

Stefan joined the other Polish pilots at the bar and looked around.

'Has anyone seen today's arrivals from Poland?' he asked casually in Polish.

The others shook their heads. 'No,' said one of them, 'I heard that an army car was waiting as they arrived and they were whisked off pretty quickly – two men and one woman, apparently.'

'That's a pity,' said Stefan, as he took a sip of beer. 'They did the same a few weeks ago; I heard there was a woman carrying a baby on that trip.' His shoulders sagged a little in disappointment.

'Does anyone fancy going to the pictures tonight?'

There were three cinemas within reach at Hornchurch. The pictures were a good way to wind down, and the other three Poles, who did not speak much English, found it a useful way to improve their vocabulary. They gave a nod and, finishing their drinks, filed out, discussing what cinema to go to.

Just two months ago they would not have been allowed to leave the airfield. After the squadron had covered the evacuation from Dunkirk, the Luftwaffe had concentrated their attention on destroying the English airfields. The fighter pilots were in the air three or four times a day, and the whole of fighter command was stretched to the limit. By August it was not Spitfires or Hurricanes the RAF was short of, it was pilots.

But just when it was getting almost impossible to carry on, the Luftwaffe changed tactics and started to bomb London and the big cities. Now, in October, the bombing raids were made at night and, so far, fighter command had not been able to adapt to night fighting. The threat of invasion was still very real - nobody was convinced it was cancelled - just postponed for the winter.

The Poles usually stuck together, and Stefan would go along to act as interpreter. In the air their lust to kill Germans had led to disciplinary action against them. As soon as enemy aircraft were spotted, they would break formation and go tearing off on their own. The squadron leader had found that the worst punishment he could inflict was to ground them for twenty-four hours for each breach. It had been a tough decision to make, because they were so desperately needed in the air; but it had worked, and 275 Squadron now had an enviable reputation for its efficiency in the air.

Stefan had not found training to be a pilot easy. The average flying hours with an instructor before going solo had been ten hours, and Stefan had still been struggling to get to grips with the process after fifteen hours. Only on the final test, when he had become resigned to almost certain failure, and so became more relaxed, did he finally twig how easy it all was. After that there was no stopping him; he

54

soon became an expert flyer. And when they moved to Grantham for gunnery training, he showed himself to be a formidable marksman.

This, he knew, was thanks to his father's tuition as a boy. As a gunnery officer from the 'Great War', his father had made sure that both his sons knew how to shoot. Out on the Pripet Marshes, he had taught them about trajectory, velocity, wind speed and all the other things to be taken into account when firing a gun at any distance.

The tuition had paid off. In his Hurricane, Stefan seldom missed anything that came within his sights. And every time he fired a gun his father's voice was never far away; advising and encouraging him; and his thoughts would follow from his father to his mother, and then to his brother, Igor, and he would worry what had happened to them.

*

It was almost a year after Max had travelled to Birmingham that Anna took that same journey to find her son. She found the house occupied by female ATS, who were part of the squad manning the nearby anti-aircraft battery. But they knew nothing about who lived there at the start of the war, and suggested that she enquire at the shop across the road.

The shop had some 'fallen' apples for sale and she bought a pound. She asked the man who served her if he knew where the occupiers of the house at the outbreak of war might be. The shopkeeper, noting her foreign accent, looked at her curiously. Noting the look, Anna explained.

'Before the war started my son was a student lodging in that house. I only arrived in England a short time ago, and I want to let him know I am here. Also, I hoped that he might have heard from his father, and perhaps his brother,' she said, and then, more quietly, added; 'It is the war, you understand, it has split us all up – like so many others.'

'Where are you from lady?' the shopkeeper asked.

'From Poland,' said Anna.

The shopkeeper gave her a sympathetic look. 'All I know is that the students left to join up – in the army I think. Then the owners left, and the house was taken over by the army.'

'The army - he enlisted in the army?' said Anna, 'yes, that is what Stefan would do.' She paid for the apples and took out a piece of paper.

'Thank you for your help - if he returns could you give him my address? I have put his name there. It is Stefan – Stefan Radovak.'

'Of course I will lady, and I'll tell the wife to look out as well.'

Anna thanked the shopkeeper and took the long journey back to London. She was hopeful that the army would be able to tell her where Stefan was. She would start enquiries tomorrow.

Later that day, when they closed the shop, the shopkeeper told his wife about the Polish woman who had been enquiring about her son. This jogged the memory of his wife.

'That's funny, there was a foreign army officer in here about a year ago asking about who lived across the road. Probably not connected – there was three students living there. But he didn't leave any name or address, so we can't tell, can we?'

'No, we can't,' he said, and shook his head. 'It's a bugger, this war, tearing families apart.'

CHAPTER 8

After a role call they were herded into columns and marched off into the biting wind. The rumour spread that they were being taken to a prisoner of war camp in the forest near Katyn. They walked three abreast along a track that looked as though it had only recently been made. There were some who spoke in low voices as they walked, but most trudged along in silence.

Occasionally there were shouts from guards; sometimes a shot rang out. They passed civilian workmen coming from the opposite direction, who carried picks and shovels on their shoulders and stepped off the track and walked alongside it, or stood aside and watched as the column walked by.

It was the way that they stared that made Igor uneasy. Not belligerent or mocking, but passive and pitying. Dusk was approaching, and Igor almost missed the gesture that one of the workmen made, but others saw it clearly. There was an angry shout from one of the Russian guards, who ran forward and clubbed the man to the ground with the butt of his rifle.

But the prisoners who had seen the gesture were already muttering to each other. The workman had raised his hand to his throat and drawn his finger across it.

As they trudged on one of the prisoners spoke in a louder voice, so that those around him could hear.

'They're going to kill us,' he said.

There was a bitter laugh from another. 'What - all of us?' he said.

Igor listened, his thoughts flashing back three years, when stories came across the Russian border that Stalin had purged his army of thousands of officers and either had them shot, or sent to a more lingering death in Siberia. One thing he had found out on the train journey they had just taken was that the three or four thousand prisoners who were now trudging through the Katyn forest were all Polish officers.

If Stalin could so callously kill his Russian officers, Igor had no doubts that he was capable of murdering Polish ones. Minutes later there was a small commotion ahead and the attention of the guards nearest to them was distracted. Seizing the chance, Igor nudged the man next to him and nodded towards the trees. Of one mind they lurched out of the column and made for the cover of the forest. Others joined them, and then there were shouts, followed by the rapid rat-a-tat of a sub-machine gun. There were screams as some were hit. Twigs and leaves showered down as bullets zipped around their heads.

The two of them stayed together and pounded through the trees. The snow was not as deep under the trees but even as he ran Igor realised that they were leaving footprints for the guards to follow. After five minutes his companion began gasping and gulping for air, and then fell to the ground. The months in the cells with poor food and lack of exercise had sapped their stamina.

'Can't go on - got to stop - leave me,' he panted.

Igor stood over him, wheezing, unable to speak. He reached down and pulled him up. They stumbled on. The shouting and gunfire continued behind them, but now seemed further away.

The daylight was almost gone when they came to the stream - a small trickle just a stride across. Igor pulled his companion after him and walked into the water and along the bed of the stream. The water was freezing cold and within two or three minutes his feet were numb. He lost track of time but doggedly placed one foot in front of the other until he heard a splash behind him and turned to see his companion lying in the stream, unable to move.

He pulled him out of the water and then lay alongside him. Spent and exhausted, he closed his eyes, knowing that he could go no further. He dimly realised that if they fell asleep in the open they were not likely to wake up. But the fear of death did not deter his intense desire to sleep.

He hardly noticed the slight trembling of the ground, or the rumbling noise, but the hoot of the train jumped him awake and forced his eyes open. The railway line was about ten or twelve metres away. His companion had also roused himself and, wearily pushing at the ground to sit up, gave a crooked grin.

They struggled to their feet and stumbled to the track, watching the end of a freight train disappearing into the darkness. Without hesitation they started to follow it. They could see a small hut at the side of the track, but what drew them to it more than anything else was the fact that it had a chimney.

The thought of getting out of the cold, lighting a fire and being able to sleep was, at that point, more important than the possibility of getting captured again.

*

Igor fumbled his hand down the door, expecting a padlock that, somehow, they would have to break. But instead he found a door handle and, turning it, the door opened with a slight creak.

His eyes focused on the bright glow from a small stove. A pungent waft of warm air escaped into the night. He heard a swift scrabbling noise and was aware of a figure, woken from slumber, reaching out for a shotgun leaning against the wall.

'Hold! - We are not armed, comrade,' said Igor quickly, in Russian.

He saw the man hesitate for a split second, and then take hold of the gun and lay it across his stomach.

'Who're you - what d'you want,' he demanded. His voice was gruff, but unafraid.

'We are Polish officers - we have escaped from the Russians,' replied Igor. He wavered from fatigue, and put his hand to the wall. There was a rickety chair behind the door and he sank down to it. Beside him, his companion slumped down to the floor with his back to the wall.

The man looked from one to the other. 'Escaped prisoners, eh', he said, 'from Katyn, no doubt - I've heard about that.'

'If we could rest here - sleep a little - we will move on in the morning,' said Igor

'Huh - they'll shoot me if they find you here - you better go,' the man said. There was no reply. 'D'you hear – you'll get me shot.' The only sound was deep breathing. His intruders were asleep.

He stared at them for several seconds and then, shaking his head in resignation, he put his gun down and lay his head back to his straw pillow.

Igor was the first to wake. Through the one tiny window he could see from the position of the weak sunlight that it was about midday. There was no sign of the man, but the stove had been well stacked, and there was a small saucepan and a battered coffee pot on top of it. Igor had no wish to steal from the man who had saved them from freezing to death in the open, but he was convinced that the contents of the saucepan and the jug had been purposely left for them.

His companion stirred and sat up; looking confused, he pushed his hand through his hair.

'Where are we,' he croaked.

Igor noticed for the first time that they wore uniforms of the same rank.

'Somewhere near Smolensk, I'd guess,' he replied. He held out his hand. 'I'm Radovak, by the way – Igor Radovak – cavalry.

The other man took his hand. 'Nikolas Solik – call me Solik - artillery,' he said. 'Thanks for pulling me on yesterday - I didn't think I'd make it.'

Igor smiled. 'Neither did I - but we've only survived one night – we're not safe yet.'

' No,' said Solik, looking around. 'Where's our saviour?'

'Not here - but I think he intends us to help ourselves to this.' Igor pointed to the saucepan and jug of coffee.

Solik stood up and looked into the saucepan, sniffed it, and pulled a face. It was a grey porridge or gruel. 'It probably tastes better than it looks,' he said.

Igor handed him a spoon, and he tasted it. Without saying anything Solik handed the spoon back to Igor, who repeated the process.

Igor's mouth twisted in disgust, and Solik laughed.

'There - what did I tell you,' he said picking up a second spoon and helping himself. 'Anyway, it's food, and it's hot, and I'm starving.'

Between them they ate the contents of the saucepan and drank the coffee - which, surprisingly, tasted very good. When they finished, Igor looked around. The timber hut was no more than three metres square. There was a rack with a variety of tools for repairing rail track, and a few pieces of old clothing and a couple of greasy caps hung from nails in the wall.

Their footwear was still damp, but their uniforms had dried on them during the night.

'We'd better get going,' said Igor, and moved towards the door. He wrestled with it, but it wouldn't open.

'He's locked us in,' he said in alarm, turning to Solik as a dreadful thought entered his head. Had he gone to tell the Russians that he had caught two escaped prisoners?

Solik looked on, his face serious. 'Let me try,' he said, and pushed hard at the door, and then pounded it with his fists. Igor inspected the rack holding the tools and selected a sledgehammer.

'Stand back,' he said to Solik, and raised the hammer above his head. As he brought it down the door swung open and the man from the hut just had time to jump out of the way as the hammer met thin air and hit the ground with a thud.

Alarm turned to anger. 'What you bloody doing - you bloody fools!' the man shouted at them.

'You locked us in,' said Solik, lamely.

''Course I lock you in - you were sleeping - did you want the bloody Russians to walk in and find you? Best to lock you in.' He stomped into the hut and slung down a canvas bag he was carrying. 'Bloody fools,' he said again, shaking his head.

Igor observed that he was about forty years old, with a stocky figure, but not fat. He wore well worn but hardwearing clothes and heavy boots, typical of a railway worker, but with a waistcoat of better quality material, which gave him an edge of slight superiority.

The man started emptying his bag. He brought out a large flat loaf, two bottles of wine, a square of cheese and, carefully wrapped in newspaper, three eggs.

'I been to the village,' he said. 'Spread the word that I seen two dead soldiers in the forest. The Russians will hear about it soon enough.'

He pulled out an old pocket watch from his waistcoat and looked at it.

'There's a train due in an hour's time – that's what I am waiting for.'

'A passenger train?' asked Igor.

' No - no passengers - it's carrying grain.'

'Grain? Where is it going?'

' Germany.'

' Germany?' Igor and Solik questioned together.

'Yes, Stalin has been selling the Soviet grain crop to Germany for years - while his own people starve.'

'And you're going on this train to Germany?' asked Igor

'Yes - to check the wheels at each stop.'

'Ah - so you're a wheel tapper?' said Igor.

The man nodded, and scratched his unshaven chin in thought.

'I need more men – mine have left to join the army. You want to go to Germany?' he said.

Solik and Igor looked at each other in astonishment. To get to Germany the train would have to travel through Poland – but they didn't want to go back to either place.

'Er - no, thank you,' said Igor

'It's not what we planned to do,' said Solik.

'Ah - so you have a plan. You're wearing Polish uniforms - you have no papers, no money, nothing - and the Russians are looking for you to kill you - but you have a plan.'

The two comrades shuffled their feet in embarrassment. 'Well - no plans, exactly,' said Igor, 'but it was Germany that invaded Poland - it would be madness for us to go there.'

'It would if you arrived there in Polish uniforms - but not as Russian rail workers.'

'Rail workers?' queried Igor.

'Yes - no one stops men working on the trains and railway lines - always look busy and you're left alone.'

'But - what would we do when we got to Germany,' asked Solik.

The wheel tapper shrugged his shoulders. 'Railways go from Germany all over Europe. My sister married a Frenchman - and that's where I'm going - to France. If I get caught the worst they can do is send me back. But a French jail would be better than here.'

They looked at him in silence for a few seconds. 'What do you think, Solik?' said Igor

Solik smiled. 'I think he's got a better plan than we have, comrade,' he said.

'You want to come to Germany then?'

Igor and Solik gave a nod. 'Yes - we'll join you, friend,' said Igor, 'your mention of getting to France is a better idea – but you'll have to show us what to do.'

'Don't worry – I'll show you - do everything I say – okay – I'm the boss. If I shout and swear - you take it. Everyone's got to see I'm the boss - okay?'

They nodded in agreement. 'Okay - you're the boss.'

The man held out his hand to each of them and they shook it. 'Call me Slav,' he said.

CHAPTER 9

Josef wiped his sleeve over his eyes; sweat was pouring off him. Every night when the weather allowed it, German bombers were pounding London and the docks with a variety of deadly devices. High explosive bombs, incendiaries, delayed action bombs, and booby traps that, if they did not kill, blew off hands and feet.

It took two of them to hold the water hose directed at the building in front of them. It was not the one that was on fire. The building that was burning so ferociously was the one next to it. Like many of the buildings that formed part of the old London docks, there was plenty of timber in them; dry, well seasoned timber that made excellent firewood. So there was little chance of saving a building that was alight; they didn't have the resources for that. All they could do was to try to contain the fire and stop it from spreading; to save those buildings that were still full of combustible commodities, stockpiled by merchants before the war started.

Josef took a quick look around him. Other firemen were concentrating on the building opposite. They were surrounded by burning buildings; many likely to collapse at any minute. It was a living hell, and the heat was becoming unbearable. He wondered how much longer it would be before they were pulled back.

Slowly, part of the building crumpled to the ground, sending up a shower of sparks and a cloud of brick dust. The men scrambled back. They played the hose on to the fallen debris for another five minutes, putting out the remaining flames. The warehouse they had been hosing stood isolated and, with luck, would survive for at least another day. The hose went dry, and they looked back and saw that they were being directed to another inferno.

After arriving in England they had been allocated accommodation in an old school; abandoned for the duration of the war. It was crowded with other Poles, mainly women and children, waiting to be transferred to different parts of the country. Josef was segregated with the other men in the school's gymnasium.

A man visited them from the Polish Embassy, who advised them that, as civilians, the only way they could get better accommodation allotted to them was to volunteer for a 'priority' occupation. They were given a list to consider.

For Anna the choice had been easy; she applied to be a nurse on the Polish ward of a temporary hospital overlooking Regents Park.

Josef, too old to be a soldier, had volunteered to join a Polish Fire Fighting Unit, formed from a group of firemen who had escaped on one of the last boats to sail for England before Poland surrendered.

Anna and Josef were now sharing a large terraced house with two other families. Josef had his own small room, and Anna and the child shared a bigger room. They had their own sitting room and a small kitchenette. The house had two inside toilets and one outside, and there was a communal bathroom. Situated between Euston Station and Regents Park, it was convenient for both of them, and there was always someone on hand to look after the child when they were not there.

A few days ago, at the beginning of November 1940, the Polish Embassy had told them that Trishka, Jak Zenski and Leon Denkov, had all safely arrived in England. At present no address could be given to them; only that they were being debriefed at an army camp in Hertfordshire, and then would be allowed a few days to recuperate. The Embassy promised Anna that they would pass on their address to them as soon as possible.

Anna was longing for Trishka to see her child again; to see the difference that a few weeks in England had made. The chest complaint that had worried them back in Poland had cleared up, and he was putting on weight. Josef was just as excited at the thought of seeing his friends together again. Although he was not related to the Radovaks', they had always made him feel he was part of the family, ever since Max had brought him to the farm at the end of the last war.

They had been comrades in that war, Max and him; Sergeants in the same battalion, before Max got to be an officer. When it was over, and Josef had found that his family had been wiped out and he had no home to go to, Max had offered him a home and a job. He had been with them ever since. The two boys, Igor and Stefan, had grown up calling him 'Uncle Josef,' and he and Max had been more like brothers, rather than master and servant.

The hoses had been dragged to another building that looked as though it could be saved. There were six of them this time, two to a hose. Part of a building had already collapsed and they were trying to keep a foothold on a pile of smouldering rubble and bricks. The air raid had been going on for about an hour now; the deep thud of bombs dropping on the city was joined with the noise of the anti-aircraft guns that had started firing as soon as the air-raid siren had sounded. Ten minutes later the earth shuddering crumps from falling bombs and the boom of the anti-aircraft guns fell silent. For a short while all that could be heard was the roar of the burning buildings, and shouting.

Then came the wailing of the all clear. Another air raid was over. A fresh crew arrived to clear up, and they withdrew wearily, treading carefully over the bricks and smouldering debris, hot and tired but satisfied that they had saved a few more buildings.

No doubt it was the noise from the buildings still burning and the shouting going on that drowned the urgent calls of warning, but as they walked wearily towards the fire engine the six of them neither heard nor saw the whole front of a four-storey building that they were passing slowly begin to fall. It fell from the top, peeling off floor by floor. They vanished from sight as the full weight of the collapsed wall crashed down on top of them.

Those who witnessed it knew immediately that there was no chance of them being dug out alive. A few months ago there had been a frantic effort to dig out anybody who was buried under the rubble of a bombed building. They still did if there was the slightest chance that someone might be alive. But from bitter experience they knew when it was a waste of time to try; when it was useless to hope. In this case they had not stood a chance.

The remaining firemen watched silently as the cloud of dust disbursed enough for them to see the pile of bricks that marked the spot where their colleagues lay dead. Shaking their heads in pity and frustration, they turned back to their duties. There was nothing else they could do.

*

When Anna pulled back the blackout curtains to let in the early dawn light, she could see a bank of dark smoke arising over the rooftops of the houses opposite. The centre of London and the docks had suffered another heavy air-raid, and she wondered how much more damage the capital could take before it became just a huge pile of rubble.

Josef would have been in the thick of it as usual. In spite of the danger and the sheer hard work of being a fireman, he was proud to be doing something useful once again, and he enjoyed working with fellow countrymen. She hardly ever heard him creep in during the small hours. Very often he was too tired to get undressed; he just fell on his bed exhausted and slept until mid-day.

She would not disturb him, unless it got too near to the time when she had to leave to do her shift at the hospital. There was a Polish mother upstairs who would look after Gregor if she asked, but Josef preferred to take over when she was working.

So far no bombs had fallen anywhere near where they were living. As she looked down the road she was, as ever, amazed to see how normal everything appeared to be. In spite of the bombing almost every night, the British got on with their lives with a relentless determination.

People were emerging from the houses and hurrying to catch the bus; and she knew that they would complain bitterly if the bus was late. She could see others who were cycling to work and, at the end of the road, was the familiar sight of the milkman with his pony trap milk cart, who had paused in his deliveries as a policeman on a bicycle stopped to speak to him. No, Hitler would not crush the British and their country as easily as he had crushed others, and she was glad to be among them.

Her great sadness though, was that she didn't know what had happened to Max and her two sons. The sadness sat like a brick in her stomach, nagging at her constantly. Hardly an hour went by without her thinking of them. Stefan, at least, she hoped to hear about before long. A few weeks had passed since she had gone to Birmingham. On her return she had put forward enquires at all the official places, but had heard nothing yet.

It had been a great relief to hear that Trishka, Jak and Leon were safe in England. They were all close friends now. It was a friendship that had grown out of need, something to cling on to, and it had become very deep rooted.

In the same way that Josef had seemed like a brother to Max, he had always seemed like a big brother to Anna. But then came Jak. Anna had taken a liking to Jak the first time she met him, and over the past year her liking had become solid and permanent. She knew, as a woman's intuition always knows, that he felt very deeply about her also. In so many small but significant ways the others had noticed the affection grow between Jak and Anna.

Josef had seen it first and had been concerned, because he knew how much Anna and Max meant to each other, but he had come to accept their relationship for what it was. They did not flirt with each other; it was not like that; it was a relationship that was purely platonic; the rare kind of love between a man and a woman that does not need to be gratified with sex.

When Anna had realised how concerned Josef was she had quietly reassured him. She reminded him that the war had changed all their lives, and there was still a long way to go before it was over. Jak knew that he could never take the place of Max; he would never try, but until she could find out whether Max was still alive, she needed someone else to lean on. And Jak also needed someone; someone like Anna, to help him through. When war tore relationships apart, it inevitably brought others together.

Anna left the window and went to make a cup of tea. She had quickly acquired a taste for English tea, which in Poland had been an expensive luxury. After pouring the water into the teapot, she started to prepare the table for breakfast before Gregor woke up. He enjoyed having cornflakes at breakfast.

She was interrupted by a knock on the front door; the milkman had reached her early today, she thought, as she grabbed the jug that she had placed ready for him to fill from his ladle. The milk bottling plant had been bombed out, so now it came 'loose'.

Opening the door she held out the jug, only to lower it, as she saw that it was not the milkman, but the policeman that she had noticed earlier. He had a little black notebook in his hand. Looking unsmiling at the jug as she lowered it, he glanced at his notebook.

'I'm sorry to trouble you Ma'am,' he said, 'but would you be Mrs Kewicz?'

It took Anna a second or two to register his mistake. Kewicz was Josef's name, and he thought that, because they lived at the same address, she was his wife. She half smiled.

'No, constable,' she said, 'I am Mrs Radovak; there is no Mrs Kewicz - there is only Mr Kewicz who lives here – Mr Josef Kewicz - he is,' she hesitated briefly, then decided to make it simple for the policeman, 'he is my brother,' she said.

The policeman's solemn expression did not change. He looked down at his notebook again. For the first time a creeping doubt took hold of Anna as she waited for his next words.

'I'm afraid I've got some bad news, Mrs Radovak..' He paused, awkwardly, before carrying on. 'I regret to say that your brother was killed during the air-raid last night.'

Anna stared at him in disbelief. Only a few minutes ago she had been convinced that Josef was in his bed as usual, fast asleep. This was why, for a fleeting moment, she thought the policeman was mistaken; but then the stark reality struck her. She turned and groped her way to a chair and fell into it, her face drained and white.

The policeman followed her from the door and looked down at her. He did not relish having to tell people that their loved ones were dead. It seemed worse when they were foreigners, who had come to England thinking they would be safe.

'I'm sorry to have brought you such sad news. There were six of them together,' he paused, trying to find words to lessen the hurt, 'It was – very quick - they didn't suffer.'

He told her briefly what had happened, and again assured her that Josef would not have suffered. He said someone would be calling on her to help with his funeral. Only half listening, Anna nodded in acknowledgement, and he left, quietly closing the door behind him. He still had several more calls to make.

When Anna heard the door close she put her hands to her face as the tears came and she started to sob.

'Josef,' she whispered, 'poor Josef.'

CHAPTER 10

When the train appeared Slav waved a hand at the driver and it slowed down to allow them to jump aboard. Igor and Solik had taken the old clothing from the hut, together with the greasy caps, to cover their uniforms and pass as genuine rail workers.

On the train they were accommodated next to the guards van. Four bunks, two either side, one above the other, each with a thin straw mattress and a threadbare blanket. The space was dirty, smelly and cramped, but Igor and Solik considered it comfortable compared to the prison cells they had experienced.

Slav told them that the journey was likely to take ten days. They soon found out why it would take so long. At night the train pulled into a siding, and shortly after it stopped the dozen or so armed guards, who supposedly protected the grain from thieves, could be seen disappearing into the darkness with sacks over their shoulders..

After they were gone, Slav also disappeared for two or three hours. In the morning he produced enough food and vegetables to last them a couple of days. In answer to their questioning looks, Slav gave a shrug.

'It's the only way we can live,' he said. 'We hardly ever get paid. That's why I wait for the grain trains - we have to trade grain for food to eat. The guards are also not paid, so they have regular customers at each stop.'

The next night Igor and Solik joined Slav with a sack of grain over their shoulder, and learned how to barter. They passed through Brest, but Slav was anxious as they continued through Poland and stopped at Warsaw. Seeing so many Germans in uniform not only made Igor and Solik tense and watchful, but they had difficulty in not glaring at them with hatred in their eyes. Slav urged them to concentrate on looking busy. When they crossed the German border some of the grain was unloaded at different locations before the final stop in Berlin.

They remained on the train as the grain was taken off and freight for the return journey was hoisted aboard. Slav went off early the next morning to find what trains were leaving Berlin towards France. He came back an hour later, excited.

'There's a train leaving for Hanover in thirty minutes,' he said. 'I've told the guard that we have work there and he has agreed to take us.'

They picked up their tools and what food they had and Slav led them across the tracks to the other train. The guard didn't give Igor or Solik a second glance as he led them to a cabin, nodded to Slav, and left them.

The cabin was much cleaner and fresher than the one they had just left, and it had a lavatory with a washbasin. When they reached Hanover, Slav used the same tactic to get them on a goods train to Bonn. But at Bonn they were not so lucky. Slav spent hours trying to find a train going to Paris, while Igor and Solik kept busy finding parts of track to 'mend.'

That night they had to find an empty truck to sleep in, and they went hungry, because the bartered food was gone. All they had left was a half bag of grain, which needed boiling, or at least soaking in water, before it was edible. Slav took a mouthful and tried chewing it - but spat it out onto the track.

'This is no bloody good,' he said, 'we got to eat.'

Taking his shotgun, he wrapped it in an old sack and left. Two hours later he returned with the sack filled with provisions. 'I only had two cartridges for it anyway,' he said, by way of explanation.

The next morning they busied themselves wheel tapping as they tried to find the destinations of various trains. It was Solik who found the faulty wheel, a clear crack in the metal. Slav went off to report it, and he came back with the two train drivers, who inspected the damage. The decision was made to uncouple the wagon and leave it for the wheel to be changed. The drivers grumbled about losing time.

'Where are you going, comrades?' asked Igor.

'Luxembourg,' came the reply.

'Luxembourg,' repeated Igor, trying to remember whether Luxembourg was in the direction they wanted to go. 'We're heading for Paris.'

'Well, you're welcome to travel with us as far as Luxembourg - there's good connections to Paris from there.'

They thought it was a lucky break, but things went wrong at Luxembourg. The rail workers and wheel tappers there wore blue overalls, and the rough foreign clothing worn by Slav and his two helpers attracted unwanted attention. They felt it was only a matter of time before they were stopped and questioned.

Slav led them out of sight among the freight trains. They found a linemen's truck that could be operated by two men sitting opposite each other, working the wheels by hand with a seesaw motion. Slav motioned to them to get in, and walked on ahead to find the Paris line. A train passed them and Slav indicated to follow it. Igor and Solik pumped the handles up and down for thirty minutes before they found a siding, and they slumped back, exhausted.

They had got out of Luxembourg without being challenged, and were on their way to France, but had left behind the remains of their food. After resting for half an hour, another train passed them. They followed it, with Slav taking a turn and Igor and Solik changing places every five minutes. They managed to keep going for another twenty minutes before the unaccustomed exercise and lack of food exhausted them once again.

'We can't do this any longer - we need to eat,' said Slav, panting. The other two, breathing heavily, nodded in agreement. Solik stood up and looked over the low hedges that grew alongside the railway line.

'Perhaps there's something in these fields we can eat, we ought to have a look around'

Igor got to his feet beside him. 'There's a farm building over there,' he said, pointing, 'we could try begging first.'

They set out together, Slav slightly ahead. 'Can you speak French, Slav?' asked Igor.

'No - but I can make it clear I'm hungry and thirsty in any language,' he said.

Igor smiled; 'I've got a few words - what about you Solik?'

'Oh -I can probably get by with simple stuff.'

Chickens scattered from their feet as they entered the farmyard. A woman carrying a bucket stopped and turned.

'*B'jour, madam,*' called out Igor, with a smile

The woman looked nervous, and put the bucket down, waiting for them to get closer.

Between them they explained that they were Polish railway workers that had left their food in Luxembourg, and wondered if she could spare something to keep them going.

She looked them over and, satisfied that they did not look like robbers, and were not likely to harm her, she nodded and indicated they follow her to the farmhouse.

Igor guessed that she was in her mid-forties, but her tied back hair was turning grey, and she looked older. Thin, but with strong sinews, she gave the impression that she did not find much in life to smile about.

But she gave them a good meal of ham and fried eggs, with fresh bread, together with a jug of cider. When they had finished, they got up and kissed her cheek in appreciation, and she looked embarrassed and pushed them away, but there was a flicker of a smile on her thin lips.

As they walked through the farmyard Igor noticed a stack of logs with an axe nearby. He made signs to the woman, asking whether the logs needed chopping, and when she nodded, they each took a turn with the axe. When they finished she gave them a bag containing a loaf, apples and cheese, and more cider.

Walking back across the fields they saw figures moving around the line truck they had left, and decided to abandon any idea of returning to it.

They continued walking through the fields parallel to the railway, and when the light began to fail they crept into a barn to sleep. The next morning they stole a few eggs from the chickens, ate the remains of the food, washed in a nearby stream, and walked on. Whenever they came to a village or a small town they got back on the railway line and walked along it, occasionally, for appearance's sake, inspecting parts of the track.

Not having a map, the names of the places they walked through meant nothing to them. It was three days before they saw a road sign at a crossroads near the railway. It confirmed that the railway line they were following was not going to Paris, but to Reims. They shook hands and slapped each other on the back and forgot about Paris, because it didn't matter any more; they had crossed the border into France.

'Where does your sister live, Slav?' asked Igor

'Nantes - it's still a good way to go. Do you want to stay together?'

Igor shook his head. 'We think we've burdened you with our company long enough Slav. We couldn't have got here without you, but Solik and I thought we would head for the nearest coast - see if we can get a boat to England.'

Slav looked doubtful. 'I'm sure there's plenty of Frenchman who would like to help you, but the Germans are the masters in France now. It will not be easy'.

'Well - we've got to try, Slav,' said Solik.

But later on, in the middle of the night, the matter was decided for them. Fast asleep in the barn they had chosen for the night, Igor was awakened by a sharp prod in the ribs. He opened his eyes to a glaring light and turned his head away as a voice in French ordered him to 'Get up.'

They had been spotted entering the barn, and the farmer had sent for the local gendarmes. They held carbines at the ready while the farmer held the torch. In answer to initial questions, Igor and Solik admitted to being Polish officers. Slav told them he was a rail worker who had fled from Russia.

Taking no chances, the gendarmes handcuffed them together and led them to their car. At the police station a Sergeant unlocked the cuffs and took down a few details before putting them in the cells. In the morning they were given a cup of coffee, and a few minutes' later three newly baked baguettes appeared, together with a small basket of boiled eggs. In turn they were then escorted to the lavatory and washroom to freshen up. At 9am, Slav was taken away for questioning; Igor was next, and then Solik.

After that they were left alone for the rest of the day, and were well fed at each mealtime. The next morning, after breakfast, a razor and shaving soap was given to them to smarten up their appearance.

At 9 am prompt, the three were taken together to a room that had a large desk and three chairs. Behind the desk sat the local inspector of police.

'Sit down,' he said curtly as they entered. He looked them over. 'Sleeping in a barn and not stealing anything or causing damage is not regarded as a serious crime - so there are no charges against you for that. But you, Lieutenant Radovak, and you Lieutenant Solik, present us with a different problem. You say you were prisoners of the Russians, but escaped, and you have travelled from Smolensk to France, which is quite an achievement. But Germany and Russia have an alliance, and I am therefore under an obligation to turn you over to the Germans.'

Igor and Solik exchanged worried glances. Igor leaned forward, his elbows resting on the arms of the chair, his face serious.

'But, inspector,' he said, groping his brain for the French words. 'It was Great Britain and France together that declared war on Germany when they invaded Poland. The fact that it was an empty gesture, because you could do nothing to help us in military terms, does not alter the fact that France was prepared to go to war against Germany. Now you are telling us that we Poles - who you professed to help - are to be turned over to our enemy. It hardly makes sense.'

The inspector shuffled uncomfortably at Igor's words. 'I'm sorry,' he said, 'but that is my instruction.' He looked at Slav. 'You *monsieur,* have entered France illegally, but so have thousands of others, so I am going to release you. You are free to go and find your sister.'

Dejected, Igor and Solik were led back to the cells

'I'm sorry, comrades,' said Slav, as he shook their hands in goodbye. 'If there was something I could do...'

'It's no fault of yours, Slav,' said Igor, 'you've been a good friend - and we are still alive - thanks to you.'

'Yes,' said Solik, 'and if we manage to escape again, we will travel by railway, as you've taught us.'

For the rest of the day Igor and Solik sat quietly, alone with their thoughts, waiting for their hated enemy to take them away. Food arrived and they ate without appetite.

Night came, and they lay awake staring up at the ceiling of the cell. The next morning there was the same routine with breakfast and washing and shaving. At 9 am a gendarme came to fetch them, and they followed him with heavy steps, resigned to their new captivity

The inspector was waiting for them in his office, together with a second man, who had a military bearing, but was not in uniform. Igor and Solik, with the same thought, looked around for German escorts.

'Sit down,' he instructed in his usual brusque way. He paused and drew in his breath.

'I have not, as yet, informed the Germans of your presence here. This is because you are to be offered a choice - an opportunity to avoid becoming prisoners of war again.'

Igor and Solik stared at him, their expressions suspicious. 'What choice is that, inspector?' asked Igor.

'When Petain signed the armistice with Germany there was one matter that was agreed upon, which was that the French Foreign Legion remained intact to garrison the French colonies in Africa.' He paused as Igor and Solik exchanged glances.

He turned to the man at his side. Medium height and fit looking, he was bullnecked, with close-cropped hair and a small moustache.

'This is Sergeant Scheider, the area recruitment NCO for the Foreign Legion. The choice you have is to join the Foreign Legion, or go to a German prisoner of war camp. If you decide on the Legion you must sign these application forms immediately and follow Sergeant Scheider out of here.'

'In effect then,' said Igor thoughtfully, 'we will be soldiers of France under the control of the Vichy government, which is pro-German.'

The inspector shrugged. 'Yes – but I can offer you no other choice.'

He passed them the forms. They had heard of the French Foreign Legion, who took recruits from any country, without questions being asked about their background. The Legion had the reputation for toughness, bravery, and fearlessness and, above all, loyalty to France and the Legion.

The form was printed in French, and Igor and Solik could not understand many of the questions. But after a brief exchange of glances, they nodded, signed the forms and handed them back. The Foreign Legion was preferable to a German POW camp.

Sergeant Scheider gave them a tight smile. '*Bon -merci*,' he said, 'you are now privates under the protection of the Legion. I have a car outside and we will leave immediately for our recruitment centre.'

The inspector stood up and shook hands with them. 'Good luck to you,' he said.

He watched from the window as they got into the Sergeant's car, and then turned and picked up the case details that had been typed out for each of them. Glancing through the papers, he then held them over his metal wastepaper bin, took out his cigarette lighter, and burned them.

CHAPTER 11

Trishka bent down and picked up the three brown envelopes that had just dropped through the letterbox. Two of them; one addressed to her and one to Leon had 'International Red Cross' printed in red across the top. They had been re-directed from the army camp where they had stayed when they first arrived in England four months ago. She noticed that the original postmark was six weeks old. The third letter was also for Leon; it had OHMS printed on it and, on the reverse, it had been rubber stamped 'Polish Forces Post'.

Ripping her envelope open Trishka took out the letter and started to read it as she walked back to the sitting room. In the background she could hear Anna washing the breakfast pots. Gregor, in a child's high chair, having finished his cereal, was licking his dish. As Anna came out of the kitchen she stopped when she saw the look on Trishka's face.

'What is it Trishka?' she asked anxiously as she saw tears fall down her cheeks. Trishka looked up.

'It's about Igor, Anna' she said. 'You remember that as soon as we arrived in England, Leon again asked the International Red Cross to try to find out what had happened to his fiancée, Olga - and Igor and Max. Well, this says that they've found out something about Igor's unit. The German Red Cross have stated that after being attacked by a detachment of Polish cavalry the German forces fought them off and later reported that there was no evidence that any survived. They also say that the identification of most of the dead was not possible because the identity tags and pay-books and most of their possessions had been taken from them before they were found' Trishka looked down again at the letter.

'It seems strange that they say that no one survived and yet they go on to say that their identity details were missing. Someone must have been alive to do that. I suppose it could have been a civilian who found them first – a farmer or woodcutter - but...' she broke off to wipe her tears away, reluctant to finish what she was going to say.

Anna waited for her to continue. 'What else does the letter say, Trishka?' she asked gently.

Trishka looked up at Anna again. 'They…they say that they found only one uniform of an officer – beside a body in a shallow grave. It…..it was a Lieutenant's uniform, Anna, and the identity number on the shirt was Igor's.'

As the words sank in Anna closed her eyes tightly. She found it difficult to accept that Igor was dead. They had been living in hope that he had been taken prisoner, but there did not seem to be any hope now. She fought back the tears and turned to Gregor, who had licked his dish clean and was holding it out for Anna. She took it and tried to compose her face as he looked at her uncertainly. She was thankful that he was too young to understand what was being said - that he would never see his father. She patted him gently on the head and turned back to Trishka.

'Does the letter say anything about Max, Trishka?'

'No, Anna, it's all about Igor. I think if they find anything about Max they will send it to you, not me.'

'Yes, I suppose so, unless there is anything about him in the letter to Leon.' Picking up the two letters addressed to Leon from the table where Trishka had put them, she carried them over to the mantelpiece above the fireplace and placed them behind the small mantel clock so that he would see them when he returned.

Leon, Jak, and Trishka had arrived in London a few days after Josef's funeral. It had been a sad reunion. The two men shared Josef's old room, and Trishka was in the other room with Anna and Gregor. The place was hardly big enough for them all, but after living together in the forest hideout for the past year, it was luxurious by comparison.

Anna had managed to get Jak a job driving an ambulance attached to the Polish Hospital. Because of her expertise in languages, Leon had used his influence to get Trishka a job with the BBC World Service. Leon had been assigned temporarily to the Polish Embassy to assist with the remaining partisans that were being flown in from Poland. This work had almost petered out and several weeks ago he had requested a posting back to active service.

That evening Leon arrived back to find Jak feeding Gregor his supper. Anna and Trishka were working their shifts and would not be back until midnight.

Jak had been eyeing the letters addressed to Leon for most of the afternoon, and almost before Leon closed the door, he called out.

'There's letters for you Leon,' and as Leon entered the room he nodded towards the clock on the mantelpiece.

'Thanks Jak.' Leon said, and greeted Gregor and tousled his hair. Looking briefly at the outside of them, he chose the International Red Cross envelope first and tore it open. Jak watched as he scanned the letter. He saw Leon's face relax a little.

'Good news, I hope, Leon?' asked Jak.

'It's about Olga, Jak. They've found that she's alive. She's been taken to a work camp in Poland - a place called Auschwitz. Yes, it's good news Jak; good to know that she's alive. I wonder what work she's doing there – I'll write to her tomorrow.'

He read the letter through again and then picked up the second letter. Jak saw his face light up as he read it.

'It's about my request for a new posting,' he said, looking up. 'I've got to report to the Polish Forces HQ at a place called Ware in two days time. They've sent a travel voucher.'

Jak felt a pang of envy. He desperately wanted to get back to a more active part in the war.

'When we arrived here, I was asked if I would consider going back to Poland to join the armed resistance. I said I would, but I've not heard anything from them – perhaps I'm too old.'

Leon gave him a grin. 'Too old at forty-five! - I don't think its age Jak; I'm sure they haven't forgotten you. If I get the chance I'll try to find out what's going on - are you still keen to go back to Poland?'

'That's where the Germans are Leon. The sheer strutting, bullying, arrogance of them; it beats me how they have managed to rise up again from being beaten to a standstill in 1918. This time they've got to be put down for good - and I want to do my part.'

Leon looked at his older friend and nodded. 'I know how you feel Jak– don't worry, they'll be sending some partisans back; it's only a matter of time. Perhaps this order I've got to report to the Polish HQ will reveal something – at least it shows that wheels are turning.'

Jak nodded 'Yes, I suppose it does, but I'd be grateful for any strings you might be able to pull Leon.'

He glanced at the clock, picked up Gregor from his high chair and went over to the wireless set they had bought second-hand; salvaged from a bombed out building. He switched it on and they sat down to listen to the news.

*

Two days later, when Leon arrived at the railway station at Ware, a few miles north of London, he was pleasantly surprised to find that a staff car had been sent to collect him. The car took him through the centre of the town and a mile beyond, before turning into a gateway set in a high stone wall. It stopped at the guarded checkpoint. There was no sign on the outside of its military function. A carved plaque set in the wall merely indicated that it was the entrance to 'Lanham's Hall.' The Polish guard on duty scrutinized Igor's' pass and waved the car on.

As the car cruised up the long gravel drive Leon looked at spacious grounds dotted with oak trees and sheep grazing on the lush green grass. The tranquillity of the place struck him. It was difficult to believe that only a few miles away so much death and destruction was taking place in the London blitz. And hearing the news each day of other English cities and towns being bombed, he had almost forgotten about the rest of England, where life went on undisturbed

The house was imposing but not as large as Leon had expected. The front was covered in wisteria and looked out on to neat manicured lawns surrounded by miniature hedges and flowerbeds. The car pulled up on the gravel outside the front door. As he mounted the short flight of steps the soldier on duty gave a brief salute and held open the door. Leon walked into the relative gloom of a large oak panelled entrance hall. A Polish Sergeant sat behind a desk just inside and Leon presented his letter of authority. The Sergeant scanned the letter briefly.

'Thank you, sir,' he said, in Polish 'If you would take a seat, the Colonel will see you shortly.'

Leon turned, and saw that there were three other Polish officers seated on a row of chairs placed either side of a heavy oak door at the far end of the hall. Walking over, he nodded to those who were seated and sat down. They nodded back politely, but no one spoke. From behind the closed door came the faint buzz of voices, but not loud enough to be overheard. The only other sound was the ticking of a grandfather clock standing in the far corner.

With three others already there before him, Leon was pondering how long he would have to wait when the door opened and a Polish officer of his own rank emerged and looked along the seated chairs.

'Lieutenant Denkov?' he asked. Leon raised his hand slightly.

'Yes,' he said, 'I'm Denkov.'

'The Colonel will see you now, Lieutenant,' he said, and held the door open for Leon to go through before closing it behind him and walking off.

Three army style desks and chairs and two filing cabinets looked out of place in such a large room. There was no other furniture. Oak panelled from floor to ceiling like the entrance hall, the desks had been placed in front of a large rectangular window that jutted out to give clear views of the grounds and the rolling Hertfordshire countryside. Polish officers occupied the chairs behind the desks.

Leon's footsteps echoed on the bare wooden floor as he came forward and saluted.

'Lieutenant Denkov, sir,' he said.

He was aware that all three officers sitting at the desks had followed his progress as he crossed the room. The Colonel was tall and well built, with iron-grey hair and a small moustache. Somehow he did not look comfortable behind a desk. With his rugged, weather beaten face, Leon thought he looked more like a countryman, a farmer, than a soldier.

'Ah, Lieutenant Denkov, please sit down,' the Colonel said. His deep voice was strong, but not loud, and seemed to command attention. The blue grey eyes were frank, friendly and penetrating.

'This is Major Voznek on my right and Captain Lopwicz on my left...' He was interrupted by a loud buzz from the telephone in front of the captain. Frowning slightly, the Colonel waited for the captain to finish his brief conversation. As the phone was put down the Colonel took two sheets of paper from the file in front of him and passed one to each of the others. They spent a few seconds scanning the sheet.

It did not occur to Leon until later that the Colonel had not introduced himself. Anxious to get on with the interview, the surname of the Colonel had been the least of his concerns.

'We were impressed with your activities with the partisans, Lieutenant,' said the Colonel, as he continued to read. He looked up. 'Were you aware that the throughput of your unit was higher than any of the others?'

'No sir, we'd no idea, but I'm pleased to hear it, and I'm sure the others will also be pleased.'

'Are you still in touch with the other partisans Lieutenant?' the Major asked.

'Only three of them, Major; we're sharing a house in London; they have civilian jobs there.' The Major nodded, and glanced down again at his sheet.

'You had two women in your group Lieutenant, did not that make things awkward for you? I see one of them had a child at the camp.' The Colonel looked at Leon as the Major put this question to him. Leon sensed that the Major, at least, did not approve that women had been allowed to join the group. He felt a sharp pang of resentment at being questioned about the wisdom to take the women with them; especially since he had just been congratulated on the success of the operation.

'Well Major, I think we might've had second thoughts if we'd known one of them was pregnant; but it didn't occur to us to ask at the time. We were desperately short of two key personnel, and the two women fitted in extremely well, as it turned out. They did an excellent job.'

'And did they get safely to England?' asked the Colonel.

'Yes sir'

'With the child?'

'Yes sir, they're safe and well.'

The Colonel nodded and gave a smile. 'Good; and do any of them wish to go back?'

Leon was pleased with this question. He could put in a good word for Jak, as he'd promised.

'Only one of them is keen to go back, Colonel; Jak Zenski, the leader of the group. He's already put in a request two months ago, but hasn't heard anything since.'

'Hmm, thank you Lieutenant; assure him that we will not forget him. The Sergeant has a list in his file of those partisans who have requested to go back. Before you leave ask him to check it and make sure his name is there; if not, give him the details. What about you, do you wish to return to Poland?'

'I would sir, if that's where I'm sent - but I would prefer something more - front line, if possible.'

The Colonel smiled. 'We thought so too Lieutenant; that's why we've called you here today. As you are probably aware from the news, the Italians have been having a bad time in the Middle East, and the Germans are expected to go and help them out - in fact to take over. As a result of this the Allied forces can expect a tougher time.

On our part, we have been asked to provide suitably trained officers and men who speak German to join special units to work behind enemy lines. As you've already had some experience behind the lines, you've been assigned to a four week training course, after which you will report to one of these special units in the Middle East - you will be advised more fully about that at the end of your training. Unofficially you will still be attached to Polish Military Intelligence.' He paused and glanced down at his papers, then looked up.

'Have you any questions Lieutenant?'

Leon hesitated. He had several that he would like to ask, but decided not to; he would let the plans that had been set for him develop. It was the kind of posting he wanted, and he was pleased to get it.

'No sir, I'm grateful for the opportunity.'

'Good, the sergeant will advise you of your training details and provide you with travel vouchers and so on. Your camp is a new one that has been set up in Hampshire - somewhere in the New Forest, as the English call it. You will not, of course, be able to tell anyone where you are going. Officially you will be stationed here, so any correspondence can be sent through this address.' He paused for a moment or two before giving Leon a brief smile.

'There's one other thing to tell you. As from today you will have the temporary rank of Captain, which will be confirmed when you've completed your training.' He smiled again at the surprised look on Leon's face.

'Congratulations, Captain - and good luck.' With that the Colonel shook his hand. Leon shook the hands of each of the other officers and left the room in something of a daze.

After checking with the Sergeant's list, and confirming that Jak Zenski's name was on it, he left the building and climbed into the waiting staff car.

Behind him the telephone buzzed again on the desk of the Captain.

'Just a moment please,' he said, turning to the Colonel. 'It's for you, Colonel.'

The Colonel reached and took up the receiver. 'Colonel Radovak speaking,' he said.

CHAPTER 12

Leon picked up the newspaper that had been left on the easy chair and sank down. He closed his eyes and leaned his head back onto the soft leather. It had been an exhausting afternoon and his whole body ached. The session had been called 'unarmed combat' and he, together with a dozen others in his group, now knew how to kill or maim someone with their bare hands, or a combination of hands, elbows, knees and feet.

Yesterday they had been taught how to kill effectively and silently with a knife. Before that there were sessions on guns, from the smallest pistols to the largest machine guns: English, German, French, Italian and others. They were shown how to strip them down, reassemble them and use them with equal dexterity. There were sessions on explosives and how to make booby traps and use them to the best effect. Each morning there had been training on secret codes and how to use and maintain a transmitter, followed by map and navigation sessions and crash courses in different languages.

It had been a gruelling three weeks since he arrived, and everyone on the course was feeling the strain. But being dog tired and still able to function and carry on was part of the training.

The camp was situated in the grounds of a stately home a few miles north of the coastal town of Lymington, in Hampshire. The accommodation huts were hidden among the trees, carefully camouflaged. The house was used as the main administration centre and as offices for the higher ranks and instructors. Some of the rooms in the house were used for lectures; otherwise it was where they came to eat, socialise and relax.

Not that the social life was great. There were about twenty women and forty men on the course and fraternization was strictly forbidden. Everyone had been issued with a basic army uniform and fatigues upon arrival, with no markings, insignia or rank. Also, they had been given a new name and told to build up a completely fictitious background and family history that would stand up an interrogation they would be put through in the last days of training. If anyone was asked questions about their origins or background they were instructed to lie; to use their new identity.

Although it was a gruelling course, Leon was impressed with what was going on. Ever since Winston Churchill had taken over as prime minister, the British had squared up to the fight with Hitler and his Nazi followers, preparing to take the fight to the enemy. The Luftwaffe had not crushed the RAF as Goring had predicted, and the Royal Navy still dominated the seas. Invasion was still a threat, but Hitler was trying to smash the English into submission with bombing raids almost every night. So far this tactic was not working.

Leon's mind drifted. He thought about his friends; Trishka, Anna and Jak; in particular Trishka. Somehow they had become much closer since the news had come from the Red Cross about Igor and Olga. He wondered how they were coping with the bombing every night. One thing he had kept to himself was the news that his whole family had been killed in the bombing of Warsaw. He had no other relations. The Radovaks' were the nearest thing he had to a family now. He was looking forward to seeing them again. After the training course he was due for seven days leave before flying out to the Middle East. He planned to spend every minute with them before he left. Perhaps he would treat them to a short holiday; get out of London for a few days

He opened his eyes and sat up. The library of the old house had filled up since he arrived. Others had found it was a useful place to wind down before the evening meal. There was a room with a bar, but he preferred to have a drink later on, before turning in for the night.

Opening out the newspaper on his lap he noticed that it was two days old. His eyes skimmed over the headline items before he turned to the back page. A small batch of portrait photographs caught his eye. The caption over them read 'Medal Honours for Foreign Pilots' and as his eye drifted over the pictures he suddenly sat bolt upright. There, in the middle of them, was a smiling pilot who had been awarded the Distinguished Flying Cross. It was not a face that he had seen before; he was staring at the name underneath – the pilots name was Flight Sergeant Stefan Radovak

Glancing at his watch, Leon got up and hurried out with the newspaper in his hand. He sprinted to his hut, found a piece of writing paper, and scribbled a few lines. With an old razor blade, he cut out the article and placed it in an envelope with his note and quickly addressed it. Sprinting back to the house he entered a small room just off the main hall. The post would be collected in about five minutes, but every letter had to be censored and he was hoping that the officer on duty had not already packed up. Luckily he was still there.

He looked up in annoyance as the door opened and Leon walked in. He recognised Leon as one of his regular letter writers.

'Too late for tonight, old chap, sorry', he said.

'But it's only a quick one, Ted, hardly anything to read at all,' and Leon pulled the note and the bit of newspaper out of the envelope to show him.

'It can go tomorrow, sorry', he said, and started to get up out of his chair.

Leon pushed him gently down again. He knew that Ted liked a drink; he was propping up the bar on most nights of the week.

'Ted, this is worth a few pints later on, I promise you. This letter's to a dear friend of mine who has been trying to trace the whereabouts of her son – that's him, there – and I've just got to get this to her as quickly as possible, there's nothing to do on it, look'

Ted glanced at it; there was nothing contentious. He opened his drawer, pulled out his 'censored' stamp and banged it down just as the door opened and the army postman entered.

'There, now let's be off', he said, as he slammed his drawer shut, locked it and moved towards the door. 'I'll see you later on then, shall I, old chap?

Leon watched as his letter disappeared into the postbag.

'Yes Ted, thanks - it'll be my pleasure.' He gave him a pat on the back as he followed him out of the door and walked with him towards the dining room.

'I'll not go into detail Ted, but that lady I've just written to has recently heard about the loss of her other son, and she fears the worst for her husband, who was in Warsaw when it fell to the Germans. She badly needs some good news for a change.'

Ted, which was probably not his real name, was feeling friendlier now he had finished for the day.

'I understand old chap, no hard feelings, but after spending the day reading other peoples correspondence I get a bit cheesed off, you know. What about a quick drink now – a toast to the young pilot and his medal.'

'That's a great idea Ted, but later, I can't drink on an empty stomach – and I'm starving.'

Ted looked at Leon and noted his tanned but haggard face 'O.K.,' he said, 'let's eat first.'

*

Reading the letter two days later, Anna sat down and wept tears of joy. She was filled with pride. Not only was Stefan still alive, he was a hero and had received a medal from the King.

She went that same day to the Polish Embassy to see if they could tell her where he was stationed. They asked her to fill out a form, which was then put upon a pile of similar forms and she was told to come back 'in a few days.' Disappointed and impatient about having to wait so long, she went to the offices of 'The Daily Telegraph', the newspaper from which the cutting had been taken. Within half an hour she walked out with the number of his squadron and where it was located.

That evening Anna wrote a long letter to Stefan, telling him all that had happened to her and Trishka since the war had started and that they were now living and working in London. She told him about Gregor and how Josef had been killed in the blitz. With tears filling her eyes she also told him that she feared for his father. After Warsaw surrendered to the Germans no trace of him had been found. She finished with the sad news that Trishka had received about Igor. Reading the letter through, Anna could not stop the tears. Apart from letting him know that she and Trishka and her baby were alive and well, it was not a happy letter.

*

Stefan did not receive the letter. The day after returning from London with his medal he was informed of his promotion to Pilot Officer. Just twelve hours later he was reported missing, presumed killed, after his Hurricane was seen to dive into the sea off the coast of France. A fellow pilot had seen Stefan following a Heinkel across the Channel and shoot it down, but was then attacked by three Messerschmitt 109s. After damaging one of them he swerved away, out of ammunition. With two of them on his tail, he was hit, and black smoke streaked from his engine. Flying into cloud to shake them off, his aircraft had reappeared, flying upside down and heading towards the English coast. Belching smoke and losing height, it finally plunged into the sea. No parachute had been seen.

*

Being a Saturday, Max was at the aerodrome when the news came through that Stefan's plane had gone down. He was waiting for him to return because they had arranged to go fishing. In his grief, Max left Hornchurch immediately and returned to Ware. He found it hard to accept that his son was dead. So many pilots did turn up after being shot down. Living in hope helped to soften his anguish.

When Max had found that Stefan was in the RAF and where he was stationed, he had telephoned the aerodrome and left a message. Their happy re-union had been saddened by the fact that neither of them had heard any news about the other members of the family. Neither dared to admit that they feared the worst.

Father and son had seen as much as possible of each other over the next months. Stefan had visited his father at his quarters at Ware. They had been to see the sights of London, including the bomb-damaged areas. They were impressed by the fact that, amidst all the desolation, London was still a vibrant city. The King and Queen remained in residence at Buckingham Palace, and London was still the centre of government. The postman, the milkman, the coalman and other tradesmen were still a common sight during the day, picking their way over the piles of bricks and rubble on their business.

Max had spent a several weekends at Hornchurch; walking the country lanes with his son, fishing together, and enjoying the company of other pilots from Stefan's squadron at the village pub. And when Stefan had been presented with his Distinguished Flying

Cross at the Palace, Max had been there. It had been a proud day for him.

*

Seven days after he was reported missing, Anna received her letter back from Hornchurch, accompanied by a letter from Stefan's Wing Commander. He regretted to inform her that there had been no further news, but urged them not to give up hope. Jak, who was standing next to her as she read the letter, just managed to catch her as she collapsed to the floor.

It was only later that Anna commented that the letter from the Wing Commander seemed to assume she had already been informed about Stefan being missing. The reference to 'them' she took to mean her and Trishka, and she wondered how he had known that.

Two weeks later, when nothing further had been heard and the Germans had not reported him a prisoner of war, Max went to Hornchurch to collect Stefan's few possessions. He stayed overnight at the same village pub where he and Stefan had spent many happy evenings together. After eating, he planned to go to bed early and rise at dawn to travel back to London. But as he started to climb the stairs to his room he heard his name called.

'Colonel Radovak - over here.' Stefan's Wing Commander was beckoning to him from the bar. He was with three of his pilots. Reluctantly Max joined them; it would be discourteous not to. He would buy them a drink and then make his excuses.

They talked briefly about Stefan, and he was urged not to give up hope. Max was only half listening, because he had now accepted that his son had been killed. But something that the Wing Commander was saying jolted his brain back into focus. He was talking about returning a letter. Max could not remember writing any letters to Stefan at Hornchurch.

'I'm sorry, Wing Commander, I cannot remember receiving a letter back from you, when was that?

'It was about a week after he went missing. Actually, I wrote it to your wife, Colonel, and returned the letter she had written to him. Didn't she mention it?

Max looked at him blankly. It took a second or two to register the implications of what the Wing Commander was saying.

'My wife – but - my wife is in Poland', he said. 'She *wrote* to Stefan from Poland?'

Puzzled, the Wing Commander looked at him. 'Poland? No Colonel, I returned it to what I assumed was your address in London. I didn't open the letter; your wife had put her name and address on the back of the envelope.'

Max concentrated on what the Wing Commander was saying, trying to keep down the excitement coursing through his body. His wife, here in England; was it possible?

He tried to keep his voice steady. 'Wing Commander, I was at the Military Academy in Warsaw when the war started, and I was flown out to England just before Poland surrendered. My wife was at our farm, near Pinsk. All my efforts to find out what happened to her and my daughter-in-law have been in vain. The news that you have given me that she wrote to Stefan from an address in England is – well – tremendous! It is incredible. If you could give me her address, I will go to see her tomorrow.'

The Wing Commander's face was blank. 'I'm very sorry, Colonel, but I didn't think to keep a note of the address. All I can remember is that it was in London. Somewhere in Camden Town, I think.'

'Camden Town?' queried Max, 'where is that?'

'Not far from Regents Park, Colonel; I think Euston is the nearest station.'

The other pilots had been listening with fascination at the conversation between the two officers. Max gave them a smile and turned back to the Wing Commander.

'Thank you, Wing Commander,' he said, 'I believe that your switchboard operator has my telephone number. If you remember anything more, please let me know. I'm sure I can find her address somehow. It is, as I have said, tremendous news you have given me. I will keep in touch. Now, if you will excuse me gentlemen, I will turn in so that I can make an early start in the morning.'

Max raised his hand in farewell to them as he made his way to the stairs. He lay awake for most of the night, waiting for the first glimpses of light to appear. The innkeeper had reluctantly agreed to provide the Colonel with an early breakfast. He was disappointed that the Colonel bolted down only half of it and was off in his car by 7a.m.

Driving as fast as the roads would allow, Max arrived back at Ware two hours later. After a busy morning, he made excuses and caught the 2.15 train to London. He had reasoned that, as civilians, the Polish Embassy would know the address of his wife and daughter-in-law. He was not sure how to get there, but he found a taxi outside the station and jumped in and said 'Polish Embassy' to the driver. To his relief, the driver merely nodded and threaded his way into the traffic.

When he arrived at the Embassy Max fully expected to have to wait whilst they traced his wife's address. To his surprise the mention of his name brought instant recognition from the lady on the reception desk.

'Mrs Radovak? Anastasia Radovak? Yes, Colonel. I have her address here, in this tray.'

As she spoke she leafed through a pile of papers and pulled one out.

'Yes, here it is,' she said, handing it to him. 'Your wife requested us to locate the address of your son, who had been awarded a medal, but she has not been back to collect it.'

Max looked down at the form. He recognised the handwriting; it was the familiar hand of his wife. She had put her address on the form, which now had Stefan's address, typed on by the receptionist.

'Thank you,' he said. 'Do you have a map of London that I can look at? I would like to make contact with my wife as soon as possible.'

The receptionist looked surprised. 'You have not been in touch before now?

'No, until yesterday I thought she was still in Poland.

As he was speaking the receptionist spread out a map of London on her desk. She pointed out to him the address he was looking for and he noted how far it was from the Embassy. He would need a taxi again, he thought.

'Thank you, you have been most helpful,' he said, as he made towards the door.

'You are welcome, Colonel - good luck,' she said. He was almost out of the door.

'Oh, Colonel,' she called. He turned, anxious to be on his way.

'The Embassy has a car; shall I see if it is available? It would be quicker for you,' she said.

Quicker! Of course it would be quicker. 'I'd be most grateful if it is,' he said.

The receptionist disappeared. Two long minutes went by before she reappeared, followed by a Polish officer. She smiled at the Colonel.

'This is Captain Linska, he knows the address and has kindly offered to drive you there Colonel,' she said.

Relieved, Max shook the hand of the Captain.

'I'm most grateful to you Captain Linska, it will be a great help.'

'Not at all, sir, please follow me. I know the way pretty well; I used to drop Lieutenant Denkov off at that address when he was working at the Embassy.'

Lieutenant Denkov? Max could not remember where he had heard that name before, but it made him wonder what he was doing living at the same address as his wife. He sat in the back of the car with growing excitement, mixed with apprehension. He was trying to recall why the name of Lieutenant Denkov sounded familiar.

The daylight was fading into dusk when Captain Linska turned into the road where Max's wife was living. Leaning forward to look, he was thrown forward as the Captain slammed his foot on the brake. Tyres squealed as the car came to a shuddering halt. For several seconds they stared at what was in front of them.

'My God,' said the Captain. The whole street of houses, except for one or two standing windowless at the far end, was just a pile of rubble.

Getting out of the car, they gazed at the scene. A few people were picking at the ruins, trying to recover possessions or, perhaps, bodies. The Captain led the way over the rubble of bricks, wood and broken furniture, towards the remains of the house where Anna had lived.

Two men and a woman had rescued a small, pitiful, pile of furniture and pots and pans from the property that had been next door. They looked up as the two men in uniform approached them.

'Do you know what happened to the people in the other house?' asked the Captain, pointing.

'No one in the building survived.' One of the uniformed men replied. 'Six bodies have been recovered so far, but we don't know the names of the dead, or where they've been taken. They were Polish, that's all we know.'

'Do you know if anyone from around here escaped?'

'Those who were in the air-raid shelters have moved into the church hall, two streets away. Earlier in the day there were three of four people digging in the ruins of the house, but they left two hours ago. I knew them by sight as having lived in the house but don't know their names.'

Max listened grimly, his face grey and drawn. To find and then lose his son had been a bitter blow. To find out that his wife had, apparently, been in England for some time but was probably now dead was almost too much to bear. Numb with grief; he could not speak.

Silently they returned to the car. Captain Linska drove it to the nearby church hall. A flustered, matronly woman in charge listened attentively to their enquiry. Consulting her records she assured them that no one by the name of Radovak was staying at the hall.

The light was almost gone as Max slumped into the back of the car, feeling very weary - weary and alone. In the gloom, tears filled his eyes. Captain Linska could see the outline of his passenger in the rear view mirror. He could not think of any words that would comfort the Colonel in his grief. No words seemed appropriate. But one act of kindness occurred to him.

'I think you have missed your train, Colonel; would you like me to drive you back?'

Max had completely forgotten that he had come by train, and he had no idea how long he would have to wait for another one. He badly needed to get back to his quarters and be alone for a while.

'That would be most kind of you Captain, if you're sure that you will not be missed.'

'Well sir, I might be missed but, under the circumstances, I think I might be excused. It is only a few miles – I should be back within an hour.' It was, he knew, an exaggeration, because the blackout would slow him down to half the usual speed.

The Colonel expressed his thanks once again and lapsed into silence. Tomorrow he must find out the names of those who had been killed at his wife's address. If there were some doubt about the identity of the dead, he would have to arrange to see the bodies. If she were not amongst the dead then there would be only two alternatives. She could be still under the ruins of the house - or alive. But if she was alive he had little time left to search for her. In twenty-four hours he would be on his way to the Middle East with a small party of newly trained officers.

The next morning, after making a number of telephone calls, Max found out that all of the dead from the house had been identified and there was no one named Radovak amongst them. He telephoned Captain Linska, who told him that he had been making enquiries at all the hostels for the homeless in the area, but without success. He assured the Colonel that he would keep looking; his wife was almost certainly still alive and would probably make contact with the Embassy herself.

'Thank you, I appreciate your help,' Max said. 'Unfortunately I will not be able to join in the search. I shall be out of the country tonight and be away for several weeks. Please leave a message with my staff Sergeant at this address if anything should turn up.'

'Yes sir, of course – and - good luck.'

That afternoon Max travelled with two of his staff officers to an airfield in Wiltshire. A long-range bomber aircraft was waiting for them on the tarmac, converted to take passengers and fitted with extra fuel tanks. They were kitted out with flying suits, flying boots and a parachute each before joining the rest of the small party. There were fifteen of them altogether. As the senior officer, Max went from one to the other shaking their hands. He said the same thing to each of them.

'I'm Colonel Radovak – and you are?' And as each one answered the Sergeant with him placed a tick against the name on his list. It was the fifth man he came to that stared at the Colonel speechless when he heard his name.

'Colonel Radovak?' queried the officer, hesitantly.

'Yes, I'm Colonel Radovak – and you are?' The officer was still staring at him.

'I'm Denkov, sir, Captain Denkov.'

Max stared at him. Denkov! Yes, he remembered him now. He had come over with the partisans and he had been sent on a training course. It was, he felt certain, the same Denkov that had been living at the same address as his wife.

'I believe you know my wife, Captain, Mrs Anastasia Radovak,' he said as calmly as he could. He noticed how the others face relaxed and softened a little at the mention of his wife.

'Yes sir - very well - and also Trishka, your daughter-in-law. They're the two women who joined the partisan group. We spoke about them briefly at my interview. I'm sorry, sir, I didn't know at the time that she was your wife. She has no idea that you're in England. She thought you'd been killed or captured in Warsaw.'

Max nodded. He was more concerned about his wife and needed to ask a vital question.

'When did you last see my wife and Trishka Captain - are they all right?'

'I said goodbye to them this morning Colonel - yes, they're all well.'

A look of relief flooded across Max's face.

'Thank you, Captain; I'm relieved to hear you say that. It was only yesterday that I found out where you were all living - only to find that the house had been bombed.' He turned and beckoned to his Sergeant. 'I must move on; we will talk later; please would you give my wife's address to the Sergeant.' He spoke to the Sergeant. 'Sergeant, please let Captain Linska at the Polish Embassy have a note of the address that Captain Denkov gives you.'

Smiling, Max moved on. There was much more that he wanted to know, but it would have to wait. His wife was alive and well and that was enough for now.

An hour later, in the diffused light of the aircraft, Leon saw that the Colonel had nodded off. He was feeling tired himself but he doubted that he would be able to sleep against the noise of the engines. They were already over the English Channel and heading towards the Bay of Biscay and the Portuguese coast. He had been told that flying at night was much easier if there was some moonlight and a coastline to follow. Scattered clouds allowed the pilot to fly over them but still see enough to stay on course. Before takeoff the pilot had explained that when they got to Gibraltar he would turn east and follow the North African coast to Egypt.

Leon reflected what a fool he had felt when he was introduced to the Colonel and had to admit that he did not know his name before that moment. Everything had happened so quickly at his interview that it had not seemed so important at the time.

And it would not have mattered so much, except that if he had bothered to enquire he could have re-united Anna with her husband six weeks ago. And so he was angry with himself; angry because it meant that Anna and her husband would not be re-united until Max returned from his present mission. With Jak Zenski on a course of training similar to the one he had just been through, Anna and Trishka and young Gregor had no men on which to rely.

Leon realised that the Colonel had been concerned that he might be emotionally involved with his wife. He needn't have worried; it was Jak he needed to be concerned about. In the last two weeks, convinced that she had lost her two sons as well as her husband, Anna had drawn much closer to Jak. With Jak about to go back to war he knew that the two of them had been sleeping together ever since she had received the bad news about Stefan. Sharing a bed did not, of course, necessarily mean that they were in a sexual relationship, but it did mean they were close to it. Unlike he and Trishka. After receiving the bad news about Igor the close friendship that had grown between them began to change. In spite of feeling some guilt about it, knowing that Olga was still alive in Poland, he had fallen in love with Trishka – and she with him.

When he returned from his training he took them all to Bournemouth for a long weekend. Bournemouth had been bombed, but nothing like the raids over London. The sun had shone and they took leisurely walks along the cliff top. They enjoyed a meal together and went to the cinema. The emotional tension between Trishka and himself had, by the evening, become overpowering; so that, later, it seemed the most natural thing to go to bed together and make love. The next day, when they were all together, they found a photographers shop, and he now had a photo of them in his wallet.

When they got back to London they realised that the trip had probably saved their lives. It was pure chance that Trishka, a few days earlier, had heard that a colleague wished to let part of a house in the suburbs, away from the worst of the bombing. With so many people having fled the blitz, there was no shortage of properties to let, and rents were cheap. They had moved just in time.

Leon's thoughts turned to what lay ahead of him in the Middle East. With all the intense training he had gone through he expected to be in close contact with the enemy. With these thoughts drifting through his mind his head dropped to his chest. In spite of the noise from the aircraft, he was asleep.

CHAPTER 13

In the fading light the small fishing boat edged towards the shore. The rocks on either side looked black and threatening, but it glided through them easily.

Down in the hold, Stefan was told by gestures to keep out of sight. He could only be sure of one thing. His rescuers, being French, were taking him to France.

He knew he was lucky to be alive. When his ammunition had run out the reflexes that seem to bye-pass any involvement of the brain, took over. He'd pushed the stick forward into a dive and, as his pursuers started to follow him, he pulled it hard to his stomach, and shot up into the clouds. He'd felt bullets thudding into the Hurricane's engine and it burst into flames. He knew the aircraft was finished and wouldn't get him back to England. It was time to get out.

With flames licking at his hands he'd gripped the stick between his legs and in three blurred and frantic movements he slammed back the canopy, unclipped his seat harness and flipped the aircraft over. He dropped straight out and the Hurricane screamed away from him, flying upside down on a long descent before finally hitting the sea. Stefan had plummeted through the clouds, dropping like a stone towards the sea as he scrabbled in panic to get his parachute open. With a jolt it opened a hundred metres above the waves.

The small yellow dingy that had recently served as a cushion had inflated on impact with the water. It was little over a metre away from him but he was being dragged under by the weight of his clothing and the parachute harness. Although a strong swimmer, Stefan began to panic as his efforts to keep his head above water sapped his energy. Somehow he got rid of his parachute harness and was trying to shake off his clothing when his hand caught on a line attached to his belt. It was a line that stopped the dingy from drifting away. Pulling on it, Stefan was relieved to see the dingy come towards him. Slinging his arms over the side, he'd hung on. His legs were like lead weights and he was exhausted. He'd started to doze.

A familiar noise brought him back to alertness. Screwing his head around he saw two Messerschmidts skimming the waves, flying back towards France with two Hurricanes on their tails. The German pilots had also run out of ammunition and were probably low on fuel. He heard the rat-tat-tat of machine guns from the Hurricanes as they disappeared from view. The incident gave him fresh energy. With one mighty effort he dragged the rest of his body into the dingy.

Stefan was not conscious when the fishermen pulled him from the sea. When he woke up he found that his hands had been roughly bandaged in clean towels. Then he remembered that his cockpit had been on fire and burning his hands as he wrestled with the controls.

*

There was a bump and a short scraping noise and the boat stopped. Stefan could hear the voices of the fishermen as they secured the boat for the night and unloaded their catch. He heard other voices join in. His French was not good, but he could understand that they were discussing the catch and were not talking about him. He had been resigned to becoming a prisoner of war, but now he began to wonder. Were these Frenchmen going to protect him and help him get back to England? He would have to wait to find out.

After thirty minutes one of the fishermen came into the small hold. He took off his thick black jumper and hat and handed them to Stefan.

'*Vous – moi*' he said, pointing his finger first at Stefan and then at himself.

Stefan hesitated, not understanding what he meant.

'You – me' the fisherman said, this time in English, 'we change.'

Still not fully understanding, Stefan put on the sweater and hat that was held out to him. The fisherman looked at him. He took off the bandages from his hands. '*Pardon monsieur*' he said, as Stefan flinched. He stood back slightly and looked at Stefan, then bent down and lifted the hatch to the engine. Putting his hand into the hatch he wiped it around the engine and brought it out covered in black grease. With a grin he pointed to his black four or five day stubble and then smoothed the grease around Stefan's chin and cheeks. Satisfied, he waved Stefan out of the hold. Stefan realised what was required. Three fishermen had gone out, and three fishermen must return. Someone must be watching them, and to get him safely ashore he must act like one of the crew.

The skipper lifted a box of fish to Stefan's shoulder as he appeared and indicated that he should walk between him and the other crewmember. Fitting in with their steps, he walked up a rocky slope away from the shore. There were no buildings and he could not see anyone about, but he dared not look around. Suddenly, out of the gloom, came a voice.

'A good catch today, Frenchman?' The voice said in poor French. Stefan caught a glimpse of a German uniform and held down an urge to jump on him. The skipper gave a friendly chuckle and replied calmly.

'Not so good today, Fritz, but here are a couple of nice lobsters for your supper'

'*Danke*' said the guard, ' *merci.*' It was an expected perk.

As the skipper handed over the lobsters the other two walked on. With a wave the skipper left the guard. The track from the shore joined a rough road, and they walked to where a small battered van was parked. Placing the boxes of fish in the back, Stefan was hauled in as the skipper went to the front of the van and hand cranked the engine to get it started. For about ten minutes the van rattled along country lanes at an alarming speed. On the approach to bends, rather than slow down, the skipper blasted his horn. They eventually stopped at a house in a small village.

The skipper took some of the fish and indicated to Stefan to follow him. Walking to the back of the house, without knocking, the skipper opened the door and went in. It was the kitchen, lit by an oil lamp standing in the middle of a large square table. A plump woman at an unglazed stone sink turned her head as they entered. Her round apple cheeks beamed as she saw who it was.

'Ah! Renē!' she said. Her eyes went to Stefan and her smile wavered. She looked back to Renē.

Renē spoke rapidly, which Stefan had difficulty following, but he could tell that the skipper was explaining what had happened and how he came to be there. He heard the words 'Royal Air Force' and his name mentioned. René turned and said in broken English.

'This - *Madame* Dubar - she look after you. Her husband, Doctor Dubar, he see to your hands' He held out his hand, but dropped it as he remembered that Stefan could not shake it. 'Good luck - if you get caught, please say you swam ashore, eh,' he said, grinning.

'Of course, and - thanks for all you've done, skipper,' said Stefan. His rescuer patted his shoulder as he opened the door and disappeared into the night. Like so many others who were about to briefly enter Stefan's life, he never saw him again.

Madame Dubar gave Stefan a smile and bade him sit down at the table. Producing a bowl of hot water and some soap she wiped the grease from his face, and then placed a bowl of hot soup in front of him, with bread and a large chunk of cheese. Until he saw the food Stefan had not realised how ravenously hungry he was. With some difficulty he managed to hold the spoon, but had to ask his host to help him with the bread and cheese. With his meal he was given a large mug of cider. The sound of a car stopping outside made him pause in his drinking. *Madame* Dubar smiled.

'Doctor Dubar,' she said, to reassure him, and went out of the kitchen to greet her husband at the front door. Stefan could hear her explaining his presence in the kitchen. She reappeared leading her husband. She is acting as though I am a special guest, thought Stefan, rather than a fugitive that could get them shot if found there.

Stefan stood up. *'Bonjour, monsieur, j'suis Pilot Officer Stefan Radovak,'* he said.

Looking keenly at Stefan, the Doctor put out his hand but noticed the burns that the pilot had suffered and realised that a handshake was impossible. Instead he inspected each of Stefan's hands in turn. Stefan saw that he was of medium build and height, he had a slight stoop, he seemed quite fit and had, a few years earlier, probably been a good athlete. His hair was grey and thinning and he had a drooping grey moustache. Perched half way down his nose was a pair of gold-rimmed spectacles, which forced him to lower his chin so that he could look over them.

'You speak German, *monsieur*?' the Doctor asked in English as he looked up. The slight smile was still there but Stefan could see that his eyes were serious, alert, enquiring.

'Ja, Ich sprechen Deutsch sehr gut.'

'Good – and French?'

'Some, Doctor - from school – I'm a little rusty,' he replied in English.

The Doctor nodded. 'We can probably help you improve, now you are in France,' he said with a smile, 'but I speak English.' He led him through the house to a room fitted out as a surgery. Over a sink he poured cold water over Stefan's hands and then sat him down. Applying a yellow jelly like ointment, he started to bandage them.

As the Doctor worked Stefan was aware of him glancing over his spectacles, as though trying to assess him in some way. He asked a few questions, and when he found out he was Polish, enquired how he came to be a pilot in the RAF.

'I was at university in England, studying engineering.' Stefan told him.

'And your family are still in Poland?'

'My father got out in time, but we've heard nothing about the rest of the family.' He explained that he had met up with his father, and how they feared for the others.

Stefan answered the Doctors' questions politely, but got the impression that the Doctor knew more about what was going on in England than he was prepared to admit. As he finished with the bandages, the Doctor remained silent for a few seconds before changing the subject.

'You will not have heard the news that was announced this morning, *monsieur* Radovak – that Germany has invaded Russia.'

Stefan blinked in surprise, then gave a grin

'Germany has attacked Russia? So much for the non-aggression pact between them – but I don't think any Poles will be sorry about it – or the British.'

'Yes, I can understand that the Polish people will be particularly pleased about it'

The Doctor cleared away the ointment and bandages.

'You know, of course, that it is expected of us to report you to the gendarmerie. We should have done it already, but you have the right to medical attention first.' He was again looking over his spectacles as he said this, watching for Stefan's reaction.

Stefan shrugged. 'Becoming a prisoner of war, Doctor, is no more than I expected. I am lucky to be alive; but if I see a chance to escape, I will take it.'

The Doctor pulled up a chair near to Stefan.

'Apart from myself, your rescuers and my wife, no one knows you are here. You could walk out of here now, if you wish. I could give you some money – but what would you do - where would you go? You would not get far without identification papers *monsieur* Radovak.' He shook his head.

'You would not know who to trust and who not to trust. At best you would soon be taken prisoner; at worst some trigger happy guard would shoot you.' He paused.

'No one can get far without papers now. The Germans demand that the local gendarmerie co-operate in checking everyone's papers, especially around the ports and at railway stations. Anyone who doesn't co-operate is arrested – or shot.'

Stefan shrugged his shoulders. 'But I'll not need papers as a prisoner,' he said.

'Yes, that's true, but you mentioned that if you found a way to escape, you would take it,'

Stefan nodded in agreement.

The Doctor leaned forward.

'If I was to suggest a possible alternative to becoming a prisoner of war, would you be interested? I should hasten to add that there would be conditions – and it would not be without danger.'

Stefan stared at him; an alternative?

'I would certainly be interested, Doctor, if there's the chance of not going to a prisoner of war camp.'

The Doctor nodded, then got up and walked over to his desk.

'Have you heard of the Todt Organization *monsieur* Radovak?' he asked, as he returned to Stefan carrying a map.

Stefan shook his head. 'Can't say that I have – who are they?'

'Well, to put it simply, they are a massive building and construction business that only works for one client, or rather, one government; the Nazi. They build roads, airfields, fortifications – anything that the German war machine requires – and they mainly use slave labour, but sometimes they employ local people.' He spread out the map as he spoke. It was a map of the Cherbourg peninsula.

'Look,' he said, pointing his finger at the top corner, 'this is where we are, near Auderville – the island of Alderney is a few miles to the west. All the Channel Islands are crawling with Germans now, and the entire coastline is carefully watched. It is just not possible to get you back to England this way. But, as I have mentioned, there is an alternative; it may not be one that will appeal to you, but it is all I can suggest.'

Stefan waited for him to continue. The Doctor moved his finger down the map; he stopped about twenty-five kilometres to the south west of Cherbourg, at a small town called Montebourg.

'Near here,' said the Doctor, tapping the map, 'the Germans, or rather the Todt have begun to build something. It is in the country at a village called Azeville,' he paused and looked up at Stefan, 'and we would very much like to know what is going on there.' Stefan glanced at the map; he had noticed that the Doctor had said 'we' and he did not think that he was referring to his wife.

'How do I fit into this, Doctor? Surely you are not suggesting that I go to work for this Todt Organization? It would be impossible anyway, without any identification papers, and whatever else they might ask for.'

The Doctor leaned back. 'You're right, *monsieur*, it would not be possible without the necessary papers, but if I tell you that these can be arranged for you, would you be interested in working there for a short time, to find out what's going on? Unfortunately, I can get the papers only on that condition; you see the person who provides the papers, works for Todt; not on the site, but as a recruiter.'

So that was it, thought Stefan; to avoid becoming a prisoner of war he was being asked to be a spy – a spy who would be employed by the enemy! A whole raft of doubts filled his mind. If he were found out he would be shot. Also, what nationality would he be? He could not pass as a Frenchman, except perhaps to a German who did not speak the language. He began to shake his head as he thought of all the difficulties he would encounter. It was lunacy; he would never get away with it.

The Doctor watched patiently as he wrestled with his thoughts. It was not an easy decision to take, he knew that, but he was not yet prepared to accept that he had misjudged his man.

'There is no need for you to decide now *monsieur,* even if you decide to do this it will take many days to arrange. Also, you need time for your hands to heal. Let me try to find out what kind of work you are likely to be given, and what identification you will have. In the meantime, you will be safe here; we can help you to improve your French, but you will have to sleep in the loft, I am afraid.'

Relieved that he would have a few days to think it over, it will do no harm to see what happens, Stefan thought. Anyway, he was not in any condition to go anywhere with his hands as they were.

There was the sound of the front door opening and closing and light footsteps. The door to the surgery opened and the head of a young woman appeared. Stefan caught a glimpse of an attractive face and waves of dark curly hair.

'*B'jour* Papa!' she said, but the smile on her face faded as she saw that her father was not alone. 'Oh, pardon' she muttered, as she withdrew her head and closed the door. The Doctor gave Stefan a quick smile.

'My daughter' he said, unnecessarily. 'She is a teacher, so she could help you to improve your French. If you will excuse me one moment *monsieur,* I'll explain who you are and introduce you.'

He got out of his chair and left the room. Stefan could hear them talking in the kitchen; first the voice of the Doctor, then the voice of his wife and, finally, what seemed to be questions from their daughter. There was a short pause, followed by footsteps returning. The door of the surgery opened and the Doctor entered, leading his daughter by the hand.

'*Monsieur* Radovak, this is my daughter, Marie – she greatly admires the RAF'

Stefan saw that the rest of her was in keeping with the attractive face he had seen a minute or two earlier. His pulse quickened at the sight of her. Her oval face was surrounded by waves of rich chestnut hair that reached to her shoulders. Intelligent clear brown eyes matched the colour of her hair, and her body was perfectly formed. Like her father, she gave the impression of being an athlete. She was wearing a dark blue dress covered in light blue forget-me-nots and black shiny 'sensible' shoes. Around her neck was a small crucifix on a thin gold chain. She was, he thought, a year or two younger than he; perhaps eighteen or nineteen years old. He was only twenty, but somehow he felt older; the past eighteen months had aged him beyond his years.

She came forward, a polite but nervous smile on her face, which turned to embarrassment at her father's words. She lifted her hand, but Stefan, as he attempted a suitable greeting in French, raised his bandaged hands in apology at not being able to shake hands. Marie gave an understanding nod at his predicament, which Stefan acknowledged with a self-conscious grin. Somehow, the small incident with the hands seemed to dispel the initial nervousness between them and, for a brief moment, their eyes met and it seemed that they were immediately at ease with each other.

The Doctor, looking from one to the other, was relieved to see his daughter's reaction. He turned to her and said something in French. It was too quick for Stefan to follow, but Marie translated what had been said with her reply in English. With a hint of coyness in her voice she said.

'Yes, Papa, I'll be pleased to help *monsieur* Radovak with his French.'

The Doctor nodded his satisfaction 'She is a teacher, *monsieur*' he said, with a touch of pride, forgetting that he had already informed Stefan of this fact.

His daughter gave Stefan an apologetic smile.

'I teach the five year olds in the village' she said in explanation.

Stefan laughed. 'Well, that's a relief – at least I'll be learning my French at the right level' he said. She broadened her smile to disclose a set of white even teeth.

'Hopefully, *monsieur,* you'll pay more attention than some of my young ones'

The Doctor smiled his pleasure.

'Marie, I've explained to *monsieur* Radovak that he must sleep in the loft - could you help mama with preparing a bed up there?'

'Yes. Papa, I'll see to it now.' She turned to Stefan. 'Excuse me, *monsieur*', she said. At the door she looked back and with a straight face said. 'Lessons will start tomorrow, *monsieur* Radovak.' Stefan gave her a grin as she vanished from view. He turned to the Doctor, and his face became more serious.

'You have a fine daughter, Doctor, but I'm concerned that the kindness and help you're giving me will put you all in danger – I wouldn't want to do that – are you sure that it's alright, my being here?'

Peering at him over his spectacles, the Doctor nodded.

'Yes, *monsieur,* so long as we're careful, you are safe here. Not only am I the local Doctor, I'm also the mayor. I know the people around here will not talk, even if they suspect something. They trust me. We're a very tight community, and intensely anti-fascist.' He glanced away for a moment before resuming.

'We're aware that our so-called leaders have betrayed us – betrayed France, to the Nazis. It started soon after Hitler came to power in 1933. Fascist sympathisers infiltrated the whole rotten political system. Even before Hitler there were those who admired Mussolini. One way or another Nazi agents made sure that France was in no position to fight when they were ready to pounce.'

Stefan was taken aback by the bitterness in the Doctor's voice. He had not taken a great deal of interest in how the French military had come to disintegrate so quickly against the Germans. But he knew how shocked and disappointed the British had been that Marshall Petain – as soon as he was made premier - had signed a peace treaty with Germany. The Doctor had obviously been fairly well informed about what was going on. Stefan would have liked to continue to question the Doctor but he was suddenly gripped with overwhelming fatigue and struggled to keep his eyes open. The Doctor noticed that Stefan was spent; he needed to sleep.

'Come, *monsieur,* I will take you upstairs – your bed should be ready by now.'

Later, Stefan vaguely remembered being helped up a staircase, and up a ladder. Marie was there, assisting him, and then he was sinking onto a straw mattress. He was asleep before his head touched the pillow. As much as he had looked forward to his first French lesson with Marie, he did not wake for sixteen hours.

CHAPTER 14

The stone cottage was set back about three hundred metres from the beach. Being on higher ground, the senior officers that were gathered on the upper floor had an excellent view of the landing craft that were approaching from the sea. The beaches on this remote part of the east coast of Scotland were not unlike those in France, which was why they had been chosen as a training ground for the invasion of Europe.

Beside each of the senior officers stood a junior officer taking notes in shorthand from the observations they were making. These would form the basis of a briefing the next day. Two of the NCOs present were women, and one of them was standing next to Max Radovak.

Sergeant Thelma Dowska had been his driver and secretary for several months now, starting just a few weeks before she became a widow. Her husband Karl had been in the same squadron as Stefan, and had been good friends. He was shot down two days after Stefan's Hurricane had dived into the English Channel.

An hour later, the exercise over, Max said his goodbye to the others, got into his staff car and was driven away by Thelma. Looking at him in the rear-view mirror Thelma reflected how he had changed over the last few months. He had lost weight, his face looked tired, preoccupied, and he didn't smile so often. She turned her head slightly and spoke over her shoulder.

'Have you heard from your wife lately, Max?' she said.

There was a slight pause as Max turned his gaze from looking out of the car window and addressed the back of her head.

'I had a letter yesterday,' he said, wearily. 'It was polite, and told me that they were all safe, and that she hoped I was OK - that was all, just the same routine letter.'

Thelma gave a nod. She knew what he meant.

When he returned from the Middle East and they had been reunited, Max had felt that his wife's feelings towards him were not the same. It was not apparent at first - yes they had slept together and made love and the joy of finding that his wife and daughter-in-law were alive and that he had become a grandfather distracted him. But Anna's questions about the whereabouts and welfare of Jak Zenski, and Trishka's questions about Leon Denkov made him realise how the war had changed them.

They had formed other relationships. His immediate reaction was frustration and anger, but he quickly realised it was no good. How could he be angry with either of them after the shock of Josef's death, and then losing Stefan so soon after hearing about Igor? They were not to blame. It was the bloody war that was to blame.

But he couldn't get it out of his head that at the time he was grieving for Stefan his wife and daughter in law were on holiday with two other men. He had not dared to ask his wife if she had shared a bed with Jak, or whether his daughter-in-law had done likewise with Leon. But he suspected that they had. And so, amid doubts and growing tensions, he had gone back to the war.

Max tried to bury his grief by working harder. Losing Stefan, Igor and Josef, and then finding that his wife had fallen for another man just about broke him up. But then something happened that changed his life.

After attending a meeting in London that stretched into the late evening, he'd emerged to find Thelma waiting with the car. But before he could get in air raid sirens started screeching, and as bombs started to fall they made a dash to the nearest underground shelter.

Elbowing their way to find a less crowded part of the shelter they were sent staggering by an earth shattering near miss above them, and Thelma had flung herself in terror towards Max. In the darkness the comforting arm that Max placed around her shoulders suddenly became an embrace.

The closeness of death coupled with the physical contact had exposed their loneliness. As the earth shook and trembled around them their lips came together and they kissed and clung to each other as though the world was about to end.

When they emerged from the shelter in the early hours of the morning the car had disappeared under a pile of bricks, so they walked arm in arm through the smouldering ruins and bomb-damaged streets to her apartment, where they went to bed and made love, and fell asleep in each other's arms. They now shared a bed whenever they could, and life was more bearable for both of them.

After driving along in silence for a few minutes, Thelma spoke again.

'Max - why don't you go to see them'

He shook his head slowly. 'I thought of that, but I doubt that it would make matters any better. There's nothing I can do about it. I know I should be grateful to those two men for looking after them and getting them safely to England, but it's still difficult to accept. Anna thought I was dead, and Trishka heard through the Red Cross that Igor was dead. Perhaps it's harsh to blame them, but it was still a shock that I wasn't expecting'

Thelma nodded. 'But they haven't got anyone now Max. The other two have gone back and may never return -you've got to forgive and forget.'

Max did not answer immediately, then nodded.

'You're right, I've got to accept what happened, but I doubt Anna will accept what has happened between you and me. If I get back with Anna, I'll have to tell her about us.'

Thelma concentrated on driving for a while before replying.

'Do you have to tell her about us Max? I could ask for a transfer, and that would be the end of it.'

In the mirror she could see the sadness on his face. He gave a small shake of his head.

'Would it Thelma? Is that what you want?' he asked.

Thelma felt something tugging inside her chest. 'No, it's not what I want Max, but the war will finish one day and everyone will have to try to pick up the pieces of their lives. You've got to try to think ahead - to the end of the war.'

There was another short silence and Thelma could see that Max was looking out of the car window, but not at the Scottish countryside. It was as if he was trying to stare into the future.

'Yes,' he said quietly, 'the war will end one day, and if we're still alive we'll have to put our lives together. But it won't be easy. We had a farm in Poland - but it's doubtful that we'll go back there. So, if we survive, we'll be homeless, stateless - and broke.'

Thelma slowed down the car as they approached the village. They had been lucky, the only place to stay had been the 'Crofters Rest,' in the centre, and they had managed to get the last of the three double bedrooms, which they shared as man and wife.

She stopped the car in the small car park at the side of the Inn and turned around in her seat to face Max.

'Keep writing to Anna, Max. She might have fallen for this other man - what's his name - Jak Zenski - but he's gone back to Poland.

Thelma climbed out of the car and opened the rear door for Max. Glancing at her as he got out of the car he gave her a small smile. Her face looked composed, so he was completely unaware of the turmoil she was in. Turmoil caused by the fact that she had fallen in love with him, and didn't want to lose him, but knew that, one-day, she would have to.

She had, from the start, regarded their relationship as only temporary, for the duration of the war at most. Such relationships were, after all, common in wartime. War made everyone realise that life was too short not to make the most of it. Normal conventions were put aside. And so Thelma thought that she was sticking to the 'rules', following the unwritten code, which, broadly speaking, boiled down to a 'love 'em and leave 'em' attitude. Right from the start she had accepted that Max was only 'on loan' – she was not out to steal him from his wife.

When it happened Max had badly needed someone loving and tender to cling to. And he convinced himself that it would not have happened with Thelma if his wife had not made the first move. Even so, he felt some guilt about sleeping with another woman. But it was much worse now that he'd fallen in love with her, because he couldn't visualise a future without her.

When he'd last seen his wife he felt betrayed. This was why he found it difficult to write. If she had been unfaithful to him, and there was no certainty that she had, he knew that his relationship with Thelma could be the end of his marriage. He felt depressed. The war had messed them up completely.

*

Anna recognised the handwriting on the envelope as she picked it up off the mat. It was from Max. It had taken him three weeks to send a reply to her letter. Trishka looked up from feeding the baby. She was concerned, wondering whether Max was coming to visit them again. She waited patiently as Anna read through it.

'How is he Anna, still working hard?' she ventured.

Anna started to read the letter once again. She nodded.

'He says that he's fine, but is heavily engaged in training exercises. He's based in Scotland now, and won't be able to get sufficient leave to get to London for some time.'

Trishka put the baby back into his cot and tucked him in.

'He hasn't mentioned anything about the baby then?'

Anna looked guilty and shook her head. 'No,' she said. 'I didn't tell him about the baby Trishka. I'm sorry, I should have done, but I thought it best not to.'

'Oh, Anna, I thought we had agreed that he should be told. He's got to know some time. He'll be angry, I've no doubt – but not telling him makes it worse. Perhaps one day he'll understand. I mean, I didn't cheat on Igor did I? It was after I heard that he was dead. But I felt so wretched, so alone, desperate I suppose, and not in my right mind. It was only the once, on that weekend in Bournemouth, and knowing that Leon was going off to war again. I had lost Igor, and then the thought of losing Leon – I couldn't bear it.'

Anna held out the letter for her to read.

'Trishka, I *do* understand. After all, I nearly did the same with Jak. Yes, we shared the same bed. But that's all we did - just shared a bed - there was no sex between us. It was just so nice to be in a man's arms again and, like you; I thought I might never see him again. I wish we had made love now.' Tears came into her eyes and she wiped them away with her hand.

'But I do miss him. And I miss Max. I love them both, Trishka – I know it's wrong, but I can't help myself. I was stupid. When Max was here he sensed that I'd fallen for Jak – I could feel it. I should have kept quiet but realised too late. And he was upset when you asked him about Leon. He would have walked out anyway if he had known that you and Leon had slept together and you were pregnant by him.' As she finished speaking she could see tears falling down Trishka's cheeks.

'I know, Anna – what a mess I've made of everything,' she said, 'And I might never see Leon again, or you see Jak again – we have not had a word since they went away. If only we knew that they were still alive it would help. I wrote to Leon to tell him about the baby - and every month since - but not a word from him.'

Anna nodded. 'I know,' she said, 'but that doesn't mean that they are not still alive. They did warn us not to expect any letters - we would probably only hear something if they were wounded, or taken prisoner, or dead.'

Trishka put her hands to her cheeks to wipe away the tears. 'Oh, what a bloody mess! Do you think that Max will ever forgive me? Perhaps it would help if I found somewhere else to live,' she said.

Anna stared at her for a moment in disbelief. She reached out and put her hands onto Trishka's shoulders. 'You mustn't talk like that Trishka. How would you cope on your own with two youngsters to look after? The two of us together only just manage as it is. It would be the worst thing we could do - to split up. No, you mustn't even consider it - we must stick together, come what may.'

'But - what about Max....?

'Never mind about Max,' said Anna quickly. 'We're all the family he's got left - he knows that. The next time I write to him I shall say that there was nothing between me and Jak that I am ashamed of, and Jak has now gone from my life and I doubt that I will ever see him again. And I'll tell him about the baby - he's got to know some time, and I'm sorry I didn't tell him before. You were right, the sooner he knows, the sooner he's likely to accept it. '

CHAPTER 15

On the first night that Marie gave a French lesson to Stefan the session was fairly formal. She concentrated on finding out how much French Stefan could speak by asking him questions about himself and his family. She was pleasantly surprised to find that, after two hours, Stefan could understand most of what she said. He was hesitant and lacked confidence with his replies, but she was convinced that, with practice, he would become fluent enough to fool most Germans, if not the French. She gave him 'homework' to do, and he concentrated hard, because he thought that she was the most attractive woman he had ever met and he wanted to impress her.

He was not disappointed; Marie was impressed with his progress. They got on so well together that, by the fourth night in the attic, they were giggling and laughing so much that Doctor Dubar came up to warn them to keep down the noise.

By the sixth evening, there was a small amount of talk to start with and then silence. This was because they were kissing and petting on the bed, with whispering and giggling in between. On the sixth night they made love; sensuous, passionate, delicious lovemaking.

The bloom that falling in love gives to a young face, together with the extra sparkle in the eyes, did not go unnoticed. At the breakfast table the Doctor exchanged knowing glances with his wife at the sudden change in their daughter. They knew what had happened, but were pleased, because the only other self appointed suitor that had been pushing their daughter for attention was a German officer from the local garrison - a brash, arrogant Nazi, with airs of superiority and a veneer of charm.

Marie had kept him at arms length by telling him that she was already engaged to a Frenchman - a soldier who had been captured by the Germans at Dunkirk. Which was partly true, but her fiancé had not been captured, he had been killed.

On the eighth day after Stefan's arrival, when the Doctor was changing the dressings on his hands, he looked over his spectacles at him.

'I have had some news today. A work permit can be obtained for you with the Todt. As you have some knowledge of engineering this would be a supervisory position, making sure the work is in accordance with the plans'.

Stefan gave a nod but could not think of a suitable reply. Could he get away with posing as a Frenchman? Surely he would soon be found out.

'A work permit,' he repeated thoughtfully. 'As much as I would like to help you Doctor, I doubt that I can pass as a Frenchman. What about my identity papers, how good would they be?'

The Doctor gave him a small smile.

'We can provide you with identity papers. You would be taking the identity of someone your age. His father was a Frenchman and his mother was Polish of German extraction. They are all dead, but only the parents have been registered as dead. The papers of the son are in order and we also have a ration card. It is a good cover, if you are interested.'

Stefan nodded again, it sounded more promising than he had expected.

'Also,' continued the Doctor, 'working for Todt would give you some credibility. You will be given a Todt uniform and have the right papers. With these you are not likely to be stopped and questioned, except at check points, like everyone else.

This was probably true, thought Stefan. It seemed that the Doctor had carefully considered all the angles.

'Where would I live, Doctor, would I have to live on the site?

Doctor Dubar gave him another smile.

'You would be lodged with a local farmer in the village of Azeville, not far from the site. They are good people; you will be safe there until we can move you on.'

'Move me on?' queried Stefan. 'How long will I be there? Does that mean that I will not be coming back here?'

It seemed that the plans the Doctor had for him meant that he would not see Marie again. His first reaction was to tell the Doctor that if it meant not seeing Marie again he was not interested. He quickly stifled this thought; Marie had known all along that he could not stay there indefinitely, that he would have to move on. Was this why she did not resist his advances? No, he did not think so. What had happened between them was genuine, not contrived. He was convinced that Marie would be just as distraught to learn that, having just found each other, they must part.

The Doctor finished tying the bandages and looked up.

'Your hands are healing well, *monsieur*. We will be able to take the bandages off in a few days.' He stood and started to tidy up, a thoughtful expression on his face.

'I have to say that, regretfully, it will not be wise for you to come back to this village or this house once you have left it. You must remember why we did not pass you over to the Germans as a prisoner of war. It was because you preferred to escape back to England if possible, and this is what we are working towards. This business we are asking you to do at Azeville - it is important for us to know what is going on, but it is also part of your escape plan. You will not be there longer than is necessary, I assure you – perhaps only a week or two'

Stefan felt guilty. Whoever else was involved besides the Doctor and his family, they were all risking their lives to help him. He decided not to put forward any more doubts. He would go along with their plans.

'Can you tell me where I shall be going when you move me on?'

'Not for certain - but once you have settled in and shown how keen you are – and it is important that you do this, however much you hate the Germans - the intention is to get you promoted. Even if this fails, we will try to get you moved to the Todt regional headquarters in Paris.'

Stefan pondered these words. The Doctor made it sound as though all he had to do was to go along with the plan and everything would fall into place. He doubted that it would be easy; and then another thought occurred to him.

'How long do you think it'll be before I get back to England?'

Stroking his chin, the Doctor went over and looked at his wall calendar.

'It could take anything from three to nine months. I'm afraid there is no way of telling at this stage. The important thing is not to make any moves until we are quite ready; until everything has been planned out.'

The thought of working for the Germans at all was against Stefan's every instinct; nine months would seem an eternity. But he knew he had to do it.

'When do I start, Doctor,' he said.

'You will have to report to the site at Azeville in seven days.'

Stefan gave an involuntary gulp. The Doctor reached over and patted his knee.

'You can do it *monsieur* - you can do it. We cannot beat them yet, but we can fool them.'

That evening, when Stefan told Marie about the plans that had been made for him, tears came to her eyes and she sank her head to his shoulder.

'*Cherie*,' she whispered. 'I knew it would have to be, but I can hardly bear the thought of losing you now. We have had so little time together.'

She lifted her head and kissed him and then looked into his eyes.

'I love you so much, Stefan.'

'And I love you, Marie. But I will not be many miles away – perhaps we can still see each other until I get moved on.'

'I will speak to Papa - if it can be arranged safely, I am sure he will do it.'

Marie decided not to mention it to Stefan, but she was concerned that Hans Gruber, the German officer, would call on her again before long. She did not want to go out with him, but was afraid that, if she continued to decline his invitations, he could turn resentful and dangerous. Now that Stefan was going, she did not wish to stay in the village. This is what she wanted to talk to father about; to see if he could find a way for her to keep in touch with Stefan; to be nearer to him.

The Doctor listened gravely to his daughters' request but when she had finished he slowly shook his head. He saw the pleading in her eyes and spoke as gently as he could.

'I am sorry, my dear, it is just not possible. It would be very dangerous for you to be seen with him. If he got arrested, they would arrest you also. It is safer to stay here in the village teaching the young ones.'

'But papa, what if Captain Gruber asks me again to go out with him? I think he's likely to turn nasty if I keep refusing him.'

'Hmm, I had forgotten about Gruber,' said the Doctor thoughtfully. 'We must find a way of keeping him from pestering you without causing offence.'

'If that is possible,' said Marie, with doubt in her voice.

The Doctor leaned forward and gave her hand a squeeze

'Let me give it some thought, I'm sure we can work something out.'

*

At daybreak six days later Stefan embraced a tearful Marie and then left the house pushing a bicycle. Dressed as a typical Frenchman, he mounted it calmly and peddled out of the village. In his pockets he had a map together with his new identity papers and his instructions to report to the office of the Todt Organisation at Montebourg.

He was heading for Cherbourg first; from there he would take the road south to Valognes, then to Montebourg. The Doctor had suggested that he would be less conspicuous on the main roads, where people on bicycles were a common sight.

He had to stifle his panic when he reached the outskirts Cherbourg and came to a queue of people at a checkpoint. It was a usual routine for locals by now, but it was a tense moment for Stefan. As he stood there, the wheel of his bicycle touched the one in front of him. A young woman turned around with a slight look of annoyance on her face. He apologised and she gave him a quick, forgiving, smile. The smile helped to calm him down.

As he waited he watched the actions of those in front of him. By the time it was his turn he passed over his papers and looked slightly bored as they were scrutinised. With an expression of equal boredom on the face of the gendarme his papers were handed back to him and he was waved on. Trying not to hurry, he rode off, elated that he had got through his first big test.

Hot, tired and hungry, he reached Valognes in the early afternoon. He had to go through another checkpoint before taking the road to Montebourg. His papers had been scrutinised more closely this time, and his heart had thumped as he forced his face to maintain a slightly bored and uncaring expression. Following the instructions that the

Doctor had given him, he soon found the house where he was to stay the night.

A small, thin, drab old lady opened the door. She said *'Bonjour'*, gave a nervous smile and led him to a dingy room on the first floor. There was a wrought iron single bed, a square bedside table with a small candle on it, a washstand with a bowl and water jug, and a small wardrobe.

'You are very lucky, *monsieur,* that I have a room for you. The town is full of soldiers and workmen. The soldier who lodges here is on leave this week. He has left some of his things in the wardrobe and has taken the key, so I'm sorry that you cannot use that.'

Stefan bristled inwardly at the thought of having to sleep in a bedroom occupied by the enemy, even for one night, but he pretended to look around with satisfaction.

'Thank you - this will be fine. I am, as you have been informed, only here for one night, two at the most. When does your soldier return?'

'The end of the week, *monsieur*, you can stay another four nights if you wish.'

'You're very kind, but I expect to be working at Azeville from tomorrow and have arranged accommodation there.'

The old women looked at him shrewdly.

'I know, *monsieur*, you will be staying at my brother's farm. You will be working for Todt at Azeville?'

Stefan raised an eyebrow, wondering how much she knew.

'You know about Azeville - what is being built there?'

She lifted her hands slightly and shrugged her shoulders.

'I know that the Germans are building something there. It is my brother's land that they have taken to build it on. Good farm land – just taken – and no payment – it's disgraceful.' She paused and looked at him a little nervously, wondering if she had said too much.

'That is all I know *monsieur*. I've two other lodgers who are working for Todt - you will meet them later, when we eat - they might know more.' She walked towards the door. 'We eat at six thirty, *monsieur*,' she said, as she closed the door behind her.

Stefan took off his shoes and eased himself onto the bed. The mattress was hard and lumpy, but the sheets were clean. He put his hands behind his head and tried to work out a strategy to follow. If

120

the other two Todt workers were French they might immediately spot him as a fraud. He decided to develop a sore throat before dinner, which would excuse him from saying too much. He took a deep breath and tried to relax. It had been a long day, pretending to be a Frenchman for the first time; but he suspected that each day would seem long from now on.

He woke to the sound of footsteps clambering down the stairs. Glancing at his wristwatch he saw that it was six twenty. He went over to the water jug and bowl and dashed water over his face. Looking briefly into the small shaving mirror over the bowl, he smoothed his hair down slightly and left the room. At the top of the stairs he paused for a second to collect himself to his new identity, and then descended with a noisy clatter.

Following the sound of voices he entered a small room that had been set out for the evening meal. The first thing that met his eyes was the back of two soldiers wearing SS uniforms sitting at the table. Panic gripped his insides as he hesitated. He was saved by a short laugh from the other side of the table. Sitting opposite the soldiers were two men in sand coloured uniforms. They each had a white armband with a black 'Org Todt' printed on it. The older one spoke.

'Ah, you must be Pierre Limone - we have been expecting you. Don't worry about these two,' he said, waving a casual hand at the soldiers who were craning round to look at him, 'they're OK.'

Stefan glanced at the two faces. Both had fair hair and blue eyes; good Aryan stock. He gave what he hoped looked like a relaxed grin. It was the first time he had been addressed by his new name and he was taken slightly off guard. He was trying to think what to say, when the older man saved him again.

'I am Jorge Kranik and this is Henri Dewitz – and our friends here are Wilhelm and Heinz.' Jorge was not only older than Henri, he was almost twice his size; and where Henri was fair skinned and looked like a dapper bank clerk, Jorge was swarthy, with dark hair and a moustache; an outdoor man. But it soon became clear that they were the best of friends.

Speaking with an affected croak in his voice Stefan continued to grin as he held out his hand for a brief handshake to each of them.

'Pleased to meet you all - sorry about the voice – sore throat,' he said, pointing to it

From the names they had given him it sounded as though neither of them were French. The two SS soldiers seemed friendly enough; or, if not friendly, unconcerned. He assumed that they already knew that he was a new recruit for the Todt, and he was accepted as such.

After a few courtesy questions about where he had travelled from and his journey, the conversation turned to the German invasion of Russia. The two SS men enthused about the progress of the Germans against the unprepared Russians.

Stefan learned that they were German Czechs, and he had to force his face to smile as they talked about their admiration for the 'Fuhrer'. He also noticed how skilfully Jorge led the conversation and kept it relaxed and friendly. At no time was Stefan not included in the table talk but, somehow, Jorge contrived it so that he did not have to say much.

By the end of the meal and the last of the wine and cider Stefan felt that he had been 'accepted'. Jorge and Henri told him that they were Poles with German ancestors, hence their allegiance to Hitler. But Stefan suspected that Jorge, at least, was not what he seemed. His friendly attitude towards him could be passed off as mere 'comradeship'; being part of the 'Org Todt' but he had the feeling that Jorge was there to 'keep an eye' on him. Whatever his suspicions, however, Stefan dare not ask Jorge. That would be admitting that he himself was not who he said he was.

The next morning Stefan followed Jorge and Henri on his bicycle to a Todt warehouse on the outskirts of the town, where he was fitted out with his uniform. As soon as he had it on he felt more secure. They carried on through the country lanes and reached Azeville at lunchtime. Jorge led the way to a large field of bare earth. About twenty men were scattered over the field measuring and driving in wooden pegs. In the corner of the field next to the road were three wooden huts. A black Citroen saloon was parked nearby. Stefan followed Jorge and Henri as they dismounted outside one of the huts, parked their bicycles and entered.

Inside were three tables and chairs. Two were strewn with papers and occupied by men in Todt uniforms, who looked up as they entered. Jorge went to the man wearing the uniform of a supervisor, stood to attention and said 'Heil Hitler!' Stefan and Henri did the same. The supervisor was middle aged, tall and thin, pale and bespectacled. His disdainful expression seemed to be a permanent feature.

'Heil Hitler' he returned casually and without enthusiasm. Dismissing Jorge and Henri he turned to Stefan and fixed him with pale, watery blue eyes.

'So, you arrive at last. I was promised extra help over three weeks ago' He spoke poor but understandable French. Pointing to the empty desk, he continued.

'That is where you will work - but first, I will explain what we are doing here, and what is expected of you.'

Turning to a large plan of the field pinned to the wall behind his desk he beckoned Stefan to his side. He talked for about fifteen minutes, mainly about the need for precise measurements for the military establishment that was to be built there. The site covered about five acres but, when he finished talking, the supervisor had not given any indication what the installation was to be used for. Their job was to ensure that the site was excavated accurately. When that was done they would move to another site and a specialist construction team would move in. Stefan was disappointed that he had not found out what the site was to be used for. But he reminded himself it was only his first day. He was kept busy until 6pm, when he was allowed to leave to seek out the farm where he was to stay. Azeville was not a large village and it did not take him long.

His room at the farm was a small attic with a single creaky bed; washstand, small chair, and chamber pot. There were nails in the walls and on the back of the door for hanging clothes. A candle on the washstand was the only lighting. There was no electricity. When it was dark lighting was by oil lamps and candles.

Stefan thought that the best thing about it was the wonderful view from the small window; a view of peaceful open fields toward the Normandy coast, two or three kilometres away.

The farmer and his wife were civil enough, but serious and worried looking. Apart from one old cowman they had no other help. Each day they were up at the crack of dawn and always seemed to be working long after Stefan had gone to bed.

The job at the site was easy and by the end of his forth day Stefan was bored. Much of each day was spent supervising the digging of foundations. Apart from one or two locals most of the workers on

123

the site were slave labourers; prisoners of war as well as various nationalities from the countries now occupied by the Germans. Six SS stood guard over them.

He found that his superior, Herr Vroond, was Dutch. The other assistant in the hut was a Polish land surveyor named Karl Jervitz, who had volunteered to work for Todt rather than languish in a prisoner-of -war camp. Stefan had to pretend that he did not speak Polish very well but, as Karl did not speak French, Stefan offered to teach him more French in return for teaching him some Polish. Not surprisingly, Karl Jerwitz was impressed with Stefan's quick grasp of Polish as he struggled with French. The only other thing they had in common was that they both played chess, which helped them to pass the long evenings.

Stefan missed the protection and friendship of Jorge and Henri, who had returned to Volognes. He never saw them again. But even more he missed Marie. Each night he thought about her and ached to be with her again. On the third day he had his first letter from her. It was full of concern and tender love for him, and she told him that on Saturday morning she intended to cycle to Cherbourg and then take a train to Montebourg. Could they meet at the station? She would be able to stay the night if Stefan could find a room. Overjoyed, he cycled to Montebourg and went to see the old woman who, fortunately, had a room vacant for Saturday night.

The days dragged out but, when they finally met, it was a blissful reunion. The weather was fine and they strolled arm in arm out into the countryside. It was the first time that they had walked in the open together, and Stefan enjoyed moving amongst the Germans that were about. They hardly gave him a second glance.

'Tell your father that he was right about the uniform, Marie', he said, 'it's excellent camouflage.'

That night they had an early, leisurely, supper. When it was over they went to bed and made love and then slept entwined until the sound of church bells awoke them. They went to church, and then walked and talked into the afternoon. Marie asked him about his family, and he told her, adding gloomily that his father was probably convinced that he, also, was now dead. For his own security, news of his rescue had not been transmitted to England. The Doctor had told him that if the Germans intercepted the message they would not give up searching for him.

As they parted at the station Stefan gave Marie a message for her father. So far, he told her, he had not found out the purpose of the building work that was going on at Azeville. Marie nodded and kissed him, promising to visit him every weekend, and Stefan promised to be at the station, waiting for her.

He stood on the platform and waited until the train disappeared from view. When he turned and started to walk away he suddenly felt very lonely.

CHAPTER 16

On the next weekend Stefan cycled to Montebourg and waited at the station as arranged. But he waited in vain. He left when it was dark and the last train from Cherbourg had departed. He slept alone that night in the room he'd arranged for them to share. The next morning, worried, he returned to the farm at Azeville.

A letter from Marie was waiting for him. He read it through twice, a puzzled frown across his face. Marie could not come to see him again until certain '.....difficulties at home had been dealt with.' What could she mean? If someone was ill, or had an accident, surely she would have said so. Had someone found out that he had stayed with the Dubar's, and they were now under suspicion? Stefan felt sick with worry that the 'difficulties,' were connected to him.

His first impulse was to telephone Marie from the public box in the village. But the Doctor had warned him that calls were being intercepted at the local exchange. All Stefan could think of was to write to her, confirm his love, and hope that the 'difficulties' she referred to would be soon resolved.

Stefan posted the letter on his way to work the next morning. Although he arrived at the site punctually, he found Herr Vroond standing outside the hut waiting impatiently for him to arrive. As he dismounted from his bicycle Stefan could feel the eyes of his superior watching him. Had he been found out?

He fought down a feeling of panic that he was about to be arrested. But he relaxed a little as he glanced around. If he was going to be arrested there would be members of the Gestapo, or the SS, present, but there was no one else except his Polish co-worker, Karl Jerwitz, who was just emerging from the planning hut and locking the door. Herr Vroond tapped his leg with the short leather switch he always carried.

'Come, both of you, we have been allocated new sites. We will inspect them today and find somewhere else to live. This site is finished for our work - we will return this evening to pack and we leave it tomorrow. Get in the car.' As he finished speaking, Herr Vroond pointed his leather switch to the rear seats of the Citroen, opened the drivers' door and climbed in. As the others got in the car he turned and passed a map over to Stefan.

'Here,' he said, 'all the sites are marked on this map and are numbered. See if you can guide us to the next one without getting us lost.'

Stefan looked down at the map. A number of small circles with crosses in them had been marked, stretching down the whole Cherbourg peninsular as far as Caen. Several were a few kilometres inland, but most were near the coastline, and some seemed to be on the beach. As he stared at the map, Stefan just saved himself from letting out a gasp of surprise. The words 'Top Secret' were stamped in red at the top, and his excitement mounted as he realised what he was looking at. He'd found out the secret of the site at Azeville for Doctor Dubar - and much more. Azeville was part of a much bigger plan; it was just one site in what Stefan guessed to be a vast programme of coastal defences.

Herr Vroond was looking at him in the rear view mirror, a trace of a smile on his lips.

'I have been instructed that we must clear and lay out these sites much more quickly from now on. The Führer wants his Atlantic Wall completed as soon as possible,' he said, with a slight emphasis on the word 'Führer.' To Stefan, it sounded slightly mocking, or even contemptuous.

Nodding, Stefan shared a glance with Karl Jervitz. So he had guessed right.

'Yes, Herr Vroond, we understand,' he said, and passed the map to his companion for a quick look. Looking out of the car window at the passing hedgerows and fields of the Normandy landscape, Stefan concentrated on keeping his face calm and unconcerned but, inside, he was jubilant. It was the kind of information that the British would be very pleased to receive, if the Doctor could get it back to them. Unfortunately, he had no idea how he was going to let the Doctor know.

Marie was the messenger, and now, after the letter, he had no idea when he would see her again. They had agreed that nothing was to be put in writing, and he must not telephone, so how could he communicate? He could perhaps give the Doctor a hint that he had some information in a letter to Marie, but it was no good writing to

127

Marie again until he could tell her his new address. Karl passed the map back to him and Stefan quickly assessed the direction they were taking.

'We are heading for the vicinity of Sainte-Mere-Eglise, Herr Vroond, is this correct?'

'Yes, that is correct – we will locate the first site - notice there are three or four in that area - and then we will find our accommodation – although that can wait until tomorrow if necessary. I would prefer to get back to Azeville before dark and clear the huts. As I said, we must pack our belongings ready for departure tomorrow morning. I will pick both of you up outside the church at eight o'clock. Is that understood?'

'Yes, Herr Vroond,' they answered in unison.

'What about our bicycles, Herr Vroond - have we got to leave them behind?'

Herr Vroond, negotiated a bend in the road before he replied.

'Certainly not - they will be needed, I will bring rope and we will tie them to the roof.'

'Thank you, Herr Vroond,' said Stefan, 'that is most kind of you.'

After exchanging a small smile with Karl, Stefan sat back in his seat, watching the map and occasionally giving directions to Herr Vroond. There was nothing more he could do until he had a new address to write from. His eyes rested on the back of Herr Vroond's head. There was something about him that Stefan liked. The man was taciturn, poker faced, gruff, a stickler for detail and something of a slave driver. No doubt considered by the Germans to be ideal attributes for the job he had been given. But behind this façade Stefan suspected that there was another Herr Vroond, someone with more warmth and understanding and intelligence and, more importantly, not a Nazi.

*

Marie glanced nervously at the clock. Soon she would have to meet and be nice to Captain Gruber. Her father had explained exactly what they were going to do, but she knew it could be dangerous for them if it didn't work out. There was a tap-tap at the front door. He had arrived; it was too late to change anything. Marie heard her father open the door.

'Captain Gruber! How nice to see you again!' said the Doctor with deceptive genuineness. 'Please – do come in. Go through to the sitting room – Marie is there. What can I get you to drink Captain?'

Captain Gruber, as Marie had anticipated, had not given up. He had called on the weekend that she had spent with Stefan.

His previous efforts had been rebuffed, but now he was back and determined not to be put off again. Village gossip had told the Doctor that the Captain had slept with many French girls since his posting to Cherbourg six months ago. Intimidating charm, a few bars of chocolate, and a packet or two of cigarettes was all it took. Rumour had it that it was the chase of the ones that resisted that aroused him the most, and he now had a sizeable bet on with his fellow officers that he would be sleeping with Marie before his next leave.

Her father had told her what had happened when he'd called the previous week. The Doctor had answered the door, and seemed pleased to see him.

'Ah! Captain Gruber,' the Doctor had exclaimed, with a smile, 'do come in; come in,' and stood aside for him to enter.

'I am sure that you have called to see Marie – not me – eh Captain?' he chuckled, ushering him to a chair.

'Unfortunately, she is not here,' he had said, lowering his voice, 'but I'm glad you have called Captain, because - well - I am worried about Marie, and I would appreciate your help in making her see sense.'

Intrigued, Captain Gruber had been all attention. Of course he would help the stupid Doctor if it meant that he would get his way with Marie all the quicker.

'Worried about her, Doctor?' the Captain enquired. 'Has anything happened to her? I shall, of course, help in any way I can. Please, tell me what I can do.'

'What has happened – you may well ask,' said the Doctor with down turned mouth 'She has taken up with a young Frenchman, Captain, a nobody, and she has gone off to spend the weekend with him. That is where she is now, with him.'

Captain Gruber had suppressed a smile.

'How can I help, Doctor - I assume you do not approve of this Frenchman?'

'It is someone she knew as a teenager – he grew up around here. He works for the Todt Organisation now – but I don't think he is the right man for her. She needs to get him out of her head. If you could help in any way, I would be very grateful. If you could take her out – to the cinema, dancing - you know what young girls like to do'

'But she may not wish to go out with me, Doctor – nothing would give me greater pleasure, I assure you, but she may still be reluctant.'

From the leer on the Captains face Doctor Dubar knew that he had taken the bait, and was no doubt anticipating what he'd do after the outing.

'Yes, Captain, but I'm sure she will come around in the end. If you are willing to be patient, I'm sure she will take to you.'

'What do you propose then, Doctor?'

'Well, Captain, for a start, can you come and dine with us next Sunday? You will be my guest. Marie will be here, and we will have a nice meal together. I suggest that you do not ask her out on this occasion – just concentrate on getting her to like your company without – well – without any pressure, eh? Then you must come again the following week. I will make sure that she does not go away again. Ask her out then, eh?'

And so Captain Gruber had fallen in with the Doctor's plan. Seducing Marie Dubar was turning out to be more fun than he had anticipated.

*

Gruber had not come empty handed. He brought English chocolate for Marie, English cigarettes for her father, and a bottle of 'Johnnie Walker' whisky – bounty from Dunkirk, he told them smugly.

Madame Dubar excelled herself cooking an exquisite meal. Marie, reserved at first, relaxed as the meal progressed; smiling, and then laughing, at Gruber's jokes. As the evening progressed, she seemed quite happy sitting next to him on the settee.

When it was time to leave, Hans Gruber said, 'I must thank you all for a most congenial evening. I shall look forward to seeing you all next week.'

130

As the Doctor walked him to his car he could see the satisfied smile on the Captains face

It took about twelve hours for the powder that had been mixed into Gruber's meal to start working. Awaking with a raging thirst, he broke out into a feverish sweat, followed by crippling stomach pains, vomiting and diarrhoea. After two days he was taken to hospital, where the Doctors puzzled over what was wrong with him. A week later, gaunt and white faced, he was discharged from hospital but relieved of all duties for another week. The vomiting had stopped but he was still suffering from diarrhoea and stomach pains. With no appetite, and no strength or enthusiasm for wenching, he managed to send a message to Doctor Dubar to say that, because of his illness, he could not visit.

Doctor Dubar went to see Gruber, appearing to be most concerned to learn about his illness. He left him a bottle of medicine to try, in the hope that it would help him to get well. Three days later the Doctor received a letter from Gruber, to thank him for the medicine. It had had a most beneficial effect. He was feeling so much better that he looked forward to coming for another visit on the following weekend.

Still pale faced, but feeling almost back to normal, Gruber turned up for another meal. Marie, he was pleased to find, was very sympathetic and much friendlier towards him. He was determined now to make up for lost time. Once he had her alone, he did not think it would take him long to seduce her.

At the end of the evening, after the best meal that he had managed to eat since his previous visit, he was delighted when Marie agreed to meet him on the following Saturday.

On the following Friday, however, there was another message from the Captain to say that he was in hospital again. The Doctor, as before, went to visit him, taking another bottle of medicine. Unfortunately, it did not have the same effect as before. Gruber got worse. After a month, deathly pale and thin, he was sent on leave to convalesce.

*

Stefan wrote to Marie from his new address, telling her that his 'boss' Herr Vroond, had requisitioned an abandoned farmhouse on the outskirts of the small town of St-Mere-Eglise. They had a room each and there were spare rooms for any 'guests' that they might invite. He also told her that, in spite of the workload they had been given, he had some 'good news' to tell her when they next met. His 'good news,' if anyone wished to question it, was that he had been 'promoted,' and was now in charge of his own site. But he hoped that Marie and her father would interpret his remark differently and realise that he had got the information that the Doctor wanted.

*

Two weeks after receiving his letter, Marie caught the train from Cherbourg to St-Mere-Eglise. Stefan was waiting at the station. At the house she was introduced to Herr Vroond and Karl Jervitz, who discretely went off to the cinema together, so that she and Stefan could be alone. Marie told him about Captain Gruber and how her father had dealt with him. Concerned at first, Stefan ended up doubled over with laughter. Later they went to bed and lay in each other's arms and kissed and talked into the small hours before they made love again and finally fell asleep.

The next morning Stefan gave Marie a small flat parcel wrapped in brown paper. He watched as she opened it. It was an old school atlas of France, the date on the inside cover was 1878. Stefan smiled at the look of puzzlement on Marie's face.

'I'm sure you already have a more modern one in your classroom, Marie, but this one is rather special and is really for your Father. It has been carefully marked.'

Marie flicked through the pages. 'But – will he know where to look?'

'Yes, after I've told you all about it,' he said, reaching out to take it from her.

As soon as he had found out about the sites, Stefan had racked his brains to find a way to convey the information to the Doctor without arousing any suspicion if it got into the wrong hands. Simply sketching a copy of the map and placing crosses on it was much too risky, he decided.

132

On the day before Marie arrived he had found the answer to his problem. Near the church in the town centre he came across a second-hand bookshop and, browsing inside, found the old school atlas. One whole page of the atlas was devoted to the Cherbourg peninsular. Stefan promptly bought it, returned to the farm and locked himself in his bedroom. Taking a pin, he made random pinholes on each page of the book, as though by a previous owner. The only page that he took time over was the one that displayed Normandy. Then he wrote a note in French and put it inside the book.

Dear Marie
I found this atlas in an old bookshop and thought it might be of some use in your classroom.
Kindest regards – Pierre

Stefan opened the atlas to the page showing the Cherbourg peninsular and held it up to the light. He had carefully made a pinhole at each of the sites that were on Herr Vroond's map. Marie was to tell her father that the site at Azeville was just one of dozens that were under construction in Normandy. Also, it was his guess that these sites were only a fraction of the fortifications being built along the whole coastline from Denmark to the Bay of Biscay, and probably to the Spanish border. They were part of Hitler's 'Atlantic Wall' against an Allied invasion

CHAPTER 17

After he had been declared fit enough to return to duty following his mysterious illness, Hans Gruber had been posted to Jersey. Jersey was considered a good posting, mainly involved with 'training' the local gendarmerie to Nazi doctrine. He had managed to seduce two or three of the local girls there, but still smarted from the fact that Marie Dubar had escaped his clutches. And so, six months later, when he got posted back to Normandy, he had relished the thought of continuing the chase for Marie. His thin lips smiled as he recalled the expression on the face of Doctor Dubar when he turned up on his doorstep after so many months.

'Captain Gruber!' the surprised Doctor had exclaimed. 'How - how nice to see you again. How are you?'

Not waiting to be invited in, Hans Gruber had stepped forward, forcing the Doctor to stand aside.

'*Guten Tag, Herr Doctor*,' he said in German, before reverting back to French.

'Actually, it is Major Gruber now,' he said, with a smirk. He took off his hat and placed it on the small hall table and dropped his leather gloves inside it. The Doctor forced a smile.

'My congratulations to you Major, a well-deserved promotion I am sure,' he said, pointing the way to the sitting room. '

The Major gave him a curt nod in acknowledgement. He came straight to the point.

'I have been away in Jersey for a few months, but I am back now, and would like to see Marie, if that is possible.'

'Please, sit down Major. Can I get you a drink? I still have some of the whiskey that you brought on your last visit.'

Hans Gruber shook his head. He did not wish to admit to the Doctor that, since his illness, he had not been able to drink alcohol. 'No, nothing, thank you *Herr Doctor*.' he said. ' I have come to see Marie, that is all. Is she at home?' He sat down and crossed his legs, waiting for the Doctor's reply.

The Doctor sat down and faced him. 'Marie, I regret to inform you Major, does not live here any more. She went to work for the Todt Organisation, and now lives in Caen.'

The Doctor saw the eyes of the Major register disappointment, almost malice, before he forced his lips to a small smile. He affected a nonchalant shrug.

'Aah - that is a pity – I was *so* looking forward to seeing her again. Caen, you say? Chased after her Frenchman, did she?'

'I'm afraid so, Major,' said the Doctor, adopting a glum expression. 'At least, I think that was the idea, but I'm not sure that they are seeing much of each other. He was, I understand, travelling a great deal in his work. But she did want to do something for the war effort – and there was nothing here.'

'Hmm,' said the Major thoughtfully. 'This Frenchman, what is his name?'

If the Doctor was alarmed by this unexpected question, he did not show it. He pretended to think for a moment.

'Pierre,' he said, slowly. 'Yes – Pierre – Pierre Lamont,' he continued, deliberately mispronouncing the surname.

'Hmm – and I seem to recall you mentioning that he used to live around here,' Gruber said, still deep in thought.

Alarm bells were sounding inside the Doctor's head, but his face was passive. He knew that this line of questioning was dangerous, but he could not think of any way to divert it.

'Am I right, Doctor?' asked Gruber, as he drew out a cigarette case from his inside pocket, opened it, and proffered it to Doctor Dubar.

The Doctor, realising that he could do nothing to avoid the question, gave a nod and smiled as he took a cigarette. 'Yes Major, it was the village of Vauville, five or six kilometres south of here. But he moved away after he lost both of his parents in a tragic fire.'

'Fire? What happened?'

'The house burnt down, and they went with it,' said the Doctor, as he lit the cigarette. 'Very tragic.'

'Hmm,' said Gruber. He drew on his cigarette and slowly exhaled the smoke.

The Doctor waited. Gruber gave a quick nod and stood up.

'Well, Doctor, I have seven days leave from tomorrow and I was planning to go to Paris and hoping to take Marie with me – I'm sure she would have enjoyed that. But, since Caen is on my route, I would like to have her address so that I can visit her and pay my respects. Who knows, if she can get some leave, she might still be able to join me. If not I may decide to stay in Caen.' Gruber smiled at the Doctor as though he was doing him a favour. He moved towards the door. 'Now, if you would be so kind as to give me Marie's address, I will say goodnight'

He watched the Doctor go to his desk, consult his address book and write out the address on a piece of paper.

'Here you are, Major,' he said with a smile, 'I am sure Marie will be most surprised to see you again.'

Gruber took the piece of paper and waited while the Doctor opened the door and stood aside as he walked out.

'*Gute nacht, Herr Doctor,*' he said.

'*Bonne nuit, Major - bon voyage,*' the Doctor replied in a friendly voice. Closing the door, the smile dropped from his face and his expression became serious. He stood for a few seconds, then went back to his study, sat down at his desk, took a piece of blank paper and started to write to Marie.

*

The next day Hans Gruber reached the outskirts of Bayeux just as the light was beginning to fail. He was pleased with the black Renault that he had 'requisitioned' from a Jewish tailor on Jersey. It was a comfortable car and only four years old, and made a nice change to being driven around in a staff car. The journey had taken him longer because he had first driven to Vauville and spent an hour or two talking to the mayor. He had left Vauville with a smug smile on his face..

He stopped at a barrier, showed his papers and drove on into the town, deciding to spend the night there rather than travel on in the dark to Caen. He could continue his journey in the morning and plan his surprise more effectively.

Gruber found a room at the small hotel next to the railway station that was reserved for German officers. Feeling hungry, he ordered sirloin steak for his evening meal, the most expensive item on the small menu. It proved impossible to eat; so tough that he suspected it to be from a horse that had died of old age, and he barked his displeasure at the *patron* and refused to pay. Tired after his long day, he decided to turn in early, and was dozing off when the Cherbourg to Paris train trundled into the station and kept him awake. He cursed and stared up at the ceiling, thinking about Marie. A small smile played on his lips as he tried to picture Marie's face when he told her what he had found out about her Frenchman. Happy with his thoughts, he did not hear the train start and continue on its way to Caen. He had fallen asleep.

Among the passengers that got off the train at Caen was a man in a black overcoat wearing a black homburg hat and carrying a black leather holdall. Hurrying ahead of the other passengers he jumped into the solitary taxi and gave the driver an address.

Ten minutes later the taxi stopped in a quiet side street near the centre of Caen and the passenger got out, paid the driver, and asked him to return in ten minutes. Turning, he rang the doorbell of an apartment that was situated above a shop. He listened as footsteps descended a staircase. The door was unlocked and opened just enough for a face to look out. The eyes opened wide.

'*Papa!*' exclaimed Marie in surprise.

Doctor Dubar moved forward and she stood aside to let him in. He kissed her on the cheek.

'Hello, my dear,' he said as he started to climb the stairs. ' I have sent you a letter - it's about Gruber - he is on his way here, but I heard this morning that he had called at Vauville and spent some time questioning the mayor. I feel Stefan is in danger of being exposed, so decided to travel down by train to warn you. Gruber has got to be dealt with. Is Stefan here?'

Marie started to climb the stairs after her father. 'No Papa, I'm not expecting him for another two days. Gruber? – I thought he was in Jersey,' she said, confused.

'Well, he's back - and it's Major Gruber now - and he wants to continue the chase after you,' said the Doctor grimly.

'*Merde,*' said Marie quietly to herself, then out loud, as another thought struck her. 'But where is Gruber - is he likely to come tonight?'

'He might, but I doubt it now. He'll probably come tomorrow. I can only stay ten minutes; I must catch the next train back to Cherbourg. Now my dear, sit down and listen carefully.'

He quickly explained how to handle Gruber when he arrived and what to say to him. She must, at all costs, be agreeable and friendly towards him. He handed her some pills and a small piece of paper on which was typed the name, address and telephone number of a local Doctor. He repeated the plan again, kissed her goodbye, and hurried downstairs just as the taxi that had brought him there arrived to take him back to the station.

In the apartment Marie sat down, white-faced with worry, thinking over what her father had told her she must do. She waited until midnight before she felt safe enough to go to bed, but she did not sleep well. The next morning she left the apartment early to go to work.

When Marie returned in the late afternoon she saw a black Renault parked at the kerb opposite her apartment and guessed that it was Gruber. She ignored it, reached the door of the apartment, pretending to fumble in her handbag for her key. Behind her she heard the car door open and close and footsteps approach.

'Hello, Marie,' said Major Gruber in his silkiest voice.

Marie turned and pretended surprise. 'Hans!' she said. 'What a surprise! What are you doing here? How did you know my address? Have you been posted to Caen?'

Gruber smiled at the list of questions that Marie flung at him in her confusion.

'One question at a time, my dear Marie. First of all, you will notice that my few months away have not been wasted; I am now Major Gruber.' He pointed to his new insignia with a grin. 'With regard to your other questions - no, I have not been posted to Caen, I am on leave. When I called to see you at your home, your father explained that you now worked for Todt in Caen, so he gave me your address. I am on my way to Paris for a few days and thought I would call in on the way to see you. But now that I have found you, perhaps we can spend some time together. I would very much like to renew our friendship.' He took hold of her hand and bent down and kissed it. His hand was cold and damp and she resisted the impulse to pull away.

She gave him a small coy smile, pretending to be a little flustered and embarrassed. Finding her key she unlocked the door and opened it.

'Congratulations on your promotion Hans – please come in.' She waited for him to enter, closed the door and started to climb the stairs. She remained silent until they entered her apartment and she had closed the door.

'I hope we can remain friends Hans, but my father should have told you that I have a boy friend. He also works for Todt - although I've seen little of him lately.'

'Ah, yes, your Frenchman. Your father did tell me about him Marie,' said Gruber, his expression becoming more serious. 'Tell me, how well do you know him - his background I mean?'

Marie gave a shrug. Although she was expecting such a question, she was finding it hard to keep calm. Gruber was dangerous to Stefan and to them all, and she must play her part.

'His background? Well, I went to the same school as his brother. Not that I remember much about that, I wasn't interested in boys then. His grandparents had a farm near Vauville and they brought him up after his parents died. He was at an agricultural college when the war started. Apart from that, not a lot,' she said. 'Why do you ask?'

Gruber ignored her question. 'What is the name of your Frenchman - what do you call him,' he said.

'His name? It's Pierre - Pierre Limone,' she said in a puzzled voice. 'Look, Hans, can you tell me what all this is about?'

Gruber had sat down. He tried to look serious and sympathetic about what he was about to say, but what Marie saw was superiority and arrogance.

'I am sorry to have to tell you Marie, that I suspect your Pierre is not who you think he is.'

Marie opened her eyes wide and put her hand to her mouth. She stared at him. 'What!' she said. 'I –I don't understand. What do you mean Hans?'

Enjoying himself now, but keeping a straight face, Gruber continued. 'I think we will find that he is living under a false name with a false passport. You see, I have found that Pierre Limone died from a kick in the head from a horse, but his death was never registered. Your Pierre has taken his identity. I have proof of this. I'm sorry, but it is my duty to arrest him and turn him over to the Gestapo, he is most probably a spy.'

Marie's face paled, she did not dare ask Gruber how he had found out.

'He is not living here Hans. He works away, I don't see him very often,' she said, realising now why her father had made his rushed visit. She shook her head. 'I can't believe it, I'm sure there's some mistake.'

'Well, perhaps there is Marie,' said Gruber, in a conciliatory tone, 'perhaps there is. We shall see.' But he knew very well that there was no mistake – he was convinced that Pierre Limone was an impostor, and he was looking forward to arresting him – unless Marie could persuade him not to.

And that was what he was hoping for. He had thought it all out. It seemed a perfect solution, and it was so simple. Looking at her he was convinced that she would succumb to his wishes. If Marie would agree to become his mistress he would not arrest her boy friend. Not that he intended him to escape being arrested. No, he would leave it for a week or two before informing the Gestapo. By then she would be well in his clutches. He gave a shrug.

'Anyway, there is little that can be done until I have had the chance of speaking to him. In the meantime perhaps you would care to join me for an evening meal. Is there a restaurant nearby that you can recommend? '

Marie looked thoughtful for a second or two. 'Thank you Hans - yes, there is one not far away which is quite good. If you would give me a few minutes to change out of my uniform and freshen up, we could get there before it gets too crowded. Here, you might like to read the newspaper while you are waiting.' She walked into the bedroom. 'Isn't it dreadful,' she called out. 'Thousands of Italians have surrendered in the desert. The Fuhrer will be angry with that, don't you think? '

Major Gruber picked up the newspaper and scanned the front page. He scowled.

'The cowardly swine,' he said, 'they have let us down in the desert and would like to pack it in. They have been useless to the Führer and to Germany.'

Marie smiled to herself as she listened to his remarks. When she was ready, she took two of the tablets that her father had given her and pushed them into the finger of one of her gloves. Taking a last look in the mirror, she braced herself and put on a sweet smile.

'I'm ready,' she said, as she emerged from the bedroom, 'shall we go?'

By asking Gruber to tell her about his stay on Jersey, all Marie had to do during the meal was pretend to be enraptured with his conversation. He was complimentary about how the Todt Organisation - with the aid of Russian slave labour - had built such massive fortifications. The Channel Islands, he gloated, 'were an impregnable fortress.' While he spoke, her hands were busy beneath the table retrieving the tablets from her glove. When she reached for the wine bottle she had no difficulty in dropping the two tablets into his glass as she poured the wine.

As they walked back to her apartment she linked her arm with his and listened with feigned interest as he talked about himself and his promotion. He was obviously pleased with her friendliness towards him. He gave her hand a squeeze and smiled.

'I hope, Marie, that you will not send me away tonight. I have been so looking forward to seeing you again.'

Marie looked at him. 'Have you Hans? I thought that you had forgotten all about me,' she said. 'But what about Pierre? I can't believe what you told me is true. It *must* be a mistake, and I can't - well, I can't sleep with you - knowing that he might be arrested. I can't do it, Hans.'

Gruber nodded his head as though he understood. It was what he had expected her to say, and it was the opportunity that he'd hoped for.

'Well, if your Frenchman is living under a false passport it is my duty to arrest him, I am sure you see that.'

'Yes, I do, but he's working for Germany. He's been promoted and is highly regarded by his superiors. I can't sleep with you knowing that as soon as Pierre returns you are likely to arrest him.'

There was another nod from Gruber; everything was going exactly as he had schemed.

'Yes, yes Marie, I can see that it is very difficult for you. Please forgive me. Perhaps we can find a way. Even so, I think I must stay with you until he returns.'

By this time they had reached the apartment and Marie was concerned that the pills she had given him did not seem to be working. Then she saw Gruber pass a hand over his forehead.

'That wine has gone to my head a little,' he said, as he reached out and pulled her towards him.

'Marie, I cannot bear the thought of sharing an apartment with you but not sharing your bed. Please believe me that I do not wish to harm your Frenchman, but if I do not arrest him -which is my duty - are you prepared to give him up and come and live with me?'

Marie pulled herself away from him. 'Would you do that Hans - would you let him go,' she said.

'I would, my dear, if we could be together.'

'You would keep your word?'

'You have my word that I would not arrest him,' he said, looking steadily into her eyes, because he knew that he would not – it would be the Gestapo who would do the arresting.

She smiled at him, appearing to give in. 'All right Hans, I will give him up if you agree not to arrest him.'

'And you will come to live with me?'

' Yes,' said Marie.

Gruber kissed her.

'My dear, you will not regret it, I promise you.' He knew full well that it was a promise that he did not intend to keep and she would, in time, bitterly regret her decision. 'I'm tired out,' he said, giving his head a shake, 'it has been a long day. Do you mind if we go to bed now, my dear.'

Marie paused for a brief second; she knew there was no choice. 'All right, Hans, I'll get ready,' she said, and walked towards the bathroom.

When she emerged from the bathroom ten minutes later she found that Hans had undressed and was in bed. He was fast asleep. She sighed with relief and went over to him and patted his cheek.

'Hans – Hans,' she said softly, but there was no response.

Picking up her handbag she pulled out the piece of paper that her father had given her. Taking it she went downstairs to the telephone that was fixed to the wall under the staircase. She asked the operator to connect her and as she was waiting the door behind her opened and someone climbed the stairs. Marie could not see who it was, but assumed it was the owner of the shop, who lived on the top floor.

Just then the Doctor answered at the other end of the line. Marie gave him her address and asked him to come urgently, as her father had told her to do. She put down the receiver and started back up the stairs.

*

When Marie got to the apartment she was startled to see a figure standing looking at the discarded uniform and the man lying asleep on the bed.

Marie let out a startled cry. 'Stefan!'

Stefan turned, his face wooden. 'What's going on Marie?' he said.

Marie's brain was in the whirl, she didn't know how to begin.

'It's Gruber – he was here when I got back from work.'

'Gruber - isn't that the Nazi from Cherbourg who was chasing after you?'

'Yes – he forced Papa to give him my address. He's found.......'

'He's a bloody Major in the SS,' interrupted Stefan, staring at the uniform. 'A bloody Nazi in our bed!' he continued in disbelief. 'What's wrong with him?'

'I –I've given him a sleeping pill – he found out that you have a false passport. I had to agree to sleep with him. He was going to arrest you.' Marie was letting the words tumble out but realised that Stefan was hardly listening. Without another word he walked over to the wardrobe, took out a kit bag and started filling it with his clothes.

'Stefan, what are you doing?' said Marie. Stefan continued packing, and Marie went over to him and placed her hand on his arm.

'Stefan I can explain - please let me explain,' she said.

He pulled his arm away. 'You have, Marie. You've just said that he was going to arrest me so you agreed to sleep with him to save me. Do you think he would have kept his word? I don't think so. But I've got to get out of here – I can't hang around for him to wake up.'

'But Stefan, I wasn't expecting you back until tomorrow – and I didn't intend – I don't *want* to sleep with him.' she said trying to hold him back. He gave her a quick squeeze then pulled himself free. He looked at her and shook his head.

'Marie, I really do have to move quickly. You and your father have taken big risks to keep me alive – but don't think that you have to sleep with a Nazi to protect me. I can't stomach that. I came back early because we're being moved to Honfleur.' He turned and went into the bathroom and came out with a clean towel and soap and put them in the kit bag. 'I was hoping we could spend the night together before I left, because I'm not sure when I'll see you again.'

He pulled an old Michelin tourist map of Normandy out of his pocket and handed it to her. 'Here, make sure your father gets this, I've pin holed all the sites I've worked on after Bayeux. And tell him that these are only the big sites – I'm not involved with all the machine gun positions.' He tied up the kit bag, slung it on to his shoulder, kissed Marie on the cheek and moved towards the door.

'Sorry to have to part like this Marie.' He nodded towards the bed. 'But, believe me, I'll take my chances at being arrested, so you don't have to sleep with any bloody Nazi to try and protect me.' He went out and closed the door behind him, leaving Marie speechless, her eyes full of tears.

She listened as his footsteps went down the stairs and the front door closed. Her brain numb, she stood, unable to grasp what had happened. Looking over at Gruber lying in her bed the thought crossed her mind to take a knife from the kitchen and sink it into his heart.

Stefan had brought her back to her senses. She should have known that he would not want her to prostitute herself on his behalf, especially not with a hated German. But it was too late now, unless – and it was a tempting impulse - she packed a case and dashed after him. Instead, she sat down and cried.

A few minutes later the Doctor arrived and she went to let him in. Like her father he also wore a black overcoat and hat, but he was tall and thin and pale and had a drooping moustache – more like an undertaker than a Doctor. He looked at her keenly.

'Where is he?' he asked brusquely.

Marie pointed upstairs and led the way. The Doctor stood by the bed and looked down with contempt at Gruber. He slapped his face but there was no response. He opened his small bag and prepared a hypodermic syringe, inserted it into the nipple of Gruber's left breast and gently pressed down until it was empty.

'There,' he said, ' it is done'

'What is done, Doctor? – What's going to happen now?'

'Tomorrow I will have to inform the military hospital that Major Gruber has had a heart attack during the act of making love and has died.' he said with a straight face.

'Died?' Marie gasped out, 'but - *has* he had a heart attack?' she said, feeling a flush of relief flood through her body.

'Yes, I have just given him one. He will not recover. This is the bastard who seduced and debauched my daughter. He has done the same to many other women – and you were to be his next victim. He had it coming to him. Don't worry - it is undetectable. But you will have to pretend that he was your lover and you are grief stricken that he has died.'

Preparing another syringe, he injected Gruber in the arm.

'If anyone asks, you only saw the second injection – understand – only the second.'

Marie nodded, numb with shock.

'Tomorrow you will be asked questions. If anyone asks you about Pierre Limone, you gave him up months ago and don't know where he is. Understand?'

'Yes,' said Marie quietly, 'I understand.'

'And you must not try to follow him or contact him.'

Marie stared at him for a second or two. 'I'm not sure I can promise that. I love him and he has just walked out and left me. I must see him again – to explain – to make him understand that I had no intention of sleeping with Hans Gruber – that it was part of a plan to get rid of him.'

The Doctor narrowed his eyes. 'Limone is in great danger. You will not improve his chances if you follow him - and you will endanger yourself. You say he has just walked out on you – he was here, tonight?'

'Yes – he left just a minute or two before you arrived. I wasn't expecting him – but when he saw Gruber asleep on my bed, he packed his clothes and left.' Tears filled her eyes at the recollection.

'*Merde*,' said the Doctor. 'He should not have come back here. The Gestapo are already making enquiries about him. If they followed him here.......'

'The Gestapo?' Marie interjected. 'Are you sure?'

'Yes. The restaurant where you ate this evening - you have been there before.' It was a statement not a question. 'You have been there before with Pierre Limone.'

'Yes – we ate there a few times.'

The Doctor nodded. 'The *patron* is a collaborator. He pretends to be friendly, patriotic – gets people to confide in him. Limone introduced himself as a Frenchman but hearing him talk the *patron* became suspicious that he was not a Frenchman – so he reported it to the Gestapo.'

Marie's face was deathly white. 'Oh my God,' she whispered.

The Doctor closed his bag. 'If they question him, it is all over – it will not take them long to trace his false identity back to your father. Did he say where he was going?'

'He said they are being moved to Honfleur tomorrow.'

'Honfleur?' said the Doctor thoughtfully. 'That might give him a bit more time.' He lifted his bag and made for the door. 'I must leave you now –I will report the death immediately, so you may not have long to wait before a military Doctor arrives. It is up to you to play your part.' Opening the door, he turned and glanced back at the bed. 'Good luck to you,' he said, and gave her a reassuring smile. 'Just keep your head, you'll be all right.'

Marie stood staring at the door to the apartment, her brain and emotions in a whirl as she listened to the Doctor's hurried departure from the building. She sat down and faced the bed, half afraid that Gruber would wake up. Then she looked at the uniform that he had so hurriedly discarded and, finally her eyes rested on the case that he had brought up from the car. Getting up she went over to the uniform and searched the pockets. She replaced everything exactly as it was until she found a small notebook in black leather with a swastika on the front of it.

She flipped through to the last few pages. Her face darkened as she struggled to read his German handwriting of the visit he made to Vauville. It was clear that Gruber had intended to arrest Pierre, but '*Erst Marie*' exposed his deception. A chill went down her spine as she read the last entry. Printed in capitals with a circle around and a question mark was the name of her father, Doctor Dubar.

She looked again at the pages of the notebook and could see that several pages had previously been torn out. Without hesitation she removed the last few pages and tore them into small pieces and walked to the bathroom. Dropping the pieces into the lavatory she flushed it and watched it disappear. Replacing the notebook in Gruber's uniform, she undressed, put on her dressing gown, sat down, lit a cigarette, and waited.

CHAPTER 18

Sergeant 'Scarlet' O'Hara leaned his elbow out of the three-ton truck and narrowed his eyes to a squint. The spotter 'plane that patrolled that section of the desert had reported a sighting of 'persons unknown' and he had been sent with a dozen men to investigate.

The midday sun seared down and the shimmering heat distorted his view. There was an escarpment about a mile away and the space in between was strewn with mines. He turned to his Indian driver and took up his binoculars from his lap.

'Stop here - let's have a look through the glasses.' Swivelling his head he addressed the men in the back.

'Five minutes to stretch your legs and have a pee - if anyone sees any movement over yonder, give me a shout.'

As they scrambled out of the truck he lifted his binoculars and started a careful scan. After two minutes he lowered them to give his eyes a rub. When he raised them again he was just in time to see a flash and a plume of sand and something more solid shoot into the air and fall back. A couple of seconds later came the boom of the explosion. Someone had detonated a mine. He focused on the spot and could see five or six figures. One was lying on the ground - the others were standing still.

He turned to his men, who were looking in the direction of the explosion. He pointed a finger. 'You four - get the mine detectors and follow me - the rest of you stay here, stay alert, and have your rifles near you.'

He led his small party towards the minefield and they started the slow process of waving the mine detectors in front of them, carefully lifting the mines and placing them in rows either side of the pathway they were creating.

An hour later they had covered about half the distance. Sergeant O'Hara took another look through his binoculars. He could see that they were not Germans or Italians, but they were not British or Australian either, and the funny hats they were wearing were not the turbans that the Indian soldiers wore. Then he recognised them. They were wearing kepis.

'They're frogs,' he said to himself.

But finding out that the soldiers waiting to be rescued were French did not help him to decide whether they were friend or foe. He knew that a regiment of legionnaires had joined General De Gaulle's Free French army to fight with the Allies, and less than two months ago many of them had been involved with holding up Rommel's advance at a desolate place called Bir Hakeim in Libya.

The French had suffered a non-stop bombardment by the enemy ground and air forces for weeks, and it was only when they were running out of ammunition and water that they decided on a desperate attempt to break out. In the dead of night, using up the last of their ammunition, over 3000 had broken through the German lines and rejoined the Allies. But many had been left behind.

O'Hara was also aware that the bulk of the Foreign Legion was still loyal to the Vichy government, who had demonstrated often enough that they were pro-German. When he got closer he raised his hands to his mouth.

'Who the 'ell are you?' he shouted.

'Legionnaires,' came the hoarse reply.

He decided that it didn't matter what side of the military fence they were fighting on. They were soldiers who needed help. He pointed to the figure on the ground.

'Is there anything we can do for him?'

There was a shaking of heads. 'No – nothing- he's gone.'

They were speaking English, but not with a French accent, he noticed

The last mines were cleared and the five men moved to the cleared pathway. O'Hara and his men could see what a terrible state they were in. They wore ragged shorts and short-sleeved shirts, and the sun had burnt and blistered all the exposed skin. But it was their faces that had suffered the most, and their lips looked like pieces of dried, cracked, leather.

'How long since you ran out of water?' asked O'Hara

'Almost two days,' one of them croaked, 'but we didn't have much to start with.'

O'Hara passed his water bottle to the Sergeant. 'Here – pass this around. We'll have a nice cup of tea when we get back to the truck.'

Taking one mouthful each, they held the water in their mouths before letting it trickle down their throats, repeating the process until the water was gone.

Walking slowly back through the minefield, the senior NCO of the group introduced himself as Sergeant Igor Radovak, and explained that they were Polish. He introduced the corporal, Nikolas Solik, and the others, who had got to Algeria by various means and joined the Legion, rather than be captured by the Nazis.

Sergeant Radovak told him that they had fought against Rommel at Bir Hakeim, and on the breakout had been captured. They had managed to escape during an air raid by the RAF, and had been walking in the desert for eight days.

As he walked, Scarlet O'Hara decided what to do. Going strictly by the book he should take these men back to base immediately for a debriefing. But he had seen men before who were suffering from dehydration and malnutrition. Very often, having reached safety, they died. In fact, he had nearly died himself a few months ago, when he got captured by the Italians but managed to escape. And what happened when he crawled half dead out of the desert? They had insisted on the debriefing him before he was allowed a rest, a shower and shave, or something to eat.

No, he would take these men directly to the military hospital. They were not in any fit state for a debriefing yet. Bloody debriefing could wait. Also, he had a great respect and sympathy for Poles. His best mate was one, before he got killed at Tobruk.

*

Igor drifted slowly back to consciousness. His head felt fuzzy and when he opened his eyes a large fan above his head was waving from side to side. He squeezed his eyes shut for a few seconds and opened them again. The fan looked normal. He turned his head and looked around.

He was in a ward with twelve beds, six either side. There was an atmosphere of quiet calm and an overall smell of antiseptic. Nurses in crisp white uniforms were in attendance at several beds.

'Good morning,' said a voice, in Polish.

Igor turned his head. A man in the next bed with a bush of thick curly hair was smiling at him.

'Good morning,' he replied. 'This is a different place to the one I remember - where are we?'

'Cairo – you've been here four days - flown in from somewhere.'

'Four days?'

'Yes - the three of you have been under sedation.'

Igor let this sink in for a second or two. There had been five of them - where were the others?

'Your comrades are over there,' continued his neighbour, pointing his head across the ward.

Igor raised his head and looked across. There was no movement from the two beds. He decided to go over to see them, and folded back the sheets and swung his feet to the floor. He took one step and his legs buckled under him, and he grabbed at the end of the bed to stop falling.

There was a chuckle. 'Don't worry,' came the voice, 'you haven't lost the use of your legs.'

'It feels like it,' said Igor, as he tried, unsuccessfully, to walk again but fell back onto the bed.

'It's a combination of the drugs wearing off and not using your legs for a few days. If you call a nurse, she'll bring you a pair of crutches.'

'Crutches?' questioned Igor, alarmed.

The other man grinned. 'You'll only need them for a day or two – they'll stop you falling over as you get your legs back to strength.'

His neighbour introduced himself as Nik Blewzki. They were in a recuperation ward, and he was recovering from a severe attack of malaria. He mentioned that he was attached to a 'reconnaissance unit'

Igor found that the legionnaires in the other two beds were Solik and Corporal Norkz. Upon enquiry, a Doctor told him that two legionnaires had died within hours of being rescued. An hour or two later Solik woke up, and soon joined Igor walking around on crutches to strengthen their legs. Corporal Norkz did not wake up; he died in his sleep two days later.

Intelligence officers visited them and listened to their story, asked questions, and took notes. They were told where to report when they were discharged from hospital.

As they recovered the three men became good friends. They played cards, chess; talked and walked, until, eventually, they were told that they would be discharged on the same day.

Igor and Solik found that their shorts and shirts had been laundered and their boots cleaned, and they were given shaving kit and a toothbrush. They had no other kit. As Nik pulled on his shirt Igor noticed his shoulder flash - it was just three letters – PPA.

When they left the hospital, a jeep with a pair of mounted machine guns was waiting for Nik.

'Can I offer you a lift anywhere,' he said, 'where's your billet?'

'We haven't got one - we've got to find somewhere tonight,' said Igor, 'we report to regional HQ tomorrow.'

Nik scratched at his chin. 'Well, there are two spare bunks in my tent you could use tonight.'

Igor and Solik glanced at each other in surprise. 'Great - thanks Nik,' said Igor, 'that'll save us the trouble of wandering around looking for somewhere.'

*

As the jeep sped along the main road out of Cairo they gazed in awe at the spectacular sight of the Pyramids, even though it was partly spoilt by the burnt out tanks and trucks that littered each side of the road.

The jeep turned off the main road onto a rough dirt track. Five minutes later they pulled up in the shade of a cluster of trees around a small ancient looking well. Among the trees five tents could be seen. Two three-ton trucks, together with three other Jeeps, were neatly parked nearby. A few men, mainly shirtless, were scattered about, doing various odd jobs; some shaving; some mending; some cleaning equipment. One or two looked up with curious eyes at the two strangers. Nik Blewzki introduced Igor and Solik to each of them in turn as they passed. He led them to his tent, which the two newcomers could see was well sited - catching the early morning sun but, by mid-day, well in the shade.

Nik pointed out the two spare bunks.

'I'll introduce you to the skipper when he returns,' he said. 'We eat at six, normally – in the meantime, make yourselves at home.' With a nod and a grin he walked out and left them to settle down.

'A good Polack,' said Solik, taking off his boots.

'We were lucky to bump into him, Solik, my friend - but I'm curious to know what this little group do. Did you notice their shoulder flashes – PPA?'

Igor took his boots off and put them under the bunk, patted the pillow and put his head down. 'Yes - I'd like to know what PPA stands for,' he said, as he closed his eyes.

The sound of laughter woke them up at six thirty, just as everyone was finishing their meal. There were a few more men about; looking out - Igor counted twelve. Nik spotted them and beckoned. As they walked over to him they saw that he was standing next to a tall, thickset, older man. He was dressed the same way as the others but as they got closer they saw from the single crown on his shirt that he had the rank of Major.

'Before you eat, I thought you should meet the skipper,' said Nik. Turning to the other man he continued.

'These are the two I told you about, Popski. They needed a bed for the night, so I offered them my spare bunks. They're Polish legionnaires. This is Sergeant Igor Radovak, and this is Corporal Nikolas Solik.'

The Major shook them by the hand. He looked at them keenly and smiled.

'Forgive the manners of this insubordinate pup. My superiors know me as Major Vladimir Peniakoff – but around here I'm known as Popski, or skipper, and perhaps a few other names at times. But, as guests, call me Major.'

In spite of his Russian name, the Major spoke perfect, educated, English, with unhurried confidence. Igor and Solik were pleased that they could understand his English so well. He pointed in the direction of the food.

'Why don't you get some food and bring it over to my tent. We can have a talk there, and I have some whiskey we can share.'

As they ate, the Major poured a measure of whiskey into three enamel mugs and handed them out. He told them that he was curious to know their story. When Igor explained that they had escaped from Russia, the Major raised his eyebrows.

'Did you, by Jove,' he said, 'would you like to tell me about it?'

The Major listened in silence as Igor and Solik explained how they had been captured, about the train journey to Smolensk, and how they had escaped and eventually got to France, where they joined the Legion rather than being turned over to the Nazis. When they had finished, the Major reached over and poured another measure of whiskey into their mugs.

'That's a fascinating story, gentlemen. What are your plans now – or rather, what are you hoping for? Do you want to get back to the Foreign Legion?'

Igor lowered the mug from his lips. 'We have to report back tomorrow, Major. We assume we'll be sent back to the Legion.'

The Major stroked his chin. 'Hmm,' he said, 'do you want to go back?'

The two men exchanged looks. 'We have no choice,' said Igor, 'we had to sign on with the Legion for five years.'

'So long as we're in the front line fighting Germans, we don't mind where we go,' said Solik.

The Major nodded. 'But getting you back to the Free French might be difficult. Look, it's getting late now - I'll give you the up-to-date positions of our forces in the Middle East in the morning – you should know that - then I'll drive you to HQ. I know one or two chaps there - I can put in a word for you for a good temporary posting.'

Igor and Solik expressed their thanks, said goodnight, and walked to their tent in silence. As they reached it Igor put his hand on Solik's sleeve.

'Are you thinking what I'm thinking?' he said.

Solik nodded thoughtfully.

'Probably, Igor – if this little band goes anywhere near the front line, why not see if we can join them? I like the look of the Major, and the whole bunch of them.'

'Yes, so do I – but Nik told us it was a special unit of some kind, although they were not specialists – but I think he was being modest – or cautious. The snag is, we can't expect the Legion to let us go.'

154

Still deep in thought, they entered the tent and prepared for sleep. Igor put his hands behind his head on the pillow and stared absently at the roof of the tent.

'We still don't know what PPA stands for' he said, just loud enough for Solik to hear.

But before Solik could respond, a tired voice came out of the darkness.

'PPA stands for 'Popski's Private Army,' it said, and then trailed of with, '- now can we get some sleep?'

Igor cursed himself silently for his thoughtlessness. It didn't sound like Nik's voice - and then he remembered that the tent had four bunks.

'Thanks,' he said into the dark, 'sorry to disturb you.'

There was the sound of a suppressed chuckle from the direction of Solik's bunk, followed a few seconds later by a low snore.

Igor turned on his side and grinned to himself. 'Popski's Private Army,' surely that was a jest. It was hardly likely that the British would create a special unit of just twenty or so men, put a Russian Major in charge, and name it as his 'Private Army.' It might, though, be the nickname the men had chosen to use. He would find out the truth in the morning. He closed his eyes, pleased that, after tomorrow, wherever they were sent, they would soon be back in the war.

*

Unable to drop the habit of waking up at the crack of dawn, Igor and Solik finished their ablutions before the rest of the camp roused.

After breakfast, Popski - or rather, the Major, as they still respectfully called him - spread out a map on the ground and anchored each corner with a stone. For the next fifteen minutes he gave his two guests a concise breakdown of the desert war up to that point, concluding with the direction in which Rommel and his troops were now retreating.

'Tunisia, gentlemen – that's where he's heading. There,' he said, pointing with his finger, 'near Gabes, is a defensive position that the Italians built a few years ago. I think Rommel will try to stop the Eighth Army long enough at that point to enable fresh supplies of armament and equipment to reach him from Germany and Italy Then he will counter attack.' He glanced up. 'Any questions?'

Igor looked thoughtfully at the map.

'What about French West Africa, Major – are they still pro-German?'

Popski gave a wry smile. 'That's a good question – so far they have followed the Vichy line – talking neutrality but acting pro-German - but Churchill and Roosevelt are putting the pressure on to change their minds.' With that he picked up the map and folded it up. He looked at his watch.

'Now, I must get you to your appointment for a posting.'

True to his promise, Popski took one of the jeeps and drove Igor and Solik to Eighth Army HQ. As they sped along the Cairo Road, Igor tried to think of a way to open up a conversation that would lead to asking about the PPA. But Popski drove in silence, seeming to be lost in thought, and so Igor kept quiet.

When they got there he asked them for their papers and suggested that they waited in the reception area while he 'chased up a few contacts.'

Thirty minutes later Popski re-appeared. He had extra papers in his hand and a broad grin on his face.

'No need for you to go back – you have been assigned to my unit,' he said.

He chuckled at the surprised look on the faces of Igor and Solik.

'Your unit?' asked Igor, in a disbelieving voice.

'The PPA?' asked Solik.

'Yes, gentlemen, you are now formally attached to PPA – otherwise known to only a few as Popski's Private Army.'

Igor and Solik looked at one another in surprise. Convinced that they would not be eligible, they had made no overtures at all – and they still had no idea what Popski and his private army actually did. But their surprise turned to a grin and Igor held out his hand to the Major.

'Thank you, Major – we would be pleased to join the PPA – but we were under the impression that it was a specialist unit for which we did not qualify. Can you tell us more about it?'

'Yes, of course, and please call me Popski, or skipper, from now on. And you're right – you are not qualified yet – but we can deal with that. We have all had to learn new tricks. I should mention, however, that there is a downside to your attachment to PPA.' He gave them a smile. 'You have to agree to start as privates.'

Igor and Solik grinned at their new CO. 'That's not a problem, Popski, we had to start from the bottom again when we joined the Legion,' said Igor

'Good,' said Popski, and motioned to them to get back into the jeep.

'Sorry to drop that on you, but it's not as bad as it sounds. Several others in the group have also had to accept demotion – temporarily – and agree to work up within the unit. If it doesn't work out and you leave, your previous rank will be re-instated.'

He paused for a moment as he started the engine, then he turned to them again.

'Let me explain my position. PPA is, in fact, a new unit – it was only formed a few weeks ago. Before that I was in charge of a patrol attached to the Long Range Desert Group – or LRDG – working behind enemy lines – mainly observing troop movements, armaments and location of ammunition and petrol dumps – all that kind of thing - very useful, but not all that exciting. So when I met some friendly Arabs, who told me about an Italian airfield and a large petrol dump, I arranged for the Arabs to do the observing while a few of us went off and blew up a few planes and destroyed the petrol dump.'

Pausing to steer the jeep back onto the road back to camp, he continued.

'Although we suffered a couple of casualties, the operation was very successful. So instead of getting an anticipated reprimand for my action – I didn't tell HQ what I was doing until it was over - HQ has given me my own unit, with orders to spread 'alarm and despondency' behind enemy lines. I am still responsible to the head of LRDG, but have more autonomy. The order that established PPA states that it will consist of just twenty three men – a Major; a Captain; two subalterns; four NCOs and fifteen other ranks. So, when I tell you that I already have all my officers and NCOs and thirteen other ranks in place, you will understand that the rank of private was all I could offer you – which takes me to full strength.'

They gave him a nod in agreement

'Then privates we will be – and thanks for your confidence in us Popski.'

'Not at all – you are just what I was looking for. You are survivors – you have already proved that – and now we are up to full strength we can begin our training. We've got to be ready to move out in three weeks.'

Igor smiled; a growing excitement coursing through his body. His thoughts went back to his first battle and the dash into the forest, where his wounded comrades had been finished off with a bullet in the head while he had lain hidden under a tree.

CHAPTER 19

Nik Blewzki leaned forward and touched Igor lightly on the shoulder and pointed. Raising his field glasses, Igor could see a line of trucks driving away from an outcrop of rocks behind a low escarpment about two kilometres away, close to the main highway. 'Highway' was, perhaps, too grand a word for the ribbon of tarmac across the arid desert. The trucks were covered and obviously heavily laden. As they lumbered towards the road Igor focussed his glasses at the spot where they had appeared.

'It looks like there are a few rocks out there, but I reckon the rest of it is camouflage.'

'I think you're right, Igor – and damn good camouflage – we've been staring at it for hours and didn't twig it.' They scanned in silence for a few minutes.

'Hello, there's a few more trucks leaving,' said Igor, the glasses still at his eyes, 'if we don't act quickly there wont be anything left to blow – it must be petrol'

'Well, if it's not petrol it must be something else important – so we need to blow it anyway,' said Nik, reaching over to the wireless set.

'I'll report back to Popski with the co-ordinates – he'll want to see this – he might want to do it tonight.'

Igor smiled grimly as he continued to look through his glasses. Yes, he thought, let's do it tonight. Get it done, then on to our next job. He began to hum softly to himself. Nik glanced up at Igor's profile and, with a small shake of his head, smiled as he busied himself with the transmitter. He knew the tune well. Igor hummed it every time there was a chance of action against the enemy. All Poles knew it. It was the Polish National Anthem.

Nik reflected on how Igor had changed over the past five months. The few weeks training with LRDG and the SAS had turned him into a formidable warrior. His skills in explosives and detonators, mine laying, booby traps, and other sabotage tricks had made him equal to, if not better, than most in the unit. He could drive and maintain any of their vehicles, and Popski had taught him more about navigation and map reading. No one surpassed his proficiency with weaponry.

Not only did he hit every target he aimed at, he could also strip down and re-assemble blindfold all the machine and hand guns that they used, together with most of those captured from the enemy.

Apart from his undoubted skills of war, Igor had delighted Popski with his scrupulous attention to detail. After the unit training had started, many of the men had groaned at Popski's fetish for detail and order. As trained soldiers, they felt they should be allowed some latitude as to how they arranged their kit, so long as it was in good order and they could, given time, find what they were looking for.

This attitude was not good enough for Popski, who insisted that everything had to have its particular place, no variations allowed. Igor had seen the logic of this. Nearly all of their actions against the enemy were at night.

By having everything exactly in the same place on each vehicle, any one of them could use a vehicle and not have to think where to find extra ammunition, grenades, or anything else. Without as much as a glance they could reach out a hand for whatever was needed. So now they could all unload any vehicle and reload it blindfolded. When in camp, relaxing, they had turned this chore into a game. Split into teams, they would compete against each other against Popski's stopwatch.

Only half the sun was still visible on the horizon when Popski sidled in beside them, followed by Solik, who was now his driver. Nik explained what they had seen as he handed his glasses over and indicated the direction.

As he pointed another six trucks appeared and headed for the tarmac road. Popski focused on them.

After a second or two, without lowering the glasses, he said. 'Get on the transmitter to camp. Give them the map reference, and tell them to take the remaining jeeps and intercept those trucks eight or ten kilometres down the road, and destroy them.' After a few more seconds he lowered the glasses.

'Can't see any sign of barbed wire. What do you think Igor?'

Igor shook his head. 'We don't think there is any barbed wire, Major, but it's well camouflaged and is obviously an important dump. It could be weapons or ammunition - but petrol would be our guess.'

'Hmm,' said Popski, 'protected by a minefield then?'

160

'Yes, Major, we reckon it must be.'

Igor had got into the habit of addressing Popski as 'Major' when any action was imminent.

'And they are using it at night to avoid being spotted by the RAF.'

'It seems so.'

Popski nodded. 'So, carefully camouflaged, waiting for darkness before using it – the Desert Fox has gone to a lot of trouble to protect this dump.'

The others nodded but kept quiet, waiting for him to make his decision. They knew that Popski never went into action without careful reconnaissance and preparation - and a job like this ought to be carefully prepared beforehand. They needed to know the size of the dump and, apart from the assumed minefield surrounding it, what other defences it had. To attempt the job tonight would be risky, foolhardy even, but Igor knew – they all knew – that Popski was under orders to destroy as quickly as possible whatever could be found of the enemy's supplies and stockpiles - in particular, petrol dumps.

Since the battle of El Alemain, Rommel had been pushed relentlessly towards Tunisia. Then had come the news that a combined American and British force had landed in French West Africa and, pushing east, had been expected to finish what Montgomery and the Eighth Army had started. But Rommel's battle hardened Afrika Korp, although badly weakened, had given the raw Americans a bloody nose and taken hundreds of prisoners. More seriously, the Germans had captured vital supplies of food, petrol, trucks, guns and ammunition, and even tanks - enough to keep fighting for another two or three weeks. Rommel's own supplies from Germany and Italy had virtually dried up, a result of the combined actions of the RAF and the Royal Navy in the Mediterranean.

'There's another convoy just arriving, skipper,' said Nik.

They watched as a line of tiny subdued headlights left the road and trundled from sight behind the escarpment.

'A dozen of 'em, I think' said Popski. 'If the dump is protected by a minefield, they seem to know exactly where to leave the road to go through it.'

161

For the next fifteen minutes they watched the dump in silence. Then a flash of yellow and orange light lit up the evening sky to the left. It was in the direction of the road, about eight kilometres away. Several more flashes followed in quick succession. Seconds later the sounds of the explosions reached them.

'There go the loaded trucks,' said Nik.

'Yes – and from the way they went up it looks like we're dealing with petrol,' said Popski. He continued looking at the distant fire for a few seconds, lost in thought. Then Igor saw him give an almost imperceptible nod, as though coming to a decision.

'The other jeeps should be with us shortly. While we're waiting perhaps you should check your daisy chains and the rest of your kit,' he said. 'Solik and I will take a walk over to the road. If you hear two shots it means we're in trouble and for you to get out quick.'

Nik gave Igor a nudge with his elbow. In spite of the risks, Popski had decided to attack without delay.

'Right, Skipper,' Nik replied, and joined Igor as he headed towards their jeep. Daisy chains – small explosives linked together and set with a time fuse, were ideal for this type of work, and Igor was an acknowledged expert in setting them.

An hour later Popski finished his briefing for the attack. With Popski in the lead, three jeeps would wait for the next convoy of trucks to appear, and then tag on to the end just before they left the tarmac road. The remaining jeeps would be ready to cover their retreat, if necessary. The only disguise they used was to put on a German forage cap. Apart from a discrete number in a style used by the Germans, the jeeps had no other markings.

After thirty minutes more trucks appeared. Popski let them get ahead a little way before he led his jeeps on to the tarmac and closed up behind them. As they approached the dump they could see that subdued lights illuminated it. Carefully screened from the approach road and from above, it was hard to distinguish that there was any light at all until they were within three hundred metres. Two guards materialised out of the shadows and stopped the lead truck. Metallic clicks came from each of Popski's jeeps as machine guns were cocked for action. But the convoy was waved on. They gave a similar half salute, half wave, that they saw the other trucks give to the guards as they passed. Igor and Nik, in the last jeep, caught the blank stare of the guards as they followed the trucks into the gloom of the dump. One swivelled his head to follow them. They held their breath for a few seconds, but no alarm was sounded.

Peeling off from the trucks they parked in the shade of one of the camouflaged piles of oil drums. It was one of the largest, about a hundred drums. A quick inspection revealed that the piles ranged from ten up to one hundred drums – each pile covered with camouflage netting to make them blend in with the natural outcrop of rocks nearby. Popski silently pointed the direction that each pair should take. Their instructions were to place as many explosives as possible within a deadline of thirty minutes.

They would meet back at the jeeps and wait for the loaded trucks to leave and follow them out. It was an audacious plan and, as Popski had pointed out at his briefing, even if successful it would not be enough to destroy the whole dump. But that was not the intention. Before they had started out Popski had transmitted the location of the dump to HQ, requesting that the RAF fly out at first light to finish the job. The smoke from several hundred oil drums would make it an easy target to find.

Thirty-five minutes later they were back in their jeeps waiting for the filled trucks to appear. Tension mounted as they heard voices. As the voices got nearer they could hear part what was being said. It was clear that a patrol of guards had been sent out to locate the three unidentified vehicles that had entered the dump behind the last convoy. Igor knelt behind one of the Browning machine guns, finger hovering over the trigger. Nik reached behind him and quietly picked up a grenade. Igor gave his forehead a quick wipe with the back of his hand. The night was cold but sweat was running into his eyes. Popski's instructions were not to shoot first; in fact, not to fire at all unless there was no other alternative.

If they were challenged the plan was to try to bluff a way out by shouting at them in German. If that failed and shooting started the chances of getting out alive were very slim. Just one stray bullet hitting an oil drum would send them into infinity. But to be captured would be a worse fate. The voices, grumbling, arguing, sounded very close, perhaps a few metres away. Then came another sound that silenced them. The grinding engine noise of laden trucks. There was a curt order and the voices grew fainter as they hurried towards the sound of the trucks.

Popski started his jeep and edged out of the shadows. The other two followed, Igor and Nik in the rear, behind the two New Zealanders. Popski paused in the shadows at the spot where they had peeled off from the trucks as they came in. The heavy trucks passed in front of them. Popski waited until the lead truck reached the entrance, stopped, and was then waived on.

As the last truck moved away the three jeeps were close behind. Igor heard shouting behind him. Turning his head he saw the guards were running towards them, shouting for them to stop. Igor waved back with a grin, which faded as he saw the guards drop on one knee and point their rifles. He swung the Browning around. The jeeps were almost at the entrance and the guards there were trying to see what the commotion was about. Bullets hit the rear of the jeep and Igor responded with a short burst from the Browning.

'Heil Hitler,' he murmured.

The guards at the entrance were raising their rifles. Popski and the New Zealanders were already through, but the guards seemed determined to stop the last jeep. Nik drove straight at them. Three of them managed to dive out of the way but he hit the forth just as the guard pulled the trigger of his rifle. The bullet hit the front tyre and sent the jeep swerving to the right, off the track. Igor could hear Nik cursing and swearing as struggled to regain control, but the jeep continued to the right.

Nik's voice was the last thing that Igor remembered of that night, except for the mind-numbing, ear shattering explosion, and a feeling of floating in the air before blackness engulfed him.

CHAPTER 20

Was this death? How could he tell? Igor's whole body ached and he was too weary to care. Out of the blackness came visions of ghostly people in white, people speaking German; people he hated. He tried hard to shut them out, but they floated in and out of the blackness for a long time. Until, eventually, he heard a different voice, a man speaking in a language that sounded vaguely familiar but was not German. Where had he heard it before? He listened to the rumbling voice more intently. Some words he could understand, they were a peculiar kind of English. Then he remembered. He had heard this kind of voice when he was training with the LRDG. One of the Sergeants had been difficult to understand, and when he had asked him if he was foreign, the Sergeant had grinned.

'Ya'could sa' tha', chum - I'm Scottish,' the Sergeant had replied.

The voice seemed near, and Igor felt an urge to see who was speaking with a Scottish accent. He opened his eyes. A white blur hovered over him.

'Ah, welcome back t' the land o'the livin',' said the voice. Igor's vision began to focus. He saw a man with a mop of brown hair and a beard, through which he could see a line of white teeth smiling down at him. The man was wearing a shabby white coat, not buttoned, and beneath it army issue shorts and a khaki shirt.

'You're – Scottish?' was all Igor could think to say to him.

The man continued to smile. 'Now I wonder how ye knew tha,' he said, emphasising his accent.

Igor tried to smile. 'I've been dreaming Germans – it's a relief to hear English.' His voice was just a croak. The inside of his mouth felt like dry paper.

The man picked up an enamel mug from a wooden box at the side of the bed, put his arm under Igor's shoulder, raised him slightly, and put the mug to his lips.

'Here, ha'e a drink o'wata,' he said.

Igor gave a nod and drank until the mug was empty. 'Thanks,' he said.

The Scotsman put the mug down.

'I'm Captain McIntyre,' he said. 'I'm the MO in charge o'the prisoners ward here on Crete. We're in one o'the buildings of an auld Benedictine monastery' He paused. 'Ye've bin under sedation f'quite some time.'

By this time Igor had realised that he was heavily bandaged and one leg and an arm were in plaster.

'How badly injured am I Doctor,' he asked, quietly.

'Well, th'good news is tha' you still ha'e all ye limbs. But ye've a broken right leg, a broken left arm, a bad flesh wound to ye thigh, a few other flesh wounds – and a he'd wound which mae affect ye left eye.'

Igor winced and closed his eyes, or rather, his eye, because he had not realised until now that his head and left eye was bandaged. He let the extent of his injuries sink in. At least he had not lost any limbs. Then he recalled the other words that the Captain has spoken.

'Prisoners ward?' asked Igor. 'Am I a prisoner?'

'Afraid so – but only since yesterd'y.'

Igor looked at him, uncomprehending. The Scotsman smiled.

'Until yesterd'y the Germans thought ye was one o' theirs. Ye must 'ave lost your dog tags. They brought ye all the way t' Crete with a batch of their own wounded. Ye were given plenty of drugs t' keep the pain down and they've patched ye up pretty well. Ye're a lucky fella – ye lost a lot o' blood - if they had realised ye were English I doubt that ye would be alive now. They don't lavish such good care on prisoners. But yesterd'y ye got tipped out of the German ward and into mine'

Igor stared at him in silence as this information sank in. He found it hard to believe that, by mistake, the Germans had saved his life and brought him to Crete. Where was Crete? He was not sure, but had an idea that it was a Greek island. A flash of memory brought back the last moments in the jeep, the bullets flying and the deafening explosion. And then he remembered Nik. What about Nik?

'There was two of us, Doctor, is there another prisoner – another that came here like me?'

The Doctor shook his head. 'No' that I know of – but the fact that ye mate didna make it to Crete, laddy, doesna' mean he copped it.' He poured more water into the mug and handed it to Igor. 'Ye know that they'll be wanting to talk to ye, now they know ye're English and not German.'

Igor gave a small groan at the thought of being interrogated by Germans.

'I'm not English, Doctor – I'm Polish,' he said.

'Polish?' The Doctor raised his eyebrows in surprise. 'They'll be even more upset that they looked after ye so well. But ye'r English is pretty good - I'd let 'em think that ye're English if I were ye.'

'I doubt if I can pull that off for long, Doctor,' said Igor. 'What made them realise their mistake – that I was not German?'

'So far as I can make oot, t'was dark when they found ye - all covered in blood. They thought ye wa'dead until someone heard ye muttering in German.'

'Muttering in German?' Igor questioned in astonishment.

The MO nodded. 'That's what I wa' told – repeating a couple of words over and over'

'A couple of words?'

The MO gave a nod.

'The medical orderly that travelled with ye said ye were muttering 'Heil Hitler' – and that's why they assumed ye was a Nazi.'

Igor gave a low chuckle.

'Do ye remember now?' asked the MO.

'No, I can't remember, but I do understand. 'Heil Hitler' has become my – well, kind of personal battle cry,' he said, still smiling at the irony that the two hated words had saved his life.

'Aah,' said the MO. 'I see - well, as ah said, t'was dark, ye wa' soaked in blood, so they stripped ye'r clothes off, put 'em in a kit bag, and tha' travelled with ye. A couple of days ago someone ha' the bright idea to tak' all the kit of the wounded and give it a wash and brush up. That's when they found ye bush shirt wasna' German – it had an Allied shoulder flash with PPA on it. They asked me if ah knew what it meant, but ah told 'em I'd no idea. That's what they want to talk to ye abaht.'

In his native Polish, Igor cursed quietly to himself. He was determined not to tell the Germans anything about the PPA. He knew that Hitler had called covert operations behind enemy lines 'gangsterism,' and prisoners from such units would be classed as commandos - and shot.

Igor felt trapped. He doubted that he could stall them for long, certainly not long enough for his injuries to heal and try an escape. It would probably be months rather than weeks. Also, Crete was an island, if he escaped he would have to go into hiding or leave by boat. Either way he would need plenty of help, and there was no way that he could make contacts while confined to a bed. Igor gave a low groan and cursed again. Captain McIntyre could see that his patient was clearly anguished at the thought of being questioned.

'I've no wish to know what PPA stands fer, or what kind of operations ye were on, but can I assume tha' if the Germans find oot about it, they're likely to shoot ye?'

Igor gave a slight nod. 'I think that's a fair assumption, Doctor,' he said, then, after a pause, 'but you might as well know that PPA stands for Popski's Private Army.'

The MO gave a disbelieving grin.

'*Who's* Private Army?' he said. 'Ye don't think they'll fall fer tha', do ye? I've never heard o' the British going in fer private armies.'

'Maybe not, but PPA does stand for Popski's Private Army - and that's the only true thing I'm going to tell them – if I have to – but I think I'll try them with 'Polish Pioneers Auxiliary' to start with, and see if they swallow that.'

'To be frank with ye, tha' sounds more believable.'

'When is the questioning due to start?'

'Tomorrow morning'

Igor gave a grim smile. 'That gives me a few hours to think up a story,' he said.

'Right – and if they ask me again I'll stick with th' Polish Pioneer's. I need to know ye name, rank and number for th' records – that's all. Don't tell me anything else – and I'd advise ye not to talk to anyone about ye past, no matter how friendly they are. Ye can't be too careful. Just concentrate on getting back t' full strength – some prisoners have escaped from Crete, but ye haven't a chance unless ye're fit.'

After Igor had given him the required information Captain McIntyre nodded, then turned and walked away with a thoughtful expression on his face.

The wounded prisoners were housed in a stone building about the size of a small church. The only light during the night was from two candles at either end set on upturned wooden boxes. Apart from an occasional groan and the low sounds of men sleeping, all was quiet. Igor's head was throbbing and he was in a fitful half sleep thinking about his interrogation when he felt the bed move. He opened his eye to see dark figures silhouetted around him.

'What the….. ?' he said.

'Shhsh,' came a whisper, close to his ear, 'we're moving you.'

The bed was lifted at each corner and transported to the far end of the ward.

Another bed was moved out and his bed put into the space. Igor had an impression that the other bed was occupied as he watched it being taken to the place that he had just vacated. The figures melted away into the gloom

'What's going on?' he hissed.

One of the figures came back and put his mouth close to Igor's ear.

'The chap in the other bed has died,' he whispered. 'The MO asked us to move you here – he'll explain in the morning.'

Mystified, Igor watched the figure disappear from view. He lay there wondering what the MO was up to. By changing the position of the beds, the MO had, in effect, changed his identity. Who was the dead man? What was his name and rank? What injuries had he suffered?

He couldn't sleep now. The hours dragged by as Igor stared into the black gloom of the high ceiling. The more he thought about his predicament the more frustrated and depressed he became. He was alive but he was helpless. Not since the war began had he felt so useless. It looked as though he was out of the war for good.

At last a pale dawn light seeped through the high windows. There was a metallic clank and the creaking of a door being opened. Two round shadowy women entered carrying trays. On one tray were a number of mugs - on the other small bowls. In the dim light Igor's first thought was that they were nurses but, on closer inspection, he realised they were nuns. Moving quietly from bed to bed, they placed a mug and a bowl on the upturned wooden boxes that served as bedside cabinets. There was movement at several of the beds where the occupants were mobile enough to feed themselves.

Igor was hungry and thirsty and watched patiently as the nuns came slowly towards him. When they arrived at his bed he was mortified to see them pass it by. He gave a short cough and one of the nuns turned towards him with a surprised look on her face. She said something to her companion and they returned to his bed and gave him a mug and a bowl.

The nuns continued to talk quietly to each other as they helped him with his breakfast of mint tea and watery porridge. He couldn't understand them but it seemed clear that they thought from their previous visit that the occupier of this bed had died. When they had finished feeding him they smoothed his pillow and blanket, gave him a kindly smile and walked away, shaking their heads.

Igor watched them go, sweating with frustration and worry. They were bound to talk. Whatever plan the MO had in mind, it was fast falling apart. Where *was* the MO? What was going on?

A medic entered the ward, accompanied by another nun. He looked like any other prisoner in his worn bush shirt and shorts, except for the Red Cross armband he was wearing. They moved among the beds, checking bandages, gently washing, dealing with bedpans. They ignored Igor.

He decided to call out to them but at that moment Captain McIntyre walked through the door. With him was another man in a white coat carrying a clipboard. From his superior attitude Igor guessed that he was a German Doctor. The Captain walked to the bed with the dead man in it. The German made an inspection, nodded his head, took a pen from his pocket and wrote on his clipboard. McIntyre stood nearby, watching impassively.

The German Doctor finished the form and signed it. Tearing the sheet off he handed it to McIntyre, who acknowledged with a curt nod of his head.

Without another word the German Doctor turned and walked out. Only when he was well out of sight and hearing did Captain McIntyre's face relax into a smile. He came and stood at Igor's bed.

'I've just got a death certificate fer ye, so no need t'worry about bein' interrogated.'

Igor cast him a doubtful look.

'The nuns who brought breakfast thought I had come back from the dead. The news of the miracle is probably all over the Island by now.'

The smile faded from the Scots Doctor's face.

'The nuns? I'd forgotten about them.' He shrugged.

'Don't worry, by the time they come back ye'll be dead again.'

'Dead *again*? What d'you mean Doctor?'

The Doctor shook his head. 'Sorry to keep ye in th' dark – but must dash now – ye're interrogators are due any minute'

'But – you just said I would not be interrogated,' said Igor, bewildered.

'Ye won't be – if everything goes t'plan – jus' stay quiet, man. Only a couple more hurdles an' ye should be out o' here.' The MO moved towards the door, and then he was gone, leaving Igor shaking his head with worry.

Ten minutes later the MO returned leading an immaculately uniformed Gestapo officer accompanied a Sergeant. The MO had the sheet of paper in his hand that the German Doctor had given him earlier. It was Igor's 'death certificate.' They stopped at the bed where the dead soldier lay. Igor could see the MO shaking his head and shrugging his shoulders. The two Germans looked briefly at the dead man, scrutinised the death certificate, requested the MO to sign a form, and then walked briskly from the ward.

The MO followed them out, but was back five minutes later with a huge grin on his face. With him he had three New Zealand medics. They stopped at the bed where the dead man lay and, taking a corner each, they carried it down the ward towards Igor, and three minutes later his bed was back in his original space. The MO leaned over him. 'Now just lay quiet until we've got ye into yer coffin,' he whispered.

'Coffin?' spluttered Igor, 'what the …..'

'Keep calm, man,' interrupted the MO, 'it's just a big basket - there'll be enough holes in it t'breath through. Ye want to escape, don't ye? Well, a coffin's the quickest way out o' here - and no one'll come looking for ye, cuss ye're dead, don't ye see?' He waved the bit of paper in his hand.

'Yes – but….,' began Igor.

The Doctor held up his hand. 'As I said, don't ye worry. When I've got the second death certificate we c'n get moving with th' burial. I'm going t' leave it a couple of hours before I tell the Germans that another prisoner has died.'

'But won't the German Doctor realise that it's the same body?'

'The same Doctor would, but the Germans have four Doctors here – although they're not all German – anyway, they take it in turns to issue death certificates, so we're not likely to get the same one again for a wee while.'

At last the antics of the MO were making sense. It was a neat trick that he was pulling on the Germans, and Igor suspected this routine had been used before.

There were questions that he would have liked answers to. The main one being that he would still need medical attention. Had the MO arranged for him to be cared for on the outside?

'We've arranged for ye to be looked after when ye leave,' said the Doctor, as if reading his thoughts.

CHAPTER 21

Stefan, now first deputy to Herr Vroond, was clearing his desk in the site office when he looked up and saw a black Citroen saloon stop at the barrier. He expected it to turn around and depart, because instructions had been given that only vehicles bringing in materials and supplies were to be allowed entry. Herr Vroond had built up an enviable reputation within the Todt Organisation for efficiency and discipline, and now that he had left Stefan in charge while he had a few days leave, Stefan was determined to maintain his high standard.

When he saw the barrier being raised he frowned and watched the car as it navigated its way through the excavations and stopped next to the site office. First the passenger door and then the driver's door opened and two men emerged. One was slightly shorter than the other but both were thickset, muscular and brutish in appearance. They were wearing black leather overcoats and black trilby hats, the favoured civilian attire of the Gestapo.

A few months ago Stefan's first reaction would have been to panic and run. But a cool contempt had replaced his fear. Over the months he had heard plenty of stories from the slave labourers about German atrocities in Poland, organised by the Gestapo and the SS. And on all the sites he had worked on he had seen for himself the brutality of the SS. They beat up prisoners or shot them on the slightest provocation. This was why he had already decided that, if either the Gestapo or SS captured him, he would find a way of killing himself.

He took a deep breath to steel his nerves, then sat down at Herr Vroonds desk, bent over the file in front of him and started to write. He continued looking down as the two men entered without knocking. There was a clicking of heels.

'Heil Hitler,' they snapped out in unison.

Feigning surprise, Stefan looked up at them, rose to his feet and flicked up his hand.

'Heil Hitler,' he snapped out, with an enthusiasm that was mocking rather than genuine.

They looked at him suspiciously as they sat down, one in the chair in front of him and the other on the corner of his desk.

'What can I do for you, gentlemen,' said Stefan in perfect German as he sat down again.

Still looking at him, the one in the chair undid the top button of his overcoat, reached inside and brought out a black notebook. He opened it, flicked through to find the page he wanted, and then glanced at the nameplate on the desk, which said ' *D. Vroond, Camp Commandant*'

'You have a man working here, Herr Vroond - a Frenchman by the name of Pierre Limone?'

Stefan strove to keep his face stony calm while his stomach churned. They had assumed him to be Herr Vroond and he grasped at the straw they had given him. 'Yes, he is one of my deputies,' he said calmly.

'Would you please send for him, we wish to ask him a few questions.'

'Questions? Is he in some kind of trouble?'

The one in the chair gave a shrug. 'Perhaps not,' he said, 'we just need to check his papers.' The one sitting on the desk smirked.

Stefan glanced at each of the hard, arrogant, faces in front of him. He knew he was finished if he could not come up with a satisfactory answer. They looked at him, waiting, and an idea came to him just in time - a single ruthless audacious cold-blooded idea that, with luck, might work. There was no choice – he had to try it.

'Very well, if you do not mind waiting for a while gentlemen, I will fetch him.'

'Wait for a while?' snapped out the one sitting on his desk in annoyance. 'For how long?'

Stefan looked at him calmly. 'Limone is not working on this site today - he is at our other site, about two kilometres away. I will have to fetch him.'

The Gestapo men exchanged glances. 'No need,' said the one in the chair, 'just give us directions, we will collect him ourselves.'

Stefan smiled and shook his head. 'I'm afraid I cannot do that - give you directions I mean. You see, it is a secret site - ordered by Field Marshal Rommel himself after he took over control of the Atlantic Wall. You would need the authority of someone of higher rank than the Field Marshal to get near it.'

'Don't be absurd,' snapped the one in the chair. 'We wish to question a possible traitor - that is all.'

'I understand gentlemen - but, as I said, if you do not mind waiting, I will go for him.' Stefan paused. His lips tightened as he plunged ahead with his plan. He looked at them and could see that they were still unhappy. He gave a shrug, as if in surrender.

'Very well, if you are in a hurry I will escort you there. I could then return with him – or, if you wish to retain him - in his vehicle.'

The Gestapo men glanced at each other, surprised at the offer.

'That would be appreciated.' The one sitting on the desk stood up. The other pulled himself out of the chair.

'Yes, good cooperation is essential in these matters,' he said..

'Not at all,' said Stefan, giving them another disarming smile. 'If you would like to turn your car around I will just finish signing these papers and join you.' As though the matter was settled he picked up his pen and started writing; listening as the two men made for the door.

As soon as they were gone he put the pen down and opened a drawer in Herr Vroond's desk. He lifted out a small automatic pistol, checked to see that it was loaded, and slipped it into his pocket. Picking up his cap and gloves, he went out of the door and locked it.

He walked towards the car; the rear door open, waiting for him.

'Thank you, gentlemen, we can proceed now,' he said, sinking onto the rear seat. 'You know,' he continued, conversationally, 'it is fortunate that you came today, because our work here is finished. We hand over the site to the next contractors in the morning. So, if you had left it until this time tomorrow, you might have missed your man'

They grunted, and he saw them give each other a grim smile. 'Not for long, we assure you,' said the driver.

*

Stefan directed the Gestapo driver along country roads until they came to a track that went through thick woods. He had ridden this way several times on his bicycle. The branches of the trees hung over the track, blocking out the daylight. Silent and eerie, it was a place where the seasons came and went and the years passed by with little disturbance from human beings. He leaned over and tapped the driver on the shoulder and pointed.

'There is an entrance that you must turn into just ahead,' he said. ' I suggest that you slow down or you will miss it.'

The driver slowed the car to a crawl and they moved along in silence. A minute passed by.

'How much further is it?' the driver snarled.

At that moment Stefan saw what he was looking for.

'Not far now, gentlemen,' he said quietly. There was a metallic click, which the two Gestapo might have just had time to recognise as a safety catch being removed before Stefan pulled the trigger. The first bullet hit the driver above the ear and a spray of blood appeared on the windscreen in front of him. The next bullet hit the other man in the right eye as he was turning around in alarm. Stefan fired another shot into each of them. The car rolled to a stop, the engine still running.

Stefan leaned over and switched off the ignition. Getting out, he opened the driver's door, dragged out the dead body and pushed it on to the rear seat. Getting into the driving seat he started the engine, and drove the car at a small gap in the trees that was just wide enough to let the car through. He crashed forward, breaking down small saplings as he went. The car travelled about thirty metres before it hit a larger tree and stalled. Stefan got out, walked back to the track and looked towards the car.

Satisfied that it was hardly visible, he straightened up the bent and half broken saplings as he retraced his steps. Dragging the two bodies out, he stripped them of their leather overcoats, their automatic pistols and all means of identification. Taking them by the legs he pulled them, one at a time and in different directions, further into the wood. In each case he found a fallen tree, scooped out the leaves and soft earth beneath it, and pushed the body into the depression. Kicking earth and leaves over it, he finished off by throwing a few rotten branches on top.

Stefan returned to the car and opened the boot. Taking out a tyre leaver, he used it to rip off the number plates. Making sure that there was nothing left inside the car he locked the doors and threw the keys into the undergrowth. Next he gathered up fallen branches and leaned them against the car and on top of it. He circled around the car a couple of times and filled in a few gaps, then, picking up the leather overcoats, the trilby hats and number plates, he walked off. A few minutes later he came across another fallen tree. Digging away the leaves and earth, he pushed in the overcoats and number plates and covered them over. A few metres further on he scooped another hole and threw in the identity cards and the pistols. Having second thoughts, he picked out the pistols and put them into his pocket.

Sixty minutes later he was back at the site. He walked up to the guards on the barrier, his face stern.

The two guards saluted, which Stefan ignored.

'Your orders are to let in vehicles carrying materials and supplies, are they not?

The guards exchanged nervous glances. 'Yes sir,' they said together.

'Then why did you disobey those orders and let through a black saloon car?' he shouted at them. The guards looked at each other again.

'But...' said one, and paused, clearly surprised. The other butted in.

'They were Gestapo, sir, they said it was most urgent....'

'Rubbish!' Stefan shouted. 'You should have checked with me before letting them pass.'

'But...' said the first one again.

'No 'buts' – you have disobeyed clear orders,' said Stefan, glaring at them. He then appeared to relax a little.

'You are aware that we have to hand over this site tomorrow, and your log book of vehicles entering the site now shows that one of those vehicles was unauthorised.'

Concern crossed the faces of the guards.

Stefan shook his head, as though in thought. 'Even if I am prepared to overlook your incompetence, others may not.' He pointed towards the small hut at the side of the barrier. 'Let me see your log book,' he said, walking towards it. The entries of all vehicles let into the site were, as he suspected, made in pencil. He looked down the list and turned back to the previous day. He saw that one vehicle had made several visits over the past few days.

'Have you got a rubber?' he said.

'Yes, sir,' said one of the guards, searching in his pocket.

'I am sure that this vehicle here,' he said, pointing to the regular visitor, 'has made a visit today but you have not got it listed. I suggest that this is where it should be,' and tapped the spot where the black Citroen was entered.

The guards looked bewildered, until one of them gave a slight smile as he understood. He clicked his heels together.

'Yes sir, I will make the necessary correction at once,' he said. 'Thank you for pointing this out to us.'

'Right – so you have not seen any Gestapo visitors in a black Citroen, and let them into the site?'

'No sir,' said the guards together.

'No, and neither have I – is that understood?'

They nodded with relief as Stefan started to walk away.

'Good, I will inspect the log tomorrow before we hand over. Make sure it is corrected.'

*

The next afternoon Stefan boarded the 3.15 p.m. train to Paris. It was crowded, but he managed to find a seat near a window. Placing his kit bag between his legs he glanced around at the other passengers. Nearest to him was a woman with a teenage girl; the others were soldiers in uniform. He leaned his head back and closed his eyes. Although his Todt uniform protected him from suspicious looks, he had found that pretending to be asleep was the best way to avoid eye contact or conversation when travelling on a train. A few minutes after the train started he was asleep.

An hour later he woke up with a start as someone jostled against him. He half opened his eyes and what he saw sent a cold shiver down his spine. Quickly he closed his eyes again. The passengers had changed. The woman with her daughter had gone, and now, sitting next to him and in the seat opposite were two men in the familiar black leather overcoats and black hats of the Gestapo. The one opposite to him had been looking at him intently, as if waiting for him to wake up. He was trapped and he wondered how they had managed to find him so quickly.

Stefan felt a tap on his knee and opened his eyes. The Gestapo man opposite to him was leaning forward. He had drooping cheeks and big bags under his eyes. Stefan guessed his age to be about fifty. Old for the Gestapo, he thought.

'You are Pierre Limone?' he said, his voice low and gruff.

Stefan sat up, frightened but trying not to show it

He looked at the man and then at his companion.

'Why do you want to know?' was all he could think of saying.

They scowled at him.

'Please show us your papers,' said the one sitting next to him, and held out his hand.

Looking from one to the other, Stefan realised that he had no other choice but to do as they requested. He pulled his identity card from his pocket and handed it over. It was looked at briefly, and then passed to the other man with a nod. Giving it a brief glance he put it into his inside pocket

'At the next station you will get out and come with us,' he said.

'But - my orders are to report to the Todt headquarters in Paris,' said Stefan.

The two smiled at each other. 'Those orders are now cancelled,' said the Gestapo man next to him.

Stefan shrugged his shoulders in resignation, determined not to show any signs of panic. Not knowing what else to do, he laid his head back and closed his eyes again. At his waist he could feel the hardness of one of the pistols he had taken from the Gestapo the day before. He would go with them quietly but, once they were clear of the station, he would have no hesitation in using it on his new captors. It would be dark by then, with a good chance of getting away. He could then make his way back to the station and resume his journey.

Thirty minutes later the train stopped at the last station before Paris. The two Gestapo men got up and made sure that Stefan was between them as they left the train.

At the barrier they flashed their passes and made it clear that Stefan was their prisoner. A flustered guard waved them through. As they left the station a black Renault with a small Swastika flag on its bonnet pulled up beside them. Without a word they opened the rear door and pushed Stefan inside. One got in beside him in the back and the other next to the driver.

Stefan slid his hand to the pistol in his pocket. He was looking out of the window of the car, waiting for a stretch of road with less people on it. Sweat trickled down his forehead, but he felt cold, and steeled himself not to tremble. He would shoot them first, and then, if he got caught, he would shoot himself. The car turned a corner into a suburban road lined with trees. It was quiet, with plenty of shadows. Stefan felt for the safety catch of the gun as he slowly drew it from his pocket. With a swift movement his hand was held in a vice like grip. The gun was taken from him. There was a gruff chuckle in the darkness of the car.

'There is no need for that *monsieur,*' he said, as a handcuff was snapped onto his wrist.

A few minutes later the car turned into the drive of a large house and stopped at the steps to the front door.

The driver got out and opened the rear door next to Stefan.

Getting out of the car, Stefan stared up at the building. In the dim light he could just read a sign over the door that said *'Ecole Musique.'* There were no lights from the building; in the shade of the trees it looked cold and sinister. The car driver knocked on the door. Three quick taps, a slight pause, then another tap. It sounded familiar, but Stefan was too busy trying to think of a way to escape for it to mean anything.

The door opened and they entered a wide hallway that went the whole length of the building. The only light was from a few small candles. Stefan was led to a door that had a light shining under it. The Gestapo man undid the handcuff as the door opened. Resigned to being interrogated and tortured, Stefan gritted his teeth.

The room was lit by an electric light that caused him to squint, but then he saw the man who stood aside for them to enter. Stefan's jaw dropped.

'Doctor Dubar!' he said in astonishment, 'what – what the hell are you doing here!'

The Doctor gave him a smile and motioned to a chair next to a table in the centre of the room.

'We have been waiting for you, *monsieur* Stefan. It was necessary to get you off the train because the Gestapo are waiting to arrest you at Paris.'

Stefan looked bewildered. He pointed to the two men who had arrested him on the train.

'But – what about these two?' he said.

Doctor Dubar smiled. 'These men are not Gestapo – they are *resistance,*' he said.

'I regret having to make you think that they were genuine Gestapo, but as you will appreciate, it was the best way to ensure that the true Gestapo did not get to you first. Also, I regret that we could not tell you. It was important that you believed you had been arrested. Your reactions had to look real.'

Stefan shook his head in disbelief. His legs felt weak and he sat down at the table.

'I'm sure my reactions looked real enough, Doctor,' he said. 'I was ready to shoot these two, and then myself if necessary.'

The resistance men beamed at him. The one who had taken the pistol from him took it out of his pocket and held it out.

Stefan waived it away. 'No, you can keep that, I've got another one in my kitbag,' he said.

Doctor Dubar sat down on the other side of the table, his face serious.

'We know that you were taken away by the Gestapo yesterday, but you returned to the site. Can you tell us how you got away from them?'

Stefan nodded, and told the Doctor all that had happened. When he had finished the Doctor was silent for several seconds.

'You are a very brave man, *monsieur* Stefan. And you are sure that the bodies will not be found?'

Stefan nodded his head wearily. 'I doubt if they ever will be – even if someone stumbles on the car,' he said. 'But what now, Doctor, if I'm not going to Paris?'

'Your work with Todt has finished. It is too dangerous to remain as Pierre Limone – he has got to disappear. We have got to create a new identity, and get you back to England.'

Stefan gave a tired grin. 'I'm ready for that, Doctor.'

'Good, then I will show you where you will sleeping until we have your new identity and papers.' The Doctor got up and led the way out into the hallway and the up a staircase to the top floor. He stopped outside a door and handed Stefan a key.

'You may be here for several days, please do not look out of the windows or leave the building. Food will be brought to you – all you have to do is relax.'

The Doctor gave him a reassuring smile and turned and went back down the stairs.

Stefan opened the door and found himself in a well-furnished bedroom. There was a door leading off which he took to be a bathroom. Two candles and the flames from a fire in the grate lighted the room. He threw his kitbag into a corner and went into the bathroom. Returning, he kicked off his shoes and flung himself onto the bed. He stared up at the ceiling for a few seconds, everything that had happened racing around in his head; then he closed his eyes.

He started to drift into sleep, but something brushed against his lips.

'*Bonjour Cherie,*' came a whisper in his ear. Was he dreaming? Then he saw her. She was bending over him.

A great feeling of warmth and yearning swept through him. 'Marie, my darling,' he murmured. He reached out and took her in his arms and kissed her. The tension finally left him as he pulled her down beside him. He nestled his head against her breast and blissful erotic thoughts drifted into his mind as he fell asleep.

*

A rough shaking of his shoulder woke him up. Instinctively he reached out for Marie. She was not there. In the seconds between sleep and wakefulness he realised that she had never been there. There was another shake.

'Wake up, *monsieur*! Wake up! The Germans are searching the houses, we must get out!'

Stefan focused his eyes as he leapt out of bed. It was one of the men from the train, who beckoned as he made for the door. He carried a carbine and Stefan's Luger was pushed into his belt. He spoke calmly.

'They are in the next building. Follow me. There is an escape tunnel in the cellar.'

Stefan did not bother to reply. He grabbed his shoes and kit bag and followed the Frenchman down the stairs and through a door to the cellar. In a corner a heavy wooden bench had been pulled away from the wall. The Frenchman ducked behind it and crawled into a low tunnel about a metre square. Stefan followed him. The Frenchman struck a match and lit a small candle. Placing it down, he picked up a rope that was attached to the back of the bench.

'Help me with this, *monsieur,*' he said as he started to pull on it.

Stefan took hold of the rope and together they heaved. At first their joint efforts had little effect. They changed position and heaved again, and slowly the bench slid back into position. The end of the rope was tied securely to an iron ring set into the wall. On hands and knees they crawled slowly through the tunnel, the Frenchman leading the way with the candle. The air was cold and musty. The floor of the tunnel was bare earth and over time bits of brickwork had fallen from the roof and sides. After twenty metres Stefan had to grit his teeth against the pain in his knees as he crawled over the debris.

'What about the others, have they got away?' he gasped out.

Before replying the Frenchman paused and leaned against the wall for a rest.

'Yes, *monsieur*, the Doctor left during the night, the others are in front of us.' He waited, as though expecting another question. But Stefan merely nodded, so he resumed crawling.

They stopped twice more to rest and rub their knees before they came to the end of the tunnel. It was similar to the other end; a cupboard had been pulled away from the wall and they crawled into another dank, dark, cellar where a candle had been left burning.

'Does anyone live here?' asked Stefan, rubbing his sore knees.

There was a pause. 'Not any more - it belonged to a Jewish family - relations of mine. They have been taken away.'

'I am sorry to hear that, my friend,' said Stefan quietly.

The man nodded and putting his shoulder to the cupboard pushed it back against the wall.

'Come,' he said, 'we must get out of here. They might also decide to search these houses.' He led the way up wooden steps to a trapdoor that had been left open for them. They emerged into the kitchen of a house that was in the next road to the one they had just left. The Frenchman closed the trapdoor and rolled a piece of linoleum over it. The house was a shambles; it had been looted. Everything of value had been taken and the rest broken or vandalised. The Frenchman shook his head sadly at the mess.

'The Germans took the best,' he said quietly, 'and others took the rest.'

He looked cautiously out of the door, tucked the carbine under his coat and signalled for Stefan to follow him.

They walked down the short drive to the road, where the Frenchman turned to Stefan.

'Here we must part,' he said. 'You will stand a better chance alone. If you get to Paris, get a taxi to the Hotel Sorbonne; ask for Claude and say that you have been recommended by Jules. Do not say this to anyone but Claude.' He raised a hand and started to walk away. 'Good luck to you.'

'Thanks – and good luck to you,' said Stefan, and turned and walked in the opposite direction. After a few steps he stopped and swivelled around. He was about to a call out, but checked himself. He had suddenly realised that he had left his kitbag in the cellar, but he could not expect the Frenchman to take any more risks on his behalf. For the first time since arriving in France he felt alone and vulnerable. Doctor Dubar had always been in the background, watching out for him, but now the connection was broken. Not only that, he had also lost contact with Marie.

As he reached the main boulevard he looked back. A few pedestrians could be seen, but no one in uniform. A lorry appeared at the far end coming his way. It was a military lorry. Crossing to the other side of the boulevard, he entered a café and sat down at a table away from the window but where he could see out. He ordered coffee and a croissant and picked up a newspaper that had been left on the table and pretended to read.

The lorry turned into the boulevard traffic. There were six soldiers on board. They were looking intently at the pedestrians as the lorry was driven slowly along. Stefan watched it disappear out of sight. Letting out sigh of relief, he ordered a second coffee and stared unseeing at the newspaper as he focused his mind on his next move.

He had no spare clothes, shaving kit, boots – or weapon. On the plus side he was wearing the better of his two Todt uniforms; he had his travel papers and Todt credentials for his new job in Paris, and a reasonable amount of money. The downside was that he was stuck with the identity card for Pierre Limone, a man wanted by the Gestapo. But it was all he had. Dare he risk going on to Paris? And if he got to Paris, dare he turn up at Todt headquarters? No, as the Doctor had told him, his work with the Todt was finished. But his only contact was what the Frenchman had given him, and that was in Paris. He decided on Paris, where his uniform might still be useful.

Getting up, Stefan paid his bill and asked directions to the station. If he took a late train and got there when it was dark, he might be able to give the Gestapo the slip. It was a risk, but he had to take it.

*

When he got to the station Stefan hung back, pretending to be engrossed in the timetable. From there he had a good sight of the barrier. There were two ticket collectors and two gendarmes. But the gendarmes, with one ticket collector, were scrutinizing the papers of new arrivals. The other ticket collector was checking the tickets of those going onto the platform.

He decided to catch the 4 pm train to Paris, which meant that he had nearly four hours to kill. Leaving the station, he retraced his steps for about two hundred metres, where he had passed a cinema. He bought a ticket and went in. The films were newsreels combined with a third-rate propaganda films. He stuck it for ninety minutes before walking out.

Making his way back to the station, he showed his ticket, bought a street map of Paris from a kiosk, and went into the station café. It was crowded, and soldiers took up most of the tables. But there were two tables with Todt Organisation employees sitting at them. He could see that he was higher in rank to any of them. He ordered a cup of coffee and took it over to the table that had a spare chair.

'Mind if I join you, comrades?' he said with a smile and, not waiting for an answer, sat down. The three at the table nodded and gave him a half smile.

'Is anyone heading for Paris?' he continued, as he took a sip of coffee.

They looked at each other and one of them spoke up. 'Yes,' he said, 'we are all heading for Paris.'

'Good,' said Stefan, and smiled again, 'so am I.' He nodded in the direction of the other Todt workers. 'Perhaps we can travel together - get a compartment to ourselves.' He inclined his head towards the other table. 'Do you know them?'

'No, we've only just arrived,' said the one who had spoken previously.

Stefan pushed his chair back. 'I'll go and ask them if they will join us on the train.'

He went over and introduced himself, then pointed back to where he was sitting, giving the impression that he was already part of the other group. They looked across and gave a nod. Stefan returned to his seat and picked up his coffee.

'They think it's a good idea, and appreciate the offer,' he said, as he raised his cup.

He could hardly believe his luck. There was safety in numbers. Breaking the ice with the other Todt workers was easy; you just asked them where they were from. After that he concentrated on questions about their home and family. He found that there was one Pole, a Dutchman, and a Finn. By the time the train arrived Stefan knew much more about them than they knew about him.

As they got up to leave he waved to the other table and, as the train came to a stop they spread out, ready to jump in and secure an empty compartment for them to share. Stefan was conscious that he was the only one without any luggage, but he casually remarked that he had 'sent it on' in a trunk.

As planned they managed to get into one compartment. Stefan got his favoured corner seat where, once they were settled, he put his head back and closed his eyes, discouraging any further conversation.

'Wake me up when we get to Paris,' he said. But he had no intention of falling asleep; he was too tensed up concentrating on acting the part of being relaxed and natural. So he feigned sleep, and when one of them eventually shook his shoulder with the words, ' - wake up we're here,' he made a show of waking up slowly and reluctantly, so that they all left the compartment ahead of him. He would have preferred to stay with them, but he could not risk going through the normal exit from the station.

The train was almost empty before he moved. Leaving the compartment he walked through the coaches towards the back of the train. When he got to the end coach he opened a door on the opposite side to the platform and jumped down onto the track. Before he moved he looked carefully around him. He could see men working on the lines, but there was no one close to him. He walked casually across the tracks and away from the station. Like any other station in a big city, it was in a built-up area and he did not have to walk far before he found a low fence into a garden, and beyond that a road.

He walked back towards the other side of the station and hung around until a taxi turned up.

'Do you know the Hotel Sorbonne?' he asked the driver.

'*Oui monsieur.*'

Stefan opened the car door and got in 'Take me there, *sil vous plait,*' he said.

The name of the hotel had little association to its actual location. It was nowhere near the Sorbonne but situated in a narrow street on the other side of the River Seine. Paying off the taxi, Stefan entered the dim interior. There was a small, unattended, reception desk, lit by a single light bulb under a yellow, fly blown, shade. Opposite the desk, through an archway shielded by a beaded curtain, was a bar.

The rattle of beads as he went through caused a couple of heads to turn curiously in his direction. Three of the five tables were occupied. Two German soldiers sat at one; at another was a man in a Todt uniform with young woman and, at the third, another man and woman in civilian clothes. A candle stuck in the top of a bottle lighted each table. The bar was lit by a similar light and shade to the reception desk. Behind it was a man wiping glasses. At the far end of the bar a woman drinking alone eyed him casually as he walked in.

'*B'jour monsieur,*' said the barman.

'*Bonjour,* I am looking for Claude.'

The barman put down the glass he had been wiping. He gave a small nod 'Yes, *monsieur* I am Claude,' he said, 'can I help you?'

'I would like a room; I have been recommended by Jules,' said Stefan.

The barman looked at him thoughtfully for a moment.

'Can I get you a drink, *monsieur*?'

'Yes, I'll have a *demi* please.'

The barman filled a small glass and placed it in front of Stefan.

Stefan took a sip and put the glass down. 'Do you have a room?' he said.

'I'm sorry, but I do not have a vacant room. The best I can offer you is to share a room with two others.'

Stefan took another sip of beer. 'Perhaps I could see the room?' he said, knowing that he had no choice but to accept the offer. He had nowhere else to go.

There was a nod. 'I will get the key, *monsieur*,' said the barman, and went through the beaded curtain towards the reception desk.

As he left the woman at the bar got down from her seat and walked toward Stefan.

'Are you looking for some - company, *monsieur*?' she said.

Stefan gave her a smile and shook his head. 'Not tonight, *merci*, perhaps another time.'

She gave a shrug, glanced at the beaded curtain and moved closer to his ear.

'That is not Claude, *monsieur*,' she whispered. 'Claude has been taken away. This one is a *collaborator*.'

For a second or two Stefan could do nothing but stare in shock at the woman as she walked through the curtain and out of the hotel. He had the urge to run after her but instinct told him that that would be the wrong move. Picking up his glass, he forced himself to remain calm.

Two minutes later – long enough to make a telephone call, thought Stefan. The barman claiming to be Claude appeared at the curtain and gestured to him. Stefan placed his glass down and followed him up to the first floor.

He was shown into a large bedroom with three single beds, well spaced out. The outer two were clearly taken. Each bed had a small single wardrobe and a side table with a candle on it. The barman pointed out that the room had a bathroom with a shower and lavatory.

Stefan pretended to consider it for a moment, and asked the price. Not that he now intended to stay. His only thought was to get out of place as quickly as possible.

'Thank you,' he said, 'I'll take it.' He took a couple of steps towards the door, but stopped. 'I'll follow you down – I need to use the bathroom. Leave the key, I'll lock up.'

And without waiting for a response he walked into the bathroom and closed the door.

He held his breath and listened. The barman hesitated for a few seconds; then Stefan heard his footsteps receding down the stairs. Stefan breathed out with relief. Opening the bathroom door he looked more closely at the luggage of the other two occupants. A cheap suitcase and a civilian pair of shoes indicated that one was a civilian. A German soldier occupied the other bed; the uniform of a corporal was hanging in the small wardrobe. He walked across the room to the window and looked out. Below was a narrow alleyway. The window opened with a push.

He was about to climb through it but hesitated. Going into the bathroom he picked up the shaving kit, pushed it into the kitbag of the soldier and threw it out the window. He squeezed himself out and, legs dangling, hung onto the windowsill for a second or two before letting go. With legs bent to take the impact, he landed safely and rolled over. He slung the kitbag over his shoulder, paused at the end of the alleyway, and then walked with unhurried strides in the direction of the river.

At the end of road, on the corner facing the Seine, was a small restaurant, which reminded Stefan how hungry he was. He walked in and sat down at a table where he could see the passing traffic and ordered a *plat du jour* and a bottle of wine. The wine arrived first and as he poured it he saw a black Mercedes turn the corner and head in the direction of the Hotel Sorbonne.

When his food arrived he ate it quickly, paid the bill, and left. A glance over his shoulder confirmed that the Mercedes was still parked outside the hotel. He hoped that the barman calling himself 'Claude' was being questioned and would be arrested for allowing him to escape. He crossed the road to join the pedestrians sauntering along the bank of the river. Many of the walkers were in uniform, and most with female companions. He felt that his best protection was to be among them.

After an hour the kitbag was making his shoulder ache. He walked on doggedly until the light was failing and there was no one about. He wondered whether he was breaking a curfew. He had reached the suburbs and the path beside the river ran through trees and grass. Looking around for somewhere to bed down for the night he found a bench in a quiet spot. Putting the kitbag under his head, he stretched out and closed his eyes. As he started to doze he began to turn over and woke up with a jolt as he rolled off the bench.

Stefan resettled himself and began to doze, but a minute later spots of rain on his face roused him. Cursing, he sat up and looked around. Apart from a few trees and a rhododendron bush there was no other shelter. Picking up the kitbag he walked to the rhododendron, remembering from his boyhood hiding and making a 'camp' inside one of a similar size. As he reached it he saw at the waters edge below him four rowing boats tied to a wooden stake. One had a black tarpaulin over it. He walked down for a closer look.

By now the rain was coming down steadily. Pulling the boat with the tarpaulin clear of the water, he untied the knots and crawled inside. He lay down; listening to the drumming of the rain inches above his head, thinking he was in for a sleepless night.

He woke to the squawking of ducks on the river. Peering out into the early morning light he saw that the sky was clear. He climbed out and stretched his stiff limbs. From the kitbag he took out the razor and shaving brush and had a cold shave. Sorting through the kitbag, he found it contained a typical assortment of soldiers kit; spare underwear, socks, two shirts, a pair of civilian shoes, slightly big for him but wearable, a forage cap, a bar of soap and two tins of sardines.

Wrapped in an army issue towel were two packets of cigarettes, a box of matches, and a leather wallet containing 100 francs. With it was a picture of a girl in a Bavarian dress. Finally, at the bottom, was a leather holster containing a Webley .45 revolver, with twelve bullets. It was the kind of handgun that a British officer carried. The holster had a dark, almost black, stain on it that looked like dried blood.

Stefan was hungry again. Across the river he could see what looked like shops and a café. He looked thoughtfully at the rowing boat. From the leaves and twigs gathered on it, it looked as though it had not been used for some time. He untied the rest of the tarpaulin, rolled it up and put it in the boat. It was then that he noticed a black swastika stamped on the rear end. He gave a grim smile, pleased to find that he wasn't stealing the boat from any local. The oars were inside the boat, and with them a fishing rod and line. Placing the oars in position, he pushed the boat out and jumped in.

Rowing to the other side of the river, he tied up at a small jetty and walked up a flight of steps to the road. The café was closed, but the *boulangerie* next to it was just opening. He bought a loaf of bread on his ration card, some cheese, and two bottles of cider. Returning to the boat he rowed away, heading south.

He had no idea where he would end up, but now had somewhere to sleep at night, and the river, he felt, was safer than being on land. He concentrated on his rowing, to give any onlookers the impression that he was on a mission, carrying out orders, and had a destination to reach.

CHAPTER 22

With a roll of fishing net over his shoulder the Greek, who proudly boasted to have an Irish mother, walked casually along the quay. In spite of the heat he wore a dark blue woollen sweater, unbleached canvas trousers and a blue serge cap. He was not a tall man, but his shoulders were wide, and behind his black beard and moustache his face was weathered and sunburnt.

Beside him, dressed as a local peasant, with a similar moustache and dark hair showing from under a battered panama hat, Igor kept pace, walking with the aid of a stick. It was nearly mid-day, and Crete's Suba Bay shimmered in the withering heat. The sun reflecting on the water dazzled Igor's recently wounded eye, causing him to squint. Passing a line of nondescript fishing boats, they picked their way through heaps of tackle. Beyond the quay ships with German or Italian markings dominated the harbour. In the middle of the harbour the top half of a sunken British cruiser lay at an angle.

'Which one is yours, Rico?' asked Igor, in English - the only common language that they could use.

The Greek lifted his head slightly, pointing ahead with his nose. Three boats further on he stopped and threw the net on to the deck of an old caique. Igor looked at it in disbelief. Of all the boats that were tied up, it was the scruffiest and looked the least seaworthy. There was a gaping hole where the mast should be.

'Is this it? Do you think this can get us there?' Igor asked.

'Yes, this is my '*Marbella*,' said the other, with some pride. 'She's a good boat –she will get you there.'

Stepping carefully on to the boat, Igor judged that it was thirty foot long. The deck was cluttered with piles of fishing gear that, to Igor's eyes, looked unusable.

'How many will it take?' he said.

The Greek fisherman lifted a shoulder. 'Twelve,' he said, -'ten better.'

He lit a cigarette as Igor continued to look around.

'It's gotta good engine,' Rico assured him, patting the handrail, 'English – 'Perkins' – you know?'

Igor shook his head. He didn't know. 'What about the mast – and have you got a sail?'

Rico lifted his shoulder again. 'I getta sail, if you want – but it'sa good engine.'

'But the engine needs fuel – have you got enough to get us to Italy?'

'We have a ration – enough to fish t'ree time sa week - but I can get fuel - it cost money – but I can get it,' he said.

Igor picked his way through the clutter on the deck and peered down the hatch.

Rico came and stood beside him, and then went down the steps to the cabin.

'Come – I show you the engine,' he turned and beckoned, 'come'.

After a slight hesitation Igor followed. As he reached the cabin he found Rico lighting an oil lamp and, as the light penetrated the gloom, he was not surprised to see that the cabin was as untidy as the deck. Ignoring the look of disdain on his companion's face, Rico grinned as he moved to a small door, unbolted it, and then squeezed through.

'Come, Tommy, look – see engine,' he called.

Curious to see the condition of the engine, Igor put his head through the opening. All he could see was a pile of old tarpaulin. Rico hung the oil lamp on a hook and, with a sweep of his arm, turned back the tarpaulin to reveal what was underneath.

The look of surprise on Igor's face brought a low chuckle from the fisherman.

Completely out of character with the rest of the boat, the engine house was tidy and the engine gleamed. Only engines that have received fastidious and tender care could gleam like that. It exuded reliability and power.

'What you t'ink, Tommy, okay, eh?'

Igor had told Rico his name twice but Rico had simply said 'Okay Tommy,' and so Igor had given up and accepted that, on Crete, he was 'Tommy.' Looking at the engine, he gave an admiring nod.

'Yes, Rico – the engine looks good – very good,' he said. 'I'll be talking to the others tonight – can you be there?'

'Of course – if you want my '*Marbella,*' there'll be much to do – much to buy. You have plenty money?'

'Just tell us what you need tonight – and how much it will cost.'

The two men returned to the quay. Igor took another look at the boat. With its peeling paint and unkempt appearance it gave the impression of being distinctly unseaworthy. But he understood now why it looked such a mess. After the Germans took over the island they had requisitioned all the best boats in the harbour. A few months later they took more. Rico had noticed that only the cleanest and tidiest boats were taken, and so he made sure that his boat looked the most unappealing.

They started to walk back towards the harbour town of Canea. Not much had been done to repair the bomb damage that the town had suffered during the invasion, but the streets had been cleared and the occupiers had restored the water and electricity supply. There was a checkpoint at the end of the quay but as Rico drew near he greeted the guard in Greek - a local policeman.

After a little banter and backslapping, with Igor smiling and nodding in the background, they went on their way, with Rico explaining that the guard was an old schoolmate.

'It seems easy to get on the quay during the day, Rico,' said Igor, 'but how are we going to get twelve of us on to the boat? Even if we get through the checkpoint there are too many soldiers and sailors about during the day for them not to notice.'

Rico walked along in silence for a while.

'It must be done at night,' he said.

'At night! But what about the curfew – if we're caught we'll be shot.'

Rico gave a small smile. 'Yes, that is the risk you mus' take Tommy,' he said, 'but I 'ave a little idea – I will speak with my sister.'

Igor looked at him with some surprise. 'Your sister - how can she help us?'

Rico smiled at him. 'I tink she can 'elp plenty - I bring her tonight,' he said.

Accepting that Rico would not expand on his idea until he had spoken to his sister, Igor did not pursue the matter. He walked along in silence, engrossed with the thought of escaping from Crete. It had taken over three months for his wounds to heal and he was keen to get back to the war. He had been out of it too long and he still had scores to settle.

Not long after Igor had arrived on Crete, Rommel and the Axis army had surrendered in North Africa. In July the island had buzzed with the news that the Allies had landed on Sicily and then, just a few days ago, that they had landed in Italy.

When they reached the town they took the narrow side streets. From a small bakers shop Igor collected two loaves and some goats cheese he had ordered. They walked on in silence until they came to a small café, almost hidden amongst the terraced houses. There was a 'closed' sign on the door, but Igor opened it with a key and walked in.

'Come up for a drink before you go, Rico,' said Igor.

'OK, Tommy,' said Rico, ' just a quick one, then I mus' go – I 'ave much to do.'

Igor walked through the cafe and mounted a narrow staircase at the rear. At the top of the stairs was a small landing with three doors leading off. Opening the first door he came to, he stood aside as Rico followed him.

It was a fairly large room, with a single bed in the corner behind a muslin curtain. In the centre, a table and four chairs. A pair of glazed doors opened out to a small balcony with views over the rooftops towards the harbour. Igor went to the table and picked up a bottle of wine and two glasses. Rico sat down as Igor poured the wine.

''ow many you got so far, Tommy?' Rico asked, as he took the glass from Igor.

'Six at present - you can take six more, did you say?'

Rico shook his head doubtfully. 'Better if four.'

Igor nodded. 'How long will it take to get the boat ready, Rico?'

Rico screwed up his face. 'That depends 'ow soon we get supplies. I need money to buy fuel – and food. Maybe 'ave to pay others, to – you know - look other way. It depends on whether you 'ave enough money. If all okay, maybe – two weeks.'

Igor nodded thoughtfully. 'I've been promised some money Rico, but I've not met the man who has promised it. He'll be here tonight with the others. I've been told that he is a Jew who came here from Italy to avoid being persecuted by the fascists. He brought his wife and daughter with him and they took a lease on this café. Then, after the Nazis arrived, one day when he was out, they came and took away his wife and daughter. That was a year ago. He's been in hiding ever since.'

Rico nodded gravely, rose from the chair, swallowed the rest of his wine and put his glass down.

'OK, Tommy – I must go now - see you tonight,' he said.

Igor listened as Rico's footsteps went downstairs and out of the cafe. He sat looking out towards the harbour and thought about when he had escaped from the prisoner's ward in a coffin. He would like to have seen and thanked Captain McIntyre for his escape, but he had managed to raise enough money to buy cigarettes and a few other items to send him as a small token of his gratitude.

The MO had been as good as his word; Igor had been taken to the house of a retired dentist who, with his wife, had carefully nurtured him back to health. There was an ugly scar on his thigh and another to the side of his left eye that pushed his eyebrow up slightly. Fortunately his eyesight had not been affected, except that his eye was much more sensitive to sunlight. He'd moved into the cafe two weeks ago, and let the grapevine know that he was planning to escape to Italy. It was known that the Islander's were hiding a number of Allied soldiers.

It had not taken long for the word to get around, and he soon had visitors. Sergeant Kirby was the first, then Corporal Stone, Private Richards and another called Stephens. Except the Sergeant, who was Australian, they were all New Zealanders who had been hidden by the locals since the occupation. Next came an RAF pilot, Flight Sgt Fletcher, a Welshman. And then word from a Jewish merchant of means who offered to provide money for the escape, so long as he was included.

Igor began to prepare for his visitors. He went down to the café and brought up more chairs and another table. Going down again, he returned with wine and glasses. On a large plate he placed the loaves and the cheese. Satisfied, he went and lay down on the bed. Putting his hands behind his head, he stared unseeing at the ceiling, trying to figure a way to get the required supplies and everyone on to the boat if Rico's idea with his sister did not work out.

Igor woke up with a start as he heard the door of the café being rattled. Getting up he hurried down the stairs. It was the New

Zealanders and the Flight Sergeant. Pointing to the staircase, he bade them to go up and help themselves to a drink. He took a look outside – and froze. Walking towards him was policeman. Had he seen the others arrive and was coming to investigate? Igor stood rooted to the spot. As the policeman got nearer Igor tried to collect himself; he leaned back against the wall of the café and waited. The policeman stopped in front of him.

'Iss everythin' okay, Tommy?' he said, in poor English.

Igor nodded and gave him a grin; his attempt to look like a local peasant had not fooled this man.

'Yes – fine - I'm just waiting for a few friends'

'I know – I know. I bin asked keep eye out – make sure you not disturbed.'

Igor raised an eyebrow. 'Who arranged that - Rico?'

The policeman smiled. 'Rico? No, not Rico,' he said, shaking his head as he walked on, hands clasped behind.

Reassured, but intrigued, Igor went back into the café and up the stairs. He found that the New Zealanders had helped themselves to the wine and the bread and cheese. They greeted him cheerily.

'Did you hear the news, Polski? The Yanks have landed in Italy!'

'Yes, I heard - great news – are you all still as keen to get away?'

They nodded.

'You bet.'

'When can we go?'

'Have you got a boat lined up yet?'

Igor looked around at their faces and grinned. It was obvious that they were all keen to join him.

'I'm expecting others to arrive soon who are vital for the escape. But I can tell you I've seen a boat today that looks promising.'

There was a knock on the door downstairs.

'Help yourself to more wine, chaps, it sounds as though the others have arrived,' said Igor as he headed towards the staircase once again. He returned leading Rico and an attractive, plump, woman in her mid-30s. Under her arm she was carrying what looked like a bundle of washing. Rico introduced her as his sister, Linda.

Igor made the introductions, and Linda, a nervous smile on her face, sat down at the table. As Igor poured out more wine the door opened, and in the frame stood a tall man, pale and thin. He had a

197

black beard, and his dark penetrating eyes glowered at them from under bushy black eyebrows. They looked at him in surprise, wondering how he had got there. The man gave a small smile.

'I am sorry to startle you,' he said. 'I came in the back way. My name is Lubin.'

He was wearing a pair of immaculate cream linen slacks and a black shirt. On his feet was a pair of shiny black shoes, in his hand a black wide brimmed hat. Igor gave him a smile and put out his hand.

'I'm pleased to meet you Mr Lubin,' he said, realising that this was the man who had promised to provide the money for the escape. 'Now we can get down to business.'

Igor told them about the boat, explaining that, at first sight, it did not look seaworthy, but he was convinced that it was in better shape than it appeared. He asked Rico to tell them how much money he needed for fuel and provisions. Rico told them the supplies would cost between 250 –350 drachmae; he would also want 200 drachmae for the hire of his boat, and a further 50 for his sister. As soon as the money was provided he could start making the necessary purchases. He would aim to get everything bought and on board the boat in ten to twelve days. It would take at least another day to get everyone on board. So, if there were no hitches, they could leave at dawn in fourteen days.

There was a short silence after Rico finished speaking.

'That's buggered it,' said one of the New Zealanders. 'We haven't got that kind of money.' The others were shaking their heads.

Igor looked at them. They were not aware that Mr Lubin had promised to fund the escape, and he had the impression that they were not meant to know. Also, he was not sure whether Mr Lubin would be prepared to pay such a large amount.

'600 drachmae is a lot of money, Rico,' said Igor, slowly. '*If* we find this amount, can you assure us that you will not ask for any more?'

'You 'ave my word, Tommy,' said Rico. 'No more.'

Igor looked across the table and caught the eye of Mr Lubin, who gave a small nod.

'Okay, Rico, the money will be found. The next problem is, how can we all get on board without being detected. You said you had an idea about this, and that it could only be done at night. Can you tell us what you have in mind?'

Rico smiled and glanced down at his sister.

'Yes, Tommy - as I say - it 'ave to be at night, during curfew 'ours. This is where my sister can 'elp.' He placed his hand on this sister's shoulder. 'Show what you 'ave in the bundle, Linda.' he said.

Linda cleared a space on the table, placed the bundle upon it and opened it out. Tightly rolled inside were three German uniforms. One had the rank of a Sergeant; the other two were corporals.

They looked at the uniforms, and then back to Rico, waiting for him to continue.

'She do some repairs for Germans and Italians.' he said, by way of explanation. 'During curfew, soldiers take their girlfriends and whores along the quay. I can find girls, and with these you can get on the boat.

There were grins all round the table. Igor nodded in approval.

'It sounds like a good idea, but if you only have three uniforms, how will you get the uniforms back to the others.'

'When first three on board, I wrap uniforms in fishing net and carry back for next three,' said Rico.

'And what about the girls,' asked Igor, 'how will they get back?'

'They be okay – they come back with me - when we 'ave finished they sleep on other boats. They done it plenty times.'

'Good, but are the owners of the uniforms likely to want them back before we've borrowed them?'

Linda smiled and spoke for the first time. Like her brother, she spoke poor English with an Irish accent. 'It's not likely,' she said, 'these three I 'ave for several months. I t'ink the owners 'ave forgotten them.'

The fact that they would most likely be executed if they were caught wearing German uniforms was completely ignored.

Igor nodded. 'Good - I think that's it - I suggest we meet again in seven days time for the final briefing. In the meantime we need to find three more passengers.'

Mr Lubin cleared his throat. 'Excuse me,' he said.

Heads turned towards him.

'I will be bringing three others with me, so that will make ten, will it not?

Mentally, Igor cursed. It was thoughtless of him not to have asked Mr Lubin if he had others in his party. He moved over to him and placed a hand on his shoulder.

'Yes, of course Mr Lubin - bring them along to the next meeting.'

'Thank you, I will,' he said. 'Now, if everyone will excuse me, I must leave,' and then, turning to Igor, 'perhaps you could see me to the door.'

Igor nodded and followed him down the stairs. At the bottom Mr Lubin paused and pushed a brown envelope into Igor's hand.

'This is 650 drachmae,' he said. 'I suggest that you do not part with it all at once – and keep half of Rico's money back until we are landed in Italy.'

'I'm sure I can get him to agree to that, Mr Lubin and, well – thanks for what you are doing.'

The other man placed a long slender hand onto Igor's arm.

'I have faith in you Tommy Pole, just get us to Italy – that's all I ask,' he said quietly, and disappeared into the darkness. Before the others left Igor warned them not to talk about the escape to anyone.

*

The next few days dragged by. Igor could do nothing but hope that Rico was making the necessary purchases and getting them to the boat. On the seventh day they met again in the café. This time Mr Lubin arrived first with his three passengers. Igor had expected them to be fellow Jews, but they turned out to be three Australian soldiers he had been hiding.

Rico and his sister arrived next with the German uniforms. When the rest of the party arrived a dress rehearsal took place. The uniforms did not fit everybody, but Linda assured them that she could do some quick alterations when the time came.

Rico confirmed that most of the supplies were on board and everything should be ready by the twelfth day, as arranged.

'What about the girls Rico?' said Igor, as he handed over more money.

Rico nodded his head. 'They come when we're ready.'

He then pulled a map from his pocket and spread it on the table. It was part of a larger nautical map that covered the area between Crete and the lower half of Italy. They crowded around as he pointed with his finger the route they would take. He intended to remain in sight of the islands as they sailed north but not to make a landing unless it was essential. Rico told them that the only luggage they could take would be in their pockets.

'Has anyone got any questions?' asked Igor. ' Better ask them now if you have because this is the last meeting before we embark.

There was only one question; how long would the journey take.

Rico shrugged his shoulders. 'Five days - if all goes well,' he said.

Before they left Igor went over the details once again, making sure that everyone knew exactly what was going to happen and what they should do. The last to leave was Mr Lubin, who told Igor to contact him through the policeman he had met in the street, should it be necessary.

Over the next few days Igor's excitement changed to tension. The Germans had started another campaign of house searching in the town, and several arrests had been made. He thought it was only a matter of time before they reached the café. He was comforted by the fact that the policeman in the pay of Mr Lubin was frequently to be seen in the street outside.

On the thirteenth day Igor spent most of it watching the clock, unable to think of anything but getting safely on board the boat. As dusk approached the party gathered in the cafe. Rico arrived with two attractive young women. A few minutes later four more arrived. Igor guessed their ages as between eighteen and thirty. They knew what was expected of them, and after Rico had paid them half of what he had promised, they started to pair up with the soldiers. Rico departed, making his way to the boat. The first three put on the German uniforms over their own and then, each with a girl on their arm, two minute's apart, they started off. There was nothing the others could do but wait anxiously for Rico to return with the uniforms. As it was not yet curfew, the three girls would follow him back.

Igor had arranged to be the last to leave. He planned to walk down to the quay alone, wearing the Sergeant's uniform. Having no uniform of his own, all he had underneath were the peasant clothes the dentist had given him. Rico had arranged for a girl to meet him near the quay. As Igor stepped into the street and locked the cafe for

201

the last time a figure came out of the shadows and fell in step beside him. It was Mr Lubin's policeman, still keeping an eye on him, and Igor was pleased with his presence.

As they got nearer to the harbour Igor was surprised to see how many German and Italian soldiers were walking about. But no one took any notice of the German Sergeant and the local policeman walking together. As they approached the quay in the failing light a girl came out of a doorway and linked her arm with Igor's. She was dark and slim and beautiful and gave him an affectionate kiss on his lips. The policeman turned away into a side street, his job done.

Igor and his girl were only one of many couples walking along the quay. There had been no problem at the checkpoint; as Rico had observed, soldiers in uniform with a girl on their arm were just waved through.

When they reached the boat Igor stopped and took the girl into his arms and kissed her while he looked around to see who might be watching. He was beginning to wish he'd met her earlier than the night he was due to depart. Near to the boat was a pile of fishing net and they sat down on it. They kissed again, and the girl lay back and pulled Igor down beside her. By now the quay was bathed in bright moonlight. Looking over his shoulder she gave him a slight push when it was clear and he casually rolled away from her and heaved himself onto the boat. He noted that the clutter had all gone. After a few minutes the girl sat up and started combing her hair. Satisfied that no one was observing her she got up and walked slowly away. Igor raised his head slightly and watched her depart, a small sense of loss stirring in his loins.

Keeping low, Igor crept across the deck and eased down the steps to the cabin. A small glow from an oil lamp revealed the others cramped together on boxes with their backs to the wall. All were now wearing their own uniforms, except for Mr Lubin, who had added a black goatskin jerkin over his black shirt.

In whispers they welcomed him, but there was little further conversation. It had been a tense day and they were exhausted. Igor sat on the floor and leaned back against steps of the hatchway. He closed his eyes, his thoughts and senses still lingering on the soft seductive lips of the girl he had just embraced. Gradually, the sounds of sleep began to fill the air, and it was not long before he joined them.

*

They were aroused by the sound of the diesel engine starting up. The first glimmer of dawn was showing through the open hatchway. He rose and tried to stretch some of the stiffness out of his cramped limbs. The scar on his thigh always ached in the morning, and he massaged the skin as he put his head through the hatchway. All he could see was the outline of several other fishing boats proceeding towards the open sea. He felt reassured; there was safety in numbers.

'Okay, Tommy, you can 'ave a look now,' he heard Rico say. 'Put on the clothes down there – we're being watched.'

Igor found the clothes hanging on hooks in the cabin. They were old and threadbare but were typical of what the local fishermen wore. Pulling them over his other clothes he found a hat that fitted and returned to the deck.

Rico gave a nod of approval. He took the stub of a cigarette from the corner of his mouth, lit another one with it, and flicked the stub into the sea. His face looked strained as he stared ahead, concentrating on keeping his place in the small flotilla.

'You can all take turn on deck, Tommy,' he said, 'but only two each time – and use the same clothes. They 'ave their telescopes, so better not look back – always face the sea.'

Igor nodded and went back to the cabin. A few of the others were now awake and he gave them Rico's instructions. One of the Australians dressed and followed him back to the deck, and they walked around the small space, stretching their legs. Igor noticed that Rico had obtained a mast; it was wrapped in a sail and tied to the starboard side of the deck. The sun had appeared on the horizon, turning the sea to a blazing gold, and the flotilla was sailing straight towards it. Igor's spirits rose the further they got from the land, but a niggling worry entered his mind. Something was wrong and he could not pin down what it was. Then it dawned upon him.

'It's a spectacular sunrise, Rico, but we're sailing east – I thought our route was north.'

Rico took the cigarette from his mouth and smiled.

203

''ave patience, Tommy. My friends 'ave sailed with me for past two weeks. The sun blinds those who watch. As others drop their nets, we go into the sun – and disappear. Then we turn north.'

Igor grinned at the cleverness of Rico's plan. He seemed to have thought it out very carefully. He returned to the cabin so that someone else could take a turn on deck.

Two hours later they were sailing north with no land in sight. The sea was calm and they sat around on deck, ate some food and talked, enjoying their new freedom. Igor organised a roster so that each took a turn at steering to give Rico time to rest and eat. He checked the food and fresh water. There was not as much as he would have liked but, with care, he calculated that they had enough for the next seven days.

On the third day they passed several islands, but at a distance. In the afternoon the sudden appearance of an Italian plane sent them scuttling for the hatchway. As soon as he saw it Rico slowed the boat and threw out the fishing nets. It circled over them for several minutes. The three that remained on deck gave it a wave. It flew off but the incident put them all on edge.

The sky became overcast and the sea choppy. Some were sick and no one felt much like eating. It was calmer on the forth day, and they were lounging on the deck about mid-day when Rico gave a shout.

'Get below - there's a boat – starboard side.'

Igor stayed on deck, and Rico pointed out a distant speck as he lifted the binoculars hanging around his neck. His face was grim as he recognised what it was.

'A German torpedo boat,' he said grimly. 'They don't take prisoners. They'll either kill us before sinking the boat, or sink the boat and leave us to drown'

Igor disappeared down the hatchway to tell the others. There was a stunned silence for several seconds, followed by curses. They could not outrun an MTB - the escape attempt was over. Returning to the deck, Igor found that Rico had slowed the boat down and, rather than try to outrun the patrol boat, he was steering straight towards it.

'No point in letting 'em t'ink we're not friendly,' he said, grimly.

They watched in silence as the German boat drew nearer. When the distance had closed to about two hundred metres, Rico, conscious that they were being closely watched, wore a look of unconcern on his face as he spoke again.

'Go below, Tommy, and open the box Mr Lubin is sitting on.'

Without hurrying, Igor went down the hatchway. As the space between the boats narrowed three sailors with automatic rifles appeared. An officer in a peaked cap holding a loudhailer stood behind them.

'Identify yourself – where are you from,' he called out, in Italian.

Rico had been studying the map that morning and knew the islands that they had passed.

Cupping his hands together he shouted back in poor Italian that they were fishermen and named one of the islands.

The German officer looked down and consulted his chart. He was not satisfied. He spoke to his crew and they raised their rifles.

'Heave to - we are coming aboard,' he called.

Rico shrugged his shoulders and cut the engine. The gap grew smaller. At three metres the German sailors were staring at the remaining space and preparing to jump when a small black object arched through the air and landed with a clatter onto the deck of the torpedo boat. The sailors just had time to look around in surprise and identify a grenade before it exploded and they were blown over the side into the sea. A second grenade, and then a third, quickly followed. Another sailor appeared at the machine gun that was mounted on the deck. Face furious, he swivelled it around and fired a short burst before the third grenade exploded in front of him and he dropped from view.

Igor, leading the New Zealanders and Australians, emerged from the hatchway, each holding a grenade. Several more grenades flew through the air in quick succession and landed on the patrol boat. As they exploded it quickly became a total wreck. Two of the grenades must have gone down the hatchway, because there were muffled explosions from the inside of the boat. They waited, tensed up for some retaliation, but none came.

'Let's go aboard and finish it off,' said one of the New Zealanders, handling another grenade.

Rico shook his head. 'Better to stay away,' he said.

They waited in silence, each with a grenade ready to throw. The only sound was from the swell of the sea lapping against the sides of the two boats.

'Blimey, we must've killed 'em all,' said someone, in awe.

There were one or two nods in agreement but no one spoke. They stood in a line along the deck, still not believing that the skirmish was over. Igor looked for the two who had been thrown into the sea with the first grenade. He spotted them drifting face down, about twenty-five metres away. The explosion had probably not killed them outright, but they had been stunned, and because they had landed face down they were likely to have drowned by now.

The enemy boat slowly began to list, indicating that one of the grenades had caused damage below the waterline. One of the New Zealanders shook his head.

'Yeh,' he said, 'I reckon we've killed the poor buggers.'

'Poor buggers be damned!' said the Sergeant, grimly. 'What d'you think they were going to do when they found us lot on board? At best we would have been prisoners again – but more likely shot.'

There were several growls of agreement from the others as they continued to watch the enemy boat. A few minutes later someone remarked quietly, 'There she goes,' as it slowly disappeared beneath the waves. Rico started his engine and pulled away.

As they turned from watching the boat sink they found Mr Lubin sitting near the hatchway holding a bloodstained handkerchief to his neck. A bullet from the machine gun had grazed him. Sergeant Kirby fetched the first aid kit from the cabin and attended to him.

'You'll be all right, cobber - it's only a flesh wound,' he said, reassuringly.

But a few minutes later he took Igor aside 'He should be OK – but he's bleeding a lot' he said, quietly. 'I'll keep my eye on him.'

Igor gave a nod. Now that the tension and the excitement of the short battle were over, Igor had time to reflect on the fact that there had been some armament on the boat. He went over and patted Rico on the back.

'You didn't tell me that we were armed Rico. Were the grenades included in the price of the trip?'

Rico nodded and gave a chuckle. 'I thought it best we 'ave something, Tommy. They cost nothing – the British hid 'em from the Nazis – and we found 'em.'

Igor gave him an approving nod. They had been lucky in engaging Rico for this expedition.

'Have you got anything else – guns?' he said.

'I 'ave a revolver and a few bullets, that's all.'

'And a few grenades left, but not enough to repeat the same kind of action, Rico.'

'No, but in two days we shall be there – God willing.'

But they quickly found that their luck had run out. A storm hit them an hour later, turning the sea into a cauldron of twenty-foot waves. Rico turned the boat into the wind and used all his skill and concentration to ride each wave. Just one slip that allowed the boat to be broadside to one of those waves would have floundered them.

The storm raged for several hours, and for that length of time Rico stared through the driving rain, spinning the wheel one way and then the other with a dexterity that would have attracted considerable attention, had anyone been there to see it.

When the storm abated they knew that they were off course but had no idea how much. Igor took over the steering as Rico went below to get some food and sleep. The sky was grey and overcast for another four hours before the clouds thinned out and a watery sun came through. There was no sight of land in any direction but, with sight of the sun, Igor steered the boat due north once again. A little later Sergeant Kirby came and stood beside him.

'Mr Lubin's lost a lot of blood. It doesn't look much of a wound, but it won't stop bleeding. He's in a bad way.'

Igor turned to him, feeling guilty that he hadn't checked on Mr Lubin since the storm started.

'Take over the steering – I'll go and have a look at him,' he said.

Clambering down to the cabin Igor found Mr Lubin stretched out on the boxes. His face was waxen, and there was a towel wrapped around his neck soaked with blood. Igor pulled up another box and sat beside him. Mr Lubin stretched out a thin white hand and placed it on his arm.

'I think I might be dying, Tommy Pole. I have always bled very easily - since I was a child,' he said quietly, trying to smile through thin pale blue lips.

Igor took his hand, not knowing what to say. He had come to respect Mr Lubin, who in spite of his dark brooding appearance, had proved to be a kind and generous man.

'Try to hang on Mr Lubin, we've been blown off course by the storm, but I'm certain we'll be in sight of the Italian coast within the next few hours.

Mr Lubin closed his eyes.

'I hope you will be Tommy, but I might not be with you by then.' He gave Igor's hand a slight squeeze and lay quiet.

After a few minutes, with a sympathetic shake of his head, Igor returned to the deck, trying to think of something that would help keep Mr Lubin alive; but there was nothing.

He took over the steering once again. Three hours later Rico was back on deck. He scanned the horizon with his binoculars before moving over to stand beside Igor, who told him the bad news about Mr Lubin.

Rico shook his head sadly.

'I'm sorry to 'ear that Tommy,' he said, but in a voice that was a little distant, as though his thoughts were elsewhere

Igor looked at him. He could see that his face was weary, his eyes worried.

After a few seconds Rico continued. 'The storm used a lot of fuel,' he said. 'We've enough for ten more hours. Also, a bullet hit the water tank. We're down to the last litre or two.'

The news sent a stab of despair through Igor and he suddenly felt drained of energy.

'Any idea how far we've got to go before we sight land, Rico?'

Rico shook his head. 'I 'ave no idea – we should 'ave sighted land 'ours ago.'

Igor, his face serious, gave a nod. 'Here, Rico, you'd better take over again while I break it to the others.'

Most of the men were lounging on the deck, dozing or playing cards. When he finished telling them the bad news they rose to their feet and stood silently gazing towards what they thought was the direction of Italy, each hoping to be the first to sight land. Igor went below, deciding not to say anything to Mr Lubin.

He lay as Igor had left him, his eyes closed. Igor thought he was dead, but his eyes flickered open and, recognising Igor, he slowly stretched out his hand towards him. Igor took it, but realised that he was trying to give him something. It was his wristwatch.

'For - you,' he whispered.

Igor glanced at it - it was a gold Rolex. He slipped it into his pocket. 'I'll look after it for you Mr Lubin.'

Mr Lubin attempted to raise his hand again but could not, so he beckoned Igor to come closer. Igor leaned his head towards him.

'I am - going,' he said, and paused, as though the effort to speak was too much. Igor leaned closer as he opened his mouth again.

'Take – the money,' he gasped, 'take the clothes, shoes – share them out – useful.'

His eyes looked briefly at Igor, and then went blank. Igor sat watching him for a minute or two. When he lifted his hand there was no pulse; Mr Lubin was dead.

Igor gently closed the staring eyes. 'May your God speed your journey, my friend,' he said quietly.

He sat holding Mr Lubin's hand for another half minute before he placed it to his chest and made his way back to the deck to inform the others.

Most of them had anticipated the bad news. They had seen for themselves that the wound would not stop bleeding. They discussed whether to keep his body until they reached land, but decided that he would probably have preferred to be buried at sea.

Two of the New Zealanders went below with Igor and carried the body to the deck. They took off his clothes and shoes and wrapped his body in a piece of sailcloth. Two empty fuel cans filled with seawater were used as weights. Standing in two lines, with the body between them, Rico read a prayer in Greek before they committed Mr Lubin to the waves.

Igor looked at the clothes lying on the deck, together with Mr Lubin's shiny black shoes. As he folded them up, he found a wallet in the trouser pocket. In it were identity papers, two letters in Italian, a photograph of Mr Lubin's wife and daughter, 1000 Italian liras and 250 drachmas. Igor told them what Mr Lubin's dying words had been and solemnly shared out the lira between them. He gave Rico the drachma, which was little more than was still owed to him.

'Does anyone want any of his clothes?' said Igor.

The others looked at what Igor was holding up. The black shirt was stiff with dried blood, and there were spots of blood on the trousers. Then there was the black goatskin jerkin with three leather buttons down the front, and the black shoes. The soldiers shook their heads. They were wearing their old uniforms and army boots and had no need for any civilian clothing. Igor looked at Rico.

'Nothing to fit me, Tommy - why don't you 'ave 'em.'

Igor shrugged his shoulders. 'Okay,' he said, 'but I doubt I shall use them, I hope to be back in uniform myself before long.' He wrapped the shoes in the trousers, rolled up the leather jerkin and tied them into the shirt.

The sun was beating down as Igor shared out the last of the water and food. No one felt like talking. Two hours went by before Rico turned and beckoned to Igor.

'We must use the sail, Tommy. Save the fuel 'til we sight land - easier to dock with the engine.'

They got the sail up just before sunset, and as the wind filled it out Rico turned off the engine. In the fading light he stared hard through his binoculars. The flight sergeant went to stand beside him. Rico pointed something out. Straining his eyes, all that could be seen was a feint smudge on the horizon. It looked like a low cloud, but might be land. He shouted to the others, and they continued watching as the sun went down and the smudge disappeared into the darkness.

The thought that the smudge might be land kept them awake for most of the night, but as dawn approached they all fell asleep. They roused themselves to find Rico was still at the wheel, but the boat was hardly moving. They were surrounded by a sea mist and visibility was down to about fifty metres. The sail flapped listlessly against the mast

The eerie silence was broken as Rico started the engine.

'We gotta keep movin',' he said with a shrug. 'No good waitin' for wind.'

The water having gone, thirst, rather than hunger, was the main problem. For the next three hours the boat chugged through the mist.

210

They sat around the deck, eyes closed, chins on chests or heads laid back. Then someone looked up.

'It's getting lighter. Don't you think its getting lighter?'

One or two opened their eyes but, before anyone could answer, the boat came out of the mist as though through a curtain. A hazy sun filtered down onto a calm sea, and they scrambled to their feet and gave a choking cheer from parched throats. It was a coastline, five or six kilometres away. Rico grinned and nodded in relief. If the fuel ran out now he could send up a distress flare. They had made it. An hour later they approached a small bay. Tiny figures could be made out on the beach.

Igor, with the binoculars to his eyes, gave a curse.

'They're not locals, they're in uniform. Italian by the look of it,' he said.

He passed the binoculars to the Sergeant. The Australian peered through them keenly. A minute later he gave a chuckle.

'They're not Eyeties,' he said, 'they're Yanks!'

With a broad grin on his face, Rico steered the boat towards the small bay. The men crowded forward, impatient that the boat could not go any faster. Some began to wave and then, as they got nearer, to shout. More figures gathered on the shoreline, watching curiously. As the boat got within earshot they heard an exclamation.

'They're Limey's' said a Yank, in astonishment.

'Say, fellas',' he shouted, 'you're too late – we already took this Island.'

'Island?' shouted Igor, 'which Island?'

'Sicily – say, how long you fellas' been out there on your fishin' trip?'

Unable to wait any longer, laughing and shouting, the New Zealanders and Australians jumped overboard and waded ashore. Igor, smiling with relief, watched as Rico nudged the boat against the jetty, jumped out and tied her up. Igor rubbed his thigh, suddenly aware that his old wound was paining him. Picking up Mr Lubins' bundle of clothes, he stepped off the boat and stood beside Rico, patting him on the shoulder.

'Thanks Rico,' he said. 'You were right. Your *'Marbella'* is a good boat.'

'T'ank you, my friend,' Rico said with a smile. Then he nodded towards the shore. 'Looks like we'll be taken prisoner.'

Igor followed his gaze. Beyond the soldiers who had greeted them, six Americans in combat uniform had appeared and were walking towards the shoreline. With semi-automatic rifles resting in the crick of their arms, the helmets on their heads displayed the letters MP painted in white. The soldiers stopped and formed an arc and a Sergeant spoke to each of the new arrivals. They were told to stand in line, and the Sergeant turned and waited for Igor and Rico as they walked down the jetty. He gave them a tight, businesslike, smile as they approached him. His eyes flitted to the bundle that Igor was carrying. He came straight to the point.

'Line up over there fellas', with the others. We gotta search you guys before we leave the beach. First of all, has anyone got any weapons?'

They shook their heads, except Sergeant Kirby, who drew his hand from his pocket holding a grenade, held it up for a second, before dropping it into the sand.

A few knives then appeared, and scissors, and nearly everyone had a shaving kit of some kind.

The Sergeant swept his eye over them. 'Is that all,' he said.

'Yes, I'm sure that's all Sergeant,' said Igor.

The Sergeant turned to him. 'Who are you, buddy?' he asked.

Igor hesitated for a second. He almost blurted out that he was a private in a special unit attached to the Eighth Army, but decided to revert back to his proper rank.

'I am Lieutenant Igor Radovak. A Pole. I was wounded in the desert and taken to Crete by the Germans. As soon as I was fit enough I planned this escape.'

The Sergeant looked at him suspiciously. 'Yeah?' he said, and nodded at the bundle Igor was carrying. 'What's in the bundle?'

Igor was suddenly conscious that, to the American, he appeared to be a Greek peasant. 'These?' said Igor, holding them up. 'These are the clothes of the man who paid for the escape. He died of wounds after a German torpedo boat tried to board us.'

The Sergeant's eyes opened wide. 'An MTB *tried* to board you – and you fought them off?' There was disbelief in his voice.

Igor nodded and smiled. 'Better than that,' he said, '- we sank it.'

The Sergeant stared at him, then turned and took another look at the tatty boat that they had arrived in. 'You *sank* it? You sank an MTB with *that?*"

Igor nodded again. 'Well, Sergeant, we sunk it *from* that – with a few of those,' he said, pointing to the grenade lying on sand.

The Sergeant shook his head. 'Cheeze-us,' he said, and glanced around at his men. 'You hear that guys? This Greek says he's a Polish officer and they sunk a German MTB!'

The rest of the MPs had heard. They were grinning and shaking their heads.

At this point Sergeant Kirby joined in. 'Yes Yanks, we sank the bloody thing all right.'

'We sure did,' said a New Zealander, which was echoed by the other escapers.

The Sergeant looked them over. 'OK – OK,' he said. 'Tell it to the interrogation guys – now, lets get movin'.'

With Igor and Rico at the rear, the escapers walked two abreast off the beach, laughing and joking with their escorts, and asking endless questions. 'Where can I get a beer?'- When do we eat?'-'Am I looking forward to a tubbing.' -' What are the girls like?'

Igor smiled, but his thoughts were elsewhere. He turned to the MP walking alongside him.

'We've some catching up to do with regard to the war – can you tell us what's been going on?'

The American gave him a grin. He replied in a drawl from the American deep South that Igor found difficult to understand. 'Sure – yoh wouldn't have heard, I guess, with y-all too busy sinkin' mo-toe torpeedo bo-ats. But while yoh-all been out there enjoying yo'selves, Italy has surrendered - and yesterdee we landed at Salerno.'

Igor stopped short. 'Italy's surrendered?' he said, his voice loud enough for the others to overhear.

'Sure thing, buddy - announced by General Eisenhower himself.'

Hearing this, the rest of the escapers gave a cheer. 'Bloody 'ell,' someone piped out, 'we might be home by Christmas.'

The MP sergeant shook his head. 'Not until we've licked the fuggin' Nazis we won't,' he said grimly.

CHAPTER 23

As Igor came through the door the same thin, bespectacled, Captain was sitting behind his desk. He glanced up and waved a piece of paper.

'A message has come through for you at last Lieutenant Radovak,' he said.

Igor stopped in surprise. After seven days of debriefing and interrogations and general disbelief about who he was and his attachment to PPA, the use of his proper rank and name came as a shock. The Captain had frankly told him that his whole story seemed 'a bit far fetched,' and that he'd never heard of PPA.

Igor snatched the piece of paper that the Captain was holding out to him. A broad grin crossed his face as he read it.

'Delighted to hear of your resurrection. Please assume original rank of Lieutenant and join Captain Rowan's unit now refitting at Taranto.
Peniakoff (Major)
C.O. PPA.

Igor looked in triumph at the officious Captain, whom for days he had wanted to throttle, sitting there with a sheepish smile on his face, filling his pipe with tobacco.

'Well done, Lieutenant,' he said. 'No hard feelings I hope - only doing my job, you know.'

'How did you find him?' Igor asked.

'I suddenly remembered an old chum of mine from the desert – Roy Farran. He belongs to another cloak and dagger unit. I asked him if he had heard of PPA, and it seems that he knows your Popski quite well. More importantly, he knows his call sign and offered to get a message to him. That's his reply.'

Igor looked beyond the Captain to a map of Italy on the wall. 'Where is Taranto?' he said,

The Captain scraped his chair back. 'Here,' he said, tapping at the heel of the mainland.

'And how do I get there?' said Igor, staring at the spot.

'Ah, yes - I can arrange that. A transport 'plane goes from here twice a day.'

'Good –what time is the next one?'

'Err – midday- but that one is full. I can get you on the next.....'

'Full!' Igor's voice raised a notch. '*Full?* - Captain, you've kept me hanging around here all week wasting my time. I *want* to be on that midday 'plane.' He prodded the desk with his finger. In fact, he had not been wasting his time at 8th Army HQ in Messina; he had been doing a lot of hard walking and physical exercises to get back into shape.

The Captain bristled at being spoken to in such a way by a lower rank. He placed his pipe down carefully. Then he looked up and saw the glint in Igor's eyes and the expression on his face. The eye contact lasted for a few seconds; it seemed longer. Then the Captain lowered his gaze. He knew he had lost. And he knew why. This man in front of him was a soldier in the true sense of the word - a warrior, a killer of the enemy. Not a deskbound clerk like himself, who in three years had not fired a shot, except on the practice range.

He picked up the flight schedule and looked at it.

'Hmm - I suppose I can take off some of the freight until the next flight,' he said, stroking his chin.

'Thank you - I would appreciate that Captain,' said Igor, as though it was settled. 'What time shall I be at the airport?'

The Captain assumed a businesslike attitude.

'Rendezvous back here at 11:30 hours. There are six other passengers and transport will be available to take you to the airfield.' He sat down and took up a pen. 'Now, I must decide what freight to take off to make room for you.'

Igor hesitated. 'How do I contact Captain Rowan when I get there? Do you know where they are billeted?'

The Captain looked up and smiled. 'Haven't the foggiest,' he said. 'You cloak and dagger chaps never broadcast your whereabouts. But don't worry, someone will be there to meet you.'

'Will they? How can you be sure?' asked Igor.

'Pretty sure - some of the freight on the plane is addressed to your Captain Rowan. All you have to do when you get there is sit on it until someone turns up to collect it. They know it's coming today.'

At 4 am on the third day of his arrival at Taranto, Igor stood with the rest of the unit as Rowan spread out a map of Italy. Copies were handed out to the four drivers of the Jeeps that formed the patrol.

For the next thirty minutes Rowan explained the route they were to take and their objectives. Basically it boiled down to keeping out of sight of the enemy and finding out where they were dug in and the strength of their armament. They were to make contact with local resistance groups, use them for intelligence gathering and give them whatever assistance possible to harass the enemy. At all times they were to pass themselves off as a reconnaissance unit for an armoured division coming up behind.

Finally Rowan stopped speaking and looked up. 'Any questions?'

'What about the follow up Skip,' someone asked, 'how far behind us will they be?'

'Not far, but it depends on how strong the Germans are and how much intelligence can be passed back. But don't forget, they've got to come up the main road. They will have to put up with blown bridges, mines, ambushes and a few other delaying tactics. All the things that we avoid by going across country.'

'Do we know who's bringing up the rear?' someone else asked.

'I understand it will be the Canadians - a light armoured division,' Rowan replied.

They all nodded in approval, they had worked with the Canadians before.

'Any more questions?' Rowan looked around the table. 'No?'

He folded up the map. 'There is something else I must tell you. Some bad news I'm afraid.' he said. 'We have just received a radio message that Popski has been in a scrap and been wounded, and a couple of his men killed. His unit is on its way back and I've been told to wait for it to arrive and take over as leader.'

Someone said 'Bloody 'ell!'

Rowan handed the map to Igor. 'Sorry to land this on you at such short notice Igor, but as my second in command, you will be leading the patrol.'

Igor, shocked by the news, simply nodded and took the map from him. Then he remembered something.

'Any idea who got killed?

Rowan looked at him. He knew what was on his mind.

'Yes, one was Corporal Gibbs, and the other – I'm sorry to say Igor – was Popski's driver, Solik.'

Igor stared at him. Solik dead - he shook his head, not wanting to believe what he had been told. Feeling tears coming to his eyes, he blinked them back.

'Thanks for telling me, skipper,' he said quietly, and walked away. He needed to be alone for a while.

*

They had found - Popski had found - that the best way to the high ground travelling north from Taranto was to use the dry shallow beds of the mountain streams. Narrow, stony, but navigable, this was how the jeeps threaded their way through the enemy lines. Within ten days they had 'liberated' three villages from the Germans, not by force, but by bluff. The Italians, having surrendered to the Allies, restored the monarchy, and arrested Mussolini, were glad to be out of the war. And the peasants they met on the road and at the farms they passed were all eager to give information about the Germans.

More partisan groups had also sprung up, and when one local group made contact and told them about a village that was garrisoned by a company of Germans, Igor had called his men together to outline his plans.

'We've got orders not to seek to engage the enemy, except in self-defence,' he said, 'but that doesn't mean we can't give them a scare and spoil their sleep.'

His plan was to place the jeeps in camouflaged positions about a thousand metres above the village and about half a kilometre apart. One of the Browning machine guns from each jeep was taken off and set up in the gaps. Before it got dark all the guns were carefully sited on that part of the village where the Germans were garrisoned. Using ordinary bullets, each gun fired a ten second burst of gunfire towards the target as a wake up call. When it was dark they changed to tracer bullets and randomly sent further bursts of gunfire towards the village. Then they changed position to the flanks of the village and repeated the operation. In all they managed to fire from twelve

217

different positions during the night, giving the impression that the village was surrounded on three sides by hostile forces.

The next morning the partisans came and told them that the Germans had left before dawn. The locals mobbed them when they entered the village in triumph but, in spite of many invitations to stay and enjoy a hero's welcome, Igor pushed on. The same tactics were successfully used on two other villages. And then they were told about another village about twenty kilometres away that had a river running through it - and a bridge, and they had been told to try to secure all bridges intact.

The following morning, just after daybreak, they were in position above the village. Leaving the jeeps out of sight under the trees, they walked to the wall that surrounded the olive grove and those with field glasses leaned their elbows on the wall and scanned the narrow road that snaked down to the village.

A minute went by. 'Can't see any sign of a bridge,' muttered Igor, eventually.

There were a few grunts from the others as they concentrated. Finally he lowered his glasses but continued staring towards the village.

'No,' he said, 'not a sign of it - but it's there – we know that.' He glanced at his watch - the gold Rolex Mr Lubin had given him. 'I know it's still early, but there's usually some locals about by this time. It looks too quiet.' He paused. 'We'll go down and have a look on foot – three on one side and three on the other – not on the road – through the trees.' He beckoned towards a young Italian standing nearby. 'Antonio, you and Caesar come with me.'

Antonio was a local partisan and a dedicated communist, aged nineteen. Thin, pale, with an intelligent face, he was the son of a local landowner and fiercely anti-fascist. He had volunteered to join the unit as a guide and interpreter. Apart from his native Italian and local dialect, he could speak German and fairly good English. His dog, Caesar, was a black Rottweiler.

When the Germans had first entered the village where they lived, Caesar had made the mistake of barking at them and attacking their feet as they marched along. The Germans had kicked and clubbed the dog unconscious and left him for dead. Since then Caesar could sense the presence of a German soldier a hundred and more metres away, no matter how well they where hidden.

With an automatic rifle, a revolver, and a few grenades each, the six men started out. They kept to the cover of the olive trees that stretched down towards the village. A weak sun mottled the ground with soft shadows. Birds twittered and fluttered about them as they passed by. It was a pleasant early autumn day; a day that seemed to make a mockery of war.

Igor spotted the bridge at the same instance that Caesar started to whine. Antonio instantly threw himself to the ground and the others joined him. The split second of early warning saved them as the rattle of a machine gun shattered the silence. The bullets ripped through the trees and branches and leaves showered down on the men clinging to the soil underneath. No one moved, spoke, or shouted out. They were pinned down and they knew instinctively that their only chance to stay alive was to play dead. Igor resisted the temptation to move his head and look up, and willed the others to do the same.

He could not see Antonio or the dog but when the machine gun stopped firing - the only sound was from Caesar, who continued to whine. Then came the sound of rifle fire from the other side of the road, and the machine gun responded. After a long burst it stopped and there was silence again. In spite of the intense temptation, Igor kept his head down to the ground. He speculated on what the Germans would do now. They probably thought that partisans were attacking them, but would they venture out to investigate? He knew that there would be no assistance from the rest of the unit because his orders had been, in the event of an ambush, to remain hidden until dark and then take the jeeps back to a safer position. He cursed silently for not being more cautious. He should have waited until dark.

An explosion broke the silence. It sounded like a grenade. Then came another, followed by rifle and automatic gunfire. There were shouts, and yelling, and it was coming from the other side of the bridge. After a few seconds the German machine guns started firing across the bridge in retaliation.

Igor scrambled to his feet. 'Come on!' he yelled, and ran forward. As he got to the road he was relieved to see his men emerge from the cover of the trees and fall in behind him. As they approached the bridge they could hear a machine gun but had no idea where it was. Caesar bounded past them towards a large bush at the side of the bridge and started barking. Crouching low, Igor ran forward, pushed at the bush and felt concrete. He found an aperture and lobbed in a grenade. There was a muffled 'crump' and the firing stopped. He pushed in another grenade and swung round to see the others running across the bridge. A machine gun was still spitting from a similar bush on the other bank. He watched as the men reached it. There were two more muffled explosions, then silence.

Igor walked across the bridge, stopping in the middle to look over the side. He beckoned his men to join him and pointed downwards.

'Looks as though they had it ready to blow, we'd better get those wires cut,' he said. 'Keep your eyes open for booby traps.'

As he spoke, men with rifles began to appear from the trees on the far side of the bridge. There were six of them, all dressed in the assorted garb of partisans, except for one, who seemed to stand out as the one in charge. He had a scruffy but regular military uniform, and a shoulder flash with 'Canada' on it.

Walking up to Igor and noticing his rank, he gave a quick salute. 'Corporal Spencer, sir,' he said.

Igor returned his salute, then stretched out his hand and gave a grin.

'Lieutenant Radovak' he said. 'Thanks for coming to our assistance corporal. We were in a tight spot before you arrived.'

The corporal gave a sardonic smile as he shook hands. 'We didn't come to your assistance intentionally, sir,' he said, 'we've been planning to take this bridge for a couple of weeks. We were just getting into position when the firing started, and when the skipper saw that it was not aimed at us, he decided to attack right away.'

Igor nodded. 'I'm glad that he did.' He looked over the corporal's shoulder.

'Where is your skipper, I'd like to thank him and have a chat.'

'I'm afraid he's been hit sir.' He nodded towards the other side of the bridge. 'He's under a tree – in a pretty bad way by the look of it - and we've got very little first aid kit.'

Igor started forward. 'Well, we've got plenty – let's go and take a look at him.'

220

The skipper was lying in the shade of an olive tree. His face was covered in blood, his tunic was also soaked and there was no sign of life. Igor felt for his pulse and gave a nod - he was still alive. A quick check revealed that bullets had hit the side of his head, his shoulder, body, and right leg. Igor gave him a shot of morphine and did what he could to stop the bleeding. Then he noticed his insignia – a Captain – and, more surprisingly, a shoulder flash with 'Poland' on it.

He looked up at Corporal Spencer. 'How did you come to be working with the partisans corporal, are you escaped POWs?'

'No sir, we were parachuted in about two months ago to organise local resistance. There were six of us – three Poles, two English, and me. Since then we've had two killed and two wounded. Now the Captain's gone, there's just me.'

Igor straightened up. 'Well, he's not dead yet, but I doubt that he will last the day. To stand a chance he needs quick and proper medical attention– and that's something we can't give him.'

Corporal Spencer shook his head. 'No sir, there's only an old retired Doctor in the village, and he's got no facilities or medical equipment.'

'Hmm, that's a pity,' said Igor, 'but take him along anyway – at least he'll be able to clean him up and arrange a decent funeral. I'll leave some medical supplies.'

Igor's driver came up and reported that they had found the German transport, together with their equipment. Igor turned to the corporal.

'I'm sure the partisans will find that useful, corporal,'

'Thank you sir, yes they will.'

'Right, we'll just say hello to the locals and have a meal, then be on our way. I take it that you'll be able to hold the bridge until the Mounties arrive?' He gave a grin. 'There are some fellow Canadians behind us somewhere – a Light Armoured Division - they should be here in a couple of days..'

The corporal grinned. 'That's good news, sir. Yes, we can hold it, we'll bring in more men.'

'Good,' said Igor, and started to turn away.

'There's just one more thing, sir, if you wouldn't mind,' said the corporal.

'Yes?'

'I – well, I wonder if you would take the Captain's personal possessions and send them back to his family. It would be better coming from you, if you see what I mean. And, well, I may not make it, the way things are going.'

Igor gave a nod. 'Yes, corporal, I'll do that, it's the very least I can do.'

Corporal Spencer bent down and took the Captains watch, ring and wallet and handed them to Igor. 'Thank you sir,' he said, solemnly. 'I know he had a letter from his wife in his wallet, you'll find her address on that.'

*

That evening, when they returned to their concealed camp in the hills, Igor prepared his report for transmission, joined the rest of the men for the evening meal and then headed for his tent. He wanted to write to the next of kin of the fellow Pole who had rushed to his aid that morning and probably saved his life and the lives of his men, at the cost of his own.

Seating himself next to a candle he opened the wallet. He found that blood had seeped inside and was still sticky. As he pulled out the man's identity card a small photograph fluttered to the ground. He picked it up, noting that it was a family group, and held it as he read the man's name and looked at his photograph. Fair-haired, tall and good-looking, Igor saw from his date of birth that he was two years his senior.

Returning to the wallet he pulled out a letter written on flimsy blue 'airmail' paper. He noted that the postmark was London. Again, blood had soaked into it and as he opened it out he saw that only the middle was readable. The address of the sender had been obliterated. Disappointed, he put the letter down and picked up the photograph. It showed two men standing behind two seated women. A small boy sat on the lap of the younger woman. The man standing behind the younger woman was the wounded Captain. Igor thought the woman to be about the same age as his wife, Trishka, and they were similar in appearance. He leaned nearer to the candle for a closer look. Then he got up and found a torch and held it to the photograph. His eyes widened.

'Good God!' he said out loud, 'it *is* Trishka – and that's mother!'

He continued staring at the small snapshot, questions with no answers racing through his head. He turned it over, and on the back was the stamp of a photographers shop in Bournemouth, England. Only two things were clear. First, the picture told him that his wife and mother had, somehow, got to England. Secondly, they had clearly thought that both he and his father were dead, and found other men to take their place. There was no other explanation.

He picked up the identity card again, the name seemed more important to him now.

'Denkov,' he read out quietly. 'Captain Leon Denkov.'

Slowly, he sat down on his bunk, still staring at the small photograph on the identity card. Of one thing he was certain. Even if he had the address of his wife, he knew that he could not write a letter.

CHAPTER 24

May 1944

Thelma leaned forward over the steering wheel. 'What's the address again, Max? There's been so much bombing around here I can't see any road signs to go by.'

Max looked at the piece of paper in his hand. 'It's off the Finchley Road,' he said, 'between West Hampstead and the Cricklewood Road. A place called Fortune Green.'

Thelma slowed the car. 'I think this is Finchley Road, so it's around here somewhere,' she said, her eyes squinting in concentration.

After Scotland, London looked bleak and war-torn. There was a different feeling about it too. The uniforms of many different nationalities were noticeable, but the Americans, who were everywhere, seemed carefree and relaxed; enjoying the experience of being in England and walking out with local girls. Different to the British, whose expressions after four years of war had become strained and war weary.

Max reflected that the war had changed dramatically in 1943. Germany was crumbling against the advances of the Russians in the East and the Allies in the West. No one knew when the invasion of Europe was to take place, but everyone knew it would be soon. The whole country seemed to be on edge; waiting for the final push towards victory.

Max had to report to a secret location on the south coast by 6 am the following morning, but before that he was determined to spend a little time with his wife, and see Trishka and his grandson. It might be the last time he would see them, because he did not expect to survive the war. Although efforts had been made to stop him, and he had pretended to give in gracefully, he was determined to fight alongside the men that he had trained so hard. He was tired of fighting the war from behind a desk.

He leaned forward. 'This looks like it, Thelma, pull up at number seven.'

From inside the house, Anna heard the car draw up to the kerb and stop. Through the lace curtain she saw that it was a military car, and she felt her heart thump when she saw that it was Max. She watched as his female driver got out and open the rear door. As Max got out she could see that he was much thinner, but he looked fit and, as always, handsome in his Colonel's uniform.

She was about to turn and go to the front door when she saw something that stopped her. It instantly deflated her joy and made her heart pound harder. She saw his driver say something to him, something confidential and with a reassuring smile, and at the same time place her hand on his arm. It was the kind of small, intimate, gestures that lovers make to each other.

Anna turned away from the window and waited for the knock on the door. She quickly suppressed her anger. It would be disastrous to make a scene; that was the last thing she wanted, so she would have to pretend that she had seen nothing, did not suspect anything. She braced herself, determined not to let her feelings show. When the knock came she opened the door and tried to look surprised at seeing him. She gave a warm smile

'Max! What a lovely surprise!' she said, and moved forward to embrace him.

He gave her a kiss and a long hug. 'Hello, Anna, it's good to see you too.' He kissed her again.

'How long have you got Max? Have you some leave? Can you stay a few days?' Flustered by his kisses, she blurted out the questions too quickly.

Max smiled, pleased to see her reaction to his embrace.

'No, Anna, I regret I'm not on leave - I've only got a couple of hours.'

Anna did not bother to ask any more questions, she knew it was pointless.

'Two hours - that's a pity,' she said, 'but please, come in,' and stood aside for him to enter. She looked out at the car. She wanted to meet the woman who had shown such affection to her husband.

'What about your driver, Max,' she said innocently. 'Why not ask her in as well. If you're able to stay for a full two hours she will have a long wait sitting in the car on her own.'

Max hesitated. He had not expected this - not anticipated that he would have to introduce his wife to his mistress.

'Err, she may wish to go and visit someone herself whilst I'm here,' he blustered. But seeing the look of reproach on Anna's face, he added, 'Okay, I'll go and ask her.'

Anna watched him from the door as he went to the car and spoke to Thelma. They talked for almost a minute, then the drivers' door opened and Thelma got out. Max led her towards the door.

'Anna, this is Thelma, my driver and trusted right arm. Thelma, this is my wife, Anna.'

Each looked keenly into the other's eyes as they shook hands. Anna tried to keep her face composed, but instinct told Thelma that Anna was aware of her relationship with Max.

'Please - come in,' said Anna, and ushered them into the sitting room. 'I was just about to make a cup of tea, would you like one?

Max looked at Thelma. Anna knew that he was feeling embarrassed, a telltale flush was creeping up his ears

'Thanks, I'd love one,' said Thelma.

'Yes, thank you Anna. We've just driven down from York and haven't managed to stop anywhere.'

Anna raised her eyebrows. 'You mean you haven't had anything to eat or drink all day?'

They shook their heads. 'No, I wanted to get here before the blackout,' said Max, 'so I bullied Thelma into driving without a break.'

Thelma gave Anna a quick smile. 'He didn't really – bully me I mean,' she said.

Anna nodded, slightly surprised to find herself feeling grateful to Thelma, rather than jealous and antagonistic.

'Well, you'll need something to eat as well. We haven't got a lot of choice, what with the rationing, but I've got eggs – so how about eggs on toast?'

'Thanks, Anna, that sounds good,' said Max.

Thelma nodded in agreement. 'Yes, thank you,' she said, and then swayed on her feet. Anna put a hand out to steady her.

'You look exhausted, sit down while I fetch the tea.'

Thelma nodded gratefully, but asked. 'Could I use the bathroom first, and have a glass of water?' She couldn't tell them the real reason for feeling feint - not now. Not ever.

'Of course,' said Anna, pointing to the bathroom. She turned towards the kitchen.

'Trishka has taken the children to the pictures,' she said over her shoulder. 'To see the *Wizard of Oz*. She should be back soon.'

'I hope so,' said Max, 'I would like to see her and the children before we leave.'

Max had accepted that Trishka was hardly to blame for getting pregnant by Leon Denkov. She had been told that Igor was dead and Max was convinced that, although she and Leon had been living in close proximity since the beginning of the war, they had not slept together before she became a widow. But now he had some bad news to tell her - to tell them both. He had thought about not telling them anything, but decided against it.

He got up and went into the kitchen. Anna glanced over to him and gave him a smile. 'I'm sorry I can't offer you a better meal than this,' she said.

'That will be fine, Anna, I hope we'll not be leaving you to go hungry,'

'No, we can get plenty of eggs - several of our neighbours keep a few chickens. We either barter or pay the price.'

Max stood awkwardly at her side. Anna guessed that her husband had something to say. She turned and looked at him.

'What is it Max?'

Max hesitated. 'It's Leon Denkov, Anna, we've heard that he's been killed in Italy. '

Anna stared at him, her face distraught. 'Oh my God,' she said, and stood silent for a few seconds. Max saw tears come to her eyes. 'Poor Trishka,' she said quietly. 'First Igor, now Leon.'

Max nodded. 'Yes, I'm very sorry, Anna. He was a good man.'

Anna put the eggs and toast onto the plates. Max was anticipating her next question. If he knew about Leon, Anna would expect him to know about Jak Zenski, but would be reluctant to ask. He decided that there was little point in not telling her what he knew.

'I'm afraid the news from Poland is not good either. We have not heard from Jak Zenski and his party for several months. He was involved with organising Polish resistance, and the Nazis have been ruthless in smashing it. We don't hold out much hope for him'

Anna felt a wrench at her insides. She nodded. 'Thank you for telling me, Max,' she said, putting her hand on his arm. 'I'd rather believe that he is still alive, because you know that I feel very deeply for him. I don't think we would still be alive and in England but for Jak and Leon.' Then she raised her hand to his cheek. 'But Jak was not my husband, you are.'

Max gave a nod and squeezed her hand, and then followed her back to the dining room, carrying a glass of water for Thelma.

As they ate Thelma told Anna how her husband and Stefan had been such good friends, which brought tears to the eyes of them both. Turning to other subjects they talked about the progress of the war, and Poland, and the farm, which they doubted they would ever see again. And then Max looked at his watch. It was time to go, and Trishka and the children had not returned.

'She'll be sorry not to have seen you Max - she must have stayed to see the film through again. Can't you stay a little longer?'

Max shook his head. 'We've still got a long drive ahead of us, Anna - I doubt that we will get any sleep as it is. Tell her I'm sorry not to have said goodbye, and how sorry I am about Leon.'

Anna got up and went and kissed him. 'Thank you Max, I'll tell her.'

He put on his coat and moved towards the door. As Thelma went to the car he reached into his pocket and brought out an envelope.

'Put this in a drawer – just in case. It's my will – for what it's worth.'

Anna looked at the envelope, reluctant to take it.

'Oh, Max,' she said, and put her arms around his neck. 'Take care – I don't want to read a will, I want you to come back.'

He kissed her and put the envelope into her hand. 'Don't worry, I'll be careful,' he said, knowing that being careful was no guarantee against being killed.

CHAPTER 25

June 6th 1944

At five minutes to one in the morning the dim light snapped off and the hole in the 'plane opened. Below it the vague outline of the coast of France could be seen. Flak burst all around the plane in great globes of red and purple as it coasted in towards the dropping zone.
Max took a gulp of the cold night air whipping through the fuselage and glued his eyes to the spot where the red light would show. It came on. The combined noise of the flak the engines and the wind made even shouting impossible, so Max went down the line, tapped each man on the arm and gave a thumb up sign. Within seconds the light changed to green

There was a rapid shuffling down to the hole and one by one they jumped into space. Max felt a jerk as his parachute opened and when it stopped twisting he looked down for his landmark; a church with a wood beyond that was to be the rendezvous point. But the wind caught him and pulled him to the east. He wrestled with his straps, but it was no use, and he came down in an orchard not far from a farmhouse. His harness caught in the branches of a tree and he was left dangling. He slapped at it and dropped to the ground, landing heavily on his left foot. He grunted with pain and cursed as he rolled on the ground.

Reaching out to the trunk of the tree he pulled himself up and wiped the sweat off his brown-painted face. He put his left foot out and took a step, only to collapse again as pain seared up his leg. Cursing again, he sat with his back to the tree and looked helplessly into the darkness. Dare he crawl to the farmhouse to ask for help? Machine guns and small arms fire started up all around him, and he groped around for his automatic rifle. His hand found it as two figures loomed out of the darkness and stood in front of him.

'*Bonjour monsieur, Vive le France,*' said a low voice. Then, in English, 'you are hurt?'

Relieved that they were not Germans, Max answered. 'Yes, left foot buggered up I'm afraid.'

Without another word, while his companion quickly gathered up the parachute and Max's equipment, the Frenchman bent down and pulled Max to his feet. With one arm around each of their shoulders they walked him towards the farmhouse and stopped near an outside wall. A small pile of logs was kicked aside, revealing a trapdoor. Pulling it open, Max was carried down to an underground cellar.

'My men will be looking for me,' said Max, as they lowered him against cellar wall.

'We will get word to them – give me the name of an officer.'

'There is Major Parwitz, or Captain Krewz, but any Polish soldier will do. Tell them to pass the word that Colonel Max is slightly injured but safe.'

Max felt a hand briefly on his shoulder.

'*Bonne* - stay quiet, we will be back,' said the Frenchman. They clambered up the steps and closed the trapdoor, leaving Max in total darkness listening to the rattle of gunfire overhead.

*

Four days later Waffen-SS Colonel Hedrick von Schtanger stretched out a jackboot and turned over the uniformed body in front of him. The disdain on his face turned to a scowl.

'Ach so, it is not just the partisan swine that we are up against, there are also Polish commandos,' he said to the Captain standing at his side. He looked up. 'What do you know about them?'

Since being transferred from the Russian front – the only two officers in the division to have survived – there was a great deal of informality between the Colonel and his Captain.

Captain Retzlin shook his head. 'Not a great deal yet, *mien Colonel*. Except that there is a rumour that a high-ranking Polish officer is leading them.'

'You think that the partisan terrorists and these Poles are working together, led by this officer?'

'Yes, *mien Colonel,* but I do not think there are many Poles - just a small group that have been cut off from the main forces.

Colonel Schtanger jutted his chin out, lips pressed together in a thin line.

'Then we must find them quickly - find them and kill them. They have caused us enough trouble already.'

His Captain looked at him doubtfully. 'That might be difficult *mien Colonel*. We cannot spare men from the front positions and our informers have clamped up or disappeared since the invasion. It is difficult to get any reliable information from the locals.'

'Clamped up and disappeared, have they! Well, we have got to loosen some tongues. Take the armoured car and twenty men to the village and round up all the inhabitants into the square. I will join you in fifteen minutes. Make sure the mayor is amongst them.' He pointed to the body of the soldier. 'And take that with you.'

Captain Retzlin nodded in acknowledgement and saluted. He turned and gestured towards a Lieutenant who was standing nearby. Ten minutes later a truck containing twenty black uniformed SS with the body of the Polish commando followed the armoured car towards the nearest village.

Von Schtanger busied himself with preparing to defend his position just a few kilometres from Caen. The situation was getting desperate. With just four functional Panzers left he was running short of fuel and ammunition, and his men had not had a decent meal in the last twenty-four hours. He'd been assured that supplies and reinforcements were on their way. That was two days ago. In spite of this his orders were to hold his ground and fight until the last man. But he knew that he could not carry on much longer. His troops might find something to eat, steal if necessary, but they could not continue fighting without ammunition. Now he had found out why his supplies were being disrupted he intended to do something about it.

Fifteen minutes later he jumped into his staff car and directed his driver to take him to the village. Progress was slow, due to the number of wrecked vehicles and holes in the road made by Allied bombing.

When he got there he found that Captain Retzlin had gathered about forty residents into the centre next to the church. The adults looked sullen and scared, and most of the children were crying at the black uniformed SS that stood guarding them. Captain Rezling, pistol in hand, had singled out the Mayor, and was pointing to the body of the dead soldier that had been dumped on the ground. Von Schtanger stepped out of his car.

Ignoring the mayor, he walked up to Captain Retzlin. 'Has he told you where these scum are hiding?' he said.

'No *mien Colonel*, he says that he had no idea there were Allied soldiers nearby, or how many, and denies there are any partisans in the village working with them.'

*

Three hundred metres away, through a ventilation slit high in the wall of a tall stone barn, Max eased his injured leg into a more comfortable position as he looked down at the scene below through the telescopic sight of a captured sniper rifle. He was not intending to use the rifle and risk giving his position away, even though the rifle was fitted with a silencer.

Focusing the sight on the dead soldier on the ground his face was grim as he recognised it as one his men. The twenty men – now nineteen - that he had left were out of the village with the local partisans attacking a radio and communications headquarters. He assumed that was where his man had got killed. He moved the sight to the mayor, who was shaking his head with a shrug. If he was denying all knowledge of any partisan or commando activity, Max knew he was not telling the truth, because the mayor was the partisan leader. But what the mayor did not know, or any of the other villagers, was that Max had returned quietly to the village during the night and was hiding in the barn.

He moved the sight to see the strutting SS Colonel shouting and pointing towards the people lined up in front of them. The mayor still shook his head, at which point the Colonel spoke to the Captain and took out his pistol. The Colonel gestured with it towards the hostages. The mayor shrugged his shoulders once again and, turning his back on the Colonel, started walking towards his villagers. The Colonel screeched at the mayor to return, but he kept walking.

The Colonel pointed the pistol at the head of the retreating mayor. Max saw the head of the mayor jolt forward as the bullet struck. Some of the women screamed as the mayor fell, his body jerking in his death throes. Max blinked with shock.

'You murdering bastard,' he said out loud, and his reflexes took over. He focused the telescopic sight on the Colonel's head and pulled the trigger. The rifle gave a soft 'pop,' no louder than an air gun.

Colonel von Schtanger was about to say something to the hostages when the bullet hit him an inch above his ear. He stood with his mouth open for about three seconds before he slumped slowly to the ground beside the body of the mayor. There was a stunned silence as the SS troops turned and saw their Colonel lying on the ground with blood slowly forming a pool around his head. With no sound to go by they were unsure what had happened. The Captain was the first to recover and started to give orders to shoot the hostages. That was when Max fired his second shot, and the bullet hit Captain Retzling between the eyes.

Having started, he realised that he had no choice but to keep on firing, even though he only had eighteen bullets left. He knew his only chance was to kill or maim as many of the enemy as possible before they had time to pinpoint his position and organise an attack. Through the telescopic sight he sought out the next officer. He found the Lieutenant just as he was beginning to point in the direction of the barn. Like the others he fell with a bullet in the head.

Some of the soldiers were now running towards the armoured car. Waiting until the first one was climbing aboard before firing, Max saw him clutch at his neck and fall. Two more who tried to mount the armoured car also went down.

Max looked up quickly; a Sergeant had worked out the direction from which the shots were coming and was shouting orders, trying to rally the men into an attack on the barn. He put his eye back to the rifle and fired. The Sergeant threw up his arms and dropped to the ground. The villagers had scattered and taken refuge in the church. Now they were safely out of the way Max could shoot more freely. He picked out the ones who were trying to assume command. Some were firing back, but they were firing at the open window of the adjoining building.

He loaded his last five bullets. Then the machine gun of the armoured car started to rattle. Someone had reached it. Max ducked as the bullets sprayed against the wall of the barn before concentrating on the window of the next building. He could just see the top of the head of the machine gunner and took careful aim. He fired and the head disappeared. Then he saw what he had been hoping for. The truck behind the armoured car started to reverse. Those still standing ran towards it and jumped aboard - they were pulling out.

He took two more pot shots at the windscreen of the truck before it got out of range. He raised his head. The SS staff car, its doors gaping open, was at the centre of the carnage. The armoured car had also been abandoned. But he was pleased to see that, apart from the mayor, there were no civilians among the bodies strewn about. There were slight movements and groans from one or two of the fallen SS, but they were beyond fighting. He patted the polished wooden stock of the Czech-made rifle with approval and stood it carefully against the wall. He felt sad that it would have to be discarded, since it was doubtful that he would find any more ammunition of the right calibre.

Wincing, he shifted his injured leg, then reached down and lifted up a basket and placed it beside him on a wooden box. Taking out a bottle of wine, he took a few gulps and dipped again into the basket. Wrapped in a piece of clean linen was a *baguette* filled with cheese and he took it, broke it in half, and took a bite.

As he ate he saw the villagers emerge from the church. Some of the men started collecting the firearms that were scattered about; others checked the bodies and began to strip them of anything useful. Any SS that were still alive were dispatched with a bullet to the head. Max continued to eat. He felt no pity for the dead SS. The defenceless mayor had been shot in cold blood and they had come very close to murdering all the villagers without a second thought. His only concern was that the SS would return with reinforcements before he could get the civilians safely away.

But the SS did not return. The next day Canadian Infantry walked into the village, and with them about fifty of Max's Polish commandos. After they were reunited with the rest of his men, Max was taken away in an ambulance and flown back to England.

CHAPTER 26

The clouds looked like lead and it was bitterly cold. There had been some flurries of snow, but it looked like a heavy fall was about to start. The men were wearing everything they had to keep warm. Igor had found Mr Lubin's old clothes useful after all, especially the goatskin waistcoat. He hitched the blanket tighter around his shoulders and read the message through again before pushing it into his pocket. He glanced over to where Spencer was busy stripping down and cleaning the two Browning's on the jeep he'd been assigned to.

Four weeks ago they had saved Spencer's life after he and his partisans had walked into a German ambush. He had been the only one still alive when Igor's patrol arrived on the scene; still firing his Bren gun even though wounded. As he recovered from his wounds the Canadian had gained the respect and friendship of the whole patrol. Possessing all the specialist skills that they had, plus a few more, his modest and quiet self-assurance had quickly made him 'one of them.'

It was time for the evening meal and Igor walked over to him.

'Grub up, Spencer,' he said. 'Have a wash and join me over there will you?'

The Canadian looked up and grinned. 'OK skipper,' he said, 'just finished.'

No one could recall the time when Spencer had started calling Igor 'skipper' rather than 'sir.' It had seemed the natural thing to do, and was part of the measure of his acceptance that no one had noticed, or cared.

Igor waited until the meal was over before he pulled out the message that he had received earlier. The men looked at him expectantly. A rumour had been whispered around.

Igor opened it out and glanced up.

'As you know, Popski returned to duty a couple of weeks ago, and it seems that he's been busy relocating our HQ further up the coast to Bari. He's recalling all patrols to rendezvous at the new HQ within the next seven days.'

He paused and returned the grin that the men gave him. They had been working behind enemy lines for three months and were ready for some leave.

Igor's face then became more serious. 'There's one other thing that I've to mention,' he said. 'We took on Spencer here when he was wounded, and since his recovery he's somehow become a useful member of the patrol. But, strictly speaking, now that we're being recalled, we should be saying our goodbyes to him, because, as you're aware, Popski is the sole recruiter for PPA, and I've no authority to add him to our patrol.'

Someone murmured 'Too bad', and the others nodded in agreement.

Igor turned to Spencer. 'But I think we all agree, Spencer, that we don't really want to push you out. So, unless you want to go back and recruit more partisans, I'd like to take you back with us and introduce you to Popski, and see if he'll take you on.'

Spencer gave an appreciative nod. 'Thanks, skip, I'd like that,' he said.

'Good,' said Igor. 'But if Popski does take you on, you'll probably have to lose your stripes and start as a private.'

The Canadian gave a shrug. 'That's OK – I've heard that you had to start at the bottom when you joined PPA'

Igor gave a grin. 'Yes - and it was worth it, believe me.'

*

When they reached Bari three days later, they found that the new HQ was a small hotel overlooking the sea front, previously occupied by the Germans. The men were billeted in nearby villas. Popski greeted them and showed them around. He kept his left hand in his pocket, giving him a casual appearance. When he took it out they saw that he'd lost his hand, and in its place was a stainless steel hook, which was covered in leather cut from a glove.

Seeing Igor's glance, he said. 'You'll be surprised how the barrel of a sub-machine gun nestles into it very handy.'

When Igor introduced Spencer to Popski, he took him by the elbow.

'Come and have a drink, both of you, and tell me what you've been up to.'

Thirty minutes later, after listening quietly to Spencer's story, Popski turned to Igor. 'And I assume you explained to corporal Spencer that, if accepted into PPA, he would be starting as a private?'

Igor smiled. 'Yes, Popski, I've told him that.'

'Hmm,' said Popski, and took a sip of whiskey. 'Well, corporal, I have to tell you that I do not need any more privates.'

He paused just long enough to see the look of disappointment on both their faces, and then smiled.

'But what I *do* need is a Sergeant - someone who has already shown his mettle, and can mould others into our ways. So, if you would like to join us as a Sergeant with Captain Radovak's patrol, I'll be pleased to confirm your appointment and advise your old HQ of your transfer. My new orders are that I can recruit who I like – and no questions – which is helpful.'

He sat back in his chair as the two men grinned at each other. The Canadian held out his hand to Popski.

'Thank you, sir – or may I call you Popski?'

'You may call me what you like, Sergeant Spencer, so long as it comes with a measure of respect and affection.' Then he looked at Igor.

'And in case you think that it was a slip of the tongue when I just called you 'Captain' – it was not. I think you, and a few others, are well overdue for promotion, and a list of the new promotions and the makeup of the new patrols will be on the notice board in the morning. In the meantime, congratulations.' He held out his hand.

'Thanks, Popski,' said Igor, as he shook hands. He wanted to say more. He wanted to tell Popski that he would willingly serve under him in any capacity. Rank was not his criterion. But he suspected that Popski already knew this. To Popski his promotion was pure necessity. There was a rumour that the strength of PPA was to be increased to 100 men. If this was the case, he badly needed experienced men to train the new recruits.

*

237

After the patrols had arrived and were settled in, Popski disappeared to Taranto to interview potential recruits. He returned five days later. Out of a total of 125 men who had expressed an interest to join PPA, he had selected just 24.

The new men arrived in ones and twos in the days leading up to Christmas. No time was wasted in starting their training, and all the existing members of PPA had a part in the training programme. On 28 December, the news came through that the Canadians had broken through the eastern flank of the Gustav Line and taken the town of Ortona. On 29 December Popski called everyone together for a briefing. He stood in front of a large map of Italy. South of Rome, a red line had been drawn across Italy. Popski pointed to the red line.

'This is where the Germans have decided to make a stand. It's called the Gustav Line. Here in the middle is a place called Monte Cassino, which is an old monastery on top of a mountain. It commands the whole Po valley, and the route to Rome. It will not be easy to take.' He moved his pointer to the eastern side of the Gustav Line.

'But here, near the coast, the Canadians have broken through and taken Ortona. And this is where we will be heading, and will infiltrate behind the enemy lines from this point. Initially, there will be five patrols going out, known simply as; a, b, c, d and e. I will be leading 'a' patrol. To save time, we will be travelling up the coast by sea. Because of the distances involved, we will have to be supplied from the air. The objectives will remain the same, namely, to gather intelligence of enemy positions and their strength, and report back to Eighth Army HQ, who will, I suspect, organise bombing raids. I'm sure that there will also be plenty of action as the opportunities arise, but always remember that we are not there to take on the German army by ourselves, our priority is intelligence gathering, and supporting local resistance. We will be leaving in twenty four hours.' He paused and looked around. 'Any questions?'

Everyone looked thoughtful but no one raised an arm.

'Very good, if anyone thinks of a question, raise it with your patrol leader. There will a final briefing of patrol leaders and senior NCO's two hours before departure. Thank you gentlemen - and good luck.'

They had cheered when the news came through on the 4th June that the Allies had taken Rome. And then, yesterday, the 6th June, they had celebrated again when they heard that the Allies had landed in Normandy. And so they were in a relaxed mood that morning, when rejoicing locals surrounded them as they entered another village. Wine, eggs, flowers and anything else the villagers had, was pressed on them.

A middle aged man climbed onto the bonnet of Igor's jeep with a bottle in his hand, yelling 'Viva America, Viva Churchill' before he appeared to slip off. Simultaneously a single shot was heard and there was a brief two-second silence as the crowd realised that the man had been shot. In unison, the women screamed and went scurrying for cover. A second shot shattered the steering wheel of the jeep an inch from Igor's hand, and Igor heard Spencer behind him mutter 'I've got him.'

There was a click as he cocked the Browning and swung it around towards the church tower. But he was a split second too late. A third bullet ripped into his head and he was thrown backwards onto the road. He died instantly. At the same time a Browning from one of the other jeeps opened up at the bell tower of the church. Rushing the church, they found the bodies of three Waffen –SS. Two had sniper rifles.

The mayor told them that the three Germans had been captured by the partisans and left in the village for Allied interrogation. That was two weeks ago. But with the news of Rome falling to the Americans, and the D-Day landings in France they had been released and told to make their way back to Germany. Instead, knowing where the sniper rifles were hidden, they had obviously decided to continue with the war.

Mortified at the stupidity of the villagers, Igor had the body of Spencer wrapped in a blanket and in silence he led his patrol out of the village.

*

Igor put his pen down and read through the letter once again. He wiped at the moisture in his eyes. It was addressed to Spencer's

239

father, telling him that his son had been killed in action. Igor told him of the high regard they all had for him, and how he had talked affectionately about his 'old man' and the farm, and what plans they had to improve and expand it when he got back home.

Over the last few months Igor and Spencer had become close friends. On the days when the weather was too bad to operate, Spencer would bring out his small travelling chess set and they would sit for hours as they battled the moves. And Spencer had showed Igor one of the letters his father had written. In it his father had said that, apart from sitting on a tractor, his back was now so bad he couldn't do much work, but Italian and German POWs were working the farm OK. He just hoped that, when the war ended, his son would be able to get back home before the POWs were sent back to Europe.

Igor signed the letter, folded it, and put it into an airmail envelope. Sinking down onto his bunk, he silently cursed the whole bloody German race for starting the war. They must have realised by now that they could not win, but kept on killing.

CHAPTER 27

Max felt a kiss on his cheek and opened his eyes. Anna was smiling down at him. She was in her matron's uniform, and the faint smell of carbolic soap and antiseptic told him he was in hospital.

'Hello, Max,' she said. 'I had a telegram two days ago saying you were missing in action. So when they brought you in on a stretcher last night I nearly passed out- but they told me you were only asleep. They had given you a sleeping pill for the journey.'

Max smiled and reached out to squeeze her hand, and then pulled her down to kiss her. Her face was pale and weary, but she looked happy to see him.

'I thought I was dreaming for a moment,' he said. 'It's good to see you Anna - but I don't know why they've brought me here, all I've got is a sprained ankle.'

'No Max, you've got a broken ankle. It's in plaster now, and you'll be out of action for a few weeks. You're due for a rest anyway.'

He nodded, groaning inwardly at the thought of being inactive while the war was still raging in France.

'It'll give you the chance to get to know your grandsons,' Anna continued.

Max brightened a little at this thought, but was anxious that his recent experiences behind the lines in France should be reported as soon as possible. And he wanted to see Thelma again. She had wept when they parted just before he left for France. Like Anna, she had thought he would not come back. But he wanted to let her know that he'd survived the first onslaught and was back in England.

'There's some breakfast on the way,' said Anna, and lifted up a walking stick. 'After that you can get up if you like and try walking up and down with this. I'll hang it on the bedpost here.' She gave him a quick wave as she turned to attend to her other duties.

'How long do I have to stay in hospital?' Max called after her.

'Only until the end of my shift,' she said, turning back. 'We need your bed. Then you can come and spend a night or two with us before you decide what to do. You're welcome to stay longer, but I don't think having your ankle in plaster is going to keep you away from the war for long.'

After breakfast two officers from British Intelligence visited Max, and for the next two hours he gave them a detailed report on his experiences.

At the end of her shift Anna arranged for an ambulance to take them back to her house. He spent three happy days getting to know Gregor and his little half brother Simon, as well as making his peace with Trishka. On the fourth day he telephoned his old HQ and arranged for a staff car to come and pick him up.

'I would like my old driver, if available,' he said. 'Sergeant Dorska.'

'Sergeant Thelma Dorska? I'm afraid she's not with us any more, sir,' said the voice at HQ, 'Corporal Butler will be your driver, unless you have any objections.'

Max had no idea who Corporal Butler was.

'Err, no objections,' he said, 'that will be fine. Has Sergeant Dorska been posted?'

'She hasn't been posted sir, she resigned from the service and left last week.'

He was taken aback by this news, but tried not to let it show in his voice. He could find out more when he got back to HQ.

'I see,' he said, 'thank you - goodbye,' and put the phone down.

He continued staring at the phone for a few seconds. If Thelma had left last week it meant that she must have made her request before he left for France. He was a little annoyed that she had not mentioned her plans, but was confident that there was a letter waiting for him somewhere, explaining her actions and giving her new address.

Anna was on duty at the hospital when Max was picked up. He left a note to say that he had reported back to duty. Anna assumed that Thelma had picked him up, and the main reason for returning to duty was to be with her. Jealousy and anger swelled inside her at this thought. How could he do this to her? She had felt that an unspoken forgiving had taken place. Max had forgiven her for falling in love with Jak, and she had forgiven him for falling in love with Thelma.

But she felt cheated. It had been easier for him to forgive her because he knew it was unlikely she would ever see Jak again. But Thelma was here, in the UK, waiting for him, and he'd gone back to her. Anna sat down and cried as she read his note again. It was kind and loving and said how much he had enjoyed the last few days together. But he had gone back to *her*. What could she do? She did not want to upset him by showing her anger; she was afraid she might lose him altogether if she did.

Anna stood up as she heard Trishka and the children come through the front door. The problem of Thelma would have to wait, she decided, probably to the end of the war. The war was not over yet, and she dare not think what she would do if he didn't come back.

*

Ten days later she had a letter to say he was back in Scotland. Two weeks after that Max turned up at her house on a Sunday morning. His ankle was out of plaster but he still needed a walking stick to help with a slight limp. Anna guessed that he had come to tell her that he was off to war again. She embraced him on the doorstep and gave him a kiss on the cheek, and then her eyes went to his car.

'You should have warned me you were coming - you could have stayed for Sunday lunch.'

'I'm sorry Anna - there was no time. I've got to fly out again tonight, but wanted to see you before I went.'

'Surely you've time for a cup of tea – and your driver, Thelma, isn't it?'

Max glanced at his watch. 'Yes, thanks Anna, we could do with a cup of tea – but that's not Thelma, it's my new driver, Corporal Butler – I'll just go and ask her.'

He left Anna staring after him. For weeks she had assumed he was continuing his affair with Thelma. Had she been wrong all this time? She watched as he escorted his new driver up the path and introduced her. She smiled her welcome.

'Pleased to meet you Corporal Butler - come in and sit down while I put the kettle on.' She couldn't wait another second to learn where Thelma was. 'What's happened to Thelma, Max, has she been posted,' she called out from the kitchen.

There was a slight pause before he replied. 'Err, no - after I left for D-Day she resigned from the service, I'm not sure where she is Anna, no one seems to know her new address'

Anna came back into the room. 'Oh, so you haven't seen her or heard from her – how strange – I hope she's all right.'

The first flash of relief that her husband had not seen Thelma since he came back from France was replaced with irritation. If Max and Thelma had not been lovers after all, she had put herself through a lot of unnecessary worrying.

Max noticed the look of puzzlement on the face of his new driver as she listened to their conversation. Corporal Jane Butler was a smart blond and a competent driver, married to an American pilot.

He smiled at her. 'Sergeant Dowska's husband was a friend of our son Stefan,' he said. 'They were in the same squadron - and were both shot down over the English Channel within two days of each other. Unfortunately, Thelma – Sergeant Dorska - also lost the rest of her family in the blitz.'

Jane Butler looked concerned. 'Oh, how awful,' she said. 'I spoke to Sergeant Dowska several times before she left - I had no idea.' She shook her head.

'It makes me feel - well - guilty somehow. I haven't lost any of my relations, and Johnny, my husband, has done so many missions he's now been grounded for the rest of the war.'

Max glanced up at Anna. 'No need to feel guilty, corporal, just be thankful,' he said. Then he had another thought. 'Did Sergeant Dowska, by any chance, leave her new address with you?'

'No, sir,' she said, and paused. 'No, wait - I'm sure she left a temporary address until she got settled. It will be on her file.'

'Hmm, I had a look in the file, there was nothing.'

'Well, I'm fairly sure she left an address with someone. Would you like me to try to find out?

He nodded. 'If you could, corporal, I'd be grateful. But even if you come up with an address, I won't be able to do anything about it until I get back.'

Anna, listening in, was pleased to learn that Thelma had gone but, strangely, she felt an urge to help. She handed out the tea.

'If there *is* an address for Thelma, Max, would you like to write her a quick letter and leave it with me – I'll send it on for you.'

Max, sipping his tea, looked at Anna in surprise over the rim of the cup. He lowered the cup and gave a nod.

'Thank you, Anna, if you have a piece of writing paper, I'll write a few lines – just in case. I'd like to think that she's OK – I was surprised that she left as she did.'

Anna nodded thoughtfully. 'She probably had her reasons,' she said, and began to wonder what those reasons could be

CHAPTER 28

Northern Italy, April 1945

Leaving the jeeps well hidden, Igor walked up the sloping ground with his two Sergeants and stopped in the shade of an olive tree. For the past four months PPA had been trailing the remnants of a division of Waffen-SS, the same unit whose snipers had killed Spencer. In their retreat they had left a trail of death. Every village or small town they had passed through had witnessed atrocities. From shooting captured partisans out of hand, they had progressed to shooting all the males they could find, young or old.

Popski had advised all PPA patrols to report if they spotted them, but not to engage. But Igor's interest in them was personal, and he'd carefully plotted all the places where they had been sighted. Even so, because of the need to pursue other activities, the trail had been lost for several weeks.

But, two days ago, they had come across a group of partisans who had been badly mauled by retreating SS, and he decided to follow the partisans' directions and see if it was the same division

Not that he wished to confront the SS head on, but having been recently re-equipped with ammunition and supplies by air, he intended to prod the enemy at a distance. He doubted that they were getting fresh supplies of any kind. They were a spent force but, being fanatical Nazi SS, were still ruthless to anyone who got in their way.

From higher ground, Igor scanned the village. There was no sign of life. He decided to take two jeeps into the village and leave two in reserve.

'It could be a trap, skipper,' said Cooper, the leader of the second jeep.

'Yes, it could be,' said Igor, thoughtfully, 'but I've a hunch that the place has been abandoned. Anyway, we'll soon find out.'

From experience, Igor knew there was little point in a slow approach on these occasions. A fast moving vehicle was harder to hit, so he drove as fast as the rough road allowed. Entering the village they skidded to a halt in the square. Igor looked around and his eyes stopped at what looked like bags of laundry spread out in the shade of a large tree near the church. Getting out he walked over. It was not laundry. They were bodies.

There was a creaking from the direction of the church, and the four of them instinctively crouched down and pointed their sub-machineguns towards the noise.

An old woman emerged through the door. She was wearing black, with a grey shawl covering her shoulders and white hair. She slowly descended the few steps from the church and walked towards the tree where they were standing. Without speaking she looked down at the bodies, shaking her head. She was weeping. Igor took her arm and led her to a nearby seat. He spoke to her in Italian.

'Can you tell me what happened?'

She continued shaking her head, and Igor began to think that she might be deaf. Then she took a corner of the shawl and wiped her eyes.

'Those devils have killed my husband and all these people,' she said, pointing. 'My husband was the mayor,' she added.

She spoke as though Igor and his men had not yet seen the bodies.

'Are there any Germans still in the village?'

'No, they have left - took all the food they could find, shot everybody they could find, and left.'

'Have they killed everyone but you?'

She lifted her hands in despair 'I think some ran away, I don't know.'

'How long is it since they left?'

She took a few seconds to answer. 'An hour – two? - I don't know.'

'Did you see which direction they took?'

She nodded. 'They took the road north, but stopped at Graziano's farm.'

'How far away is that?'

'Oh, about a kilometre - perhaps a little more.'

' And you're sure that they stopped there?'

'Yes, I was hiding in the bell chamber. You can see the farm clearly from there.'

'How many were there?'

She gave a slight shrug. 'Twenty - thirty - I'm not sure.'

Igor beckoned to Cooper. 'Get the other two jeeps to join us -we'll go and take a look at these bastards.'

The woman looked up at him.

'How many men have you?' she said.

'Ten,' he said.

'Ten?' she croaked out in disbelief, and shook her head, 'that is not enough.'

'Well, we'll see,' said Igor. 'Did you notice their uniforms?'

She spat on the ground in disgust. 'They are SS – the worst kind.'

While waiting for the other jeeps, Igor questioned the woman about the farmhouse and the terrain surrounding it. Learning that there were sufficient trees to give cover on two sides, but the front of the house would be more exposed.

As the other jeeps arrived she got up from the seat.

'I will come with you.' she said. 'I show you where to take cover - I know that farm well - I played there as a little girl.'

Igor looked at her doubtfully. 'No, it'll be too dangerous for you – just tell us where.'

'Dangerous?' she said, scornfully. 'What do I care? My husband is dead - my sons dead - the villagers murdered. My only wish is to see those swine killed.'

She looked around at them with pleading eyes, her face full of grief.

Igor relented. 'All right, show us the way - then you walk back here. Is that understood?'

She nodded. 'I will get my basket,' she said. She returned carrying a large wicker basket with three loaves of bread in it. Igor helped her into the back of his jeep and they set off.

The farmhouse was built of stone, with small windows and a solid looking door. Three trucks and a staff car were parked nearby. The woman showed them the best position for the jeeps. They were hidden from view, yet every angle was covered and no one would be able to escape without being seen.

As they got into position they were astonished to see the woman walking with her basket towards the farmhouse. They held their breath and waited. The woman was within twelve metres of the door when there was a rattle of a machine gun. She stopped, dropped her basket, and crumpled slowly to the ground.

'The buggers have gone and shot her!' gasped out Mac, Igor's driver, his finger twitching on the trigger of the 50mm Browning.

Igor, his face grim, held up his hand. 'Hold it – we can't help her now. I think she wanted to die. She did that to try to help us, and she has. Did you see the hay flying off that stack to the right of the farmhouse? They've got a machine gun hidden in there.'

'OK, skip, I've got it covered – just say when.'

'Give them a minute or two – see if they show themselves.'

They didn't have to wait long. About half a minute later the door of the farmhouse opened and two unkempt SS soldiers came out and walked towards the body. Talking and grinning to themselves, they bent down to pick up the loaves of bread.

Igor ground his teeth in anger. 'Right, let them know we're here.'

'My pleasure, skip,' said the other quietly, as he squinted down the sights of the Browning and closed his finger to the trigger.

The two SS were still grinning as the bullets ripped into them and slung them to the ground beside the woman. Then the Browning was directed to the haystack and raked it for a full eight seconds before stopping. The second jeep fired, concentrating on the farmhouse door. The door was blasted away, leaving just a few shards of splintered timber hanging on the hinges.

From one of the windows of the farmhouse a machine gun sprayed the trees to the right of Igor's jeep. They were firing blind but had managed to get the general direction. The third jeep opened up, concentrating on the window from which the firing was coming. The firing stopped abruptly. The fourth jeep fired at each of the remaining windows in turn. Suddenly there was silence.

Igor scanned the building through his binoculars. There was no movement, but he was suspicious that a counter-attack was being planned. Thirty seconds later they heard a dull 'stonk' and a mortar bomb exploded somewhere behind them. Two or three more, closer this time, followed it. From Igor's position there was no sign where the mortar was hidden. He was about to order his driver to reverse out of range when they heard a Browning open up from one of the other jeeps. After that the mortar bombing ceased. They waited again in silence.

'Switch to tracer bullets, Mac - we'll start firing at the roof. If we can set it on fire, we'll smoke them out. The others will catch on to what we're doing.'

Smiling, Mac changed the ammunition to tracer. It took him ten seconds.

'Right skip, ready when you are.'

'Okay, commence firing.'

After a quick spray of the nearest window, Mac directed his fire at the roof. Tiles started flying in all directions, then the tracers were hitting the rafters. When he stopped firing, thin wisps of smoke could be seen rising from the roof. By this time the other jeeps had followed Igor's lead. When they stopped firing the roof was well alight, and a slight breeze was fanning the flames into a crackling blaze.

As they watched, a white flag on a stick appeared in the open doorway. It was waved from side to side and then the soldier holding it emerged. After a few seconds he stepped aside, and out strode an SS Colonel, wearing a surprisingly clean and well pressed uniform. Tall, blond and fair skinned, he was holding his hands up level with his head, but still held a pistol in his right hand.

'They're surrendering, skipper,' said Mac, in an unbelieving voice.

Igor slung a sub machine gun over his shoulder and took out his revolver.

'Maybe – maybe not - bring your sub and stay two strides behind me - we'll go and see what he wants.'

He walked several paces to his right, so that he did not give his true position away. Then he strode out of the trees towards the farmhouse.

The German watched his approach. A small mean mouth twisted into a lopsided, arrogant smile. As Igor and Mac got within hearing distance, he spoke in perfect English.

'I am sorry to say that we have run out of ammunition, gentlemen, we are unable to continue the fight.'

Striving to remain calm, Igor continued walking. He stopped three metres away.

'Drop your weapon, Colonel - I assume you are surrendering.'

The Colonel glanced at Igor's shoulder flashes, noting his rank.

He stood up straight, his hands still above his head. 'I will only surrender my weapon to an officer of higher rank than myself.'

His face white with fury, Igor stared at him. This was the closest that he had ever been to a Waffen-SS officer - a live one anyway. A thought flashed through his mind how such an educated man had

250

become such a ruthless and dedicated killer. When surrender was only considered after they had run out of ammunition and could not kill any more.

'I am the highest rank you will get. Drop your weapon Colonel, and order your men to do the same and come out with their hands up.'

The SS Colonel looked at him scornfully. 'I repeat, I will only surrender to an officer of higher rank than myself.'

'And I repeat, Colonel – you, and the rest of your men, will drop your weapons.'

By now the grim smirk had disappeared from the face of the Colonel. His eyes narrowed at the impudence of the scruffy looking Captain in front of him.

'You speak English with an accent – are you not English?'

'No – Polish.'

The Nazi Colonel raised his eyebrows slightly. A flash of contempt crossed his face

'Polish!' He spat out the word with disgust. 'I will not surrender to a – Polish Captain, I will only surrender to…'

He didn't get any further. The barrel of Igor's revolver flicked up and he shot the Colonel through the heart. As he fell a stick grenade arched through the air from inside the farmhouse. Igor was pushed aside as Mac shouted 'Look out, skip!' and flashed his hand at the grenade, caught it, and lobbed it straight back through the open doorway. He flung himself to the ground as it exploded. Getting up, they began firing their sub-machine guns through the open doorway as they backed away. Running towards the jeep, there was a crashing behind them, and they turned to see that the explosion had caused the ceiling of the farmhouse to fall in, followed by the roof. They watched it burn.

There was a burst of gunfire from the rear of the farmhouse. Reaching the jeep, they went to investigate. Ten SS soldiers had been shot dead as they tried to make a dash from the rear of the house, firing as they went.

That evening, Igor reported to Popski that the SS Division was no more.

CHAPTER 29

July 1945

Max waved his convoy of fifteen Jeeps and assorted trucks to a stop as they came to a crossroad. A column of POWs walking towards a nearby railway station blocked the way. Most of them were in some kind of uniform but others were in rags. They all looked wretched and miserable, hungry and dirty. Some were limping along with makeshift crutches, others had their arms in a sling, and many had bandages around various parts of the body. All of the bandages looked dirty and needed changing, and Max wondered how long it would be before they received any further medical attention.

As the end of the column passed a POW with a bandage around his head looked towards the jeeps, which all had a small Polish flag attached to the bonnet. The prisoner raised his arm and waved it about, like a half-hearted Nazi salute, and then he raised his other arm and waved them both. A guard went up to him and pushed him forward roughly with the butt of his rifle. Max shook his head. He gestured to a British Sergeant standing nearby.

'That's a sorry looking lot, but they don't look German.'

The Sergeant gave him a salute. 'No sir,' he said, 'they're Poles. Some were fighting for the Russians; some were fighting for the Germans against the Russians, and the rest were slave labourers. They're on their way back to Poland.'

As the column disappeared from view, the prisoner with a bandaged head was still looking back and waving an arm in the air.

'Poor devils,' said Max, with a shake of his head, 'they're going back to a miserable life.'

The Sergeant looked at him. 'Surely not, sir,' he said. 'Those who were fighting on the German side might have a rough time, but those who were fighting for the Russians should be all right. And the slave labourers didn't have any choice, did they?'

'Those who were fighting for the Germans will probably be shot immediately,' said Max, 'if not, they'll end up in a Russian gulag with the others and worked to death. A Russian soldier is allowed to die fighting, or get wounded fighting, but not to be taken prisoner, wounded or not. To the Soviets it is a crime to be taken prisoner. So those Poles who fought for Russia will not be set free, at best they will become slave labourers like the rest. That is Stalin's way.'

The Sergeant looked at him with some doubt. He glanced at Max's shoulder flash.

'I see you're Polish sir, aren't you anxious to get back home?'

Max gave him a rueful smile. 'Not so keen as I was, Sergeant - Hitler has been kicked out of Poland, and Stalin is taking his place. That's not what the Poles have been fighting for.'

He nodded his goodbye as his driver started the engine and the convoy moved on again. The pitiful plight of his fellow countrymen continued to fill Max's mind. The war was over, but for millions the suffering would continue. He had no wish to go back to Poland if it was to be run by the USSR. A combined feeling of helplessness and weariness engulfed him, and keen as he was to get to Calais and over the Channel to England, he decided to camp overnight and make an early start in the morning.

*

Max was up at 6 am and shaving when the early quiet of the morning was disturbed by the sound of motor engines. He turned curious eyes towards the road.

As the noise got louder four vehicles came into view, travelling fast. In the lead was an ex-German staff car. The cross on the door had been roughly painted over with a white USA star, and on the bonnet fluttered two small Union Jacks. Behind the car were three British three-tonners filled with soldiers, who waved as they passed.

The small convoy carried on for another two hundred metres before a wave from the staff car brought them all to a shuddering halt. They could hear the curses of the soldiers in the trucks as they were thrown into a pile by the sudden stop.

The passenger door of the staff car opened and a soldier emerged, shouted something to each of the trucks, and started walking back. Max could see that he was not an officer, but as he got nearer he recognised him as the Sergeant he had spoken to the day before. He stopped to speak to the guard that had been posted, who pointed him in the direction of Max's tent.

Max towelled his face and reached for his shirt and tunic. He finished dressing just in time to return the Sergeant's salute as he stopped in front of him.

'Good morning, Sergeant, what can I do for you?' he said.

'Good morning, sir - sorry to disturb you - I thought you would be at Calais by now, and I was pushing ahead to try and catch you before you embarked.'

'What's the problem, Sergeant?' asked Max, giving his batman a nod as he was handed a mug of tea.

'Well, it might be nothing, sir, but there was a bit of disturbance when we got the prisoners to the station yesterday. Some of them tried to make a bolt for it when they saw that we were handing them over to a bunch of Russian guards.'

'Hmm,' said Max, taking a sip of tea. 'I'm not surprised, but there's nothing I can do about it Sergeant.'

'I didn't think you could, sir, but one of the prisoners pushed a note at me and begged me to give it to the Polish Colonel – Dofak, I think he said. He could only whisper because his head was covered in bandages. As you were the only Polish Colonel I'd met, I thought I'd let you see it. Would you be Colonel Dofak sir?'

Max shook his head. 'No, not Dofak - I'm Colonel Radovak. Where is the note, Sergeant?' he said.

The Sergeant produced a crumpled cigarette packet from his pocket and handed it over.

Opening it out, Max could not distinguish anything legible. There were several marks, black smudges, as though from a burnt matchstick. Puzzled, he turned it around. As he stared the outline of letters began to form. In places the black had fallen away, but the indentation of three short words were just readable. His eyes widened. There was a slight tremble to his hand as he handed the cigarette packet back to the Sergeant.

'What do you think it says, Sergeant?' he asked, quietly.

'I looked at it yesterday, sir. It was clearer then. So far as I can make out, it just says 'I am Stefan.' Not much of a note really, sir. Does it make any sense?'

The Sergeant handed the message back and Max looked at it again.

'It might be just an incredible coincidence, Sergeant, but I had a son named Stefan. He was an RAF pilot and was reported killed in action three years ago.'

The Sergeant raised his eyebrows and a look of concern crossed his face.

'Blimey, sir, and you think that might be him?'

'I can't see how it can be, Sergeant. Which direction was the train taking?'

'To Paris first, sir, that's all I know - then, I'd guess, on into Germany towards Poland.

Max nodded. 'The way the railways have been knocked about, it's not likely to be travelling fast. It shouldn't take long to catch up with it. It might not be my son, but I must find out.'

'Of course, sir - is there anything I can do?'

'I don't think so Sergeant, err – sorry, I don't know your name'

'Higgins, sir.'

'Well, I'm very grateful to you Sergeant Higgins, but you carry on with getting your men back to England.' He held out his hand. 'And good luck to you.'

Sergeant Higgins shook hands and saluted. 'Thank you sir,' he said, 'and good luck to you.'

As the Sergeant walked back to his waiting trucks, Max began to gather his men together to explain what had happened. He told them of his intention to take his jeep and try to catch up with the train.

As he finished speaking his second-in-command, Major Kruwicz, glanced at the faces of the men and sensed what they were thinking.

'I don't think that's such a good idea, Max,' he said.

On May 8th, when Germany had finally surrendered, Max had let it be known that he was through with giving his men any more orders, except for appearances sake in front of others. In effect, it made little difference to his men. They were so disciplined that the unit ran like a well-oiled clock. And so, like all soldiers who live and fight and suffer together for any length of time, they had become very protective to each other. This protectiveness started with their CO, Max Radovak, which was why his second in command was voicing his objection to his senior officer's plan to go off on his own.

Max raised an eyebrow. 'But I've got to follow this up, Frank. It shouldn't take me long, and this is a personal thing, I can't expect you to get involved and miss the boat back to England.'

Frank Kruwicz shook his head. 'I didn't mean not to go, Max, of course you must. But it's not a good idea to go alone - I think we should stick together.'

It took another five minutes to decide the issue. Fifteen minutes later Max waved his goodbye to his second-in-command and left with an escort of four jeeps on his mission. Progress was slow, since the roads were still in a poor state, and they were congested with lines of trucks full of soldiers heading for the Channel ports. There was a knot of apprehension in Max's stomach. After three years of believing that Stefan was dead, he found it difficult to think that he might still be alive. And if he was, how had he got caught up with POWs on the wrong side?

It took two days to catch up with the train. They spotted it first from the top of a hill as it trundled slowly towards Frankfurt.

Gathering the men around his jeep, Max consulted his map, located the next station and pointed it out as the place to make for. He finished with the words that he had always used after a briefing.

'Any questions?' he said.

His driver, Corporal Milzik, had a doubtful look on his face.

'Yes sir, can I ask what the plan of action is when we get there?'

'Plan of action, Milzik? Well, I'll locate the officer in charge, explain to him that I would like to see if the writer of the note is my son – and if he is, bring him back with us.'

Corporal Milzik shook his head. 'With respect, sir, I can't see it being that easy. Sergeant Higgins, who brought you that note, said that the prisoners had been handed over to Russian guards. If that's the case, I doubt that they will let a bunch of Poles waltz in and take one of their prisoners just like that. The Americans might get away with it, or the British, but not us.'

Max put a hand to his chin. 'Hmm, you have a point there, Milzik. We can't assume that our Russian comrades will be either friendly or cooperative.' He stroked his chin, thinking.

'All right, we'll say that there's a suspected war criminal on the train that we have been instructed to bring back.' He glanced around. 'Anyone got a better idea?'

256

The men shook their heads.

'Right, we should get to the next station well before the train, so it will look more official if we are waiting on the platform when it arrives.'

They reached the station about twenty minutes before the train was expected. Leaving two men to guard the jeeps, the others followed Max onto the station. On the opposite platform a Red Cross train was being loaded with wounded men to take them in the other direction. A thoughtful expression crossed Max's face. The sight of the ambulances gave him an idea. He jumped down and crossed the tracks to the other side, and his men could see him in conversation with a senior nurse who seemed to be in charge. Five minutes later he started back across the tracks. He jumped up onto the platform with a huge grin on his face.

'We've got a better plan of action,' he said. 'There's an American Field Hospital about a kilometre away, and they have agreed to attend to the wounded POWs when they arrive and change their dressings. And if we find Stefan, they've got an idea how to get him away. We are appointing ourselves as interpreters and to officiate.'

Max gathered them together and told them the plan. The men grinned. With the help of the Americans they would not have to disclose that they were looking for anyone.

When the train eventually arrived and rolled to a stop, three ambulances were positioned on the platform and the nurses were standing by. A small field kitchen would provide coffee and hand out a K-ration pack to each prisoner. Max and his men were strung out, each with a sub-machine gun, giving the appearance of genuine guards. A Russian Sergeant jumped off the train first and, seeing Max, automatically gave a quick salute. Max strode up to him.

'Who is in charge, Sergeant?' he asked sharply, in Russian.

More Russian guards were appearing now, and were giving wary looks at Max and his men strung out along the platform. The Sergeant just looked over Max's shoulder and nodded. Max turned. A tall sallow faced Russian Captain was standing a few metres away, lighting a cigarette, but his eyes were fixed on Max.

'I am in command of the POWs, Colonel - is there something I can do for you?' he said, in Russian, without taking the cigarette out of his mouth. He made no effort to salute. His attitude seemed to convey that a Russian Captain was superior in rank to a Polish Colonel.

Max, with a look of distain, let his eyes travel from the Captain's face to his uniform and down to his boots and then back up to his face before replying.

'No Captain, there is nothing you can do for *me*. My orders are to see that the prisoners get medical attention at this stop. As you can see, the Americans are providing this service, so, if you will line up those prisoners who require attention, we will get on with it.'

The Russian looked surly. 'I have not been informed about this. We have stopped to take on water and bread for the prisoners, that is all.'

Max gave an impatient snort. 'I am not concerned whether you've been informed or not. My orders are to provide medical services at this station and that is what I have done. Now, please will you give the order for those prisoners who require attention to line up. The sooner we start the sooner you can be on your way.'

The Captain looked down the platform at the waiting nurses and ambulances, and then his eyes travelled to Max's men. They were all casually holding a sub-machine gun and they seemed to be looking directly at him. He was reluctant to concede to this pompous Pole, even though he held a higher rank, but he still had a long way to go, and decided not to risk any confrontation. He shrugged his shoulders.

'All right - Sergeant, get the wounded prisoners in line on the platform. One carriage at a time - and keep a close eye on them.'

Conscious that the Russians were eyeing them with suspicion, Max went and stood with his men and watched the prisoners as they got off the train. His only clue was that the POW who sent the message had bandages around his head. As if bored, he started to walk up and down the platform. He managed to get close to three prisoners with a head bandage and watch as they had their bandages changed. None had the slightest resemblance to Stefan.

Max was standing in an obscure spot by the wall when prisoners from the fourth carriage began to emerge. There were several with similar bandages to the head and he began to move forward, and then another prisoner stepped down to the platform that caused Max to stop in his tracks. He was wearing a tattered, obscure light brown uniform, and even though he could not see his face, Max new

258

instantly that it was Stefan. Quickly, he turned away and gestured to Corporal Milzik who was standing nearest to him.

Max spoke to him and the corporal gave a nod before sauntering towards one of the Russian guards keeping the prisoners in line. He put a cigarette in his mouth and offered one to the Russian. The Russian nodded his thanks and they both lit up. Corporal Milzik gave a friendly smile and began to walk away. He walked along the line of prisoners.

*

Stefan was standing with his head bowed. He felt numb with wretchedness and despair. He was sure that he had seen his father three days ago as they walked towards the train. His futile attempt to send a note had not succeeded. If only he could talk, but having his face smashed with a rifle butt made even a whisper painful. It was his damned Todt uniform that was to blame. He had hung on to it too long, so that, when the war had ended and he had surrendered to the Maquis, he made the mistake of telling them his real name before he found out that they were all communists. With his Todt uniform they instantly took him for a Pole who had worked for the Nazis. When he protested that he was an RAF pilot and had been working for the resistance, they laughed at his story. And when he had tried to escape, they smashed his face with a rifle. His sombre thoughts were interrupted when he heard his name.

'Stefan - drop down,' said a low voice in Polish. *'Drop down'*

Confused, Stefan looked at the Polish corporal walking by.

'What?' he hissed out.

The corporal stopped and spoke again, his voice urgent. *'Drop down – faint.'*

Then he moved on as he saw the Russian guard watching them. Corporal Milzik stopped and the Russian came up to him, suspicion on his face.

'What was he saying,' he said, nodding in the direction of Stefan.

'He said he felt bad and needed to see a Doctor,' said corporal Milzik. 'I told him to wait until he got to the ambulance.'

At that point Stefan collapsed to the ground. Going to him the guard dragged him to his feet. He was a dead weight.

Corporal Milzik lifted Stefan onto his shoulder. 'I'll take him to the ambulance,' he said, 'get somebody to have a look at him.' And without waiting for a response he carried Stefan off.

The guard watched with narrowed eyes as the corporal stopped at the ambulance and the prisoner was placed on a stretcher and lifted inside. He started to walk towards the ambulance but, as he reached it, the corporal re-appeared, gave him a nod and walked away. The Russian, still suspicious, looked after him for a second or two, then turned and carried on with shepherding the line.

After speaking to the corporal, Max had gone to stand near to the Russian Captain. He pulled out his cigarette case and offered one to the Captain. The Captain nodded his thanks and responded by lighting them both.

'It's going well, Captain,' said Max, 'you should be on your way soon.'

The Russian gave him a sidelong look as he pulled at his cigarette. He was still not sure about this Polish Colonel. He seemed genuine and businesslike, but he sensed that there was something else on his mind. He was about to ask a question when a female Doctor appeared from the ambulance and hurried over to where they were standing. She addressed the Russian.

'Do you speak English, Captain?' she asked.

'A leettle,' he said.

'Well, you have a prisoner who has just collapsed, and I've got to get him back to the hospital and put him in quarantine.'

'Kwar-run-teen - what is zat?'

'Isolation, Captain - it looks like typhus. Your prisoners are covered in lice.'

A look of fear came over the Captain's face. He knew about typhus. He knew that if the prisoners caught it, he and the rest of his men were also likely to catch it. An epidemic of typhus on the train would be disastrous.

'How long before you know for certain, Doctor?' Max asked.

The Doctor shrugged. 'It could be a couple of days - but it may be more.'

The Captain dropped his cigarette to the ground and put his foot on it.

'I cannot wait zat long, I am already behind time,' he said.

Max cleared his throat. He was feeling elated that he had found Stefan alive, even though injured, and to speed things up he was prepared to be generous. He moved closer to the Captain.

'Look, Captain,' he said, 'I have got to stay here for a while. There are other trains coming through. What if I keep an eye on your prisoner for you, and you take one of my jeeps and travel on ahead of the train to organise your food supplies and medical needs.' He paused, and then added reassuringly. 'I can assure you your prisoner will not escape from us.'

The Captain did not respond immediately, he pretended to be giving the proposal some thought. But Max had caught the gleam in his eye as soon as he mentioned giving him a jeep. The opportunity to escape from the train was too strong to resist. He knew what the Captain's answer would be.

'Thank you, Colonel,' he said with a curt nod, 'that seems to be a satisfactory solution.'

A minute later the ambulance with Stefan on board left the station. Max stayed long enough to clear out one of his jeeps and hand the keys to the Captain, and then he headed towards the hospital. The rest of his men were to follow after the train had left.

When Max arrived he found that Stefan had already been showered, provided with clean pyjamas, and was sitting up in bed having his face attended to. Now that the bandages were off he could see that the left side of Stefan's face was a mass of black and purple bruising. Part of his jawbone could be seen sticking through a large gash in his cheek.

Unable to speak, Stefan's eyes lit up at the sight of his father. He held out his hand and Max took it in both of his own and gave it an affectionate squeeze.

'It's good to see you, son,' he said. 'Don't try to talk, plenty of time for that.' He looked over at the female Doctor examining his son's face.

'Apart from the gash and the bruising, he's got a badly broken jaw bone,' said the Doctor without looking up, 'but once we have set it properly and stitched up his cheek he'll be in less pain - with the help of morphine. He'll have to live on soup and liquids for a while.'

'But he'll be OK to travel, Doctor?'

'Sure - but his dressings must be changed every twenty four hours for the next week at least.'

'That's fine, we can deal with that,' said Max. 'Can we collect him in the morning?'

'Yes - after we've had another look and changed the dressing - say, o-nine hundred hours.'

'Fine,' said Max, and watched the Doctor finished the bandaging. He patted Stefan on the shoulder.

'Get some sleep, Stefan, we're setting off for England tomorrow.

Feeling very weary, Stefan gave a thumb's up in acknowledgement and closed his eyes as he settled his head on the pillow.

Max turned to the Doctor. 'Thanks for all you have done, Doctor. Those prisoners needed some help. And for my purposes, the mention of typhus was a brilliant idea.'

She smiled. 'Glad to be of help, Colonel,' she said. 'We Poles must help each other when we can.'

Max raised his eyebrows. 'You're Polish? I thought you were American,' he said.

She gave a grin. 'I'm Doctor Katrina Pedrewicz. I was born in Poland, but my parents migrated to America in 1925. So I'm an American now, but I don't forget my roots.'

He lifted his arms and held her by the shoulders and kissed her on the forehead.

'Bless you, Katrina Pedrewicz,' he said, 'and also your parents.'

Slightly flustered, she smiled. 'Well, thank you Colonel,' she said, and gave him a gentle push towards the door, 'now, get out of here, you should know that kissing the staff isn't allowed.'

*

Max led his jeeps off the ship. They were directed into the 'Polish' line, which snaked towards the exits from the Dover docks. After some cheerful jostling as they settled in line, NAAFI girls appeared, walking down the line carrying big, flat-bottomed baskets; some filled with mugs of tea, others with sandwiches. Smiling and skilfully dealing with all the banter and ribaldry, they handed out the food and drink and then glided on, leaving the men laughing and joking behind them.

As they munched away and sipped the tea, the men's attention turned towards a Polish officer walking down the line towards them. His uniform was well pressed and smart and they gathered that he was part of the welcoming party.

With his mug of tea in his hand Max stood with a few of his other officers and NCOs as the Polish Captain walked up from behind.

'Colonel Radovak?' he said and, as Max turned around, gave a brief salute.

Max looked at him warily as he returned the salute. He knew this man, but could not place him.

'Captain Linska, sir, - you might recall that I drove you from the Polish embassy to where your wife was living, only to find that the street had been bombed the night before. It must be over three years ago now.'

The mention of the incident jogged Max's memory. In fact, he had not seen much of the Captain's face on that journey because he had been looking at the back of his head in the car. Even so, there was a smile of recognition from Max.

'Of course, Captain,' he said, ' it's been a long time, how are you?'

'Very well, sir, thank you, and glad it's all over.' He took a sheet of paper from a clipboard he was carrying. 'The Polish Military are taking over a number of ex-US Army camps as the Americans leave for home. You've been assigned to Camp 45, which is just outside Sevenoaks, that is where you will find the rest of your unit.' He handed the paper over. 'This should be given to the Adjutant when you arrive there.'

'Thank you, Captain,' said Max, taking the paper.

'My pleasure, sir, - as head of the Polish Rehabilitation and Resettlement Unit, I – or one of my colleagues – will be visiting the camp within the next two or three days to explain our role in helping all Polish nationals to return home.'

'Er – I think you should delay your visit for a couple of weeks, Captain. My men will be given leave as soon as they've settled in.'

A look of dismay flashed across the face of the Captain

'But we would like to get our rehabilitation visits in before they go on leave, Colonel. Could you not delay the leave for a few days?'

Max shook his head. 'No, Captain – I cannot. We have been in action behind enemy lines for several months. My men are due for some leave, and I've already agreed that they will have it. As I say, it will be better if you delay your visit until they return.'

A look of irritation crossed the others face. He inclined his head slightly and gave a thin smile.

'Of course, Colonel - I understand,' he said, and gave Max a brief salute. His eyes swept briefly to the jeeps and he saw Stefan. With raised eyebrows he walked over to the jeep.

'I see you have an injured man, Colonel - is there anything I can do?'

'Er –no thank you, Captain. This is my son, Stefan. He is the reason why my unit split up as we approached Calais. I received information that Stefan was probably still alive and on a cattle train of POWs heading back to Poland. I decided to go and find out, and I'm glad I did.'

'What an astonishing coincidence, Colonel. And where has he been since he was reported killed?

'I've no idea, Captain, his jaw has been smashed and he can't talk. I gather it was done by a bunch of French communists, because of the uniform he was wearing.'

Captain Linska looked at the remains of the Todt uniform that Stefan was wearing but made no comment. Noting that Stefan looked asleep, he turned back to Max.

'He was an RAF pilot, if I remember correctly.'

'Yes, Pilot Officer.'

'Then the RAF desk will need to register his return to the UK, Colonel.'

'RAF desk – where is that?'

'It's in Section 6 – over there,' he said, pointing to the east side of the docks.

Max looked at the multitude of men and cluttered equipment that barred the way to Section 6.

Captain Linska followed Max's eyes.

'I shall be pleased to escort him there, Colonel, if you wish.'

'How will you get through?'

'I will take him to the head of the line and go around the back way.'

'Good, I'll come with you.'

'Err, I'm sorry Colonel, but you will not be allowed back there until you are checked through. I shall have a reason for escorting your son – but not you.'

'Ah, yes, I see – very well - we will have to rouse him.'

Max woke Stefan and introduced him to Captain Linska, who explained that he would escort him to the RAF desk. Stefan listened carefully and nodded his understanding, gave a thumb up to his father and walked off beside the Captain.

Staring thoughtfully at the back of retreating Captain, Max took another sip of tea. He could not understand why, but the man's polite aloofness disturbed him. He was a changed man.

Major Kruwicz, standing next to him, followed his eyes.

'Rehabilitation Unit eh,' he said. 'Most of the men are wondering whether they've got any homes or family to go back to.'

Max nodded in agreement. 'What about you Frank, are you keen to get back to Poland?'

Grim faced, the Major shook his head.

'Not likely - my wife and I never followed the Jewish faith, but we were still classified as Jews. Two years ago the International Red Cross advised me that my wife and two daughters had starved to death in the Warsaw ghetto. No, I've no wish to return to Poland and pretend that I'm a Stalinist in order to stay alive.'

The faces of the other officers and NCOs standing nearby turned thoughtful as they overheard the conversation. Now that the fighting had finished it was time to face reality. Poland had ended up on the winning side, but it was clear that Poland would be engulfed by the USSR. The country they knew, where they grew up, was gone. So the question that was foremost in their minds was whether they would be sent back, or be given the chance to live in Britain or the British colonies. Just one thing they knew for certain. Within a few months they would be demobbed, civilians again, needing to work for a living and find somewhere to live.

Thirty minutes later Max and his men were cleared through. There was no sign of the Captain or Stefan. He took the jeeps to one side and went in search of the RAF desk. A flight sergeant was bent over some papers. 'Yes?' he said, without looking up.

Max cleared his throat. The flight sergeant looked up and, alarm on his face, stood up and saluted.

'Sorry, sir.'

'That's all right, flight sergeant. I'm looking for Pilot Officer Stefan Radovak. He was bandaged around the head. A Polish Captain brought him here. Have you seen him?'

'Err – yes sir – we checked him through ten minutes ago. We issued him with a temporary ration card and some cash, and travel documents to his old base.'

Max's face clouded over. 'But I'm his father, I've just brought him back from France. Didn't Captain Linska explain that to you?'

'Err – no sir. He just told us his name, and that he was a Polish RAF pilot, reported as killed in action three years ago, but had turned up alive. We got on the 'phone to his old base at Hornchurch, and they want him to report there as soon as possible.'

'But you saw that he was injured. He needs medical attention, and it was my intention to get him to a specialist hospital in London and also see his mother before taking him to his base.'

'Sorry sir, didn't know that.'

'Did Captain Linska and my son leave together?'

'Yes sir – the Captain was saying something about getting him a uniform.'

'A uniform - where from?'

'Well, I don't know where he could get a *new* uniform, but some of the ladies from the local church have a lot of old uniforms in the church hall which they give away to any serviceman in need – the Captain might have gone there.

'Where is the hall?'

'About half a mile down the main road as you leave the docks - look out for the church on the left – the hall is just behind it.'

Ten minutes later Max's jeeps pulled up at the church hall and they went inside. There were about twenty servicemen browsing along the rows of Army, Navy and Air Force uniforms that ran down the middle of the hut. Pedestal tables at the far end had piles of washed and ironed shirts, underclothes, pyjamas, socks and shaving kits. They found Stefan looking through some blue RAF shirts. There was no sign of Captain Linska. Max let out a sigh of relief.

'Hello, Stefan - thank God I've found you' he said, walking up to him, 'is everything OK? Where's the Captain?'

Stefan gave him a thumb up and moved closer. 'He's gone to tell you I'm on my way back to Hornchurch,' he lisped between closed teeth.'

'Oh, has he, the cheeky blighter. *I'll* get you back to base, but not before you've seen your mother and had your face looked at again. Have you found anything useful here?

Stefan nodded and pointed to a middle-aged woman in WVS uniform walking towards them. She had a Pilot Officer uniform over her arm.

'Here you are,' she said, 'try this on - and take a shirt and tie. There's a cubicle free over there.' She turned to Max. 'And what are you looking for Colonel?'

'Nothing, thank you – I'm waiting for my son,' he said, indicating towards Stefan.

'Ah – he's your son is he,' she said, looking sympathetic. 'Is he badly injured, Colonel?'

'Badly broken jawbone, but he'll be OK,' said Max, noticing her eyes follow Stefan as he walked away..

'Now, he'll need a few other items,' she said brusquely, 'lets see,' and started to sort through the RAF shirts, socks and underwear and putting them into a kitbag.

A few minutes later Stefan emerged from the cubicle. The uniform was a perfect fit. He had entered the cubicle dejected, wretched and scruffy, and had emerged an upright, dignified RAF officer once again. He raised his two thumbs, and picking up the tattered Todt uniform he had come to hate, he stuffed it into a nearby sack. He went to the WVS woman and gave her a quick embrace.

'Thank you,' he whispered.

She took his hand and patted it gently. 'I thought that would fit you,' she said quietly. 'It belonged to my son - he was shot down over Hamburg.'

CHAPTER 30

After an emotional reunion, Anna took Stefan to have his face inspected and dressed at the Polish Hospital. An X-ray indicated that the jawbone was in place and appeared to be healing well. The bandages were reduced to dressings held on with sticky plaster. He could now speak in a low guttural voice through his teeth.

That night, Anna and Max had their own reunion. But not in the way that Anna had planned it. She had been yearning to sleep with Max again but, when finally alone together in the bedroom, getting undressed, she became self-conscious and worried. There was no question that she still loved Max, but did he still want to make love to her? And should she tell him about Thelma? How she had found out where she was living - and tell him that Thelma had had a baby – a daughter – his daughter.

No, she decided, not tonight anyway. This was the night she had dreamed about, but hardly dared hope would happen. But it was more than she could have imagined, because Max had not only returned alive, he had brought back Stefan. She had said a silent prayer to God, thanking him for sparing at least one of her sons.

With so many mixed emotions churning inside her, Anna climbed into bed beside Max. She felt his warm body beside her, unfamiliar for so long, and tried to relax, to dispel the tenseness that she felt. She waited for his embrace. When there was no response from him, she turned and whispered in his ear.

'Welcome home my love,' she said softly, 'and thank you for finding our son.'

She waited for some reply, but none came – just the sound of deep breathing. Max, she realised, was sound asleep. She smiled and snuggled her head to his shoulder, and slept contentedly.

The next morning Max drove Stefan to his old aerodrome at Hornchurch, and they said their goodbyes and agreed to meet up again in a week's time. Max then took the road to Ware, anxious to catch up with what was happening at the Divisional HQ, now that hostilities had ceased.

As he drove along the country roads his mind drifted to thinking about Thelma, and he made a mental note to try to find out where she was living. He knew that their lovemaking was over, but he wanted to remain friends, and to know that she was all right.

He stopped at a village pub for a glass of beer and a sandwich before carrying on. The fields of ripening corn and wheat, the sheep and cattle grazing, and land girls busy haymaking, gave him a sudden urge to get back to farming, to the peace of the countryside. But not in Poland – here, in England, the country that he had come to love and respect. He had no idea whether it was possible, or how much it would cost. He didn't consider that Anna and Trishka and Stefan might have other ideas about the future. But, at that moment, the thought of becoming a farmer in England filled his mind, as something to strive for after his demobilisation.

When he arrived at his old HQ he was surprised to see that the number of guards around the place had increased. Stony-faces at the gate scrutinised his papers thoroughly before letting him through. At the house his papers were inspected again before he was allowed entry. Inside, the only face he recognised was that of Sergeant Lowzki, still on the front desk in the reception area. All the others he saw were strangers, who gave him frosty glances.

'Good to see you again, sir,' said the Sergeant. 'Sorry to say, sir, you've got a pile of correspondence to go through. Shall I bring it along now?

'Thank you, Sergeant - it's good to be back. Correspondence eh? Give me a few minutes to glance through my tray.'

'Right you are, sir –I'll bring it along shortly.'

Before he moved away, Max leaned over towards the Sergeant. 'There's a lot of new faces about, Sergeant. Now the war's over, I'd have thought there would be less.'

Max saw the Sergeant give a nervous glance around before answering.

'Ah – there's a lot going on at the moment, sir, all to do with getting us back to Poland as quickly as possible.'

Max thought his voice sounded a little forced. The glance had tipped him off. Something was going on that the Sergeant was nervous about. Mystified, Max gave him a nod and moved towards his office.

He found that his desk had been pushed aside and another one brought in. The nameplate on the other desk showed that it belonged to an officer of equal rank - a Colonel Manzk. A pile of paperwork indicated that it had not been used for many days.

Max started going through his in-tray, he placed one or two things aside for attention, but most of it went into the waste bin. At the bottom of the pile he came across a memorandum congratulating him on his promotion to Brigadier. It was dated two days after he had left for France. He gave a wry smile. The formal notification had somehow never reached him. Apart from the extra pay he assumed he would get for the last few months, it would be of little use to him now. He would not be fighting in any more wars.

There was a knock on the door and Sergeant Lowzki came in carrying a wire basket full of correspondence.

'Here you are, sir, all this is addressed to you,' he said, as he put the basket down.

He hesitated, 'Err, would you be staying at 'The Swan' tonight sir, like you used to do?'

Max began to sift through the first of the letters.

'I haven't made any arrangements to stay the night, Sergeant - I was thinking I might get away and stay with my wife.'

Max saw a look of disappointment cross the Sergeant's face.

'Ah, yes - very good sir - it was just a thought that if you had booked into 'The Swan' I could buy you a drink later on. I'm billeted nearby, and usually call in there for a drink in the evening.'

The remark was casual enough, but Max got the impression that the Sergeant wanted to tell him something, but not here, not in this building. Intrigued, Max decided that, even if he did not stay the night at 'The Swan,' he would have a drink there with the Sergeant.

'Well, I've already told my wife that I shall be back tonight, Sergeant, but I'll take you up on that drink later on. Shall we say about eight o'clock?'

The Sergeant smiled. 'Eight o'clock it is, sir,' he said, and turned to go. As he reached the door he stopped and turned.

'Oh - I nearly forgot, sir – there's one letter that I wasn't quite sure of, so I kept it separate.' He searched his pockets and pulled out a blue airmail letter, walked back and placed it on the corner of the desk. 'Here it is sir - if it's not for you I thought you might know where I could redirect it.' He turned and left as Max reached out and took up the letter.

Max glanced at the surname Radovak as he picked up his letter opener, but just as he was about to use it he paused, and then put it down. He sat staring at the front of the envelope for several seconds, and then he turned it over and looked at the other side. He reached for the letter opener again, but stopped, undecided. He turned it over once more, and then put it carefully into his inside pocket.

His mind was hardly functioning as he continued sifting through the pile of letters. Most were from his own men, who had written what they thought might be a last letter to their parents, wives, or loved ones, with a request that they be forwarded on should they not return. He carried on sorting through them, hoping that there might be one from Thelma, but he was disappointed.

Glancing at his watch, he saw it was almost 7.30pm. He put the letters he had opened into a drawer, and the rest he pushed into his briefcase. He was ready for a drink, and keen to hear what Sergeant Lowzki had to say.

*

The bar at 'The Swan' was busy but not crowded. Max ordered half a pint of beer and had finished half of it before the Sergeant arrived. As he walked through the door he looked around, caught Max's eye, nodded, and made his way towards him.

'The first round is on me, Sergeant – what are you drinking?' said Max.

'I'll have a 'black and tan', thank you, sir.'

'Black and tan?

'Yes, sir - half a Guinness and half a bitter together - goes down nicely.'

They took their drinks to a spare table away from the bar and sat down.

The Sergeant took a good gulp of beer and put his glass down. Max could see that he was nervous, and decided to open the conversation.

'Any idea why there are so many guards about at HQ, Sergeant?'

Sergeant Lowzki took another sip of beer and wiped his hand across his mouth.

'Not entirely, sir, it's all been building up over the past few weeks.'
Before Max could reply he spoke again. 'Could I ask you a question, sir, in confidence.'

'Yes, of course, Sergeant - ask me anything.'

The Sergeant hesitated before continuing

'Are you a communist, sir?'

Max raised an eyebrow and gave a half smile. He had not expected such a question and wondered whether he should tell the truth. His instinct was to play safe.

'Well, I read Karl Marx's book on communism years ago, and thought that - the way he put it - properly organised, it might work. But comrade Stalin has put a different stamp on it. Why do you ask?'

The Sergeant looked relieved. 'I thought so, sir, but I wasn't sure.'

'What was it you thought, Sergeant?'

'That you're not a Stalinist.'

'And has this got some bearing on the number of guards at HQ?'

Lowzki took a furtive glance over his shoulder and then leaned across the table. He lowered his voice.

'I think it has, sir, but I didn't want to say anything at HQ. You see, they've fitted the place out with microphones. They're listening to everything you say.'

Max looked at him in astonishment. 'Microphones? What the hell for?'

The other man gave a shrug 'That's what I can't make out sir - now the war's over.'

'You said 'they' – who do you mean by 'they' Sergeant?'

'Well, it started about two weeks after VE day. Electricians in Polish uniform turned up and said the electric wiring was faulty – although it was the first I'd heard of it. We had to vacate each room they worked in. They spoke to us in Polish, but I overheard them talking together in Russian. In fact I think they were all Russians, sir.'

'Are you sure about this Sergeant?'

'Pretty well, sir - and then, about a week after the electricians left, some of the senior HQ officers started being drafted back to Poland - then these new officers began to arrive. I know one or two are Poles but I'm pretty sure the rest are Russians – even though they've got Polish names and uniforms.'

'And what's their function – what do they do?'

'They're supposed to be assisting Polish nationals to get back home.'

'Isn't that a good thing – it's a big job.'

'Yes – but I don't think it's as straight forward as that sir.'

'Why do you say that?'

The Sergeant hesitated. 'Because the Polish officers that went back have disappeared,' he said.

Max, about to take another sip of beer, felt a shiver go down his spine. He put his glass down slowly.

'Disappeared? How do you know?'

'Well, I - er - overheard Colonel Manzk arguing with another officer – they were speaking Russian. Anyway, from what I could make out, Colonel Manzk had been friendly with some of the Polish officers who had gone back, and two or three had promised to let him know how things were over there, as soon as they arrived. But he didn't hear from any of them, and when he made enquiries, there was no trace of them.'

Max shook his head in disbelief. If what Sergeant Lowzki had told him was true, then Stalin was not wasting any time in taking control of Poland – and its people. He recalled the changed Captain Linska, who had met them off the ship at Dover. From what he had admitted, he was part of it. He had called it 'Rehabilitation and Resettlement,' but it seemed that this friendly sounding title might be a cover for something more sinister. Max suspected that the Polish Divisional HQ had been taken over by a branch of Stalin's secret police – either KGB or NKVD – masquerading as Poles. He wondered whether British Intelligence knew what was going on..

'This Colonel Manzk, what do you know about him? Is he Russian, or a Polish Stalinist?'

The Sergeant shook his head. 'I'm sure he's not a Stalinist – but he's a Pole.'

'How can you be sure?'

'Pretty sure, sir – first, I don't think he was a backroom officer - he was walking with a stick - as though recovering from a wound. My first reaction was that I'd seen him before – in HQ, I mean – not recently, but during the war. But it was only his face that seemed familiar – his name didn't ring a bell at all. But doesn't the name mean anything to you, sir?'

'No – d'you think it should?'

'Well – I got the impression that he knew you, sir. When the place started to get overcrowded, he insisted that he move his desk in with you.'

A look of puzzlement crossed Max's face. 'Did he now,' he said, thoughtfully. 'And where is he, Sergeant, his desk doesn't seem to have been used for a while?'

'I'm not sure where he is at the moment, sir. After that argument with the Russian, he's been away. I've had one or two phone calls from him, that's all.'

'Hmm - well, the next time he 'phones in, Sergeant, tell him I'd like to have a chat, will you? And I don't mean at HQ – here at 'The Swan' – or somewhere else.'

'Yes, sir – of course.'

Downing the last of his beer, Max was ready to go, but another question came to mind.

'What about you, Sergeant, has anyone been pushing you to return to Poland?'

Sergeant Lowzki gave a wry smile. 'No sir, I haven't been pushed at all. In fact, as soon as the war was over I requested to get back there as soon as possible.'

'I assume, then, that you have a wife and family to go back to?'

'Yes, as the war came to an end, Intelligence officers at HQ started enquiring through our contacts in Poland about family and friends. I asked them to find out about my wife and two children. At the beginning of May I was told that they were not only alive – but still living over the shop.'

'Ah – that's good - so, you have a shop?'

'Yes – it's in a small village on the outskirts of Krakow. My family have been baking bread for the village for a hundred years or more. My father had to come out of retirement when I joined up, so he'll be glad to see me back.'

'It sounds as though you are one of the lucky ones, Sergeant. And you're resigned to the fact that Poland will be part of the USSR?'

'I've made up my mind to toe the party line if I have to. I'll just keep my mouth shut and get on with my business.'

'Well – even though I would like you to stay on for a few more weeks, Sergeant – purely because I need someone at HQ I can trust – I would suggest that if you want to get back to Poland as soon as possible, you start dropping hints that you would rather settle in the UK.'

There was a blank look on the other man's face. 'How would that help sir?'

'It's the way the Russian mind works, Sergeant. My wife was born in Russia, and I've learned a lot from her. It's simply that, as soon as you said you were keen to go back, you were not regarded as a priority. They know they've got you, so they make you wait. Those being given priority are the ones who are *reluctant* to go back. Especially officers, because if the ordinary soldiers see their officers going back, they will be more likely to follow them.'

The Sergeant gave a slow nod of understanding

'They're crafty buggers, sir.'

'Yes, Sergeant, they are – always remember that the national pastime in Russia is playing chess – and the ones in power at the moment seem to like playing it with other people's lives.'

*

It was late when Max got back to Anna's, but she was waiting up for him. She had been agonising whether to tell him about Thelma, and where she was living, and had decided that she must. But when she saw his face as he came in it immediately took her mind off Thelma.

'Is everything all right Max – you look pale.'

He put his briefcase down and sank into a chair.

'Is Trishka in bed Anna?' he asked.

'Yes, she's got to go early in the morning. Why – do you want to speak to her?'

'Yes, well, she ought to be here for this. Sit down Anna – there's something I've got to show you.'

Mystified, Anna sat in the chair facing him, then looked worried. 'What is it Max – it's not about Stefan is it?'

'No, no, Anna, it's not about Stefan,' he reassured her, and brought out the airmail letter from his inside pocket. He passed it over to her.

'This letter was in my post at HQ.'

275

Anna took it from him, read the front of the envelope and gave a gasp. Like Max had done, she stared at it for several seconds, and then turned it over to read the other side.

With a puzzled expression on her face she looked up at Max.

'I – I don't understand Max - it's addressed to Igor,' she said, as though he didn't already know.

Max nodded. 'Yes – addressed to Captain Igor Radovak – and posted in Canada.'

'But – it can't be for *our* Igor, could it? They told us they'd found his body and uniform in a wood five years ago – it can't be for him.'

'That's why I decided not to open it. There are a number of families named Radovak dotted around Poland. It wouldn't be surprising if a few were also named Igor.'

Anna looked at the envelope again. 'Yes, I'm sure that must be the answer – and our Igor was a Lieutenant, not a Captain. But what's this other bit, Max,' and she leaned towards him pointing with her finger, 'there, after his name, it's got PPA Unit, Polish Forces, England. What does PPA stand for?'

Max shook his head. 'I've no idea – but it shouldn't take long to find out.'

'You don't think we should open it then?'

'No - not yet anyway – after all, it's not addressed to us,' and he took the envelope from Anna, stood up, and went and put it behind the clock on the mantelpiece. 'We'll show it to Trishka, but it can stay there for the time being.

CHAPTER 31

For several days after their return to the UK, Max spent in meetings with his fellow officers, mainly about the arrangements for demobilisation. It was the main topic of conversation among the men, together with concerns about the future. But, as arranged, he managed to get away to drive to Hornchurch the following weekend to visit Stefan. He picked him up at the aerodrome and took the road to the same pub that they used to visit before Stefan was shot down over the Channel.

In the car Max glanced at his son, who was looking much better, but seemed to have something on his mind.

'How did the debriefing go, Stefan – you must have quite a story to tell.'

Stefan gave a small, restricted, smile. 'I've had a debriefing session every day this week.' He spoke without moving his lips, like a ventriloquist. 'They want to know every detail. The trouble is, I don't think they believe me.'

'Don't believe you? Why not -have they said so?'

'No, nobody has actually *said* they don't believe me -it's just an impression I get from their reactions.'

'How many are debriefing you?'

'Three.'

'And have you finished yet?

'No – I've one session to go - then I get two weeks leave - then a final session after that.'

Arriving at the pub, they ordered drinks and found a table in a quiet corner.

As soon as they sat down, Stefan pulled out his wallet 'The only evidence I've got to back my story is this,' he said, and pulled out his worn identity card in the name of Pierre Limone.

Max picked it up and looked at it. 'This was your identity in France?'

'Yes – for about four years.'

'I'd like to hear how you managed to avoid capture for so long - but only if you feel up to it.'

Stefan nodded, and took a sip of beer. Then he started to tell his father what had happened to him in France after he was picked up out of the sea. There were several short breaks, to give Stefan a rest from talking, and to replenish their glasses.

When he had finished, Max sat back and stared with admiration at his son.

'Stefan, as your father, I believe every word of your story. But I can understand that others may not. It's pretty impressive.'

'It didn't feel like that at the time – I was just trying to survive. It sharpens your wits when you know that if you're caught, that's it – you're dead.'

He was staring at his glass, as he had done several times during his story. Max went over to the bar and brought back sandwiches, forgetting that Stefan was still confined to soup.

'What about the girl, Stefan – Marie, wasn't it - did you ever hear from her again?'

He shook his head. 'No - after I walked out on her in Caen, I don't know what happened. Doctor Dubar said that it was too dangerous for us to stay in touch. I think about her every day - I shouldn't have walked out, as I did – not like that. I still love her, but I doubt if she still loves me – if she's still alive.'

Max gave an understanding nod. He felt sorry for his son. Apart from all he had gone through, he had been forced to part from the girl he loved. He took another sip of beer and then bit into a sandwich, his thoughts still on the girl.

'If she's still alive Stefan, she might have returned home by now. Why don't you go and find out?'

Stefan looked up from his glass in surprise. 'Go back to France?' he said, 'I couldn't do that, I've only just got out of the bloody place.'

Leaning over the table, Max put his hand on Stefan's arm.

'But it's different now, son - the war's over - they'll be no Nazis chasing after you. And if you don't go back and find out, well, I think it'll gnaw away at your insides for the rest of your life.'

Stefan toyed with his glass, and remained silent for half a minute.

'You're right,' he said. 'I've got to find out if she's still alive.'

'Yes - and at the same time, if your Doctor Dubar is still alive, he could give you a signed statement about how he recruited you as a spy. Your debriefing panel would have to accept that.'

Stefan nodded, but he was frowning. 'There's a snag, though – I haven't been issued with a new identity card yet – I'll not be allowed to leave the UK without one.'

'Hmm, that's a pity,' said Max. 'How long will it be before your next leave?'

'I've no idea – I was hoping I'd be demobbed soon - but now I've decided to go to France, I'd like to get over there as soon as I can – find out what's happened to her – to all of them.'

They sat in thought for a while, and then Max gave a smile.

'Well – you've still got your false identity card. There were thousands of French citizens who were wounded in Normandy and sent to the UK for treatment. They've been gradually returning over the past few months, so no one is likely to question your French identity card – especially with your face still bandaged up.'

Stefan stared at his glass in thought for a few seconds, and then gave a decisive nod. 'Yes – I'll do that – I'll go as Pierre Limone.'

'I was only half serious, Stefan – you'll probably get out OK, but you will need a UK identity card to get back in.'

'I'll take that chance – I might get arrested, but if I find Marie, it'll be worth it.'

*

Driving back to the aerodrome, Max told Stefan about the letter that had been sent from Canada addressed to his brother Igor.

'Why don't you open it,' was Stefan's response, 'if Igor is still alive, it's the quickest way to find out.'

'You're probably right, Stefan, but I thought it better to wait until I've found out about this PPA Unit. No one seems to have heard of it – although someone has suggested that it was hush-hush unit that operated behind enemy lines.'

'Trust Igor to get into something like that - I bet it's him all right.'

Max smiled at his son's confidence that his brother had somehow survived the war. Up to now he had hardly dared to think that it might be true.

He went on to tell Stefan about his fears that the Polish Divisional HQ was now in the hands of Russian secret police. He warned him that Captain Linska or another 'Rehabilitation and Resettlement' officer in a Polish uniform might be offering to get him back to Poland as quickly as possible – but those who had already gone back had disappeared.

Stefan frowned. 'That sounds like Stalin's' work. I remember Captain Linska– I thought there was something funny about him. But they'll be wasting their time with me, I want to go back to University and finish my degree – after that I'll get a job in England if I can, but if not I'll find another country – I don't want to go back to Poland.'

CHAPTER 32

When his leave started three days later Stefan took the train to Portsmouth. He booked into a small hotel near the docks, where, upon enquiry, the receptionist said that she could arrange his passage on the 7.15am ferry to Cherbourg the next day. He then walked to the outpatients department at the local hospital to have his dressings changed. He doubted that he would be able to get them changed again until his return. Leaving the hospital, he walked through the bombed out areas of the town to the shops. When he returned to the hotel he was carrying a small suitcase filled with second-hand civilian clothes.

Over a drink at the bar, he persuaded the barman to hire him his old, but sturdy, bicycle. From a group of four nurses in the hotel, just returned from France, he bought what French currency they had, which wasn't much, but he hoped that he wouldn't need any of it.

He went to bed early but got little sleep, and was up at the first glimmer of dawn. From his kitbag he took out twelve packets of American cigarettes and two pounds of coffee that he had scrounged together, and replaced them with his folded up uniform.

Changing into the civilian clothes, he then put the cigarettes and coffee under a spare shirt in the case and closed the lid. Leaving his kitbag at the hotel, he told them that he planned to be away for three days – four at most. Tying his small case securely to the bicycle, he made his way to the ferry.

As the boat reached Cherbourg, Stefan stood on the deck looking at the devastated dock area and bombed out buildings of the town. He found that although the rubble in the streets had been cleared for traffic, the wrecked buildings were just as the war had left them. The afternoon sun failed to dispel the grey, depressive, feeling of the place. And the people walking about looked gaunt faced, poor and undernourished. The Allies had liberated them from the Nazis, but many of them had lost everything they owned.

Stefan calculated that it would take him about two hours to cycle to the home of the Dubar's at Auderville, but he had not reckoned on the state of the roads. There was little he could recognise from the time he cycled along it four years ago.

Wrecked vehicles, burned-out tanks and artillery guns, all stripped of anything useful, still littered the roads. Of the villages he passed through, artillery fire, bombs and armed combat had devastated many, while just a few seemed, strangely, to be unscathed.

A thunderstorm sent him scurrying into a nearby barn for cover and held him up for thirty minutes, but he eventually reached Auderville under a hot sun, sweating and thirsty. He hardly recognised the village. Many of the buildings were just a pile of bricks, but guided by the shattered church tower, he found his way to the Dubar's house. He stopped and looked at it, or what remained of it, because the house was a total wreck.

'Can I help you, *monsieur*?'

Stefan turned at the sound of the voice. The man was dressed in black with a white collar. It was the local priest.

'I am looking for the Dubar's, father - do you know what's happened to them?'

The priest searched his face, as though trying to remember who he was, whether he knew him from the past. Still unsure, he shook his head sadly.

'Ah, *monsieur*, the poor Doctor – he was arrested by the Gestapo and took poison to avoid torture. *Madame* Dubar was killed during the invasion of Normandy.' He paused, and then, in a quieter voice, added, 'and poor Marie, their daughter, she is gone.'

Stefan's inside lurched when he heard these words. He stood in silence for a while, looking at the ruined house, fighting back his tears as the memories of Marie flooded back.

'How did Marie die, father, was she here during the battle for Normandy?'

'Yes, she was here, my son - but she did not die in the battle.'

'Then - when did she die, father?'

The priest hesitated, as though reluctant to carry on. 'She did not die, my son - she has gone from the village, but she is not dead.'

Stefan stared at him blankly. It took several seconds for his brain to switch from the shock that Marie was dead to the shock that she was still alive.

'Alive – she's alive?' he queried, as though he hadn't heard correctly.

The priest nodded. 'Yes - she has gone to live with her aunt.'

His heart thumping, Stefan asked his next question - fearful that the answer would not be the right one. 'And do you have the address of her aunt, father.'

There was a shake of the head. 'Sadly, no, my son - all I know is that her aunt lives on Guernsey.'

'Guernsey?' repeated Stefan.

'Yes, I understand that she had an aunt and a cousin living there.'

'But – surely she wouldn't leave without letting someone know her new address?'

It was noticeable that the priest was feeling uncomfortable with his questioning. He was trying to be helpful, but gave the impression that he was holding something back.

'Yes – yes, that is true,' he said, '– but perhaps *monsieur* Pourrie, the mayor, will know.'

'And where does the mayor live, father?'

The priest seemed relieved now that he had passed any further questioning on to the mayor.

'I will take you to him - I am going that way myself.'

They walked in silence to the centre of the village, where a few shops had been patched up and were open for business. The priest stopped at the *boucherie*.

'This is the house of the mayor, *monsieur,* he is also the village butcher,' he said as he pushed open the door.

Standing his bicycle against the wall, Stefan followed the priest into the shop. The priest, who had already greeted the man standing behind the counter, was waiting to introduce him.

Monsieur mayor, this man is seeking the address of Marie Dubar – I wondered if you could help him.'

Without his slightly grubby and bloodstained blue and white striped apron *monsieur* Pourrie could have been taken for a clerk of some kind. He was the type of person that always spoke with a polite smile on his face. And he was smiling when Stefan entered the shop, as he would to a new customer. But at the mention of Marie Dubar the smile dropped and his gaze switched quickly from Stefan to the priest and then back to Stefan.

'Are you a relation, *monsieur*?' he asked, guardedly.

'No, just - a friend - we met in the war,' replied Stefan.

'You met in the war? May I ask how you met *monsieur*?'

'I was shot down over the Channel - French fishermen rescued me and took me to Dr. Dubar. The Dubar's saved my life. Look, *monsieur mayor*, can you tell me why I am being questioned in this way? The father here has told me that Marie Dubar is alive and you might know where she is living. That is all I want to know.'

The mayor shook his head, 'She did not give me any address, *monsieur,* she left very quickly, but we have found that she went to Guernsey.'

' Yes, - I have told him that *monsieur mayor*,' said the priest, 'but what about the village records in the vaults under the church - do you think there might be something there?'

The mayor looked at him, and gave a nod. He glanced up at the clock on the wall and started to take off his apron.

'There could be,' he said. 'On the application forms for identity cards, everyone had to put down their next of kin, and one other. *Madame* Dubar might have put down her sisters address on Guernsey. I will lock up now and we will go and see what we can find.'

'Thank you, I would appreciate that,' said Stefan.

As they walked towards the church Stefan was about to ask why Marie had to leave the village so quickly, when the mayor spoke again.

'May I ask your name, *monsieur*'?

Stefan almost replied with 'Pierre Limone', but checked himself.

'My name is Stefan Radovak. I am a Pilot Officer in a Polish squadron of the RAF.'

'Stefan - you say?' said the mayor, and turned to the other man 'so - she might have been telling the truth, father.'

Stefan was becoming irritated by the questions and intrigue about Marie.

'Telling the truth about what,' he asked. 'Would you explain what you're talking about? Has something happened to Marie?'

They walked in silence for another twenty paces or so before the priest replied.

'When Marie returned to the village, she had a child with her - a boy – he was about three years old.'

Stefan stopped short and stared at him. 'A child! A boy!' he said, in astonishment.

'Yes,' said the mayor, 'his name was Stefan.'

'Stefan! After me - Marie had my child!' exclaimed Stefan, more to himself than to the others.

'That is what she tried to tell everyone - Stefan was the father's name and he was a British pilot - but no one believed her.'

'Why didn't they believe her?'

The mayor and the priest exchanged glances.

'Because the surname of the child was Gruber - the name of the Nazi officer who was seen visiting her in the village,' said the mayor.

Stefan groaned. 'Oh no,' he said, and his mind flashed back to the last time he had seen Marie in Caen, when she assured him that she had never slept with Gruber.

'What happened to her?' he asked, quietly.

'She was accused of being a *collaboration horizontale*, a Jerry bag, a whore who slept with the Germans.'

'So that's why she left so quickly,' said Stefan, grimly.

There was a short silence, and then the priest spoke again, very quietly.

'No, monsieur, to our everlasting shame, we stood by as she was seized and her dress was torn off and she was beaten with sticks and her head was shaved.'

At these words, the mayor bent his head down, as though unable to look Stefan in the eye. 'It was after that, *monsieur*, that Marie Dubar left the village,' he said.

Choked with anger and sympathy, Stefan remained silent until they reached the church.

'Why did you stand by and let the villagers do that to her?'

'Oh, it was not the villagers who seized her,' said the mayor, 'it was so called *resistance* fighters who came from outside – they were communists, or ex-milici - no one recognised them – and we stood by because anyone who protested was also accused of being a *collaborator* – and they were armed and we were not. They were madmen – mad.'

Stefan stood looking from one to the other, his insides still churning at the savage injustice that Marie had suffered.

'But - she never slept with Gruber - you know that don't you?'

The two looked at him. 'No, *monsieur*,' said the mayor, 'we did not know that - and how can you be so certain?'

'Because I know that she was only playing him along to protect me - and when he found out that I was using a false identity and was about to inform the Gestapo, Dr. Dubar arranged to kill him, and Marie helped him do it.'

They stared at him, a stunned look on their faces. 'They killed Gruber?' There was disbelief in the priest's voice. 'How do you know this *monsieur* - how do you know that they killed Gruber?'

'I was sharing an apartment with Marie in Caen when Gruber turned up. I was not there at the time, but I returned to find Gruber on the bed. Marie had drugged him. She was waiting for a local Doctor to call – to finish him off.'

'And Marie Dubar did not tell you that she was pregnant, *monsieur?*'

'No, but she probably didn't know herself at the time.'

The mayor was shaking his head. 'But if she knew that the child was not Gruber's, why did she register it in his name? By doing that, she damned herself, and also the child.'

There was no doubt in Stefan's mind. 'If Gruber had died, what choice did she have. There was no choice. She had to play the grieving mistress, and say that the baby was Gruber's. She needed to protect herself and the child as best she could.'

'*Merde,*' muttered the mayor, 'what a terrible, terrible, thing has been done.

*

With the light from candles taken from the altar, it took the mayor twenty minutes to find the form that had the address of *madame* Dubar's sister on Guernsey.

He handed it to Stefan. 'You might as well take it *monsieur* - there is no point in keeping it here any longer.'

Stefan folded it and put it in his pocket. 'Thank you *monsieur mayor*, he said.

'You are going to see her then, *monsieur*?' the priest asked.

'Yes - if I can get over there. I asked her to marry me when the war was over. I want to see if she feels the same way.'

'Hmm,' said the mayor, 'that is very honourable, *monsieur*, but there is no regular ferry from here - or Cherbourg, to Guernsey.'

Returning to daylight, Stefan and the mayor blew out the candles and handed them back to the priest.

'You could try the fishermen, *monsieur*,' the priest said, 'if you have enough to pay them.'

Stefan frowned. 'I have a little French money, and some English, a few packets of cigarettes and......'

'Cigarettes,' interrupted the mayor, 'that may do it - how many have you got?'

'I brought twelve packets, as a gift for Marie and her parents.'

'Well, *monsieur*, cigarettes have more value than money at the present time. If you want the fishermen to take you, offer them four packets, but they will probably try for six. In fact, tell them that six is all you have. I suggest you do not tell them you have twelve packets.'

Stefan nodded, and decided not to mention that he also had two pounds of coffee. The priest provided a bed for the night and before it was light he was shaking Stefan awake. 'Hurry up, *monsieur*, the mayor is waiting for you.'

Dressing quickly, Stefan left a packet of cigarettes beside the bed and hurried out to find the mayor waiting for him in a battered but serviceable American jeep. The mayor had already placed Stefan's bicycle in the back. ' Hurry, *monsieur*, we must catch them before they sail.'

Stefan turned towards priest and shook his hand 'Thank you for your help, father.' The jeep was already starting to move as he jumped into it.

'Good luck, my son, and God be with you,' replied the priest, as the jeep disappeared into the darkness.

*

It happened that the fishermen were shorthanded, and accepted four packets of cigarettes and his help with the nets. When they reached

287

Guernsey Stefan helped to unload the fish they had caught on the crossing, said his goodbyes, and wheeled his bicycle along the quay towards the town. There were plenty of reminders of the German occupation to be seen, but, unlike Normandy, the Channel Islands had not been bombed or damaged by an invasion. Reaching the end of the quay, he pulled out the form that the mayor had given him to check the address of Marie's aunt. He looked around, and his eyes lighted on a building on the other side of the road marked 'Police Station.'

A Sergeant behind a desk looked up at Stefan's enquiry and, without saying a word, pointed with his pen to a roadmap of the island on the wall. Stefan studied it for a minute or two, scribbled down a few directions, mumbled 'thank you' and left the building. He was just in time to catch a ragged looking urchin about to walk off with his bicycle. 'Hey!' he shouted out. 'Put that down.' The urchin carefully leaned it back against the wall and gave him a cheeky grin.

'You shouldn't leave yer bike wivout a lock on it, mister,' he said, 'it ain't safe.'

'Scram,' said Stefan, indicated with his thumb for the urchin to be off. The incident made him realise that roadworthy bicycles were in short supply on the Island and needed to be guarded.

Following the directions he had taken down he finally stopped his bicycle at a stone cottage on the outskirts of St Peter Port. He was feeling apprehensive now at the thought of meeting Marie again. He leaned the bicycle against the privet hedge that surrounded the cottage, opened the gate, and walked up the path to the front door.

There was a well-polished brass letterbox in the middle of the door with a knocker attached to it. He knocked and waited. The sound of a voice, then music, came from the inside. A wireless was on. He knocked again, louder this time, but still there was no reply. He took a pace or two back and noticed a side gate to the back of the house. Finding it unlocked he went through. He saw a clothesline in the back garden and behind it the silhouette of a woman hanging out washing. A small boy was holding pegs for her. His heart leapt.

'Marie,' he called out, nervously.

He saw the silhouette stop moving. A hand parted the washing and a face appeared. It was not Marie.

'Pardon, *monsieur*,' she said, in French. 'I am Cathy, Marie is my niece.'

Cathy Duaqman was about forty, Stefan guessed, roughly the same height and build as Marie. She wore a scarf, turban style, on her head, but the hair on her neck was mousy coloured, rather than Marie's chestnut brown. Her face had a worn, wary look, and her eyes were suspicious. She looked more like an elder sister than an aunt.

*

After Stefan had introduced himself, she looked at him curiously and invited him into the house. She told him that Marie and her cousin, Claudine, were working for a tomato grower and would not be back for two hours. She made tea, and gave him a quick glance as she poured it out

'So, you came over from Auderville, *monsieur*,' she said, as she handed him the cup.

'Thank you – yes – by fishing boat.' He smiled down at the boy, who was playing with a small wooden aeroplane and looking at him shyly.

'Hello, Stefan,' he said, resisting the temptation to reach down and pick him up to his knee.

'You know the boys name, then?' said Cathy, with surprise in her voice.

Stefan nodded and looked at her. 'Yes – and I know his surname is Gruber.'

Claudine nodded but remained silent.

He patted his pockets and found the remains of a bar of chocolate. The boy widened his eyes at the sight of it. Stefan handed it to him, and the boy gave a shy smile as he took it. He felt a pang of guilt that he had not brought more.

'What do you say, Stefan,' said his aunt.

'*Merci, monsieur*' said the boy, through a mouth already full of chocolate.

She took a sip of tea, and Stefan was conscious of her eyes watching him over the rim of her cup. When she lowered her cup her eyes were still on him.

'If you were lovers, as you say, I'm sure she'll be pleased that you're not dead *monsieur* Stefan. But if you have not seen each other for over three years, have you thought that she might not feel the same way about you?'

'Yes, I've thought of that, but I also need to tell her that I still feel the same way about her. If she still loves me, I intend to ask her to marry me.'

'To marry you?' she said, her eyes widening a little

'Yes - is that so surprising?'

'I think it is surprising, considering the situation you are in *monsieur*.'

A puzzled expression crossed Stefan's face. He was beginning to think that Marie's Aunt Cathy was being over protective and interfering.

'I'm sorry,' he said, 'I don't understand what you mean by - situation.'

'By your situation *monsieur*, I mean - circumstances. You say you are a Polish officer in the RAF, but now the war is over you will be a civilian again within two or three months. Will you go back to Poland, or stay in England? Wherever it is you will need to find work and somewhere to live. Have you thought about these things *monsieur*? Because until they are settled, I respectfully suggest that you do not consider marriage to Marie, or any woman.'

He remained silent as her words sank in. She was right, of course. He had nothing to offer Marie as a husband. Apart from his accumulated back pay, which would help him get through his final year at university, he had nothing.

'And Marie is not in a fit state for marriage,' her aunt continued. 'She and little Stefan need time to recover from their ordeals. She is thin and weak. She hides her shaven head under a scarf and never takes it off. And, in spite of doing nothing wrong, she feels guilty. It is very sad to see. Peace and quiet is what she needs at the present time, not a husband with no job or a house to live in, whether it is England, or Poland, or anywhere else.'

He sat with his hands around the empty teacup, staring into it.

'Cathy - may I call you a Cathy?' he said, and she gave a nod. 'When I found out Marie was still alive and what had happened to her, I just wanted to find her and protect her. But you're quite right -

I can offer her nothing - nothing like she has here, with you. Yes, I can give her and the boy my love, but I can't provide much else until I've sorted out my future. So I'll not chance adding to her stress by asking her to marry me yet. But I need to know how she feels about me – and apologise for leaving like I did.' He saw her face relax a little and she gave him a sympathetic smile.

'I can see that you are a very sensible man *monsieur* Stefan. I'm sure that you would make a good husband for Marie. All that I am asking is that you give her time – and not to rush her. In fact, I think she will be pleased to see you for at least one very good reason.'

'And what reason would that be, *Madame*?' he asked.

'I think I must leave that for Marie to tell you. All I will say is that it is something to do with the boy.'

Stefan gave a nod. 'If there is anything I can do for her and the boy, I will do it,' he said.

She offered him another cup of tea, and as she was making it he went to his bicycle to get his case. He was untying the straps when he heard voices. Looking up, he saw two women walking towards him. They stopped talking and looked at him curiously. As they got nearer he could see that the taller of them was Marie. She looked pitifully thin, with a nervous, scared look about her. He realised that she had not recognised him behind the bandage and sticking plaster around his jaw.

'Hello, Marie,' he said, just loud enough for her to hear.

She stared at him, and at his face covered in plasters. Then her eyes widened and she put her hand to her mouth.

'Stefan?' she queried, her voice nervous, unbelieving.

'Yes, Marie - it's me, Stefan.' She looked so fragile that he was tempted to take her in his arms and hold her tight.

'What – how…' her voice trailed off in confusion.

'I went to Auderville - they told me what had happened to you.'

'I - I thought you were dead,' she said, her voice still uncertain 'That you were caught by the Gestapo.'

'I nearly was, but I got away.' he said.

She came forward then, and he hoped she would kiss him. Instead she looked more closely at his injured face.

'What happened to your face,' she said, concern in her voice.

'It was done by Frenchmen. I was accused of being a collaborator'

She looked at him sadly. 'How terrible,' she said. 'I was also accused. They did terrible things to me, Igor, terrible things. And did you know that my father was betrayed by a French traitor?'

'I heard that he was dead, and your mother also. I'm sorry, Marie, they were good people.'

Tears fell down her cheeks and she wiped at them with her hand. 'I do not want to go back to France,' she said.

'You don't have to, Marie,' he said quietly.

Marie nodded, as though reassured, and introduced him to her cousin, Claudine, who was shy, slim and pretty, and fifteen years old.

'She is like a sister to me,' said Marie, giving her a quick smile.

Opening the gate, she gave a nervous gesture towards the house. 'Come in and meet my Aunt Cathy,' she said.

'We've already met, Marie, and little Stefan also.'

Marie stopped and turned, her face serious. 'So, you know about Stefan? What has Aunt Cathy told you?'

'Cathy hasn't told me anything that I didn't know already. It was the mayor and the priest at Auderville who told me.'

A scared look crossed her face. Her eyes searched into his.

'He is not Gruber's son, Stefan - he is ours, yours and mine.'

Stefan smiled at her gently. 'I never doubted it, Marie, you did what had to be done.'

They were at the door of the house and Claudine went in. Marie stopped, a look of relief on her face. 'Oh, Stefan, I thought you had died not knowing you had a son. I had to pretend that Gruber was the father for protection. And then I worried that, had you lived, you would not have understood - that you would not have believed me.'

He could not hold himself back any longer. He took her by the shoulders and pulled her towards him. Her body went rigid for a second, and she started to pull herself away. But he closed her gently but firmly against him. And he felt her body relax, and she gave a deep sigh, as though a great burden had been lifted from her.

'Naming him Stefan was all the proof I needed,' he said tenderly in her ear.

She pulled away from him then and took his hand. Cathy was pouring out the tea when they entered the small dining room. She gave them a quick look and it was enough. Her fears were dispelled.

She could see they were still in love with each other. She handed the tea around and sat down.

'Well, I can see it didn't take you two long to kiss and make up.'

Stefan and Marie exchanged smiles.

'To be truthful, Cathy,' said Stefan, 'I can't kiss very well at the moment – but I think we've made up.'

Marie smiled. 'Yes, we have,' she said.

There was laughter from the garden. Claudine was playing with little Stefan.

Cathy nodded towards the garden with her head. 'She will spoil that little boy if you're not careful, Marie.'

'I don't care, Cathy, so long as he's happy,' she replied, and turned to Stefan, 'but his father might not agree.'

Stefan grinned. 'I think, whatever I say, you ladies will still compete to spoil him rotten.'

Cathy put her head back and laughed out loud. Marie also laughed, but looked at her aunt in astonishment.

'Aunt Cathy, that's the first time I've heard you laughing like that,' she said.

Cathy looked across the table at them. 'That's true,' she said, 'but since you and the boy arrived I've not felt much like laughing. I've been worried sick that you would never be the same again. And then this man walks in, and within minutes you're a different woman. I think you're through the worst Marie, and I'm happy for you. I needed a good laugh like that.'

'How long can you stay, Stefan?' asked Marie. 'Are you on leave?'

'Yes, I've got three days left - I was planning to go back tomorrow.'

'Tomorrow?' said Marie, disappointed. 'Can't you stay longer?'

'Well, I would certainly like to, but – I've got something to sort out when I get back.'

Marie and Cathy exchanged glances.

'Could you stay one extra night, Stefan?' asked Marie. 'There is a matter you could help me with.'

'I'll help you in any way I can, Marie, what is it?'

'I'm sorry – I'm talking as though it is just my problem – which it was before – but now you're here, it's a matter that involves us both.'

Stefan leaned over and took her hand. 'Tell me what it is you want me to do, Marie,' he said, tenderly.

'She's talking about getting a new birth certificate for the boy,' interrupted Cathy, impatiently.

He stared in surprise from one to the other. 'Is that possible?' he said.

Marie nodded. 'Aunt Cathy heard that it is - not officially, but it can be done – at a price.'

'But – how can it be done? Would it cancel his French birth certificate with Gruber as the father?'

'No,' said Marie, 'but I'd burn it. His new birth certificate would show that he was born on Guernsey to a different father – you.'

'That was the problem,' said Cathy, 'you have to show proof that there is a new father. There are a number of young children with German names on the Island. The mothers of most of them would like to get a replacement birth certificate, but very few local men are prepared to become a father to a German child.'

'That's understandable,' said Stefan, 'but as I'm the real father, it will be just putting the records straight.'

'Yes,' smiled Marie, 'to his proper name - Stefan Radovak junior.'

Stefan's smile faded. 'What kind of proof does the father have to provide?' he asked.

'Just your identity card,' said Cathy, and then, seeing the expression on his face, asked, 'you *have* got one, haven't you? You couldn't have got here without one.'

Stefan looked doubtful. 'Yes, I've got one – but it's the one I used in France. I came over as Pierre Limone.'

For a second or two Marie looked distraught, but then her face relaxed and she gave small shrug

'Does it really matter? Pierre Limone will not make him Polish, but Pierre Limone will still be a good father,' she said. 'It can be changed to Radovak later.'

Stefan looked at her doubtfully, then smiled and nodded in agreement. 'I can't seem to get rid of this Frenchman – he's now about to steal my son.'

He had another thought. 'But - will the new birth certificate be genuine?'

'Oh, it will seem genuine,' said Cathy, 'because it's someone in the registrars' department that fixes it. I'm told you will get the certificate, and that's all. No one must try to get another copy in the future – or the cat will be out of the bag.'

'We would take care of the original,' said Marie, firmly.

Stefan turned to Cathy. 'This official in the registrars' office – you say he wants paying. Do you know how much?'

Cathy shook her head. 'It's not money that's needed, it's other things – ration goods, black market goods, cigarettes – things we haven't got enough of. We've got a few things together – saved some ration goods. It might not be enough, but we've got to try.'

Stefan remembered what was in his case. 'I've got a few packets of cigarettes and two pounds of coffee – will that help?'

'Help!' said Cathy. 'Of course it'll help. With that we should have enough. You can go tomorrow. The office opens at 9.30am – if you get there at 9am, you'll be first in.'

'We can get it that quick?' Stefan asked.

'Yes – if you've got the right stuff. Ask for birth registrations. The man will be wearing a blue tie with white spots. Tell him what you want, and hand him the list of things you're offering. If it's not enough he will hand it back and just say he can't deal with it at the moment. That means he wants more. He doesn't say how much more – you have to get more and keep going back. When he's satisfied he'll just do it straight away.'

Still looking nervous, Marie gave Stefan a questioning glance. He smiled and nodded.

'We'll be there early,' he said.

*

As the Post Office boat from the Channel Islands entered Portsmouth harbour, Stefan's eyes drifted idly over an old 'man of war' sailing ship among the modern naval vessels anchored nearby. But his mind was more concerned about where he could buy a bicycle.

He was not too bothered - it had been put to good use. Following Cathy's instructions, they had presented the weasel-faced registrar with the list of goods they had in exchange for a new birth certificate. They had held their breath as he looked at it, and when he slid it back across the desk, saying that he could not deal with it, tears had come to Marie's eyes and she got up to go. It was then that Stefan took the list and added 'bicycle' on the bottom, and passed it back.

Weasel face had raised his eyebrows and nodded. He opened a drawer and brought out a pad of blank birth certificates. 'May I see your identity card, sir,' he said, as he started to fill it out. They looked on as he wrote. He eventually passed it over for Stefan to sign, then blotted the form, tore it off the pad and handed it over.

'You must present the certificate to obtain a ration book and new identity card in the correct name, *monsieur* Limone' he said, solemnly. 'Is there anything else I can help you with?'

Stefan had looked at him thoughtfully and picked up his well-worn and dirty 'Pierre Limone' identity card. 'Yes - is it possible to get this replaced with a Guernsey one?'

*

Later, as they left the building, Marie gave Stefan a big hug, her face happy. Yes, it had been worth giving away the bicycle, it could be replaced.

And Cathy had been right; Marie needed more time to recover. So he had not asked her to marry him. But he told her that he would be back as soon as he was demobbed. And he also told her about his decision to go back to university to finish his degree. It would take another year. She had smiled, squeezed his arm affectionately and kissed him on the cheek.

'Saying you will come back is all I need to know, Stefan,' she said. 'There's no hurry now. We're safe here, and can wait a little longer.'

CHAPTER 33

Wing Commander Chadwick glanced either side of him to confirm that the panel was ready to start, then opened the folder in front of him, looked up at Stefan and cleared his throat.

'Uh – hum,' he grunted, then paused and glanced down at the folder. 'Pilot Officer Radovak, there are one or two points we would like to clear up from your previous debriefing session. You stated that after your narrow escape from being captured in Paris, you stole a boat and rowed off down the Seine. Is this correct?'

'Yes sir, that's correct.'

'And you kept going thirty or forty kilometres without being challenged?'

'Yes – well - not entirely - but I wasn't stopped.'

'You mean you *were* challenged?'

'Yes – after I left Paris I was going under a bridge and a young soldier guarding it told me to pull over to the bank.'

'And did you?'

'No – he was a private, I was a Todt officer – not a military rank at all – but I had no choice but to try and bluff it out.'

'And how did you do that?'

'I shouted angrily to him in German to piss off - I was in a hurry.'

There was the flicker of a smile from the Wing Commander and suppressed chuckles from the others.

'And what was his reaction to that?

'He levelled his rifle and took aim - then lowered it, laughed, and gave me a rude sign.'

Major Johnson leaned forward. 'So, after your escape from Paris, would you explain how you managed to survive until the Allies arrived?'

Stefan gave a shrug of his shoulders. 'I kept to the country - I worked on farms – usually just two weeks at a time – said I was on leave. There was no shortage of work, and they gave me food. The farmers were desperate for extra help – especially when I said I was brought up on a farm. I think some suspected I was a deserter.'

'Hmm,' the squadron leader pondered, 'so you took no further part in the war?'

'Yes, that's correct.'

'But you kept your Todt uniform?'

'Yes – it drew less attention travelling between farms – and I kept up the pretence that I was still working for Todt. But I got together some old civilian clothes for working in.'

Stefan did not like the way the questioning was going. His anxiety was slowly turning to anger. He was convinced that the stupid blighters were trying to make out that working for Todt was construed as working for the enemy.

Major Johnson raised his eyes from the file in front of him.

'I was not at your previous debriefing– but you stated that a Doctor Dubar persuaded you to join the Todt Organisation?'

'Yes - Dubar said to find out what they were doing – and where. He fixed me up with the false French identity.

'And – according to your statement, you sent him maps indicating the position of German fortifications along the coast of Normandy.'

'Yes, I marked the sites on an old school atlas, and later on a Michelin tourist map.'

Major Johnson shuffled through his file and pulled out a single small map of Normandy. He held it up.

'A map similar to this?'

Stefan recognised the map immediately.

'Not similar at all, sir, – that *is* the map from the school atlas that I marked with all the sites I worked on as far as Bayeux.'

The Major glanced at the map. 'But there are no marks at all on this map – how can you be certain that it's the same one?'

Stefan reached down and picked up the faded brown envelope he had brought in with him. Smiling, he pulled out the old atlas that he had given to Marie four years ago. It was one of the few possessions that she had taken with her to Guernsey.

'I am sure, sir, because this is the atlas that it came from.' Stefan grinned at the stunned expression on the faces of three officers as he reached over and placed it on the table. 'I forgot to say how the maps were marked. If you hold it up to the light, you will see that a pinhole indicates each site.'

In silence the map was held up in turn by each member of the panel. Major Johnson picked up the atlas and turned to the page from which the map of Normandy had been torn. It fitted perfectly. A puzzled expression crossed his face.

'If this atlas was sent to Doctor Dubar, how has it come to be back in your possession?'

'I actually gave the atlas to his daughter - Marie - I've borrowed it from her.'

Major Johnson looked surprised. 'You're still in touch with Doctor Dubar and his daughter?'

'Only his daughter – unfortunately the Doctor, and also her mother, did not survive the war.'

'And when did you last see Marie Dubar?'

'Last week, during my leave.'

The Wing Commander raised his eyebrows in surprise.

'You went back to France?'

'Yes'

The men on the panel exchanged glances.

The Wing Commander shuffled in his folder and cleared his throat again,

'Er – but I have here your new identity card –which has not been issued to you yet. Can you explain how you travelled to France without it?'

'Yes – I travelled in my French name – Pierre Limone.' There, it was out in the open. Expecting them to then ask him to hand over his false identity card, he had his answer ready. He would say he'd disposed of it in Guernsey. Which was the truth, but he wouldn't mention that – with a bit of bribery - he'd exchanged it for a Guernsey identity card, which effectively gave him British citizenship. He still needed the name of Pierre Limone for the sake of his son.

He watched with apprehension as they whispered between themselves, waiting for the next question. But none came. They nodded to each other and then the Wing Commander closed his folder and looked up.

'Thank you, Pilot Officer Radovak, that clears up the points we needed. You will be hearing the results of our recommendations in due course.'

Stefan looked at them blankly. 'I don't understand - recommendation for what? Don't you believe my story?'

The Wing Commander gave a tight smile. 'I was under the impression that you knew what we were here for,' he said as he rose from his chair, 'it was merely to clarify the facts before we made our recommendations to the French that you be considered for their highest award, the *Légion d'Honneur'*

Stefan looked from one to the other. 'A medal?' he queried.

The Wing Commander nodded. 'Those maps, Pilot Officer Radovak, indicating the location of the main batteries in Hitler's Atlantic Wall, proved vital to the Allied plans to invade Normandy. You did not have to risk your life as you did. You could have chosen to be a POW and sat out the rest of the war in safety. But you didn't. That is why we think your personal contribution to the war effort should be recognised.'

They got up to leave, and in a daze Stefan shook hands with them as they walked out. He sat down and stared at the open doorway. His thoughts went back to the Dubar's – the Doctor and his wife – and Marie, and what they had suffered. He made up his mind what he would do with the medal if he got one. He would present it to Marie.

CHAPTER 34

Max had not timed it exactly, but it must have been well over an hour since he'd found Thelma's house at Eastbourne and knocked on the door. As there was no reply he sat waiting in his car on the opposite side of the road.

Apart from a quick cup of tea before starting out, he'd had nothing all day. He was just about to go and find something to eat and return later when a woman pushing a pram turned the corner. Because he was looking out for a single woman he hardly gave a second glance as he leaned forward to start the ignition. But he stopped and looked again.

As the woman got nearer he was surprised to see that it was Thelma. The last time he saw her she was wearing her smart uniform and glowing with good health. She was much thinner now, and pale, and was dressed in clean but drab civilian clothes. And she was pushing a baby in a pram.

She didn't look happy, and his insides churned with guilt as the thought flashed through his mind that he was responsible for her unhappiness. He reached for the door handle, but waited and watched as she stopped at the house and manoeuvred the pram through the gate and up the short path to the door.

The child in the pram was obviously why she had run away without leaving her address. She had been pregnant, and Max was in no doubt that he was the father. At that moment, more than anything in the world, his impulse was to take her in his arms and comfort her, and tell her that he loved her.

He waited five minutes before he got out of the car, crossed the road to the front door, and gave three short taps on the doorknocker. He then had a sudden impulse to walk away before she answered the door. But it was too late; her shadow appeared on the other side of the glass and the door opened.

Her eyes widened as she saw him.

'Hello Thelma,' he said.

'Max!' She said, as though there was some doubt about it

'Yes, it's me - how are you?'

301

His question went unanswered. 'How did you.....' she began, and paused. ' I – I thought you were dead - lost behind enemy lines on D-Day.

'Partly true – but not the dead bit.'

She hesitated for a second, uncertain, 'Thank God you're safe, Max,' she said and came forward and gave him a quick embrace and a kiss. 'I've missed you – but I didn't expect to see you again.' She turned and stepped into the hall and came back with the child. 'You might as well meet your daughter, Max – I've named her Maxime.'

*

Anna cast an anxious eye at the clock on the mantelpiece. Max should have returned by now. She wondered whether he had decided to stay the night.

She had given him Thelma's address, but didn't tell him about the baby. She thought it best if he found out for himself. What else could she do? There was no point in a confrontation. And she didn't want him to think she'd been prying behind his back. She was also pretty sure that Max would have found Thelma's address before long and she had not wanted to give him the choice of secretly going to visit her without her knowing about it.

By giving him the address she had, by implication, given her permission for him to go and see her. It was the only way she could think of to keep some control of the situation. All she could do now was wait. Wait, that is, to see if Max wanted to go back to his relationship with Thelma, which she felt was very likely when he found out that she had had his child.

If Max left her she had already decided what she would do. Max had made it clear that he wanted to live in England. Get a farm here and start again. 'What with?' she had asked, when he told her his idea. He had shrugged, 'Not to buy – just rent - I'll get a farm somehow.'

She had shaken her head in despair. Even if they had enough to pay the rent they would have no working capital; nothing to live on for the crucial first year until they had crops to sell. And it would have to be crops because they wouldn't have the money to buy livestock. She had saved about £100, but within a few weeks she expected to be out of a job, because the Polish Hospital was closing. And Trishka had also been told that her foreign language transmissions at the BBC were no longer needed. Max had not been demobbed yet, but they knew it was likely to happen within the next month or so. So they would all be out of work at the same time that hundreds of thousands of British men and women from the services would become citizens again – and looking for employment.

At the time, she had agreed with Max that they should stay in England - but, just a few hours ago, she had received some news that was inclined to change her mind. She was hoping that when Max heard it, he would agree with her.

*

There was a gentle shaking of her shoulder. 'Wake up, Anna, time to get to bed.'

Opening her eyes with a start, Anna saw Trishka standing over her. She squinted at the clock, but her eyes wouldn't focus.

'What time is it?' she said sleepily. 'I was waiting for Max – but I don't think he'll be coming back now.' She gave a shake of her head. 'I shouldn't have given him Thelma's address, it's my own fault.'

Trishka smiled down at her. 'Anna, he came back an hour ago – said he didn't like to wake you.'

'Where is he?'

'Where do you think? He's in bed, asleep.'

'Oh,' said Anna, surprised, and knew she wouldn't sleep another wink, wondering what Max would have to say in the morning.

*

The night seemed endless as Anna lay awake listening to Maxs' gentle snoring. But at the first glimmer of dawn light she finally fell asleep, and was annoyed when she awoke to find that he was already up. She was about to jump out of bed when Max came into the bedroom carrying a tray. 'Good morning,' he said, giving her a nervous smile

'Oh' she said, 'good morning Max, this is a nice surprise.'

303

Max placed the tray on the bedside table and bent down to kiss Anna on the cheek and sat down beside her on the bed. Anna was conscious of his nervousness. She felt a slight shiver of apprehension and steeled herself to stay calm.

'I wanted to catch you before you got up because there's something I have to tell you,' he said.

'Oh – what about - your visit to Thelma? Did you find her – is she all right?'

Max gave a nod. 'Yes, I found her. She's lost weight, but she's okay.' He poured out a cup of tea, added a dash of milk and handed it to her.

So, what else do you want to tell me, Anna desperately wanted to ask – but she didn't. Instead, she sipped her tea and waited for Max to continue. He cleared his throat.

'I - I found out why she disappeared so quickly,' he said.

Anna lowered her cup. 'You did? Why did she?'

Max drew in his breath, as though to gain some extra courage.

'Because she was pregnant – and it was my child,' he said, looking directly at her. He expected a shocked response, followed by indignation and recriminations. But Anna met his gaze squarely.

'I heard that she'd had a baby, Max - I was hoping it wasn't yours,' she said quietly.

'You knew? Why didn't you tell me?'

'Max, how could I - I'm your wife. It was up to you to tell me, and now you have I appreciate the fact that you've come straight out with it.'

Max ran his hand through his hair. 'Yes, well, it had to be said. I'm sorry Anna, but it happened and you needed to know.'

'Needed to know about your affair with Thelma or to know that she'd had your child?' asked Anna, striving to keep her voice level.

'Both, I suppose.'

'Would you have told me about you and Thelma if she hadn't had a baby?'

Max remained silent for a few seconds, and then gave a small shrug. 'To be honest Anna, I don't think I would.'

Anna shook her head sadly. 'No. I don't think you would either,' she said. But, strangely, she did not feel angry. She was surprised that her feelings were more envy than anger. She knew that Max had always longed for a daughter, and now he had one – but with another woman.

'What do you intend to do now Max? Do you want to go and live with Thelma?'

'No – no,' said Max, shaking his head. 'We became lovers, yes, because the war pushed us together when we were most vulnerable – when we were stressed out, lonely and wretched – and always with the thought that I wouldn't live out the war. We both needed someone to cling to - but Thelma always said she would walk away at the end of the war. The baby made her leave earlier, that's all.'

'So, it sounds like she didn't want you to find her. What was her reaction when you turned up?'

He drew in his breath. 'Surprised – shocked, more like. The last news she heard about me I was missing in action. She thought I was dead - so she was pleased to see me still alive.'

'And what about the baby – will you stay in touch for her sake – as a father?'

'I would like to, Anna, I have to admit – but Thelma has registered her late husband as the father. So she has – well, put me out of the picture.'

Anna felt a sudden sympathy for her husband and, surprisingly, some indignation.

'Can she do that? Surely it will be noticed that her husband died two years before the birth.'

'Well, she's done it. No one knows her background where she's living, so it's not likely anyone will bother to find out the actual date her husband got killed. Anyway, the only relative she has left is a cousin living in Canada, and she wants to move out there – start a new life.'

'How do you feel about that Max?'

Max shook his head slowly. 'Frankly, very sad - I've found out I've got a daughter, but I can't be a father to her, or share the joy of seeing her grow up.'

Anna didn't say anything. Her anger at Max for having an affair was gone. She felt sad now - sad for Max in his predicament.

'Well, Max,' she said quietly, 'Thelma has done what she thinks is right – for her and the baby and for you and me. How have you left it with her – will you see her again?'

He rubbed his hand over chin. 'I'd like to – but she thinks it best if we don't. I said I would send her money but she says she can manage. She agreed to let me know when she moves, and I told her the same – nothing more.'

Anna had a feeling that Max would not give in so easily to Thelma's wishes. But with Thelma in Canada her anxiety that Max might leave her had been dispelled. She felt that it was an opportune moment to tell him the news she had heard the day before.

'Max, we had a visitor yesterday. It was Captain Linska from the Polish Embassy. Do you remember him?'

'Yes, I remember him,' he said, his voice cautious. 'What did he want?'

'He came to tell us that the Germans who had taken over our farm have been evicted. It's being looked after by some displaced farmers for the time being, but he wanted to know if we would go back and reclaim it. If we don't return within three months it will be confiscated by the state – in other words, we will lose it forever.'

Max pulled a face. 'Hm – well, you know what I want to do – I want to stay in England.'

'I know – but he said that if we go back, the new government will provide us with tractors and equipment, seeds and fertilisers, to help us get started again.'

'Did you believe him?'

'Of course – why would he lie about it?'

'I don't know – but he was on the docks at Dover when we landed from France. His behaviour was very odd.'

'Odd – how do you mean?'

'He took Stefan off to the RAF section but didn't come back to tell me what had happened – which I found was to send him straight on to his old base at Hornchurch. He damned well knew that Stefan needed constant medical attention and was not in a fit state to travel alone. It was only by sheer luck that I managed to find him again. After that I've had my doubts about him. He's attached to a Rehabilitation and Resettlement Unit - getting Poles – especially officers - back to Poland – did he mention that?'

'No - but does it matter?'

'On the face of it, it doesn't – but there's something funny going on at the Polish Divisional HQ, and it's to do with this Resettlement and Rehabilitation Unit.'

'What do you mean – funny?'

'I've been told that certain Polish officers that went back have disappeared.'

Anna looked at him puzzled. 'What do you mean – disappeared – why would they disappear?'

'I don't mean gone into hiding – I mean taken by the Soviets – the KGB.'

Anna stared at him. 'But – the Poles and the Russians were both fighting to destroy the Nazis. We were on the same side – why would they arrest Polish officers who helped to win the war?'

Max looked grim. 'That doesn't mean a thing to Stalin – he's got Poland in his grasp and he intends to keep it. Any educated Pole will be considered a threat to his ideology. Have you forgotten about Katyn?'

'Katyn – where the Germans shot all those Polish officers?'

'You don't believe that do you? The Germans found them but – in spite of the Russians denial – Polish soldiers think they were shot on Stalin's orders.'

Anna shook her head in disbelief. 'No, Max, I can't believe that – it was the Nazis.'

Max gave a weary shrug. 'Well, we might never find out the truth.'

Anna nodded, and her thoughts went back to Captain Linska. 'Captain Linska left a letter for you. It's behind the clock.'

*

Captain Linska lay on his bed staring up at the ceiling. He was feeling excited and worried at the same time. The excitement stemmed from the news that his wife and daughter had been found working as slave labourers on a farm in Austria. He'd been told that they were now on their way back to Poland, and as soon as he had completed his present assignment he would be flown home to join them.

But after his visit and talk with Mrs Radovak, she had told him that her husband wasn't thinking about returning to Poland. And that was what worried him, because that was what he'd been assigned to do - get the Radovaks' to return to Poland. He'd been relieved of all other duties and told to concentrate on this assignment.

His superiors had gravely explained to him that men of the stature and calibre of Max Radovak were badly needed in Poland. Stalin had declared that he had no desire to make the country part of the USSR - they would be free to govern themselves. None of this had been mentioned, or even hinted, to Mrs Radovak, but he had an idea that there was something in the letter he had left addressed to her husband that would change his mind about returning. All he had told her was that their farm had been looked after and was ready for their return. This was what he had been instructed to say, and so believed it was true. But he had deliberately lied to her on another matter.

She was Russian born, she told him, and her parents lived in the USSR. Had they survived the war, she wanted to know?

'I'll try to find out for you,' he had promised reassuringly. But he already knew the answer. When the Germans invaded the USSR in 1941 they had burned down their village and killed everyone. The lie was another incentive to get them back to Poland.

*

Max went into the living room and returned with the envelope, tearing it open as he sat down on the edge of the bed. Anna watched as he read it through. She saw the look of surprise on his face.

'What is it, Max?' she asked.

Max remained silent as he read the letter through a second time, and then he handed it to her.

Anna narrowed her eyes slightly as she concentrated to read it. Halfway through she sucked her breath and said 'Oh, Max,' as she continued reading. When she looked up Max was staring at her, his face serious.

'What are you going to do - can you refuse to go back now?'

Max shook his head slowly. 'I don't see how I can refuse that,' he said.

CHAPTER 35

Just after mid-day in the middle of September 1945, two large American Air Force transporters touched down at a remote aerodrome in Herefordshire. One minute after they came to a halt, the front of the aircraft opened up and jeeps of Popski's Private Army trundled down the ramps.

Igor looked around him curiously at his first sight of England. There was a brief pause at the exit as an army motorcyclist joined them to lead the way to their camp. Fifteen minutes later they entered the grounds of a large country house and the small convoy stopped at a group of huts among the trees. Parking the jeeps alongside the huts, the men picked up their kit bags and looked expectantly towards Popski. He was standing up in his jeep, and he motioned for them to gather around him.

'Well, men, welcome back to Blighty - and for those who, like Captain Radovak, have not been here before, welcome to England. This is not our camp, it belongs to the SAS but, as we have never had the need for a camp in England before now, they have kindly offered to accommodate us until we're disbanded.'

At the word 'disbanded' there was a murmur from the men.

'Yes, I'm afraid so – the PPA has done it's job - there are no more enemy lines to work behind.'

There was a subdued murmuring before someone asked. 'Any idea how long it will be before we're disbanded, skip?'

'I can't give you a definite date yet – but it will be weeks rather than months. It's likely that PPA will be disbanded at the same time as you're demobbed. In the meantime, from tomorrow, you will all get two weeks leave. Anyone who wishes to stay in camp and do some local sightseeing can do so. But I'll be away in London. When I return I should be able to tell you more. You can obtain cash against pay due and temporary ration cards from the paymaster in the morning. Thanks men, that's all for now – enjoy your leave.'

The men with wives, sweethearts and families to go back to did most of the talking after that, and in small happy groups went off looking for information about local trains and buses to connect up with various parts of the country..

The men not sure of what they were going back to, or simply had no one to go back to, were quiet and thoughtful. Igor was one of these.

In Italy, before he went to sleep, Igor often looked at the small photograph he had found in Leon Denkov's wallet and wondered if Trishka had been told he'd been killed. Even if she knew, it was doubtful she would know that he had died saving her husband's life. Perhaps the best course would be, when he found her, not to say anything. Destroy the letters, the wallet and the photograph and pretend it had never happened. Could he do that? He didn't know.

Six years was a long time and, by now, she might have found another man. After all, she'd done it once, why not twice? Anyway, would she want him back after six years? And did he still want her? His love for her was based on what they had at the start of the war. But he knew that until they were face to face he would not know.

He felt sure that the child in the photograph was his. This was why, in Italy, it had seemed so straightforward. When he got to England, he would immediately go to London to find her and his son. Strangely though, within an hour of landing, the urgency to find Trishka had left him. Try as he might, he could not forget that Leon Denkov had taken his place.

He emptied his kitbag onto the bed and started sorting through his few belongings. The shorts and shirts that he had worn in Italy now looked pitiful. It was not likely that he would ever wear them again. He put them aside and picked up the goatskin waistcoat that had belonged to Mr Lubin. He held it up. It had been useful during the cold Italian winters and, like his other kit, was well worn. The three leather buttons were splitting apart and hanging off. He looked closely at each in turn, then pulled them off and put them into his pocket.

He picked up Mr Lubins trousers, rolled around the shiny black shoes. They were the only civilian clothes he had, but doubted that he would ever wear them. He put the trousers aside and tried on the shoes. They fitted reasonable well, but the heels were higher than normal. Even so, they were good quality shoes, too good to throw out. He put them under the bed.

Shadows crossed over his bed and he looked up. Mac, his driver, and two others were standing there.

'Excuse me, skip - but Evans and Shaw and me are staying in camp – we thought we would do some local sightseeing. We were wondering if it's OK to use one of the jeeps.'

Igor paused for a second, collecting his thoughts, and then gave a grin.

'Sure you can, Mac, so long as you don't mind me joining you.' Mac's request had given him an ideal excuse to delay making the journey to London. He needed more time to think, to prepare. He would see a bit of England first and buy some new clothes.

*

Trishka saw the taxi stop outside the house as she got off the bus further down the road. As she walked along she saw a British officer emerge, pay the fare, then check the number of the house with a piece of paper in his hand. He walked up the short path to the door. Before he had time to knock she was there. She noticed his rank.

'Can I help you, Captain?' she called out, 'I live there.'

Igor swung around, a startled – guilty almost - look on his face. He had recognised her voice immediately, but when he saw her he realised that he might have passed her in the street, her appearance had changed so much.

She was still looking at him curiously, without recognition, waiting for his reply.

Remembering that the scars to his face had changed his own appearance, he took off his cap and smiled. 'Hello, Trishka – remember me – Igor?'

A stunned look crossed her face. 'Igor? My God - is it really you?' she said.

Igor gave a nervous nod. 'Yes, it's me – how are you?'

Recognition finally came to her face, followed by an expression he had not anticipated at all. She looked angry.

'You've been dead for six years, Igor – and now you turn up out of the blue and say 'remember me' and 'how are you.' Couldn't you have *told* somebody you was still alive?'

311

Taken aback, Igor raised his eyebrows in surprise as his brain groped for a suitable response - and in that instance he knew. Trishka *had* changed. She had changed her hairstyle; her clothes; she wore makeup and lipstick, and she was not the girl he remembered, but a self-possessed, more mature woman. But in that instance the years apart fell away - and he knew he still loved her.

Before he could reply the look of anger was gone and he saw her lips quiver and her eyes fill with tears. She hesitated only briefly before stepping forward and flinging her arms around his neck, planting her lips to his in a passionate kiss. He held her tight, and they stayed locked together for another half minute before breaking away for air. Trishka wiped at her eyes and smiled.

'I'm sorry, my love,' she said, tenderly. 'The last three months have been agony – wondering if you were still alive. But I should have known. Do you remember the last words you said to me when we parted?'

Igor smiled at her fondly. 'Yes I do, Trishka – I said I'd be back.'

She nodded and gave him another kiss. 'Yes you did,' she said, 'but after we got to England at the end of 1940, I had a letter from the International Red Cross to say you'd been killed.' She turned to open the front door. 'So it was a bit of a shock –you turning up without warning.' He followed her through the door. 'And you *are* a Captain now – a British Army Captain,' she continued.

'Yes – I'm attached to a British unit at the moment. I couldn't find a Polish uniform. I bought this uniform a few days ago in Bath – the shop was having a clear out now the war is over - uniforms ordered and never collected. But – I'm curious – you said that you'd been waiting in agony for three months. How did you know I might be alive – and a Captain?'

Trishka walked over to the mantelshelf and pulled the airmail letter from behind the clock.

'We had no idea at all until this arrived in father's post. It's been waiting there to see if you turned up.'

He looked at the envelope, saw it was posted in Canada and realised that it must be from Spencer's father. An acknowledgement of the letter he had sent to tell him that his son was dead. He gave a small nod. 'I know who it's from,' he murmured, putting it into his pocket. Now that she had mentioned his father, he was more anxious to hear about him.

'Father's safe then – he's here - in England?'

'Yes, he got out of Warsaw before the Nazis arrived – he's a brigadier now.'

'And Stefan – is he alive?'

'Yes, Stefan joined the RAF – he got shot down and was reported dead – but like you - he's turned up.'

Igor shook his head in disbelief. 'So, we all got through it – we're all alive. But – how did you and mother get here – did you get on a boat.'

'No, we joined the partisans with Josef – we lived in the forests for a year – and then the RAF flew us out.'

'So Josef is here too – good old Uncle Josef.'

Trishka shook her head sadly, 'No, Igor– he became a fireman and was killed in the blitz.'

The smile faded from Igor's face. 'Poor Josef – he was like one of the family – I thought he was until I was sixteen.'

They were silent for several seconds, thinking about Josef. And then a thought occurred to Trishka.

'How long have you known that your mother and I were still alive, Igor?'

Igor felt a stab of guilt at the mention of his mother. 'Yes – mother – does she live with you?'

'Yes, we all live together – but you seem to have known that.' And then, without thinking, she glanced at the clock and carried on. 'She'll be back in half an hour or so – she's taken the children to the shops.'

Igor realised that any thoughts about not telling Trishka about the photograph he had found in Leon Denkov's wallet were gone. He would have to tell her – but her last remark drew a quick question to his lips. He only knew about one child.

'Children?' he queried.

Trishka silently cursed herself for the slip. She suspected that Igor was aware that he had a son - but she had planned to tell him about Leon before admitting to having another son by him. She nodded, looking nervous. 'You'd better sit down,' she said, indicating one of the fireside chairs. She sat down facing him.

'Yes, Igor - I've got two boys – one, Gregor, is yours. The father of Simon, my other boy, was also a Polish officer – one of the partisans.

We all came out of Poland together and,' she paused and looked directly into his eyes, 'and I want you to know that there was nothing at all between us at that time. I feel guilty about it now, but I felt so wretched after I heard you were dead and – well, it was after he heard that his family had been wiped out we started going out together, to console each others grief I suppose.' She looked at him, trying to read his face. 'We only slept together once, Igor – just before he went away.'

Igor could see more tears trickling down her cheeks. 'Do you know what happened to him?' he asked, gently.

She wiped at her tears. 'I had one or two letters from him – he was in Italy - and I wrote back – but then his letters stopped – and mine eventually came back unopened.'

It was time to tell her how Leon had died. He reached out and took her hand. 'Trishka – I have something to tell you – I was also in Italy and – I met Leon Denkov – just before he died. '

She stared at him as she tried to grasp what he was saying. 'You *knew* Leon – you knew about us all along?'

'No, no, Trishka,' he said, squeezing her hand, ' let me explain.'

And he told her what had happened – how Leon Denkov had come to his aid and probably saved his life at the cost of his own. Of Spencer, who had asked him to write to his next of kin, and how, when he settled down to write, he found her letter and the photograph in Leon's wallet. As he finished talking he pulled out the 'photo and her letter, his wallet, gold ring, his wristwatch, and passed them to her.

In awe, she reached out and took them from him, wiping at her face again when she saw the bloodstained letter.

'So Leon died in your arms - and then you found these –it must have been a shock.'

'Well, he didn't die in my arms, Trishka, but he was badly shot up and not conscious. As I left his men were taking him to an old Doctor in the village – not that he could do anything – he was too far gone – but just to clean him up and arrange a decent funeral.'

Trishka lifted her head. 'He *wasn't* dead then – do you think…….?' She paused.

' - That he might have survived?' said Igor, finishing the sentence for her. 'No, Trishka - I'm sure I'd have heard if he'd pulled through. And if he did pull through, he'd have let you know by now, wouldn't he?'

Trishka nodded sadly. 'Yes, he would,' she whispered.

CHAPTER 36

The remains of two black market chickens dominated the centre of the table as Anna gazed around with a happy smile on her face. Her mind went back to the last family gathering. The occasion had been Igor's wedding to Trishka in May 1939. She reflected on the six years of carnage, destruction and cruelty in between, the like of which the world had never before witnessed. They had been lucky to survive, when so many Polish families had been destroyed.

The meal had stretched out because each in turn had briefly recounted their war experiences to the others. Except for Marie, who had come over from Guernsey with little Stefan. Marie was content to listen to the family conversing in Polish, with Stefan giving her a running commentary in French. She found it hard to recall a time when she felt so happy.

Max waited until the conversation began to slow down before he got to his feet and raised his glass.

'I'd like to propose a toast - a toast to us all. Against the odds, we've all got through a bloody awful war. So – to us – the Radovaks' – including, of course, the future Mrs Radovak – Marie.'

They stood up and raised their glasses of the wine that Max had brought back from France. 'To us – the Radovaks,' they said in unison. And then Anna got up.

'And I'd like us to raise our glasses to Josef – and to Leon, and Jak Zenski – and everyone else we knew who didn't make it.'

They said another solemn toast and sat down. It was Igor who broke the short silence. He glanced over to his father.

'I'm surprised to hear you're returning to Poland, father. What kind of job have you been offered?'

Max got up and fetched the letter from the mantelpiece. He opened it out and passed it to Igor. 'Here – tell me what you think,' he said.

Igor read it through and then passed it to Stefan. 'Phew, Minister for Agriculture – that's quite a title.'

'Yes- and it'll be a worthwhile challenge. Before that letter arrived we were a bit divided about what we should do. I had it in mind to rent a farm in England – but your mother doesn't think we can afford that. We came to England with nothing – and we've still got nothing – and our army pay will stop when we're demobbed. So now we've been told that our farm is waiting for us to go back to – together with that offer – I don't think we have any other option *but* to go back.'

Stefan looked up. 'I see that the letter's from the PKWN - *Polski Komitet Lyzwolenia Narodewego* – the Polish Committee for National Liberation. Isn't that the puppet government set up by Stalin?'

Max nodded. 'I believe it is – but I understand that the committee are all Poles.'

Igor shook his head. 'They may be Poles, but they've been chosen because they're dedicated communists – more loyal to Stalin than Poland. I always thought you hated Stalin.'

'I do – but I can pretend not to for the sake of Poland. Somebody has got to do the job – and better me than a crooked communist.'

'But you can't trust any government where Stalin pulls the strings. He hates us Poles worse than the Nazis did. Have you forgotten what the Nazis found at Katyn – a mass grave of thousands of Polish officers killed by the Russians.'

'Oh, come now, Igor, that's just what your father thinks' said Anna, 'the Russians flatly denied they had anything to do with that.'

Igor looked over the table at his mother, and then he reached out and took her hand.

'Mother, do you remember a little while ago, during the meal, when I said I was captured by the Russians but managed to escape?'

'Yes, I remember,' said Anna.

'Well, I didn't say where I escaped.' He looked at her sadly, because his mother was Russian, and he knew how much it would hurt her to know the truth. 'It was Katyn, mother – I escaped from the Russians in the forest at Katyn.'

Anna stared at him for a moment. 'Did you see them being shot, Igor?'

'No, I got away before that.'

'Did you see the mass graves?'

'No – I didn't hang around.'

'Then how can you be so sure that the Nazis didn't come across a POW camp full of Polish officers and decided to kill them all?'

316

Igor shook his head slowly. 'Well, from the photographs the Nazis issued, they'd been dead for some time. But you're right, mother, I can't prove anything - although I'm still convinced it was Stalin's work. The Germans always showed some respect for officers – Stalin feared them. Don't forget his purge of Russian officers in 1937 – when he got rid of about 30.000 of them.'

Anna looked sad at these words. 'Yes, I remember that,' she said, quietly.

Max took a sip from his glass and put it down, deciding it was time to change the focus of conversation. 'What about you and Trishka, Igor, are you going back to Poland?'

'No Max,' said Trishka, quickly, 'we're definitely not going back.'

Igor nodded in agreement. 'That's right, father – we don't think there's anything for us to go back to.'

'What will you do then?' asked Anna.

Igor smiled. 'Well, I've had an offer of a job, but Trishka's not too keen on that idea - so I thought I'd look for a job with a firm of architects - and when the children start school, Trishka wants to go back to teaching.'

'Hmm, but you say you've been offered a job,' said Max. 'What kind of job was that?'

Igor reached into his pocket and out pulled the airmail letter that Spencer's father had written from Canada. He passed it over the table.

'You probably recognise this – it's the one that was in your post and you put behind the clock. It's from the father of a very good friend and comrade I had in Italy - who was killed.'

Everyone watched and waited as Max read the letter. When he finished he passed it back.

'It's pretty clear that his son thought very highly of you, Igor. But, as the old man says, he's got no son's left now to run the farm, and his health's getting worse. So his offer to pay your fare to Canada and manage his farm sounds good to me. You could manage a few thousand acres, couldn't you?'

Anna's face lit up. 'Manage a farm in Canada? What an opportunity, Igor – surely you haven't turned it down.'

'No, mother,' said Igor, shaking his head, 'I've not replied yet - but, from what I've seen of England, I'd like to settle here – and so would Trishka.'

'I think *we'd* go to Canada, given the chance,' Stefan said with some enthusiasm 'Marie's got cousins living in Quebec.'

'And there's no rationing over there - no shortage of anything – and no bombed out cities. It'll take years before Britain recovers from the war,' said Anna.

Trishka and Igor exchanged glances. 'Well, as I said, I haven't replied yet,' said Igor.

'I shouldn't leave it too long, son,' said Max. 'That letter was sent a few months ago. He might already have given up waiting to hear from you and found somebody else.'

'But – it's such a long way to go,' said Trishka. 'And we'd miss not having any family around.'

'Well, if your mother and I go back to Poland, we won't be around. What are you thinking of doing when you've got your degree, Stefan?'

'Find somewhere to live in Birmingham – where there's plenty of jobs for engineers – and settle down to married life. But this talk about Canada has made me think. I've always thought Canada was a great country, and so does Marie. With an engineering degree, I reckon I could get as good a job there as here.' He conveyed this to Marie in French, and she smiled her agreement.

Max gave a nod. 'I'm sure you could, Stefan,' he said, and looked over at Igor and Trishka. 'So it might be that within a year we could all be in different countries.'

Silence fell as they contemplated being split up again so soon after being reunited. Family had always meant so much to them. But this was a new world they were facing.

'There's another thing to consider,' Anna said, breaking the silence. 'Once you're out of the army you've got to find somewhere to live – and with so many houses destroyed and damaged in the war, there's going to be a shortage in England. The owners of this house want it back, and we're on six months notice to vacate. The job in Canada obviously includes a house – probably rent free – have you thought of that?'

Trishka smiled at Igor. 'I think you'd better get that reply off, Igor - tell him we're on our way.'

Igor rubbed his chin. 'Yes – I suppose it's the best option - I'm beginning to think training to be an architect was a waste of time.'

'Not at all, Igor,' said Anna, 'that's the second string for your bow –it'll always be there to fall back on should you need it.'

Trishka saw the look of resignation on Igor's face. 'That's true Anna,' she said, 'but I reckon Igor would prefer it the other way around - architect first, farming second.'

'Yes – but if the job's still there, with a house included – we might regret not taking it,' said Igor. He made up his mind to send a telegraph the next morning – a letter would be too slow.

CHAPTER 37

Captain Linska had arranged for a taxi to transport the Radovaks' to the airport. He had already informed them that a Swedish passenger aeroplane had been chartered to take the next batch of officers back to Poland, and he was going with them.

The taxi took them north out of London to an airport built during the war at Stansted. Captain Linska was waiting to greet them and help them with their luggage. He noted that Brigadier Radovak, although polite, was serious and preoccupied. Mrs Radovak was more talkative - sorry to be leaving England, but keen to get back to their farm and, as soon as she could get the necessary permit, to travel the ninety or so kilometres into Russia to visit her parents.

By know he knew for certain that her parents were dead, but by the time she found out it would be too late. She might curse him for lying, but not be able to do anything about it.

His assignment had been completed. He had got Max Radovak and his wife to return to Poland. Not the son, classified as dead for most of the war and only just turned up, or Trishka and the two children. Some other Rehabilitation and Resettlement officer would be detailed to get them back to Poland.

The rest of the family was no concern of his; he was on his way to be re-united with his wife and daughter. The tension and worry he'd felt as the day of departure drew near had left him. Today he felt relaxed and happy, and had exerted himself to be as cheerful and helpful to the Radovaks' as he could. Looking around he noted that, apart from Anna Radovak, there was only one other woman passenger.

After the final check against the passenger list they were led out to the aircraft. Carrying a small suitcase Captain Linska walked three or four places behind the Radovaks'. As they approached the steps to the aircraft a Polish Sergeant pushed ahead of him and spoke to the brigadier. 'Excuse me, sir - could I have a word?' he heard him say.

Max stepped out of the line. 'Yes, what is it, Sergeant?' he asked with slight irritation, indicating to his wife to carry on.

Linska, curious to hear what the Sergeant had to say, was tempted to pause and listen, but instead had to feign unconcern as he started up the steps to the aircraft. But as he brushed by he saw Max Radovak looking at a small photograph.

He waited for Mrs Radovak to find her seat and nodded and smiled as he walked on down the aircraft. Before he sat down he glanced back and saw Max Radovak enter and walk towards his wife. Relieved, he sank down and settled into his seat, and then opened the newspaper he had bought to read on the journey.

Five minutes later the engines started up and the aircraft began to move. He looked out of the small circular window next to him. There were a few people around the conning tower waving, and he saw a woman getting into a car. He turned away and lifted his newspaper – and then lowered it again as a seed of doubt entered his mind. A frown crossed his face, and he tried again to look out of the window, but the aircraft had turned and the conning tower was out of sight.

He swivelled his head around and looked behind him. Panic seized him as he scanned the faces of the passengers. The Radovaks' were not there – their seats were empty.

'Stop! Stop the 'plane,' he shouted, and started to get up from his seat.

An airhostess rushed forward and pushed him down. 'Please sit down, sir,' she said firmly, 'we're about to take off.'

'But – there are two passengers missing – we can't leave without them – where are they?'

'They got off, sir, that's all I know. Now - please sit down during takeoff,' she said, her voice louder and firmer

Linska stared at her for a second or two, then slumped back into his seat, his expression a mixture of defeat and fright.

As the aircraft left the ground and lifted into the sky the airhostess noticed that the passenger who had caused the disturbance was crying.

*

Anna held the small snapshot nearer to the window of the car.

'Yes, that's definitely it,' she said, and turned it over to read the few words of Polish on the back. Written in capitals, the short message read, 'DON'T GO – IT'S A TRAP.'

'Where are you taking us, Sergeant?' asked Max.

Sergeant Lowzki glanced at them in his rear view mirror. 'Only a few miles, sir –we're heading for a small village in the country, but Colonel Manzk said to make sure we're not followed.'

'Colonel Manzk - is this the same Colonel that has shared my room at Divisional HQ?'

'Yes, sir - I told him weeks ago that you wanted to have a word with him, and he said that he'd be in touch. He turned up this morning and told me to rush to the airport to give you that. I only just made it, sir - sorry about that.'

'It was no fault of yours, Sergeant. I'd like to have tackled Captain Linska about this - but it's probably best that he's on his way back to Poland.'

Ten minutes later the Sergeant turned off the main road and followed a country lane. The village, when they came to it, was a typical sleepy place where time seemed to have stood still for centuries. But there was a post office, a small general store, and a pub called 'The Bull.' There was also, at the far end of the village, a 13th century church with a square Norman tower, and this was where the Sergeant stopped the car.

'This is it, sir - St Peter's Church. My instructions are to wait in the car for you.'

Max and Anna exchanged a mystified look.

'Did Colonel Manzk definitely say he would meet us here?' asked Anna.

'Yes, mum - a nice quiet place, he said.'

Max opened the car door. 'Well, we will wait in the church - if he's not already there.'

Anna linked arms with Max and they walked up the gravel path to the church. The heavy door creaked as they opened it, and the subdued and peaceful atmosphere of centuries of worship descended upon them as they looked around.

'There's no one here,' said Max, quietly.

'Just Saint Peter and myself,' said a voice behind them.

They turned in surprise. The man arose from a small wooden chair in the shadows at the back of the church. He looked like a typical English countryman dressed in tweeds, and was leaning on a walking stick. He had a polite smile on his face.

'I'm very pleased to meet you, Brigadier, and Mrs Radovak,' he said, turning to Anna with a slight bow.

'And I'm pleased to meet you at last, Colonel,' said Max, holding out his hand. After they shook hands, Max took the small photograph out of his pocket.

The message on the back of this persuaded us to get off the 'plane - but the photograph is proof that we had been lied to. Can you explain how you got hold of it?'

'Yes, of course - but let me explain first of all that I am, officially, a Colonel in the KGB. Unofficially, and secretly, I am a Colonel in Polish Military Intelligence. That photograph was sent to me by one of our secret agents in Poland - someone I believe you know well, Mrs Radovak – his name is Jak Zenski.'

Anna gasped in surprise. 'Jak – he's alive?'

'Yes – he lost a foot in the war, but otherwise he's well and playing the part of a dedicated pro-Russian communist. Somehow he found out that the KGB wanted to get you back to Poland – the offer of a job in government was the carrot - but you would have been arrested, either immediately or within a short time. That is why Zenski took a picture of your farmhouse. As you can see, it's now in ruins. Your farm, in fact, has been taken over by a Russian commissar – you would have been arrested just for trying to assert your ownership. There's another thing you should know, Mrs Radovak – Captain Linska did not tell you the truth about your parents – I'm sorry to say that the Nazis wiped out the whole village when they invaded Russia in 1941 – no one escaped.'

Tears came to Anna's eyes. She shook her head. 'And Captain Linska knew this all along?'

'Yes – but he was also lied to. He was told that his wife and daughter were still alive and he would be reunited with them as soon as he got both of you back to Poland.'

'But they are dead?'

Colonel Manzk nodded.

Max shook his head in puzzlement. 'But why me in particular – I'm hardly a political activist.'

The other man shrugged. 'Who knows – except that you've never hidden your opinion of Stalin – some of the men and officers who fought alongside you may have been spies. But there's no doubt that the Russians badly want to get their hands on you.'

'Hm, but I'm not alone in detesting Stalin – most Poles share the same opinion. What about the officers who have gone back and disappeared – is there any news of them?'

'We've found out where they are. With the unofficial help of British Intelligence, we are now playing the same game.'

'The same game?'

'Yes, starting today, approximately fifty known KGB and NKVD agents in Britain will be rounded up and will 'disappear.' When the Russians protest, the British will tell them that a cache of Polish officers are responsible and offer to act as mediators. And then, after a few days – tell them that the disappearance of their own agents is in retaliation for the disappearance of the officers who returned to Poland.'

'Do you think it'll work?'

'The British think so – the Russians will be told that they will only get their own people back when the Polish officers are released.'

'Stalin will be hopping mad about that.'

'Well, he might be when we release them and he learns that they've just been on holiday.'

'On holiday - where will they be?'

'They've been booked into first class hotels on the Isle of Man. They'll be free to enjoy the full hospitality of the Island – except that there'll be no telephone lines or communication to the mainland, or anywhere else.'

Max and Anna both gave a smile. 'Good,' said Max, 'and we're grateful to you, Colonel – for being so frank.'

Colonel Manzk nodded an acknowledgement. 'I'm not sure what plans you might now have, but may I make a suggestion?'

'Of course.'

'Might I suggest that, as you are packed, you do not return to London for a few days – that you go down to Devon or Cornwall and have a break by the sea.'

'In other words, keep out of the way for a while.'

'Yes.'

Max turned to Anna. 'I think that's a good idea,' she said. 'And it'll give us some time to think about what we're going to do.'

'Hm, I'll be happy to talk about getting back to farming,' said Max with a smile.

Colonel Manzk tapped his stick down as a thought struck him.

'There's a man I know in British Intelligence,' he said, 'he's leaving shortly to go back to his civilian job as land agent to some earl. Would you like me to make some enquiries for you?'

'Yes, thank you,' said Max. 'You could leave a message with Sergeant Lowski if you hear anything.

CHAPTER 38

Ernest Spencer replied from Canada within two days of receiving Igor's telegram. It was short and to the point.

Job still open stop advise how soon can leave plus how many travelling stop will book passage stop
E Spencer

Igor replied that his demobilisation was in five days time, and his wife and two children would be travelling with him.

Three days later, around midday, Igor was inspecting Mr. Lubin's old shoes and wondering if the high heels could be lowered when there was a knock on the front door. Trishka was in the middle of doing the washing in the kitchen. 'Can you answer the door Igor,' she called.

'Yes, I'll get it,' he said, descending the stairs.

He opened the front door to find a Polish officer standing there. He had a polite smile on his face, but this faded when he saw Igor.

'Ah,' he said, 'I wish to speak to Brigadier Radovak - is he at home?'

Igor, not having met Captain Linska before, or knowing anything about him, gave a friendly smile.

'No, sorry - he doesn't live here any more. He and my mother returned to Poland three days ago.'

The Captain's eyes narrowed in thought. 'Your parents - so - you must be – Igor?' he said.

'Yes - I'm Igor - I assume you're an old comrade of my father – please, come in.' He stepped aside.

'Thank you,' said Linska, as he walked through the door. 'Yes, I have been acquainted with your parents since the early days of the war. I remember their grief when they heard you had been killed in action - and then Stefan your brother, shot down in the sea. But you have both turned up alive. It must have been a very joyful occasion when you were all reunited.'

Igor grinned. 'Yes - it was,' he said.

'And, like your parents, you will want to get back to Poland as soon as it can be arranged?'

'Er – no – I've been offered a job in Canada.'

'Canada?'

'No – Canberra – Australia,' interrupted Trishka, emerging from the kitchen wiping her hands on a towel. 'Hello, Captain Linska- I overheard what you were saying from the kitchen. I thought the Brigadier and Mrs Radovak were on the same aeroplane as yourself - didn't it go?'

With Trishka butting in with a lie about their destination Igor realised that there was something about Captain Linska that Trishka knew and he did not. Alerted, he looked on.

Linska drew in his breath and tucked his chin into his neck as he recalled the humiliation of arriving in Poland without the Radovaks'. He had been ordered to return and find them and persuade him to get on the next flight.

'Yes,' he said, 'it went - I saw them get on the aircraft - but then they got off - it left without them.'

'And you don't know why?' asked Trishka

'No, that is the reason for my call. As we were about to board the plane the Brigadier received a message. I was concerned that a crisis had arisen - a family crisis perhaps.'

He looked from one to the other as they shook their heads, puzzled.

'So you have not seen or heard from them?' he asked.

'No, we have not,' said Igor

Linska nodded. He believed them. He took a pen from his pocket. 'If you have a piece of paper I will leave you a telephone number where the Brigadier can contact me. It is important that I speak to him as soon as possible.'

*

The postcard arrived the next day. It was a view of Sidmouth, in Devon.

'It's from Anna and Max,' said Trishka in surprise, scanning the brief message on the back. 'They say they decided not to go back –.' She passed it to Igor.

'Can't say I'm sorry about that,' he said as he took it from her and read it through.

'Hm – they'll tell us all about it when they get back – but they're now on their way to Wiltshire to see about a job for father.'

'Yes,' said Trishka thoughtfully. 'It's all very mysterious - I wonder who sent that message – and what was in it.'

'This Captain Linska – you don't trust him?'

'No – not any more - he was very helpful when we first arrived in England, but your father thinks he's now being controlled by the KGB.'

CHAPTER 39

The pungent smell of leather and shoe polish wafted at them as Trishka ushered the children into the cobbler's shop. From her shopping basket she brought out a pair of Gregor's shoes, and then a pair of her own, and finally the shoes that Igor referred to as 'Mr. Lubin's'

The cobbler was behind the counter, in leather apron; with brass framed spectacles half way down his nose. He smiled politely and said 'Good morning'

'Good morning,' said Trishka. She pointed to Gregor's shoes. 'Could you put new soles on these, please.' She lifted her own shoes. 'And these need to be heeled.'

The cobbler inspected the shoes and quoted a price, and when Trishka nodded he turned his attention to the final pair. 'And these?' he said, picking them up and turning them over, 'they seem to be in good repair.'

'My husband wondered if you could reduce the heels on those - or put on new ones.'

The cobbler inspected each in turn. 'It shouldn't be difficult,' he said, 'I think they were made lower and have had extra height added.'

'Oh – good - thank you - how long before they are ready?'

'Er -seven days - I'll give you a ticket,' said the cobbler absentmindedly as he continued looking at the shoes.

'Thank you,' said Trishka, and waited. He looked up after a few seconds.

'I see that the heels have been screwed on, which is unusual - can you wait while I get a screwdriver.'

'Of course,' said Trishka.

He hurried away and returned with a screwdriver and tackled one of the shoes. There were three screws and when the final one came out the heel dropped in half to reveal a cavity. Trishka gave a gasp

'Well, bless me,' the cobbler exclaimed in surprise.

*

'Igor!' Trishka called out as she pushed open the front door.

'I'm here,' he answered, walking from the kitchen. He held up an envelope.

'This has just arrived -- there's been a cancellation – we've got berths on the 'Queen Mary' - it sails from Liverpool in seven days time.'

'Seven days,' queried Trishka, re-focusing her mind. 'But- that's the day I've got to collect the shoes.'

Igor laughed. 'Well - we can ask them to delay the sailing - or collect the shoes early - repaired or not - which shall we do?'

Trishka smiled. 'I'll go back tomorrow- see if he can do them quicker'

Gregor pulled at her coat. 'Tell him, mummy,' he said, 'tell him.'

Igor tussled his hair. 'Tell me what, young Gregor,' he said with a smile.

Gregor craned his neck back to look up at his father. 'It's a surprise,' he said.

Trishka opened her handbag and pulled out her handkerchief. She unfolded it to reveal four rings and a diamond brooch.

Igor's eyes opened wide. 'Phew -where did you get those.'

'Out of Mr. Lubin's shoes,' said Trishka, 'they were in the heels.'

Igor inspected the rings. One was plain gold; one had a single diamond; one had diamonds with a sapphire, and the other diamonds and rubies. The small brooch sparkled with diamonds. His mind went back to Mr. Lubin's final moments on the boat; when he whispered '......take the clothes - useful.'

He looked thoughtful for a moment and then put the rings down and went to his wardrobe. He took out Mr. Lubin's old trousers, searched through the pockets and brought out the three leather buttons that he had taken off the goatskin jerkin. Picking aside the frayed leather he pulled out what looked like a grey, pea sized, pebble. He held it out for Trishka to see.

'What's that,' she said

'If I'm not mistaken,' he said, 'that is an uncut diamond - and there's three of them.'

'Crikey,' she said, 'we're rich.'

'Well – all together they must be worth a hundred or two - we need to get them valued.'

*

Max licked the back of the envelope and sealed it down.

'That's my formal resignation done,' he said. 'I haven't told them the reasons for not going back - only that I've been offered employment in England and we are, therefore, giving up our rights to the farm and donating it to the new Polish State.'

'That sounds patriotic and generous enough,' said Anna, 'and doesn't give any hint that we know the truth.'

'Exactly,' said Max. 'Any suspicion about what we know and how we found out would start a witch-hunt. If there's a secret intelligence network still operating in Poland, we've got to protect it the best we can.'

A few minutes later Stefan arrived from Birmingham and they moved to the table for their last meal together before parting.

'Tell us about this farming job you've got, father,' said Stefan as he sat down

Max gave a smile. 'It isn't a job yet – and it's not farming. But it is an offer to consider.'

'Not farming? So what kind of job is it?'

'Well, it covers about fifty acres of Earl Shaftsbury's estate in Wiltshire.'

'Fifty - not big then.'

'Enough for the purpose, I think.' Max smiled

'Is there a special purpose?'

'Yes, the job is to manage the earl's pedigree stock. And he wants to expand it. Not just pedigree cattle and horses – but sheep, pigs, poultry, goats, and a few others. There's a worldwide market, apparently, for English pedigree stock, and after six years of war the demand is pretty high.'

'Sounds good,' said Igor, 'but a big responsibility. Is the pay good?'

'Enough to live on - and there's a farmhouse that goes with it, and a percentage of the profits as the stock is sold. The only snag is that

I've never worked for anyone else before. I'd rather have my own farm.'

'I know Max, we've gone through all that, but it's a good offer.' said Anna. 'And there's another thing. The earl needs a vet, and if we take the job has agreed to pay the fees for me to do a veterinary course at Salisbury.'

Igor grinned. 'That's sounds great, mother, but how long have you got before you have to decide?'

'About three months – the earl plans to start buying his pedigree stock in the spring. He's not advertising the job until February.'

'So you have some time to look around and think it over. How did you come to hear about it?'

'Connections, Igor,' said Max with a smile. 'In fact, it came through a Polish Intelligence officer – who will remain anonymous. He also gave us the news that the leader of the partisan group that your mother and Trishka belonged to is still alive.'

'You mean Jak - Jak Zenski is still alive?' queried Trishka.

'Yes,' said Anna, 'but he's lost a foot.'

'And now living under a different name,' said Max.

'Hm – your Polish friend seems well informed.'

'Yes – and to be trusted - when we leave here tomorrow he will be the only one – apart from you and Stefan – who will know our address. We want nothing more to do with Captain Linska and his so called Rehabilitation and Resettlement crowd. Poland is full of political intrigue, suspicion and treachery now – so we want to get on with a new life in peace.'

The others nodded in agreement. And then Trishka caught Igor's eye. He gave her a wink and cleared his throat.

'And we also leave in a few days - to our new life in Canada. But, before we part, there's something that Trishka and I would like to share with you. It goes back to my escape from Crete – which was funded by Mr Lubin, who died on the boat before we got to Italy.' He reached down and took off a shoe. 'This is one of Mr Lubin's shoes,' he said, 'I've had new heels put on them,' and went on to describe what had been found hidden in the original heels.

When he finished it was Anna who spoke first. 'What an amazing story, Igor - where are the rings – can we see them?'

'Er – not all of them, mother,' he said, reaching into his pocket, 'but here's one we saved for you.' He reached over and placed the diamond and sapphire ring next to her plate.

Anna picked it up. 'Oh, it's beautiful,' she said, and leaned towards Max to show him. She tried it on her finger and it fitted perfectly. With her eyes moist she looked over the table at them and said simply, 'It's lovely – thank you.'

Igor turned to Stefan and handed him the gold ring. 'And we thought you would like this Stefan, if it doesn't fit Marie you can exchange it for another.'

The ring was a wide band of heavy gold. 'Thanks, Igor,' he said, picking it up, 'that will make an ideal wedding ring.'

By this time Trishka had put the diamond and ruby ring on her finger. She held it out for Anna to see.

'We have sold the others,' she said, 'we've just kept these.'

'Yes,' said Igor, pulling two envelopes out of his pocket. 'We sold the brooch and the diamond ring, and a couple of the uncut diamonds.' He gave one envelope to his father and the other to Stefan. 'We got six hundred pounds for them - so we'd like to share it with you.' Each envelope contained two hundred pounds in white £5 notes.

'Oh,' said Anna, wiping at her eyes, 'what a wonderful present.'

Stefan raised his glass, and gulped with emotion. 'Yes, thanks to both of you,' he said, quietly, 'and especially to Mr Lubin.'

'And if you decide to sell the ring, Anna, it's valued at between £150 and £200,' said Trishka.

Anna looked down at the ring on her finger. 'We will have to be very hard up before I sell this,' she said.

CHAPTER 40

They knew that November was not the best time to travel to North America. The temperature was dropping and ahead of them was a long Canadian winter.

But for the first few days of the voyage the weather was fine and the sea calm. The liner was full of people of their own age, and there were lots of children. They enjoyed the entertainment that was provided, and they had never before seen food of the quality and quantity that was offered to them.

Igor bought a map of Canada from the on-board shop and some Canadians they met helped them to locate the area they needed to travel to, and gave them tips about trains, buses, and the hiring of cars.

But the enjoyment of the voyage didn't last. A storm struck them about three quarters of the way across. As the liner lurched and battled its way through the waves the dining rooms became empty at mealtimes as seasickness kept passengers confined to their cabins. Igor, Trishka, and the two boys were no exception. When the liner finally docked they stepped ashore white faced and queasy and thankful to be on dry land once again.

Trishka remained tight lipped, but Igor guessed what she might be thinking. The same thoughts had been on his mind for days. Why hadn't he stuck to his original idea of getting a job in England rather than travelling thousands of miles to Canada?

But neither of them voiced their doubts. In spite of what they had been through the boys were still excited that they were going to live on a farm. A big farm away from bombed out buildings, where there was no rationing and the shops had toys and sweets in them - as many as you could afford to buy.

Between them, Trishka and Igor had built up their new country into a kind of children's paradise. It was not done in a deliberate or calculating way but, having made the decision to emigrate, they had also become enthusiastic about it. The children had just picked up on their parent's excitement and held onto it. The fact that they would not see their grandparents again, or uncle Stefan - at least for a very long time - had not yet entered their heads.

One tip that the Canadians gave them was not to start on their long journey as soon as they stepped ashore. If there was no urgency, it was wise to stay a day or two in a comfortable hotel to recuperate from the voyage.

Igor and Trishka had no difficulty in following this advice. They booked into the best hotel they could find. Igor tried to telephone the farm to let Mr. Spencer know that they have arrived, but there was no reply. He tried again later, with the same result.

'If I can't reach get through tomorrow, I'll send him a telegram,' he said, in response to Trishka's worried look.

By the third day they had sorted out the transport they needed to get to the farm, which was situated between Ottawa and Montreal.

As they left the hotel it started to snow. There had been no reply to their telegram. The journey involved trains, buses and a very cold ferryboat across the St Lawrence River. They reached Ottawa in the late afternoon. It had snowed all day and traffic in the city was beginning to grind to a halt.

'We need another two days break to recover from that journey,' said Igor, as they got off the train.

'It'll be longer than two days if this weather continues,' Trishka said grimly. 'How much longer have we got to go?'

'About another hundred kilometres.'

'And Mr. Spencer still doesn't know that we've landed.'

'Perhaps his phone lines have been down. I'll try again tonight.'

He was trying hard to keep calm - to remain positive, but he had secretly become very disillusioned about the idea of managing a farm in Canada. But he dare not show it. He would not let Ernest Spencer down. He would do the job he came to do, but Trishka's support was essential.

Igor spoke to a taxi driver and asked him if he knew of decent hotel that might have spare rooms.

'Sure,' he said. 'My Aunt Mabel's gotta hotel - not big - but clean and nice.'

The hotel was on the outskirts of Ottawa next to a park. Aunt Mabel was round and jovial and quickly made them feel relaxed and comfortable. They ate the best meal they had had since arriving, and then they went to bed early.

The next morning the sky was clear and the snow glistened. They borrowed a toboggan from the hotel and took the boys to the park. They built a snowman and played snowballing amid squeals of laughter, and they went down slopes on the toboggan and laughed even when they fell off.

That evening as they got ready for bed Igor made a decision about the next day.

'If the roads are clear tomorrow I'll hire a car and go ahead to make contact with old man Spencer. Check out the accommodation he's got for us. If I start early I should be back before dark.

Trishka nodded in agreement. She didn't fancy turning up at the farm without giving any notice, or having any idea where they were to sleep when they got there. She would take the boys to look around Ottawa and do some shopping.

*

Another inch or two of snow fell during the night and it took Igor three hours to make the journey. He'd hired a station wagon with a four-wheel-drive and chains on the wheels, which clattered loudly, but kept a good grip on the snow covered roads. When he got there he almost missed the sign, which read, simply, 'Spencer's Farm' and pointed towards two posts about fifty yards from the road, sticking up out of the snow as an indication of an entrance.

There were no hedges or trees, and no sign of any track or road up to the farm - just a white expanse of undisturbed snow. But he could see the farmhouse and outbuildings about half a kilometre away. He drove the station wagon towards the two posts, but the snow had drifted and was deeper than he expected. The car stalled, and he realised that the chains and the four-wheel-drive were not enough.

He got out and opened the back and unclipped the shovel. One thing he'd learned was that - in a Canadian winter - a shovel in the car was an essential piece of equipment. He started to dig the snow from around wheels, but then he paused and looked at the buildings once again. He put the shovel back in the car, deciding to walk.

336

The depth of the snow ranged from knee to thigh deep, and he was sweating with exhaustion when he finally reached the farmhouse. He stood at the bottom of the steps to the porch to get his breath back, wondering whether it was worth the effort to climb up and knock on the door, because the place looked deserted.

It was then that he noticed a piece of paper pinned to the door. He climbed up the steps and leaned forward to read it.

Enquiries concerning the estate of **Ernest Spencer, deceased,** *should be made to*
Mr. James Spencer of Jones, McCall and Spencer, Lawyers, Victoria Buildings, Broad Street, Ottawa. Telephone Ottawa 98741.

He read it through again and stood up straight and continued to stare at it
'I'm sorry we didn't get to meet, Mr. Spencer,' he muttered, 'but what the hell do we do now.'

*

Later, when he told Trishka, her reaction was the same as his. 'He's dead?' she queried, in shock, as though she hadn't heard correctly. When Igor nodded, she fought off the tears. 'What do we do now?'

'I've been thinking about that. There's only two options isn't there? We either get on the next available ship back to England - or I try to find another job here. With option one, we would arrive in England with very little money left - and I'd still have to look for a job.

'I could sell the ring,' said Trishka.

'I know, and there's one uncut diamond left - but we couldn't live on that for long. Anyway you wouldn't have to do that if I got a job here. If we can manage until the spring, we can then decide whether to go back.'

Trishka was not so sure. 'I think I'd rather go right now - as soon as we can,' she said. ' It's turned into a disaster hasn't it?'

Igor took hold of her hand. 'I can't disagree with that Trishka. We'll find a travel agent tomorrow - see how soon we can leave.'

Trishka nodded her agreement. 'Do we have to let anyone know we've arrived - and going back? Those lawyers?'

'I don't see why they would want to know. The job agreement was with Mr. Spencer, and now he's died the agreement has died with him. I suppose it's possible that whoever inherits the farm will be prepared to offer me some kind of a job - but if we're going back to England it doesn't matter.'

'But - perhaps you should let the lawyers know we got here - as Mr. Spencer paid for our passage.'

'Yes, perhaps I should - I'll contact the one dealing with his estate - a Mr. James Spencer - in the morning. It sounds like he might be a relative.'

*

'The lawyer's office isn't far away,' Igor said to Trishka, as he helped the boys off the tramcar. 'It shouldn't take long - shall we meet in the cafe of the department store over there?'

Trishka followed his gaze. 'Yes, fine, how long do you want - half an hour?'

'Better say forty five minutes,' said Igor.

It took him ten minutes to locate the offices of the lawyer. He climbed the stairs to the second floor and entered a door marked 'Reception and Enquiries.'

A prim, middle-aged woman, wearing spectacles and with her hair tied back, stopped typing as he walked in.

She gave him an equally prim smile. 'Can I help you, sir,' she asked, politely.

'Er - yes – I haven't got an appointment, but could I speak to Mr. James Spencer please?

'I'm afraid he has a client with him at the moment. Could you call back later.'

'Yes - I suppose so.'

She opened an appointment book. 'Could I take your name, sir,' she said

'Mr Igor Radovak - and its in connection with Mr. Ernest Spencer, deceased.'

She stopped writing and looked up. 'Mr. Radovak, did you say?'

'Yes - Igor Radovak.'

She reached out for her notepad. 'If you would like to take a seat for a moment Mr. Radovak, I'll just take Mr James a note. I know that he's been hoping you would call.'

Igor took a seat as she scribbled a note and then hurried from the room.

'Yes,' she said, when she reappeared, ' if you could wait a few minutes Mr. Radovak, he won't keep you long.'

*

Trishka glanced at the clock in the café. Igor was thirty minutes late. The boys had finished their milkshakes and she had finished her coffee. She had just ordered another coffee when she saw him striding towards them.

She was expecting him to be looking apologetic, but his expression was strange, preoccupied, worried even. He sank down into a chair.

'Sorry I'm late, Trishka, but the lawyer kept me talking.'

'What about - he wasn't trying to get you to stay was he?'

'Er – no - he wasn't trying to do that at all. But we can't return to England.'

'How do you mean – can't? You said earlier that the agreement with Mr. Spencer had ceased when he died.'

'Yes - it did - but Mr. Spencer replaced that agreement with something else.'

Trishka looked puzzled. 'Something else - can he do that?'

Igor reached into his inside pocket and brought out a folded piece of paper and handed it to Trishka.

'Mr. Spencer left this letter for me with his lawyer. It's for both of us really.'

Trishka opened it out. Igor watched her face as she read it.

Dear Capt Radovak

I am writing this letter to leave with my lawyer in case I am not here when you arrive. I've been looking forward to meeting you and your wife and two boys, but have recently received some news that might make that impossible.

The pains I have had in my back for some time were not due to old age creeping on. I've been told that I have cancer and, at best .a maximum of three months to live. This has left me with the problem of what to do with the farm after I've gone. With my two sons dead I have no other relations to inherit the farm. I've thought of splitting it up and selling it to neighbouring farmers, but they don't really want any more land, they can hardly cope with what they have. And I would rather keep the farm together - the Spencer's have farmed this land for over 100 years.

So I am leaving the farm to you. I had this in the back of my mind anyway when I died, but events have brought this forward. I think that my son, who was your friend and comrade, would agree with my decision.

I wish you every success and happiness with your new life in Canada.

God bless you all.

Ernest Spencer.

Tears had come to Trishka's eyes and she wiped at them with her hand

'Poor man' she said, quietly.

'Yes,' said Igor sadly. 'I suppose I ought to be jubilant about being left a farm, but I just feel – well, unhappy about it somehow – guilty even.'

Trishka gave an understanding nod. Instead of feeling glad, she wanted to cry.

The two boys looked from one parent to the other, wondering what was going on.

Igor drank half the coffee that Trishka had ordered and put the cup down.

'The lawyer – Mr Spencer – has suggested that we stay in Ottawa until the thaw. There's nothing we can do on the farm until then – there's no livestock to worry about – that's already been sold. So, if Aunt Mabel can accommodate us over Christmas into the new year, it'll give us time to sort out the downside.'

Trishka looked puzzled. 'Downside – what do you mean?'

Igor hesitated before answering. 'The downside is that the farm is mortgaged to the bank.'

Trishka's eyes widened in alarm. '*Mortgaged* - how much mortgaged?'

Igor gave a shrug. 'The lawyer thinks only about twenty per cent of its value, but he's checking. He says Spencer raised the mortgage after I accepted his job offer. He bought a new tractor and other equipment with it.''

Trishka frowned. 'But a mortgage has to be paid for. Has Mr Spencer left any money in the farm account to cover the repayments?'

'Some, the money from the sale of the livestock is there.'

'Which will be needed to buy new livestock. Oh, Igor, have you been left a farm that we can't afford to run?'

'I hope not – I'm sure there'll be enough for us to get started. The lawyer thinks Mr Spencer also had some investments - his retirement fund. He's asked the bank to look into it but hasn't heard yet.'

She looked doubtful. 'It would need to be enough to meet the mortgage payments and for us to live on for a year – assuming we'll have *something* to sell by then.

She looked thoughtful.

'Would you consider renting out part of the farm, Igor?'

Igor shook his head. 'No, I wouldn't do that.'

Trishka looked at him in surprise. 'You wouldn't? Why not – there's over a three thousand acres isn't there?'

A worried look crossed Igor's face. 'Yes, too much for me to handle on my own – and with no money to hire any help.'

'What about your father?'

'But father said he wanted his own farm – and to stay in England, don't forget.'

'But you could make the offer.'

'Yes, but not as a tenant, it would have to be more tempting than that.'

'Like what?'

Igor gave a shrug. 'Like giving him a half share, maybe?'

Trishka smiled. 'Yes - that might be tempting enough.

*

Three days later, as they entered the dining room for the evening meal, Aunt Mabel came bustling over to meet them. She held out a small brown envelope.

'This telegram has just come for you, Mr Radovak,' she said, anxiously. And stood watching as Igor opened it.

'I hope it's not bad news,' she continued, her face concerned.

Igor grinned and passed it to Trishka. ' No, it's very good news, Mabel. We sent a telegram to our parents to see if they would like to join us in Canada, and they've decided to come.'

Aunt Mabel beamed. 'Well, ain't that just fine – I'm real pleased for you. Now, you sit yourselves down and I'll get you served right away,' she said, hurrying towards the kitchen.

Gregor sat down, excited at what he'd overheard. 'Is that right, dad - granny and grandpa are coming?'

Igor gave a smile and waved the telegram. 'That's what they say, Gregor – as soon as they can get a ship to bring them.'

Gregor gave a happy grin and turned to his brother. 'Hear that, Simon –granny and grandpa are coming to live with us.'

Grinning with excitement Simon clapped his hands together and said 'goody, goody.'

As they finished eating Igor looked thoughtful and glanced over at Trishka.

'There was one stipulation in the will, well, a request - not compulsory - but I would like to comply with it.'

'A request – what kind of request?'

'The Spencer's have farmed that land since the early colonial days. Old man Spencer requested that the name of the farm is not changed.'

Trishka, still thinking about the contents of the letter, gave a nod.

'Of course – why change it.'

Igor nodded in agreement, hesitated, and then said. There's something else I've been thinking about.'

'What's that?'

'If it's called Spencer's Farm, then the people running it should also be called Spencer.'

'I suppose so – but we can't help that, can we?'

'Well, it's not impossible – we could change *our* name to Spencer.'

Trishka looked at him in surprise, and saw his face was serious. She shrugged.

'That's fine with me, Igor. I've already experienced a change of name when we got married – and I reckon that was the smartest thing

I've ever done. But what about your parents, d'you think they'll mind?'

Looking relieved, Igor reached out and took her hands. 'I don't think so, when they know the reason. Shall we change our name to Mr and Mrs Radovak-Spencer and family, then?'

'Yes, why not,' she said, smiling, 'that sounds a good name.'

www.ingramcontent.com/pod-product-compliance
Lightning Source LLC
Chambersburg PA
CBHW060941030726

47503CB00003B/676